Dickens and the Unreal City

Dickens and the Unreal City

Searching for Spiritual Significance in Nineteenth-Century London

Karl Ashley Smith

First published 2008 by
PALGRAVE MACMILLAN
Houndmills, Basingstoke, Hampshire RG21 6XS and
175 Fifth Avenue, New York, N.Y. 10010
Companies and representatives throughout the world

PALGRAVE MACMILLAN is the global academic imprint of the Palgrave Macmillan division of St. Martin's Press, LLC and of Palgrave Macmillan Ltd. Macmillan® is a registered trademark in the United States, United Kingdom and other countries. Palgrave is a registered trademark in the European Union and other countries.

ISBN-13: 978-0-230-54523-6   hardback
ISBN-10: 0-230-54523-8   hardback

This book is printed on paper suitable for recycling and made from fully managed and sustained forest sources. Logging, pulping and manufacturing processes are expected to conform to the environmental regulations of the country of origin.

A catalogue record for this book is available from the British Library.

Library of Congress Cataloging-in-Publication Data

Smith, Karl Ashley, 1975–
    Dickens and the unreal city: searching for spiritual significance in
    nineteenth-century London / Karl Ashley Smith.
        p. cm.
    Includes bibliographical references and index.
    ISBN 0-230-54523-8 (alk. paper)
    1. Dickens, Charles, 1812–1870—Knowledge—London (England)
        2. London (England)—In literature. 3. Dickens, Charles, 1812–1870—
        Religion. 4. Dickens, Charles, 1812–1870—Symbolism. I. Title.

PR4592.L58S65 2008
823'.8—dc22   2008011811

10   9   8   7   6   5   4   3   2   1
17   16   15   14   13   12   11   10   09   08

Printed and bound in Great Britain by
CPI Antony Rowe, Chippenham and Eastbourne

Contents

Illustrations

Acknowledgements

This is a long book that has gestated over a long period of time, and necessarily there is a long list of people who have to be thanked.

It has been adapted from a Ph.D. thesis undertaken at the University of St Andrews between 1997 and 2002. This in itself was a thoroughly enjoyable and rewarding experience. I would like to thank the University, and the School of English in particular, for the scholarship funding, without which the research that went into this book would quite simply not have been possible. My supervisor, Phillip Mallett, merits special thanks for the unstinting energy, enthusiasm and intellectual rigour that he invested in that task and for the continued interest he has taken in my work since submission. Whatever else he has on his plate (and the helpings are always generous), he has always been prepared to give the work his full attention. I benefitted strongly from the advice of Dr Michael Herbert and numerous other members of the department at this stage, and must also mention the helpful comments made by my external advisors, Dr Paul Schlicke and D Gill Plain, both during the viva and afterwards. A special Dickens and the Unreal City badge must be awarded to Jill Gamble, whose name features in the acknowledgements of better books than this one! Her help as postgraduate secretary and the help of other secretarial staff was crucial at this stage of the process.

I would like to thank all my colleagues at the University of Dundee's English Department for the various pieces of advice that have fed into the process of turning this from a thesis into a book and for providing an enjoyable and supportive working environment in which to do so. I have particularly benefitted from working with my head of department, Rob Watt, on an article on Dickens's involvement in the railway-sponsored *Daily News*, which has helped me to develop some of the ideas on Providence and technology in Chapters 1 and 5.

A great deal of material from Chapter 4 was adapted into an article, focusing largely on the Victorian heroine's relationship to London's dirt, that appeared in *Dickens Studies Annual* in 2003 entitled 'Little Dorrit's "Speck" and Florence's "Daily Blight": Urban Contamination and the Victorian Heroine'. My thanks is due to AMS Press for permission to reproduce it here.

I must also thank the Carnegie Trust for the Scottish Universities for their generous illustrations grant, which paid for the pictures in colour in the centre pages of the book.

Many thanks to Steven Hall and Christabel Scaife of Palgrave – particularly for their help in sorting out illustrations while I have been in Malawi.

I must thank my mother and father, who have given me unfailing love and support at no small cost to themselves during my years when I was producing the thesis, to say nothing of before and afterwards. Finally, I must record my debt of gratitude to my wife Joy Rafferty for her constant encouragement, understanding and love – as well as the many acts of thoughtfulness she shows me each day.

Abbreviations

AN	*American Notes*
BH	*Bleak House*
BR	*Barnaby Rudge*
COO	*The Castle of Otranto*
DC	*David Copperfield*
DS	*Dombey and Son*
GE	*Great Expectations*
LD	*Little Dorrit*
MC	*Martin Chuzzlewit*
MOU	*The Mysteries of Udolpho*
NN	*Nicholas Nickleby*
OCS	*The Old Curiosity Shop*
OMF	*Our Mutual Friend*
OT	*Oliver Twist*
PP	*The Pickwick Papers*
SBB	*Sketches by Boz*
TTC	*A Tale of Two Cities*
TWL	*The Waste Land*
UT	*Re-printed Pieces and The Uncommercial Traveller*

Introduction: 'A heap of broken images'

Between Dickens's London and twenty-first century readers stands T. S. Eliot's London in *The Waste Land*. Mr Eliot's London demands to be read in two main ways. His contemporary readers recognised its various geographical and cultural reference points, so that it served as a concentrated microcosm of the modern society in which they lived. More strikingly, however, taking London as a totality, including such fluid elements of the metropolis as its crowd and its river, Eliot used it as a constantly shifting symbol in interaction with countless other symbols and archetypes, in both literary and other forms of discourse. In this way, the city allowed exploration of his emerging religious concerns with the resistance of modern life to meaning – and with the aching possibility that meaning might still be attainable.[1]

Perhaps encouraged by the fact that Eliot chose the original title of *The Waste Land*, 'He Do the Police in Different Voices', from *Our Mutual Friend*, Edgar Johnson was among the first to connect that book with the poem. In his biography of Dickens in 1952, he claims that 'The Thames of *Our Mutual Friend* is the same river that flows through the waste land [*sic*]'.[2] In both texts the river's strong historical symbolic association with revitalising power proves inadequate to the more prosaic, irredeemable conditions of modern metropolitan life, where the river is more likely to bring disease and death than regeneration. The role played by the river within the network of symbols that is Dickens's London is the subject of Chapter 6 of this book. The more fundamental issue raised by Johnson's comment is how far, not just the Thames at its centre, but London as a whole in Dickens may be read as an interrogation of the adequacy of religious symbols in the quest for renewing revelation in the modern world. Should Johnson's remark lead Dickensian critics to leaf through their copies of James Frazer's *The Golden Bough* in

1

search of particular drowned and resurrected gods and goddesses Dickens may have been evoking, as has been important in the study of Eliot? In practice they have not done so. Eliot's notes on his own poem encourage the reader to consider such sources and note the differences and continuities between the societies where these religions were practised and his own. It was an important part of his project to relocate ancient and, in the terminology of his day, primitive ritual and culture to modern contexts.[3] By contrast, although Dickens had access to a wealth of classical scholarship, Frazer's work was not yet published, nor were the anthropological methods that informed Eliot's sources developed in his time. In any case, it is obvious that Dickens's interest in classical and non-Western religious belief was cursory in comparison to Eliot's.[4]

A more fruitful approach to Johnson's own generation, still deeply influenced by Frazer's work and by Cambridge ritualists such as Gilbert Murray who had sought to apply Frazerian insights to texts in English, such as *Hamlet*,[5] might have been to seek universal archetypes and patterns of storytelling in Dickens's novels. Perhaps indeed his river is the same as Eliot's in that it objectifies the same archetype (even if Dickens was not so precisely aware of its points of entrance into literary and cultural form) and expresses the same disgust at its failure to perform its symbolic role.[6] It would be tempting even now to write about Dickens's London as a modern Thebes or Elsinore, a sick environment that must be purged of the something rotten at its heart if its fertility is to be renewed. *Our Mutual Friend* is packed with candidates for this role, whether a villain like Bradley Headstone and Rogue Riderhood sinking under the waters of death before they can renew society, or a reclaimable figure purged of his evil in the waters such as Eugene Wrayburn.

This ritualistic approach survives in an updated form in, for example, Michael Heyns's *Expulsion and the Nineteenth-century Novel*,[7] which brilliantly re-theorises it for a more deconstructionist age as a defence of Dickens against Foucauldian readers such as D. A. Miller. Heyns presents the Victorian novel as depending on the myth of a scapegoat, whose expulsion brings together a fragmented family or social group. This is inherent in the genre and is also an example of the unvoiced fears of society. Dickens is praised for emphasising the disturbing aspects of this unacknowledged convention and foregrounding its arbitrariness:

> some of Dickens's most troubling implications are generated by that which escapes the final ordering of a purposeful plot, the solution to the spiritual conundrum as much as the answer to the detective mystery ...[8]

This movement towards seeing texts as reflecting unease with unconsciously inherited archetypal patterns illuminates Edgar Johnson's comparison of Dickens's use of the Thames to Eliot's. Following this model, *Our Mutual Friend* might be seen as relying upon the archetype for his tale of changed lives and pointing boldly and with honesty to the many lives alongside it that are not changed in its presence. *The Waste Land* may be presented as a more theoretical exploration of the same complex of stories – albeit one more consciously aware of them *as* archetypes and of their origins.

It would ultimately be reductive to describe Dickens's complex representation of the city in any structuralist way, claiming, for example, that London renews itself and its inhabitants by pushing them towards literal and metaphorical drownings in the river or in the crowd or the labyrinth of streets. To read it as yet another example of literature reproducing an archetype inherent in its genres, in order to show how universal and true that archetype is, risks confirming a template in the reader's mind rather than shedding new light on the novels. Nor do I wish to pursue any Jungian line that such archetypes are present in the texts as part of a collective unconscious in order to demonstrate why we respond to these stories. Nevertheless it is still extremely useful to bear these inherited patterns in mind since they enable discussion of Dickens as a writer interacting with a complex of symbols profoundly embedded both in his genre and in other discourses of his time. These clearly re-asserted themselves in his depictions of the metropolitan world and an approach is necessary that can see Dickens critiquing them, whether consciously or unconsciously, quite as much as reproducing them.

Readers of *The Waste Land* will recognise moments when Dickens's representations of the city and its components may be interpreted as engaging at the symbolic level with his own religious concerns, as voiced elsewhere in his private and public writings. Those sharing Eliot's interest in the relevance of traditional religious symbolism in the modern world are bound to ask the same questions of crowd and river and other aspects of Dickens's symbolic city that they are accustomed to ask when they encounter them in that poem.

Indeed, these complexes of symbols and narrative structures did not come to Dickens merely as archetypes of which he was only dimly aware, but primarily through the popular religion of his own day with which he very self-consciously interacted. This links his work very strongly to *The Waste Land* which is itself concerned with a connection between ancient rituals of renewal and the Christianity, which, in a form inevitably much altered after two thousand years, was (nominally at least) the dominant religious strand in Eliot's own cultural environment. He associates the hanged God of Frazerian anthropology and in particular Apollo and Thammuz, the drowned Phoenician god, whom he uses to structure his experience of living in a city in which 'death had undone so many' (l. 63),[9] with the 'figure in the passage of the disciples to Emmaus' (note to line 46).[10] Indeed, his London is a place of decay and death-in-life because it systematically denies the decisive baptismal deaths that precede regeneration in Christianity and the mystery religions – or offers perverse corruptions of them which allow neither genuine death nor resurrection. The poem suggests that perhaps their validity, whether as symbols or as spiritual realities, has expired in the metropolitan age.

Enduring religious archetypes may have entered Dickens's frame of reference from their presence in the popular forms of Christianity of his day rather than from study of analogues and/or antecedents in the ancient world or contemporary anthropology. Nevertheless, he was acutely aware of the disjunction between the renewing power of Christianity as described in the New Testament and the sterility of its modern manifestations. His work was deeply concerned with the question of whether its discourse, including its language and symbols, still had anything to say to a modern world deeply in need of a regenerating revelation, and his borrowing of its structures and tropes was neither automatic nor uncritical. Like Eliot after him, he employed the figure of the metropolis to ask the same question of them, namely are they adequate as they recur in the modern world to afford any spiritual clarity? Dickens's London may therefore be read as an Unreal City, a symbol made up of innumerable component symbols, each one referring outward to many other networks of symbols – that allows the author to test how effectively, if at all, these symbols may function in the nineteenth and twentieth centuries. Perhaps *The Waste Land* and the critical practises it generated encourage such readings, which might have puzzled Dickens's original readers. Perhaps Dickens himself considered similar questions in the act of depicting the Victorian city and thus provided a model for Eliot's exploration of the symbolic potentialities of the London of his own time. What is certain is that we cannot speak of London in Dickens's *oeuvre*, fourteen completed novels and numerous shorter writings, written over some thirty-four years, as having the same unity of purpose as a single poem. The pleasing complexity of London itself was the product of innumerable builders with innumerable motives. In the same way, the imaginative London constructed by Dickens is the result of various local imperatives operating at various times during that period: some biographical, some polemical, some generic. This makes it very difficult, if not impossible, to perceive as a whole – and accounts for its satisfying complexity. Even the account of Dickens's London given in this book (necessarily a different thing from 'Dickens's London' itself) will be a construction, driven by numerous imperatives. These include my personal experience of London, religion and Dickens's novels, the need to be published in a realistic timeframe and the critical approaches I have absorbed over the years from my particular combination of teachers, colleagues and reading.

Why then does this book set itself the task of representing Dickens's representation of London at all? Why does it hypothesise that doing so will give an insight into his exploration of religious themes of the sort that we have come to expect from Eliot's city? Firstly, the very contradictions we have been considering in the author's presentation of the metropolis encourage both Dickens and his readers to explore the profoundest spiritual questions. Sometimes, London and certain of its aspects are represented as bringing physical death and ontological destruction of identity, issues to which Dickens applied the religious dimension of his thinking. Often London's structure and institutions are used at the levels of plot and symbolism by both author and characters to deny any revelation of the meaning which characters seek there. At other times, however, the metropolis and its constituent parts are shown as vibrant and revivifying. Moreover, they bring both practical and ontological information to light. When the reader becomes most keenly aware of these tensions, Dickens's London becomes an elaborate system, capable of doing any and all of these things and more complex than any individual (including, at times, the author) can take in as a whole. At such times, Dickens's portrayal raises questions for the reader such as whether this system reflects – or indeed may be governed by – a Providential force determining the disposal of such concealments and revelations, death and new life. At times his stories boldly assert (or at least assist) faith in a benignly unified scheme of things, however invisible to the individual perspective. At times his presentation of London seems to suggest the terrifying possibility that the individual spirit is at the mercy of a swirl of competing and contradictory forces with no authority overseeing them.

Dickens's symbols may ultimately yield more information about his grappling with religious issues than his overt statements about belief because, as an imaginative artist and not a theologian, this is the way the author did his profoundest thinking. The latter were often bland

and certainly not the product of systematic theological study, whereas his engagement with the city's contradictions led to treatments of it with an extraordinary power to stimulate thought on the profoundest issues of human existence. As A. O. J. Cockshut puts it:

> It is in his symbolism that we can most easily see the kind of development he did achieve. ... he was already obsessed with prisons, with crowds, with the mystery of money, with squalor, dirt and violence. The story of his development is partly that he penetrated deeper and deeper into the treasures of meaning that they contained. As he probed into their multiple implications, they became symbols of their own accord.[11]

In dealing with the issues thrown up by the contemporary metropolis, Dickens of necessity engages with contemporary religious and secular debates and evokes other symbolic schemes that deal with such questions. The confrontation of these with the realities of nineteenth-century London as Dickens depicts them yields richly complex results. This book addresses factors of the city that dramatise both negative and positive effects upon the spiritual life of the individual character, as consonant with the issues raised in Dickens's more direct statements on religious belief and experience. It shows how these religious concerns interact with other more immediate influences upon the representation of these phenomena of urban life to add up to an account of the city that serves a blend of spiritual, stylistic and political functions.

   After an initial summary of Dickens's general religious position, focusing on those issues I see his London addressing, the first chapters deal with those elements of metropolitan culture that mainly evoke a deadening effect on individual spiritual life. The second section deals with those that suggest life-giving, revelatory effects. It will be apparent almost from the beginning, however, that such classification becomes unstable even at a local level in the novels, never mind when each recurrent element of city life is read across Dickens's work. The final section deals with urban factors that, like London as a whole, seem to have both destructive and vitalising connotations in equal measure – even simultaneously. Here Dickens grapples most firmly with the question of how these aspects of life may be related to one another. The conclusion pans back to a panoramic view of Dickens's metropolis, the sum of all these parts, and to the reader, attempting to form an aptly bewildering series of representations of London into a whole about which something conclusive can be said. It reflects on the fact that London in

Dickens constantly resists, yet tantalisingly suggests, the idea that this can be achieved. That 'whole' sought by the reader may be a sense of Dickens's understanding of the presence or absence of order in the universe (whether or not even the universe itself adds up to a meaningful whole and what perspective can possibly exist from which to see it). On the other hand that 'whole' may have to do with how a symbolic reading of Dickens's London can impact upon our own conception of the presence or absence of that order. That this book even looks for such things in Dickens's representation of London is perhaps the legacy of T. S. Eliot. In 'Tradition and the Individual Talent', Eliot insisted that, with the introduction of truly new works of art, 'the past should be altered by the present as much as the present is directed by the past'.[12] In altering our reading of Dickens, *The Waste Land* manifests itself to be such a work. On the other hand, that these novels may be read so richly in this way is perhaps Dickens's legacy to the art of the twentieth and twenty-first centuries. The reading advanced here may well be the result of intervening texts working upon these novels. That they can perform such work upon these materials demonstrates that Dickens has contributed to the way the image of London is continually constructed to help us form our ideas of the universe at large.

1

'A revelation by which men are to guide themselves': Dickens and Christian Theology

If we are to read Dickens's London as a symbolic means for exploring broadly religious themes, some knowledge of the writer's personal religious views will be required. It is not my intention here to write a comprehensive account of Dickens's relationship to the various Christian orthodoxies – Catholic, Evangelical, Liberal-Anglican or otherwise. This would require a book in itself, with a rather broader focus than my own, and in any case, many of the critics quoted below have made useful attempts to label Dickens's position on a scale of contemporary beliefs. Rather, my intention is to summarise briefly Dickens's opinions as stated in primarily extra-fictional sources, such as the letters, speeches and *The Life of Our Lord*, about the matters the following chapters read his depiction of the city as addressing. These include the presence or absence of divine revelation and a Providential plan, the nature of mankind's death and decay and how it may be remedied.

Having done so, the main question will be how these are to be measured against the message given by the experience of reading the novels regarding these issues – after all, the tale and the teller frequently send out different signals about a piece of work. What Dickens consciously believed is not always the impression conveyed to the reader about what he felt to be true. This is not to say that Dickens did not know his own mind. Such discrepancies may arise for a number of reasons, including a need to conform to the conventions of the genre and the liberation in fiction from binding plot to the perceived laws of the universe. Most importantly, problems are resolved differently when they are engaged in imaginatively, rather than at the level of linear thought.

Dennis Walder, in *Dickens and Religion*, warns that 'Dickens articulates his beliefs by the methods of a novelist' and finds 'significant moments, images, themes' a more fruitful source of information than 'the easily abstractable, surface reflections of his views which have generally been accepted as a complete version of them'.[1] Nevertheless, in practice, he generally views the fiction as a more profound expression of the beliefs already articulated in the private and public declarations of faith. *Little Dorrit*, for example, is said to be

> a sustained attempt by Dickens to show that one can free oneself from the imprisoning forces associated with a narrow Old Testament belief ... by means of the broadly redemptive, loving spirit of the New ... But it is expressed in terms which transcend the immediately personal or social.[2]

Andrew Sanders too, in *Charles Dickens Resurrectionist*, encourages the reader to take seriously the author's defensive claims that he aimed 'to inculcate some Christian lessons in books':[3]

> It is a mistake to assume that Dickens is simply condemning the mercenary and social values of mid-Victorian England ... he is, more trenchantly, opposing a picture of a society with false values, values symptomatic of spiritual death, to those redeemed characters who offer hope of a continuing process of re-birth and regeneration ... the reality of the hope that the resurrected few may show the way to the many.[4]

Sanders, then, sees the fiction as a whole as decisively recommending a supernatural Christianity whose discourse has something positive to offer.

Not all writers on the subject, however, agree that the novels present beliefs broadly harmonious with the extra-fictional statements. Janet L. Larson, in *Dickens and the Broken Scripture*, reads the author's use of biblical texts as both supporting and undermining his stated views. Sometimes this is done consciously, she implies, sometimes unconsciously, but the effect is the same. Dickens explores at a creative level the texts upon which consolatory belief is based and suggests that often they are found wanting. Although his allusions give stable meanings within the Christian scheme of things to some events, at other times, the contrast between the words and the modern situations they are enlisted to describe can give an uncomfortable sense of their inapplicability – even meaninglessness – in the nineteenth century. According to Larson, Dickens establishes a complex dialogic between these uses of scripture.[5] The teller asserts religious faith in Providential justice and life beyond death through plot and commentary, yet finds himself resisted by the tale's constant tendency towards an agnostic pessimism, wherein 'the rituals of the church and the Bible ... no longer had the power to order feeling and inspire hope'.[6] The same conflict is to be found in Dickens's evocation of images from Christian symbolic discourse that are explored in my own study.

Larson's approach is a mirror image of Alexander Welsh's view, fifteen years previously, that the voice of the teller was Dickens's Broad Church rationalism, undermined by tales that came closer to endorsing the ideas of the more orthodox Christianity rejected by the tale in Larson's reading. Quoting Humphrey House's (problematic) remark that 'Dickens's deep and bitter hatred of Evangelicalism was not usually directed against any of its typical Christian doctrines',[7] Welsh pointed to examples of decisive transformations in Dickens's works depending on grace and faith in something outside of the self rather than good works.[8] Nevertheless, both Larson and Welsh challenge the received wisdom on the religious stance of Dickens's novels, arguing for a rigorous interrogation of the author's formal beliefs, including the symbols by which those beliefs were explored, when they were drawn into the creation of his imaginative world. The novels clearly do contain other ideas about death, new life and the sources of both than Dickens's consciously held views could allow, whether because they conflicted with his Christian orthodoxy or with his almost secular humanism. The main focus of this book is on how the symbol of the metropolis participates in the novel's discussion of these themes. In the London of his novels, Dickens constructs a symbolic microcosm of the universe which allows him to explore imaginatively the process by which things come about, sometimes in ways harmonious with his declared convictions, sometimes in ways that diverge from them.

I. Dickens and revelation

Dennis Walder begins his study by speaking of his subject's 'fundamental outlook as a liberal Protestant with radical, Romantic leanings'.[9] At first glance, this seems rather a specific identification for a man who famously insisted upon his freedom from sectarianism and doctrinal partisanship. Dickens, after all, ended his will with the desire that all his 'dear children' should live according to 'the teaching of the New Testament in its broad spirit, and ... put no faith in any man's narrow construction of its letter here or there'.[10] His respect for the personality and teachings of Jesus as recorded in the gospels was incontestable.

Equally clearly, he felt he was holding His faith in its pure form in a way that could not be reduced to denominational or sectarian labels.

Nevertheless, in the face of twenty centuries of theology, it is almost impossible to make any meaningful statement about Jesus Christ without revealing views that can be identified as siding with one existing opinion and against another. To consider the form of particular sacraments as unimportant, to take one obvious example, places one automatically in opposition to those who believe such sacraments within a particular communion necessary for salvation. Moreover, although Dickens avoided telling his children with which Christian groupings they should align themselves, he was equally adamant about which branches they should not join. He famously told Douglas Jerrold that 'I don't know what I should do, if [his son, Charley] were to get hold of any conservative or High church notions'.[11] He may have defended the rights of Catholics in *Barnaby Rudge*, but he also wrote to Angela Burdett-Coutts of 'the Roman Catholic Religion – that curse upon the world'. What he principally objected to was its restrictions upon 'Freedom' and curtailment of individual civil liberties in countries where it was practised.[12] If revelation of any order or design in the universe were to be found, it was most emphatically not going to be exclusive to any one church tradition.

His objection to the notion that observance of ritual makes a person right with God, however, did not lead him to seek revelation in the more direct forms of Christianity. The extempore prayers and sermons of the Evangelical chapels are dismissed in the 1836 pamphlet *Sunday Under Three Heads* as exhibiting a 'disgusting and impious familiarity' with the Almighty.[13] As will be seen later on, Dickens also objected to some of the characteristic doctrinal as well as stylistic features of Evangelicalism. The philanthropist George Moore saw Dickens's beliefs as sufficiently like his own to say, 'I found him a true Christian without great profession',[14] but other Evangelical readers felt Dickens's ideas of salvation to be too divergent from their own to be sufficiently Christian.[15]

He certainly did not share their conviction that the Bible was the infallible word of God, the ultimate means by which God had revealed his plan for the ages. For Dickens, it was merely a series of books in which imperfect human apprehensions of God were recorded for posterity. Annie Fields, his American hostess, recalls him speaking in March 1868 of even his beloved gospels having been assembled from 'some anterior written Scriptures – made up, perhaps, with additions and interpolations from the *Talmud*'.[16] In this conversation, Dickens also spoke intelligently of the possibility that some of the figures of speech attributed to Jesus in the gospels were anachronistic.

If Dickens could not regard the received text of the Bible as authoritative, he also saw some parts of it as more important than other parts. He felt that the Old Testament presented a different, more vindictive code than the New. In *Little Dorrit* this becomes one of the crucial points of the novel's message. The heroine works for a change in Mrs Clennam by telling her to abandon Old Testament precedents of human vengeance on the sinful in favour of New Testament mercy:

> let me implore you to remember later and better days. Be guided only by the Healer of the sick, the raiser of the dead, the friend of all who were afflicted and forlorn, the patient Master who shed tears of compassion for our infirmities. We cannot but be right if we put all the rest away, and do everything in remembrance of Him.
>
> (II 31 p. 770)

In this Dickens follows Dean Stanley's idea of 'progressive revelation',[17] by which a partial insight had been recorded by the patriarchs and a fuller one by those who had the benefit of contact with Christ. As science uncovered more knowledge about the world, revelation was continuing into Dickens's own time. He wrote to Walter de Cerjat:[18]

> what these bishops and such-like say about revelation, in assuming it to be finished and done with, I can't in the least understand. Nothing is discovered without God's intention and assistance, and I suppose every new knowledge of his works that is conceded to man to be distinctly a revelation by which men are to guide themselves.

His conception of the means of revelation may thus be expected to be more inclusive than that of contemporary fundamentalists of whatever persuasion. This optimistic view of a Providential scheme releasing more and more wisdom upon mankind as the centuries went by and the race matured to receive it is therefore an influence upon the ordered system of revelations made to the characters and readers in his novels.

Since he did not see the words on the page of the Bible as the permanent and enduring word of God, he was not particular about insisting on its doctrines about the nature of God and of Christ. His brief spell as an attender at the Little Portland Street Unitarian chapel between 1842 and 1847 is well known and his vagueness of phrase concerning the deity of Christ at the beginning of *The Life of Our Lord* is often taken as evidence of anti-Trinitarian belief:

> There is a child born today in the city of Bethlehem ... who will grow up to be so good that God will love him as his own son; and he will teach men to love one another ... and his name will be Jesus Christ; and people will put that name in their prayers, because they will know God loves it, and will know that they should love it too.[19]

This, however, is probably merely a simplification and avoidance of controversy for the benefit of his children. Elsewhere, for example, he calls Sunday the Jewish Sabbath,[20] although his fiction (for example *DS* 13 p. 162) shows him to be well aware that Saturday was their day of rest. What is really significant is that Dickens considered it more important for his children to grasp the moral relationship between Jesus and God the Father, evidenced in their behavioural resemblance, than that they should understand the exact theological relationship between them.

The same values probably lie behind his Unitarian sympathies *per se*. His 'conversion' to Unitarianism came at a time when he was dissatisfied with the lack of social action being taken within the Church of England to care for the poor in imitation of Christ. His new co-religionists, as he wrote to Cornelius Felton, '*would* do something for human improvement if they could; and ... practise charity and toleration'.[21] His rejection of High Church Tractarianism and Evangelicalism is probably referable to the fact that in the former salvation depends upon ritual, and in the latter, upon belief in the achievement of Christ. Neither places a saving value upon works. Dickens is bound to have feared that both could encourage complacency and provide insufficient obligation to perform the real Christian business of doing good. This is where the whole emphasis of *The Life of Our Lord* lies. The book concludes with the words:

> Remember! – It is christianity[22] TO DO GOOD always – even to those who do evil to us. ... It is christianity to be gentle, merciful, and forgiving, and ... to shew that we love Him by humbly trying to do right in everything. If we do this ... we may confidently hope that God will forgive us our sins and mistakes, and enable us to live and die in peace.[23]

The real revelation of order in the universe was to be found in the character of Christ as represented in his work and teachings. He seems to have left it to others to worry about the question of how this is to be apprehended if neither church tradition nor the Bible may be regarded as an accurate or authoritative reflection of these.

Dickens then can be said to belong to the Broad Church movement, within the Church of England (to which he returned in 1847). Humphrey House,[24] Dennis Walder[25] and Janet Larson[26] all use this phrase to describe the writer's position. The term was said to have been coined by A. H. Clough in conversation in the late 1840s as an alternative to High and Low Church and it soon gained national currency. Dean Stanley, whose Pauline commentaries with Jowett in the 1850s attempted to provide some scriptural grounding for the party's ideas, had popularised the term. It described a conscious movement firmly within the established Church towards greater inclusiveness of opinion, while retaining an emphasis on Jesus as the supreme example to mankind and pointer towards God. Characteristically liberal themselves, Anglicans of this school stressed, as we have seen Dickens did, the importance of the New Testament at the expense of the Old, and a special value was placed on the gospel narratives and the Sermon on the Mount in particular. Working to remedy social ills and caring for the needy were seen as the most important part of Christ's teaching and these were exactly the aspects emphasised in person and in the fiction by Dickens. In a letter to de Cerjat, the author resoundingly endorsed one of the movement's major manifestos, Benjamin Jowett and John Colenso's *Essays and Reviews* (1860):

> the importance of timely suggestions such as these ... is that the Church should not gradually shock and lose the more thoughtful and logical of human minds; but should be so gently and considerately yielding as to retain them, and through them, hundreds of thousands.[27]

Other leading figures in the Broad Church movement were admired by – and themselves admired – Dickens. Stanley preached a sermon devoted to the writer in Westminster Abbey the Sunday after his death. When the Dean published *The Life and Correspondences of Thomas Arnold*, his still more influential mentor, Dickens wrote to Forster that 'Every sentence that you quote from it [rather than the Bible itself] is the text-book of my faith'.[28] Nevertheless, Arnold was personally much more insistent than Dickens on doctrinal specificity, speaking in one sermon of the 'many' who

> habitually lose sight of [Jesus's] office of Saviour and Mediator, and regard him only as a teacher ... their opinions ... are more those of the disciples of John the Baptist, who preached repentance, than of the Apostles of Christ, who taught together with repentance towards God, faith towards Jesus Christ our Lord.

As Larson points out,[29] the opinions of the 'many' here closely resemble those recommended to Dickens's children in *The Life of Our Lord*. By this measure, Dickens's views seem rather broader than even those of this most representative Broad Churchman.

In any case, a term defined by a desire to eschew precise theological distinctions, even as a conscious stance, can be of only limited use in describing Dickens's religious thought. It will be of more practical benefit to this study to ask what Dickens thought about the theological issues that have to do with the mystery of regeneration.

II. Dickens and regeneration

The New Testament writers, as understood by most contemporary theology, both Protestant (whether Reformed or non-Reformed) and Catholic, discussed death in three aspects. Firstly, there was the present 'empty' deadness of existence with no benefit to God or to the self, from which believers are 'redeemed ... with the precious blood of Christ' (1 Peter 1:18–19). In response to this condition, Jesus said, 'I am come that they may have life and that they might have it more abundantly' (John 10:10). Secondly, there was physical death, presented as the inevitable consequence of mankind's disobedience to God: 'For the wages of sin is death; but the gift of God is eternal life through Jesus Christ our Lord' (Romans 6:23). Finally, there was eternal separation from God for those who rejected his offer of mercy: 'And death and hell were cast into the lake of fire. This is the second death' (Revelation 20:14). Christ's sufferings in the hours of darkness on the cross were regarded as a concentrated version of the torments of Hell experienced by Him in substitution for mankind:

> For he hath made him to be sin for us, who knew no sin; that we might be made the righteousness of God in him.
>
> (2 Corinthians 5:21)

As can clearly be seen from this selection of verses, Peter, Paul, John and John's Jesus are unanimous in declaring death of all three types to be referable to human sin. For this reason, they are equally unanimous in declaring Jesus Christ to be the remedy to this death. Because Christ endured all three types of death (temporal isolation from God, physical decease and the punishment of the second death) on the cross on behalf of each individual, the Apostles taught that full life on earth, bodily resurrection and life in the heavenly realm were available to all. To grasp this in faith was a revelation that provided a threefold regeneration.

Dickens's thought engages with all three of these aspects of death, but does not necessarily agree with mainstream theology as to the problem or its solution. Clearly most of Dickens's fiction is taken up with the question of how dead lives are to be made truly alive. The tendency for people to be reduced to mere inanimate things in his work has been frequently remarked upon.[30] This is symptomatic of novels such as *Dombey and Son*, where Paul, looking at the lifestyles around him, can ask, 'Floy, are we *all* dead, except you?' (16 p. 223), and *Our Mutual Friend*, where the sterility of modern life is terrifyingly universal.

Moreover, it hardly requires demonstration that physical death is a dominant issue in his writings. People of all ages, from Little Johnny to Betty Higden, must learn to confront it. The novels often narrate a search for a means of transcending it, both for those who themselves die, and also for the survivors. Dickens, like almost all other human beings, had had to deal with the death of loved ones throughout his working life. The loss of his sister-in-law, Mary Hogarth, in 1837 affected him profoundly and is frequently cited as the stimulus behind his explorations of the deaths of the pure and innocent. To this might be added the passing of his sister, Fanny, in 1848; his baby daughter, Dora, in 1851; and his son, Walter Landor Dickens, in 1863. In 1852, his friends Richard Watson, Catherine Macready (wife of the actor William) and Count D'Orsay all died within a few months of one another. No wonder he spoke of the 'tremendous sickle' that was cutting down his circle of friends.[31] There is little evidence that the second death formed any real part for him of the problem of death that had so urgently to be overcome. Humphrey House notes that

> The Devil and Hell are frequently referred to in passing, but ambiguously; they might be either literal or metaphorical ...[32]

Certainly Hell is invoked in the fiction for its concept of a Providential justice operating in a larger arena than that of this world only. When, for example, Fagin, with his 'gasping mouth and burning skin', writhes 'in a paroxysm of fear' on his last night alive and 'his unwashed flesh crackled' as if with exposure to fire, it seems an anticipation of the state into which he shall shortly pass. This is reinforced when Oliver and Brownlow arrive, hoping to 'recall him to a sense of his position' (*OT* 52 pp. 361, 364).

At other times it is used metaphorically to describe godless values and fearful conditions that characterise this present world in a way that leaves it unclear whether this, or the supernatural place alluded to, is itself the actuality of Hell. When Dickens speaks of slum dwellers as having been 'born, and bred, in Hell!' (*DS* 47 p. 737), he may be saying that their current atmosphere erodes their morals and has a bearing on their eternal destiny. Equally, he may simply be saying that the actual environment in which they live is as terrible and hopeless as the Hell that presents itself to religious imaginations.

If Dickens shared the typical views of his Broad Church allies, he is likely to have had a liberal reluctance to believe in a literal Lake of Fire. Frederick Denison Maurice, for example, a leading preacher of the social gospel ideas, was famously removed from his chair in Theology at King's College, London, for rejecting everlasting damnation in his *Theological Essays* in 1853. Tennyson, too, was a universalist who could not believe that anyone would be excluded from salvation. Such views, however, were increasing in popularity in these middle years of the nineteenth century.[33]

While Hell is an uncertain place in Dickens's writings, death does seem to have its origins in a world that has sinned against God. Although House quotes Acton as saying that 'Dickens knew nothing of sin when it was not crime',[34] the novels are full of behaviour that is legally respectable, but morally horrifying. The sense that human beings have transgressed a divine standard is overwhelming. One of the two situations in which religion enters the plot of Dickens's novels most directly[35] is when the offer of repentance is being held out to sinners, usually fallen women. Nancy speaks of her 'life of sin and sorrow' and speculates that her self-destructive love for Sikes might be due to 'God's wrath for the wrong I have done' (*OT* 40 p. 274).

Equally, Martha in *David Copperfield* correctly sees the hero's search for her as an earnest quest 'to save a wretched creature for repentance' (47 p. 585) and Harriet Carker has assumed this role for Alice Marwood with the narrator's full backing in *Dombey and Son*. Even the murderous father in *Barnaby Rudge* is urged by his wife, speaking of 'the retribution which must come, and which is stealing on you now', to 'repent'.

Whereas Rudge refuses to do so, however, Alice, Martha and Nancy recognise their position as sinners. Nancy breathes 'one prayer for mercy to her maker' (*DC* 47 pp. 322–3), explaining to her murderer that 'It is never too late to repent'.

Such widespread portrayal of sin does not, of course, mean that Dickens accepted the doctrine of original sin. Indeed he violently repudiated it. This can most clearly be seen in that its most vigorous adherents are deeply unsympathetic characters like Mrs Clennam, who notes that 'every one of us, all the children of Adam' have 'offences to expiate and peace to make' (II 30 p. 350). Mrs Barbary's insistence too that Esther has been 'born with' a fault inherited from her parents (*BH* 3 p. 31) is also taken to task by the novelist. Dickens's major objection to this doctrine seems to be the perceived long-term effects upon children such as Arthur and Esther, who believe that they are fundamentally wicked before they are able to make moral choices.

By contrast, many of the children of his novels, although by no means all,[36] seem fundamentally good. It is impossible to imagine Oliver Twist or Little Nell as inheritors of Adam's blighted nature. In the face of this, Paul's teaching seems blasphemous to Dickens's religion. Nevertheless, in adulthood such unspoiled characters are striking exceptions rather than representative human beings in Dickens's world, and they are evoked to show a spoiled world how to escape the effects of sin and death.

What, then, is the means of transcending death that Dickens and his novels recommend? Pauline Christianity insisted that a death of the old sinful and dying identity was necessary so that a sinless and deathless one could be given. The significance of the cross was that Jesus Christ had undergone the sinner's death and punishment for sin. In the Christian scheme, Calvary reverses the effects of Adam and Eve's choice to reject their relationship of love with God and afterwards with each other. There, Christ embraced the death and the terrible isolation from the life of God that human beings suffer as a result of their separation from God, which resulted in the cry from the darkness, 'My God, my God, why hast thou forsaken me?' (Matthew 27:46) The unpaid debt incurred by the parents and shared by the descendants was at last paid on their behalf, returning the proper system of relationships. Where mankind sought a self-absorbed happiness that excluded God and eternal life, God did the opposite, reaching out and renewing the vital connection. The cross is an act of complete altruism, the offended party suffering punishment for the offender, displaying God's complete love for a fallen world. By surrendering the old self, each person could identify with that death as having taken place for him or her. Christ could then identify his risen life with him or her. To help them remember this, new Christians underwent the ceremony of baptism, a symbol which, as we shall see, particularly in the chapters on the railway, the river and the crowd, was to be recast and critically re-examined for the modern world throughout Dickens's representations of London. In the submergence and re-emergence from the water, this act of self-burial and hoped-for resurrection was vividly mimed (Romans 6:1–11). Paul triumphantly declared, 'I am crucified with Christ: nevertheless I live; yet not I, but Christ liveth in me' (Galatians 2:20), but does any vestige of this aspect of the traditional understanding of the work of Jesus remain in Dickens?

In *Little Dorrit*, he makes it clear that he considers the ascetic form of self-crucifixion at any rate utterly inadequate. Mrs Clennam feels that by restricting her enjoyment of life and by suffering the effects of her disability, she is 'balancing her bargains with the Majesty of heaven' (*LD* I 3 p. 48). Her harsh treatment of Arthur's real mother, 'through ... present misery ... to purchase her redemption from endless misery' (II 30 p. 755), is justified by this same curious doctrine that suffering embraced in this life cancels out sins and reduces punishment in the hereafter. That this teaching is so obviously a mask for her own vindictiveness exposes the falsity of her own reliance upon it to cover her own sins.

It is a point worth making because it is often overlooked that Mrs Clennam is not an Evangelical. For such Christians, the idea that the sacrifice of Christ was insufficient by itself to redeem or buy back the human being from a lost eternity and that it needed to be supplemented by additional suffering would have been as deeply blasphemous as it was to Dickens. Suffering that did not directly benefit others is shown in this book to be not an identification with Christ's death but a perversion of its fundamental purpose. Arthur Clennam understands this and insists upon 'Duty on earth, restitution on earth, action on earth' in contrast with Mrs Clennam's system of reparation. Such a path is 'far straiter and narrower than the broad high road paved with vain professions and vain repetitions ... all cheap materials costing absolutely nothing' (I 27 p. 311). As Larson perceptively notices, this refers to a text in the Sermon on the Mount conventionally used by Calvinists to demonstrate the fewness of the elect, subverting it to show that the truly difficult path is that of doing practical good.[37] Larson, however, goes on to claim that even this attitude is infected with Mrs Clennam's insistence upon repayment and 'contains telltale remnants of his childhood's legalistic themes'.[38] A life of renunciation alone, Larson claims, cannot bring happiness to these characters. It is only when Arthur and Amy recognise and requite their need of each other that they find a means of transcending their world.

Little Dorrit herself at least teaches a lesson of grace, mercy and forgiveness that refuses any monetary repayment. Even if this represents an advance on Arthur's attitude, however, it is difficult to imagine the act of burning the codicil having the same meaning had Mrs Clennam not embraced something of the desire to make restitution on earth in authorising the heroine to look at its contents. For Dickens, repentance in action and reception of grace are rather more intertwined as a means of salvation than Larson's analysis allows. This is very much in the spirit of characters in the gospels such as Zacchaeus, who responds to the grace of Jesus and instantly restores fourfold the money of which his deceit has deprived others (Luke 19:8). Little Dorrit's conversation with Mrs Clennam here is one of the key points of the novel and is explicitly presented as a triumph of the heroine's New Testament theology over Mrs Clennam's Old Testament one (II 31 p. 770).

The idea of rebirth is important in Dickens and is often effected through repentance and a change of heart. Mr Dombey, Ebenezer Scrooge and Eugene Wrayburn may all be said to undergo conversions when confronted with death in one form or another, and to be reborn into an entirely new style of life.[39] It is important to remember that Dickens's novels are not tracts and that in dramatising a dimension of religious experience, the author is not obliged to exemplify a theological truth naturalistically, but may rather provide images that make the reader feel the reality of it in other ways. Nevertheless, it is worth noting that many of the characters that have to confront death are made to do so explicitly with reliance upon the work of Christ. Stephen Blackpool's death in *Hard Times* evokes the traditional Victorian deathbed confession of faith:

> The star had shown him where to find the God of the poor; and through humility, and sorrow, and forgiveness, he had gone to his Redeemer's rest.
>
> (III 6 pp. 291–2)

This orthodox statement is still somewhat ambiguous. Is the saving 'forgiveness' Stephen's forgiveness of his oppressors, for example, or God's forgiveness of Stephen? How and when has Christ redeemed Stephen and from what? Nevertheless, the knowledge that somehow He has done so seems to vitalise Stephen here in the face of death.

Our Mutual Friend provides a more explicitly Christian death in the end of Betty Higden's flight from so-called charity. The reader is told that the countryside in the rural reaches of the Thames 'brought to her mind the foot of the Cross,[40] and she committed herself to Him who died upon it' (*OMF* III 8 p. 505). Here, Dickens comes close to portraying Christ's death as being on behalf of the dying person. In the following chapter, he shows unease in the notion that Betty really is a sinner in need of salvation. When Milvey tries to console Sloppy with the thought that 'we were all a halting, failing, feeble, and inconstant crew', he responds, '*She* warn't, sir' (III 9 p. 508). Despite these misgivings about the hated doctrine of Original Sin, however, Dickens clearly feels that Christ's death has enabled Betty Higden to accept and transcend her own.

In *Bleak House*, the 'great Cross on the summit of St Paul's Cathedral' is the expression of the city's hidden meaning. Hidden by the 'red and violet-tinted smoke', it is 'the crowning confusion of the great, confused city' (19 p. 315). The implication is that 'that sacred emblem' holds the answer to the darkness and bondage which Jo's life in the mud and smog impose upon him, but that these metropolitan conditions prevent him from apprehending it. In its own architecture, the city contains the regenerating information he needs, but other aspects of the city conceal it from his view. In the same way, the Bibles carried here by the church-goers contain the same message, but Jo does not know how to read it. Jo may be prevented from apprehending its significance by men like Chadband and by all that is represented by the London fog, but it must surely have a profound meaning or else it would not strike the reader as scandalous or pathetic that it should be denied to him. Directly within his line of vision is something that might potentially give him the ability to transcend death that it provides for Betty Higden.

So what *should* the cross mean in *Bleak House*? Here, it seems to be a symbol of altruistic self-giving. What Chadband is said to obliterate is the story of Christ's 'deeds done on this earth for common men' (*BH* 25 p. 415). In so far as anyone enlightens Jo, it is Woodcourt, who shows him what Christlike altruism is, instead of imparting theological information. His recognition that the fragmented phrases of the Lord's Prayer are 'wery good' recalls their spiritual kinship with the generosity of Nemo: 'He wos wery good to me, he wos!' (11 p. 181). This works on the same principle as Alice Marwood's equation of the gospel narrative with Harriet Carker's care for her in *Dombey and Son*: 'Lay my head so dear, that as you read, I may see the words in your kind face' (48 p. 785).

The Bible and Harriet Carker's face are, then, two means of telling an identical story. Such people have earned their right to speak the message of Christianity, just as Esther's words of comfort about 'Our Saviour' are acceptable to the brickmaker's wife, whereas Mrs Pardiggle's are not (*BH* 8 p. 134). The Bible, then, is not merely a convenient text for abuse by hypocrites such as Chadband. Oliver Twist reads its pages with delight (*OT* 32 p. 211). Alice Marwood finds her place in its story (*DS* 48 p. 765), and Pip reads its pages to Magwitch as he faces death (*GE* III 17 p. 456). Acts of human kindness, including the systematic social reform the novels call for, are, then, religious acts. They are the divine operation of divine love in the world, which, to Dickens, finds its clearest expression – one might even say incarnation – in the charity of human beings. The cross seems to Dickens to be fundamentally an exemplary act of altruism, where Jesus was able to forgive His executioners, rather than the altar of a sacrifice for sin. Nevertheless, it is difficult to imagine how its apparently random suffering could have had any altruistic purpose without its redemptive element. In *The Life of Our Lord*, Dickens told his children that the disciples 'carried crosses as their sign, because upon a cross He had suffered Death', without further explanation of the significance of that death.[41] The crucifixion is also narrated without reference to Christ's suffering for mankind's sin, although Jesus's promise to the dying thief is faithfully and lovingly recorded.

It would seem, then, that if Dickens's method of participating in Christ's cross is primarily sharing in His life of self-giving practical action, then the author's religion is one of salvation by works, rather than by faith. This is the overwhelming impression created by *The Life of Our Lord*, which promises his children that 'if they did their duty, they would go to Heaven'.[42] There is, of course, forgiveness for the last-minute penitent, as was reflected in the fiction:

> people who have done good all their lives long, will go to Heaven after they are dead. But ... people who have been wicked, because of their being miserable, or not having parents and friends to take care of them when young and who are truly sorry for it, however late in their lives, and pray to God to forgive them, will be forgiven and go to Heaven too.

Two distinct categories emerge here: those who are good and need no salvation and those who are wicked and do. Dickens almost certainly saw himself most of the time in the former category. If this comes dangerously close to the complacent Pharisee and the tax collector of Luke 18:9–14, *both* of whom required justification before God, it is worth remembering that his own will concluded by committing his 'soul to the mercy of God through our Lord and Saviour Jesus Christ'.[43] Even when Dickens seems most firmly to insist that innate goodness rather than imputed righteousness is the means of salvation, however, the nature of salvation is always essentially based on the idea of conversion from one state into another:

the most ugly, deformed, wretched creatures that live will be bright Angels in Heaven if they are good here on earth.[44]

The same hope and consolation that Dickens gave his own children is repeated to Florence after the death of her mother in the contemporaneous *Dombey and Son*. Her mother has been:

buried in the ground where the trees grow ... where the ugly little seeds turn into beautiful flowers, and into grass, and corn, and I don't know what all besides. Where good people turn into bright angels, and fly away to Heaven!

(*DS* 3 p. 26)

This emphasis on transformation *via* death uses almost identical vocabulary to that of *The Life of Our Lord*, where the 'ugly' are made into 'bright angels' after death through having been 'good'. This borrows the agricultural metaphor of the Apostle Paul, who likens the buried body to a seed or 'bare grain' (1 Corinthians 15:37) that emerges from the earth as something beneficial, saying:

So also is the resurrection from the dead. It is sown in corruption; it is raised in incorruption.

(v. 42)

The same faith in bodily resurrection to a heavenly state is expressed, but Dickens guards against the assumption that this is an exact statement of his theology by semi-fictionalising the account ('"Once upon a time", said Richards ...') and putting it in the mouth of 'a strange nurse that couldn't tell it right' (I 3 pp. 26–7). Nevertheless, the rest of the book reinforces this tale of resurrections, whether it be through Walter's reappearance from the shipwreck, the transformation of Dombey himself or Little Paul's dying vision of his mother and Jesus waiting for him beyond the sea of death (16 p. 225). Within the context of the novel's world, at least, Mrs Toodles seems to have got it right.

In a less explicit way, Paul's resurrection metaphor is present behind the more Romanticised death of Little Nell. She prepares to encounter death by thinking of 'the growth of buds and blossoms out of doors' (*OCS* 53 p. 413) and, having looked down the deep well which 'looks like a grave', her last living thoughts are of the time of new growth:

> 'The birds sing again in spring,' thought the child, as she leant at her casement window, and gazed at the declining sun. 'Spring! a beautiful and happy time!'
>
> (55 p. 430)

Here the idea is rather that nature continues, even if Nell does not. Her death contributes to a natural cycle that causes other things to grow. Perhaps this is because this book's focus, unlike that of *Dombey and Son*, is primarily upon how to survive the death of a loved one, rather than upon how to transcend death and deadness. If anything metaphorically grows from the burying of the body-seed in the earlier novel, it is virtue arising in the hearts of the bereaved from memory of the dead. The schoolmaster insists that

> There is nothing ... no, nothing innocent or good, that dies, and is forgotten. ... oh, if the good deeds of human creatures could be traced to their source, how beautifully would even death appear; for how much charity, mercy, and purified affection, would be seen to have their growth in dusty graves.
>
> (54 pp. 421–2)

Nevertheless, having tested this secularised version of what grows from graves, he ultimately finds it wanting. In a letter to John Forster of 8 January 1841, he confessed that the writing of Little Nell's death reminded him painfully of his bereavement of Mary Hogarth and that 'I can't preach to myself the schoolmaster's consolation, though I try'. His intense doubts of this comfort can be seen in *The Old Curiosity Shop* as he attempts to re-iterate its precepts when Nell's passing is discovered:

> Oh! it is hard to take to heart the lesson such deaths will teach, but let no man reject it, for it is one that all must learn, and is a mighty universal Truth. When death strikes down the innocent and young, for every fragile form from which he lets the panting spirit free, a hundred virtues rise, in shapes of mercy, charity, and love, to walk the world, and bless it. Of every tear that sorrowing mortals shed on

such green graves, some good is born, some gentler nature comes. In the Destroyer's steps there spring up bright creations that defy his power, and his dark path becomes a way of light to heaven.

(72 p. 659)

It clearly remained no easy matter for Dickens to learn this lesson instead of rejecting it.

It seems that the Pauline application of the seed-into-plant analogy of the later novels, which promises bodily resurrection and reunion, had more enduring comfort for Dickens than the schoolmaster's consolation, after all. Dickens's wife, Kate, had had this hope at Mary's death. In a letter to his friend Richard Johns, dated 31 May 1837, Dickens said that she 'looks forward to being mercifully permitted one day to rejoin her sister in that happy World for which God adapted her better than for this'. The same consolation seems to have become increasingly effective for Dickens himself, and when Forster's brother died, his condolences mix the schoolmaster's doctrine of memory with a confident assertion of the Christian hope that

That end [is] but the bright beginning of a happier union, I believe; and have never more strongly and religiously believed (and oh! Forster, with what a sore heart I have thanked God for it) than when that shadow has fallen on my own hearth ...[45]

With every apparent sincerity, the writer testifies to a faith that death can be turned into the means of entering a new and transformed life available for each individual eventually to share.

III. Dickens and Providence

Dickens, then, held to a hope that revelation of God and a form of regeneration from Him were still available to modern humanity, even if his degree of trust in the traditional symbols by which these were made known varied considerably. Equally, when his trust in the reality of these benefits faded, he seems able to reapply the traditional symbols when necessary to the context of his more unorthodox thoughts. But did Dickens see the individual struggling through the universe, searching for meaning and renewal alone, or did he see an overarching scheme governing these revelations and renewals? The question becomes important when considering the tension between the exuberant and terrifying randomness of his city and the occasional suggestion that it may be governed by an inscrutable (if not necessarily benign) system. Before exploring what such representations say about the presence or absence of order in the universe as Dickens conceived it, it will be useful to discuss how Providence itself was an ongoing part of his thought. This is more directly applicable to the fiction, as most of his strongest statements on the issue come from the novels themselves.

At first glance, it may appear that Dickens did not take Providence[46] very seriously at all. Often it is reduced to the level of conversational commonplace, most memorably when Sam Weller comforts his father after the death of Mrs Weller by saying (after several minutes spent trying to think of something better), 'There's a Providence in it all' and his father replies, 'O' course there is. ... Wot 'ud become of the undertakers vithout it, Sammy?' (*PP* 52 p. 806). The humour here belies a serious concern that Providence may simply be what we should now call an ideological construct that any group in society, such as the undertakers in this case, may evoke to naturalise their position.

Dickens's satires on pseudo-religious hypocrisy and self-interest often focus on characters who abuse the notion of Providence and employ it as an excuse for inactivity at both a personal and an institutional level. The most obvious example is the fabricated letter from Mr Squeers, saying that Graymarsh's maternal aunt

> Would have sent the two pair of stockings as desired, but is short of money, so forwards a tract instead, and hopes Graymarsh will put his trust in Providence.
>
> (*NN* 8 p. 159)

Similarly, the narrator of *American Notes* explains that the American stagecoach 'has only one step, and that being about a yard from the ground, is usually approached by a chair: when there is no chair, ladies trust in Providence' (*AN* 9). Providence seems to be little more than an imaginary concept for making a threadbare attempt to cover the absence of human provision.

Barnaby Rudge, with its wider concern with self-interested appropriation of religious vocabulary, shows this concept to be very elastic. Its characters unreflectingly assume that their own habits, modes of thought and way of living are guaranteed by this higher power. John Willet, for example, believes it 'a thing quite settled and ordained by the laws of nature and Providence, that anybody who said or did or thought otherwise [than himself] must be inevitably and of necessity wrong' (*BR* 1 p. 45). Mr Dennis complacently assumes that the riots are providing him with criminals to be hanged by a dispensation like that underlying the agricultural cycle of the seasons:

> As he walked along the streets with his leather gloves clasped behind him, and his face indicative of cheerful thought and pleasant calculation, Mr Dennis might have been likened unto a farmer ruminating among his crops, and enjoying by anticipation the bountiful gifts of Providence.
>
> (BR 70 p. 629)

Only the more knowing Sir John Chester, however, is aware that people subconsciously, but no less wilfully for that, conflate a hidden divine edict with the random circumstances leading to their own getting on at the expense of others. Calling the presence in court of the Lord Mayor's brother to testify against Barnaby 'a good stroke of chance (or, as the world would say, a providential occurrence)', he shows his willingness to do so deliberately and cynically himself (BR 75 p. 671).

To take a final example from the earlier fiction, Isaac List in *The Old Curiosity Shop* observes that Mrs Jarley 'has money, and does keep it in a tin box when she goes to bed, and doesn't lock her door for fear of fire'. Encouraging Nell's grandfather to regard this as provision for gambling stakes, he considers this 'quite a Providence – I should call it, but then I've been religiously brought up' (OCS 42 p. 327). Dickens's later work explores more subtle versions of this self-deluding tendency to naturalise the exploitation of one class or individual by another with reference to a divinely underwritten scheme of things. Here, however, it is expressed in its simplest form.

Mr Pecksniff offers the first sustained indication that society may be callously invoking Providence to cover its own evasion of duty to provide in his 'short and pious grace, invoking a blessing on the appetites of those present, and committing all persons who had nothing to eat, to the care of Providence: whose business (so said the grace, in effect) it clearly was, to look after them' (MC 9 p. 147). Dickens insists that this satirical portrait has a political and not merely a personal dimension, saying of Pecksniff's statement that 'a special Providence – has blessed my endeavours':

> A question of philosophy arises here, whether Mr Pecksniff had or had not good reason to say, that he was specially patronised and encouraged in his undertakings. ... Now, there being a special Providence in the fall of a sparrow, it follows (so Mr Pecksniff might

have reasoned perhaps), that there must also be a special Providence in the alighting of the stone, or stick, or other substance which is aimed at the sparrow. And Mr Pecksniff's hook, or crook, having invariably knocked the sparrow on the head and brought him down, that gentleman may have been led to consider himself as specially licensed to bag sparrows, and as being specially seized and possessed of all the birds he had got together. That many undertakings, national as well as individual – but especially the former – are held to be specially brought to a glorious and successful issue, which never could be so regarded on any other process of reasoning, must be clear to all men. Therefore the precedents would seem to show that Mr Pecksniff had (as things go) good argument for what he said and might be permitted to say it, and did not say it presumptuously, vainly, or arrogantly, but in a spirit of high faith and great wisdom.

(20 pp. 329–30)

The quotation from *Hamlet* upon which this caricatured reasoning is based is of course itself derived from Matthew's Gospel, in which Jesus insists upon the Father's knowledge of the suffering of all creation. In context, this general statement highlights the particular idea of the verses immediately before and after, namely, that the disciples' suffering of persecution is noted and honoured above. There is a strong implication too that the persecutors are also noted and will be held accountable (10:28–32). In choosing these words as the basis for Pecksniff's spurious argument, Dickens implies that those personal and national undertakings that justify their gain at the expense and suffering of others on the grounds that circumstances have enabled them to do so are equally accountable. The concept of Providence provides an apparently religious excuse for lack of care based on a wilful misunderstanding of the Bible.

Dickens later develops this idea that appeals to Providence are part of a culpable national ideology of superiority by making the word central not only to the vocabulary of Pecksniffery, but also of Podsnappery. Mr Podsnap perhaps believes his own rhetoric, but Dickens characterises the cynicism of a nation when he observes that 'he always knew exactly what Providence meant. ... And it was very remarkable (and must have been very comfortable) that what Providence meant, was invariably what Mr Podsnap meant' (*OMF* I 11 p. 132). Podsnap draws upon the sentiment behind such songs as 'Rule Britannia' to assert his confidence that Britain has a right to world dominance and that its ways of governing came directly from God, saying, 'We Englishmen are Very Proud of our

Constitution, Sir. It Was Bestowed Upon Us By Providence'. Dickens shares the scepticism of the Frenchman listening, who laughingly remarks, 'It was a little particular of Providence … for the frontier is not large' (p. 137). Even Dickens's good characters share this tendency to attribute their own insularity to Divine decree, as when Miss Pross exclaims, 'If it was ever intended that I should go across salt water, do you suppose Providence would have cast my lot in an island?' (*TTC* I 4 p. 59).

What Dickens objects to most, however, is Podsnap's nationalisation of Pecksniff's grace, which vilifies any suggestion that the nation should provide for the poor as a rejection of God's order of dispensation. Like his predecessor, he justifies his stance by quoting Christ's words in Matthew's Gospel (26:11), this time to mean that Providence has guaranteed continuation of poverty – therefore there is no need to identify and deal with its causes:

> 'And you know; at least I hope you know;' said Mr Podsnap, with severity, 'that Providence has declared that you shall have the poor always with you?'
>
> The meek man also hoped he knew that.
>
> 'I am glad to hear it,' said Mr Podsnap with a portentous air. 'I am glad to hear it. It will render you cautious how you fly in the face of Providence.'

The narrator calls this an 'absurd and irreverent conventional phrase', and the sympathetic 'meek man' says he has 'no fear of doing anything so impossible' (*OMF* I 11 p 144). Dickens could not have made his feelings on such usage of this frequently invoked concept clearer.

Nevertheless, Dickens's satires on such absurdities must not lead us to suppose that he did not believe in the concept itself. The very same novel balances Podsnap's rhetoric with characters who unaffectedly read just such a heavenly hand in the events of the novel themselves. Lightwood says to Wrayburn, for example, 'I solemnly believe, with all my soul, that if Providence should mercifully restore you to us, you will be blessed with a noble wife in the preserver of your life, whom you will dearly love' (*OMF* IV 10 p. 723). Even Bradley Headstone, in a moment of classic tragic *anagnorisis*, recognises it in the fact that his very act of trying to separate Lizzie and Eugene by murder has led directly to their marriage:

> For, then he saw that through his desperate attempt to separate those two for ever, he had been made the means of uniting them. That he

had dipped his hands in blood, to mark himself a miserable fool and tool. That Eugene Wrayburn, for his wife's sake, set him aside and left him to crawl along his blasted course. He thought of Fate, or Providence, or be the directing Power what it might, as having put a fraud upon him – overreached him – and in his impotent mad rage bit, and tore, and had his fit.

(OMF IV 15 p. 771)

There is a force at work that turns even actions intended for harm to good.

Occasionally Dickens mocks characters' interpretation of the novel's events as acts of Providence. Mr Pumblechook in *Great Expectations*, for example, says that in Pip's 'being brought low'

> he saw the finger of Providence. He knowed that finger when he saw it, Joseph, and he saw it plain. It pinted out this writing, Joseph. *Reward of ingratitoode to earliest benefactor, and founder of fortun's.*

(III 19 p. 473)

But perhaps he has a point? If we regard Joe rather than Pumblechook as Pip's true 'earliest benefactor', Pip seems to see his own downfall as an act of justice of this sort. It gives him, after all, the opportunity to return to a proper footing with Joe and to make a new start by his own work that ultimately serves him as a blessing.

Dickens in fact saw the process of his plots as directly mimetic of the operations of a benign Providence operating in the external world, solemnly declaring to Wilkie Collins in 1859:

> I think the business of art is to ... shew ... what everything has been working to – but only to SUGGEST, until the fulfilment comes. These are the ways of Providence – of which ways, all Art is but a little imitation.[47]

Narrative existed to embody this gradual revelation of a bigger picture, whereby a force larger than the individual human being's field of vision is bringing punishment to the wicked and peace to the good. At THE END, whether the dénouement of the novel, the end of life or the end of time, this process will become clear. Dickens's conceptualisation of the novelist's art here would seem to subscribe to a vaguely defined but firmly Christian conception of history.

London, with its apparent randomness and suggestion that it forms a total system beyond the individual's power to view, becomes a crucial vehicle for exploring these Providential beliefs, showing at various times Dickens's anxieties about the reality of any overarching scheme and his desire to assert that there was one. We will also look for occasions when Dickens seems to fear that the mysterious systematisation his depiction of London invites readers to take comfort in is merely justifying the *status quo*, much as Providence itself was subject to abuse.

Enough, then, has been said to form a working idea of Dickens's stated beliefs and the beliefs expressed directly in his fiction. It is now possible to address the real subject matter of the book. It is time to enter Dickens's London, exploring the Babel of signals his novels send to the reader about the presence or absence of a Providential scheme; about revelation and concealment of meaning; and transcendence of death, new life and resurrection. The question of how Dickens engaged with the vocabulary and symbolism of Christianity here becomes crucial. Does its reflection signal belief in its enduring power or point to its inadequacies? Or is it merely an opportunistic seizure of Christian vocabulary to illustrate a secular revelation in terms to which his readers could relate like, say, Clement of Alexandria's exploitation of the mystery religions under-stood by his audience to illustrate a very different form of revelation? Raymond Williams certainly thinks so, arguing that

> Dickens ... uses the language of popular religion ... when he makes his related plea for change. ... Yet it is clear that what he has in mind is always human and social intervention, in the spirit of innocence. He rejects or seems not to know the alienated religious versions of redemption or salvation.[48]

As we examine the complex process of his engagement with religious images and modes of regeneration, the spiritual and social forms of revelation will be seen to have a more dialogic relationship in the mind and work of Dickens than Williams's diametric opposition allows.

Ephraim Sicher's recent study *Rereading the City, Rereading Dickens*[49] has paved the way here by comparing Dickens's work to other contem-porary attempts to represent the city across a range of discourses, including those of sanitary reform, apocalyptic religious pamphlets, Romantic art and poetry, and eighteenth-century satire. Sicher's con-clusions point to a writer actively promoting a literal regeneration of London's physical and human waste matter by means of engineering and social rehabilitation, yet drawing his sense of the final value of such transformations from a latent religious sensibility. He demonstrates the co-presence in *Our Mutual Friend* of archetypal religious structures and observation of the need for ontological and societal reform valuable for their own sake:

> the major symbolic patterns of this novel place [Harmon's] staged death and 'resurrection' in a mythical mode that nonetheless loses none of its contemporary social relevance, not least for the question of moral and personal identity in the city.[50]

Lizzie Hexam provides a neat example of the relationship between these discourses. She is able to provide a raising of the dead indebted to her father's socio-economic transformation of dead matter into value, but higher than it in terms of its spiritually redeeming results. The reason for this is its motivation in unselfish love, without which all other kinds of retrieval from deadness are worthless.[51] Jenny Wren and Venus too seek to recycle the dead by-products of city life into attempts to represent them in life once again, however much some elements, like Wegg's leg, seem to resist it. Sicher sees this as emblematic of the novelist's function, Dickens's ultimate expression of faith in the possibility of restoring life to the city by representing it as it is and as it might be through the revitalising power of imaginative empathy:

> The novelist too must ... conjure up an act of resurrection that will animate the drowned man, like Venus 'the articulator' who puts skeletons into artistic and anatomical shape. This secular resurrection restores the body to meaning as semantic sign in the plot and in the city's necropolis ...[52]

Dickens's very ambiguities about which type of regeneration he is providing as he undertakes this role of resurrectionist in his novels are presented as a self-conscious polyphony of discourses that allows him to explore them all by jarring contact. Nevertheless, he adds that this,

> far from distancing itself in despair at any stable meaning in an unredeemed world, does not preclude belief in another world beyond empirical verification and in a Creator to whom there is moral responsibility. On the contrary, it suggests the possibility of transcendence, as well as the consequences of blindness to it.[53]

The reader's very difficulty in separating the discourses that have formed their architectural and verbal representations signals a division between those who can see the promise of transcendence they contain and those blind to it. Indeed the form of his novels seems designed to emphasise that the onus is upon the reader to be among those who can salvage some adequate form of revelation from the polyphony for themselves. This integrated approach, recognising that Dickens interacted with social, ontological and religious forms of revelation, is reflected in my study of his London, although its focus is on his re-evaluation of specifically religious symbolism. Each chapter examines the various discourses engaged within a particular symbol which forms part of London and that, in its respective novel, plays a part in the narrative's tension between denying the possibility of transcendent revelations and working towards them. Both resistance to and restatement of the religious dimensions implicit in London's mysterious aspects will be apparent in these dramatisations of concealment and discovery of meaning.

2

'The debilitated old house in the city': London as Haunted House

Any novel centred upon a secret is conflicted between hiding information from readers and pushing onward towards revelation. Dickens's city may at first glance seem to serve only the first of these tendencies of narrative. Each individual building in the London of *Little Dorrit*, for example, including the Circumlocution Office, the Marshalsea and Mrs Clennam's house, appears designed to restrict access to information, especially about those within their walls. The cumulative effect is a metropolis whose own structure and atmosphere is experienced as an infinitely magnified reflection of such tenebrous buildings, denying the individual's attempts to fathom its secrets. Later chapters will consider the city's opposing inherent forces that push truth into the open. Here discussion focuses on how the metropolis keeps its secrets, what those secrets are and what underlies the desire to conceal embodied by the imposing conglomeration of London.

In his exploration of the urge towards concealment, Dickens consciously interacts with an earlier motif that had performed this function in relation to the plot within the genre of which it was a staple ingredient: the haunted castle in the gothic novel. In Dickens's fiction generally, but especially in *Little Dorrit*, numerous houses inherit and develop this tradition. Since the entire metropolis becomes an enormous extrapolation of their enclosed and obscuring environments, it will be helpful to look at the kinds of secrets kept in haunted houses. The gothic novel's castles employ key features from religious discourses in representing the structures that human beings erect to conceal various sorts of truth. Many of these are discernible as they are passed down to Dickens's metropolis through his individual houses. Since *Little Dorrit* is a novel that discusses religious discourse at the level of its subject matter, it is useful to see how the connotations of the gothic are adapted when its main symbol is expanded into this urbanised context.

Equally, however, modern critics have the conceptual vocabulary of psychoanalysis at their disposal and often read the gothic novel in terms of repressed knowledge about the self, repressed desires and their return in unnerving places. Dickens's interest in structures of concealment and their deadening effect on the individual may well be read as pre-Freudian examinations of a purely secular and internal human psychology. In discussing the gothic inheritance of firstly individual houses and then of the city around them, mediation between these two approaches to reading *Little Dorrit* reveals a novel richly re-formulating in religious, social and psychological terms the nuances of the genre that influenced it.

I. Castles of the ego

Dickens explicitly associates Mrs Clennam's house with the convention of the gothic castle,[1] calling it 'the haunted house' (I 29 p. 337) and comparing it to 'a castle of Romance' (I 3 p. 40). In a letter to John Forster, he refers to 'the owner of the gigantic helmet',[2] displaying some familiarity with Horace Walpole's *The Castle of Otranto* (1764), which provides an obvious antecedent for the tale of Mrs Clennam's house. In both stories, the owners of an imposing building exploit its complexities to prevent hidden information about a wronged family from leaving their control. Once the secret is out, the edifice crumbles to dust.

Another key gothic text whose books Dickens had in his library is Ann Radcliffe. In *The Mysteries of Udolpho* (1792),[3] the use of a castle by a scheming concealer was developed, with much more description of the building and the experience of wandering inside it. Crucially, both Otranto and Udolpho are fortresses that prevent outsiders from gaining access to their owners. Both Manfred and his counterpart in Radcliffe's book, Montoni, wish to be seen as powerful and rightful rulers, but under the surface is the truth that the former is an illegal usurper and the latter is the captain of a vicious gang of bandits. Montoni remains in almost complete control of everything that is seen in Udolpho and Emily's impressions of the castle could well be a description of its master, whose image it projects:

> Silent, lonely and sublime, it seemed to stand sovereign of the scene, and to frown defiance on all, who dared to invade its solitary reign.
>
> (*MOU* II 5 p. 227)

The house is an expression of power over others and a very concrete reinforcement of a public self.

Dickens evokes this motif in *Dombey and Son* to convey the barriers one man wishes to erect between his inner self and the eyes of humanity at large. Hiding behind an impenetrable public persona as the mighty man of business, Dombey refuses to let his wife and children – in fact, even himself – see behind it. His house in north-west London enables this exclusion of others from access to the self in much the same way as the Castle of Udolpho. Dickens explicitly compares it to the 'magic dwelling-place in magic story, shut up in the heart of a thick wood' of this tradition, by emphasising its darkness and enclosure behind railings. Like its owner, it constantly has 'a frown upon its never-smiling face' (*DS* 23 p. 311). It is an outward manifestation of his desire to 'shut out all the world as with a double door of gold' (20 p. 275).

In *Little Dorrit*, however, the motif dominates the novel. On the exterior, everything about Mrs Clennam's house suggests barriers, from its 'rusty' 'iron railings' to the 'jumble of roots' (I 3 p. 32) they enclose. When William Dorrit seeks admission, he enters something very like a mediaeval castle with the 'dreary, vacant sound' and grating chain of the door (II 17 p. 603). Again its refusal to disclose what is within reflects the owner's rigid privacy:

> Her severe face had no thread of relaxation in it, by which any explorer could have been guided to the gloomy labyrinth of her thoughts.
>
> (I 5 p. 44)

The exterior of the building and the exterior of the person refuse all access to the inner life, which is a characteristic feature of urban experience in Dickens.[4] The reader is taught elsewhere to compare houses with public personae when Merdle's dinner guests, set in two rows, are famously said to resemble:

> The expressionless uniform twenty houses ... all fended off by the same pattern of railing ...
>
> (I 21 p. 240)

Even the most respectable houses are designed to exclude in their featureless monotony. Intrusion into the house is an intrusion into the person (who knows what dark corners may be discovered?) and is therefore not to be tolerated.

Most writers on the gothic house and its descendants in Victorian fiction read its secrets in Freudian terms of repressed sexuality threatening to erode a respectable exterior. Leslie A. Fiedler concisely summarises this approach:

> Beneath the haunted castle lies the dungeon keep: the womb from whose darkness the ego first emerged, the tomb to which it knows it must return at last. Beneath the crumbling shell of paternal authority lies the maternal blackness, imagined by the gothic writer as a prison. ... The upper and lower levels of the ruined castle or abbey represent the contradictory fears at the heart of gothic terror: the dread of the super-ego, whose splendid battlements have been battered but not quite cast down – and of the id, whose buried darkness abounds in dark visions no stormer of the castle had even touched.[5]

The forbidding exterior provides the pre-Freudian writer with a way of discussing society's punitive and repressive norms, while the dungeons beneath enable representation of all that has been pushed under the surface to conform with them. Indeed, the cellars conceal all aspects of the self that do not fit in with the 'I' constructed by the individual in order to participate in the discourses needed for engagement in social life generally.

This astute reading identifies the reader's terror in tales of the haunted house with the perspective of the hero or heroine trapped within it – in Dickensian terms, that of Arthur Clennam, Little Dorrit and Florence Dombey. Dickens, however, is just as interested in what his 'villains' have to fear from the submerged terrors lurking in the hiding places they have built as what the searching heroes and heroines have to learn. They project a monolithic ego, structurally excluding the repressed desires that also go to make up the selves of their owners, in what amounts to an inevitably doomed denial. Indeed, his concealers have identified their own ego with the superego completely. Dombey's sense of himself as 'Dombey', which the fortified house fiercely protects, stands for the whole City's patriarchal commercial ethos. Likewise the 'wrathful, mysterious, and sad' exterior of Mrs Clennam's house (II 10 p. 525) projects a sense of herself as stoical religious sufferer that is indistinguishable from the austere religion that dominates the London Arthur walks through to get to it.

Even without accepting Freud's terminology, we can recognise Dickens's adaptation of the gothic as anticipating his interest in how human minds subtly work to conceal truths central to their sense of identity. What these egos, and the superegos that create them, repress in Dickens is the deprivation of a family of their rights. Dombey's self-image as fulfilled businessman relies upon concealing his obligation to his daughter. The size of his house protects him from the necessity of having to pay attention to Florence. He has hidden from himself and others that she has a claim on his love as rightful as any denied claim of property or money in the eighteenth-century texts. Repressing his response to Florence's love, he turns it into a hidden vacuum that undermines his being. Consequently, the inexorable laws of the narrative bring about the collapse of his marriage, business and reputation in one fell swoop. As if to underline the fact, his actual house is gutted and stripped literally bare by rapacious creditors.

Little Dorrit returns to this theme. The heroine's father conceals the debt of love and duty he owes her behind the high walls of the Marshalsea, which allow him to suppress his failure in this respect behind his 'duty' to be the Father of the Marshalsea and thus establish a spurious position for his children. He constructs an egotistical castle for himself out of these crude materials long before the castles in the air he plans in Italy prior to his death (II p. 18–19). This is ultimately compounded in a way more palpable to the reader when Mrs Clennam exploits the forbidding exterior and complicated interior of her house to hide the document guaranteeing Little Dorrit's rightful inheritance. The codicil makes the secret tangible and its whereabouts provide real reason for anxiety. Much of the novel's suspense comes from the question, 'Where is Blandois?' which really means, 'Where is the information about Little Dorrit's inheritance?' If Blandois is murdered and/or hidden in the house, then this information is within the control of its owner; if he is outside, then it is not.

The codicil also represents another denied inheritance. Should Arthur come to understand the criminal secret of this deception, he would discover the secret of his own parentage. Like Walpole's Isabella and Radcliffe's Emily, he would learn the truth about both his own identity and that of the person who has dominated him in a semi-parental role. Arthur's exclusion from such knowledge, however, has a much stronger personal significance, because he has believed Mrs Clennam to be his actual mother. He himself grew up in the building that contains the secret. 'His mother's dismal old house' (II 10 p. 596) is also 'that grim home of his youth'. The emergence of the secret from its cellar would mean the explosion of her carefully structured interpretation of their relationship as the binding one of mother and son.

Perhaps, however, rather than looking forward to Freud's stories about parent–child relationships to interpret these narratives, it might be more appropriate to look back to the story with which both psycho-analysis and the gothic engage, namely that of the Fall. The secrets uncovered in these novels often force the heroes or heroines to confront the question of guilt inherited from parental figures. Such 'original sin' must be known and addressed before their literal and ontological free-dom can be secured. The varying degrees of responsibility the younger generation assume for the sins of their elders in such novels suggest a tradition in dialogue with the story of the Fall which is still visible in Arthur Clennam's agonised conscience about the source of his own fortunes. Indeed, the discovery of parentage in Dickens is frequently a revelation that the protagonist has rightfully inherited not the parents' wealth, but their debts.[6]

The houses dramatically figure Adam and Eve's terror that their wrong-doing will come to light and that they will be cursed, initially by God and then by the offspring their action has blighted.[7] According to Genesis, the first act of hiding in human history was from the eyes of a God who has power to expose the wrong done: 'I was afraid because I was naked; and I hid myself' (3:10). The castle walls constitute an extremely sophisticated apron of fig leaves to hide the concealer's moral nakedness from view. Their age and immensity may suggest thousands of years of accumulated human strategies of denial shored up against a coming day of judgement. London's complexity too has been highly successful in obscuring the existence of this evaded responsibility. Thus in both gothic and Dickensian novels, the descendants frequently remain unaware that the atrophy and deadness of their own lives are the result of the transgressive circumstances in which their ancestors formed their identities.

For Victor Sage,[8] the house motif's fitness as a vehicle for discussing the Fall of man comes primarily from the biblical habit of referring to the body as the decaying house of the spirit in a post-lapsarian world, as for example in the final chapter of Ecclesiastes. In this reading, the fortified gothic castle fuses a sense of guilt concealed and a desperate attempt to forestall the wages of sin. Hiding the wrong done becomes an attempt to preserve a fallen life that is an increasingly eerie death-in-life. Ironically, the more defenses the concealing villains erect, the more cadaverous their houses become.

Gothic texts are often read as transmuting the story of the Fall into a mode of historical allegory. Architecturally, the figure of the castle still tends to locate the first parents responsible for today's ills in a medieval aristocracy. On the other hand, its gradual domestication into the haunted house over the course of the nineteenth century allows the possibility that more recent constructions of domesticity, so dear to the hearts of contemporary readers, may be constructed upon disobediences and injustices of their own.[9] In *The Closed Space*, however, Manuel Aguirre proposes another reading. He suggests that the gothic villain's attempts to create an environment in which they have complete control over everything that happens reflect the Post-Enlightenment culture's attempts to construct an ordered world that makes sense without deity, obeying its own inherent laws, in order to give humanity control over the cosmos. Nevertheless, there remained things that could not be understood or accounted for and these took over in the popular consciousness as objects of awe and replacements for the terror of divine retribution.[10] Ultimately, the excluded supernatural finds a way to assert its reality from within the castle itself, in the form of ghosts that insist upon declaring the truth.

If Mrs Clennam's house reinterprets the Fall in the light of its period's values in this semi-allegorical way, however, religion itself has become the structure behind which the sinning parent hides. Her house and her self-imposed confinement in it is really an attempt to exclude Providence itself by replacing its ministry with a series of self-punishments that benefit no one. As the truth emerges, this system, which is as artificially shored up as the house itself, is eroded and exposed as false.

Indeed all of *Little Dorrit*'s houses conceal a secret that could cause them to come crashing down. The Circumlocution Office and Merdle's house exist to enshrine the values of a commercial and administrated society, but both are terrified of revealing the structural vacuum at their heart. The secret enclosed in the corridors of the former is that it *does* nothing and that hiding behind the facade of Merdle's house is that he *has* nothing. The wealth that guarantees his power is illusory, just as Dombey's revered fortune has been secretly embezzled away by Carker and proves, in any case, to be of no value in purchasing the things that count in the novel. Both business houses crash violently when the truth is discovered.

If Dickens's urbanised haunted houses, then, constitute a form of symbolic psychoanalysis, they are exploring the psychology not only of individuals, but also of a society that conceals its nature even from itself. The novel engages with Mrs Clennam's brand of neo-Puritan religion by embodying it in her house and using that motif to display the suppressed truths and unspoken falsehoods upon which its ideology depends. By the same technique, he subjects to scrutiny the commercial ideology intertwined with this religion of transactions and the unvoiced denials that threaten to undermine the structure. Although the crumbling of Mrs Clennam's house has a rational explanation tacked on to it, judged by the standards of realism it is as unlikely as the collapse of Otranto. The cause of this event is rather to be traced in the laws of the book's symbolism and scheme of narrative justice than in the laws of the physical world. These stories of collapsing houses allow the reader to participate in a narrative of punitive fall following wrongdoing within a commercial nineteenth-century context, identifying strongly with the psychological factors motivating the transgressor's dread of discovery.

II. The house and the city

Arthur's first approach to his mother's residence in the novel – and consequently the reader's – is 'through some of the crooked and descending streets which lie (and lay more crookedly and closely then) between the river and Cheapside' (I 3 p. 31). This is an extended prevision of Mrs Clennam's dwelling, where 'There was not one straight floor, from the foundation to the roof' (I 5 p. 54). Seeing with any kind of perspective in both environments has been made almost impossible. Once Clennam leaves the house, he is in a structure still more labyrinthine, fragmented and bewildering. Bleeding Heart Yard is just one part of the city that is virtually impossible to navigate:

> you got into it down a flight of steps which formed no part of the original approach, and got out of it by a low gateway into a maze of shabby streets, which went about and about, tortuously ascending to the level again.
>
> (I 12 p. 129)

The dark network of passages that make up the 'proud irregularity' of Montoni's castle, in which Emily is perplexed by the 'numerous turnings' and 'the many doors that offered', in *The Mysteries of Udolpho* (II 6 245, 258), is re-figured in even more terrifying dimensions.

One of Dickens's favourite ways of describing London throughout his novels is as a labyrinth. In *Oliver Twist*, for example, the Artful Dodger and Charley Bates run through 'a most intricate maze of narrow streets' (*OT* 13 p. 74). Mrs Brown, in a later novel, takes Florence Dombey through 'a labyrinth of narrow streets' (*DS* 6 p. 75) and, of course:

> Todgers's was in a labyrinth, whereof the mystery was known but to a chosen few.
>
> (*MC* 9 p. 129)

Dickens delights in bringing naive characters such as Tom Pinch and Oliver from the country and abandoning them momentarily in the bewildering city. Florence is also lost there twice. There are so many zones in London that it is almost impossible to conceive of it as a whole. Just as the gothic villains exploit the complexity of their houses, so the city can be used as a means of asserting control over others who are ignorant of its layout. Even the normally idle Eugene Wrayburn in *Our Mutual Friend* uses his familiarity with London in this way, carefully studying its illogical structure to make Bradley Headstone undergo 'grinding torments' in following him down unknown alleys and dead end streets (III 10 p. 533).

Arthur Clennam feels that the city as a whole is a continuation of the house his stepmother uses so effectively to restrict access to knowledge. Two characteristics of London generally, its lockedness and its darkness, extend outward from these features as they appear in the house:

> the whole neighbourhood [was] under some tinge of its dark shadow. As he went along, upon a dreary night, the dim streets by which he went seemed all depositories of oppressive secrets. The deserted counting-houses, with their secrets of books and papers locked up in chests and safes; the banking-houses, with their secrets of strong rooms and wells, the keys of which were in a very few secret pockets and a very few secret breasts; the secrets of all the dispersed grinders in the vast mill, among whom there were doubtless plunderers, forgers, and trust-betrayers of many sorts, whom the light of any day that dawned might reveal; ... The shadow thickening and thickening as it approached its source, he thought ... of the secrets of the river, as it rolled its turbid tide between two frowning wildernesses of secrets, extending, thick and dense, for many miles, and warding off the free air and the free country swept by winds and wings of birds.
>
> (II 10 pp. 526)

Warding off the 'free air' makes the 'close air' of Mrs Clennam's house described immediately afterwards the atmosphere of the whole city. Indeed, London infinitely reproduces the most frustrating aspect of the rambling building: each street is a locked room or a dark corner within this enormous stronghold of darkness. It contains innumerable other people keeping London locked because of innumerable secrets, striving with varying degrees of success to build the city as their own vast house and asserting the power of their self-image over all who live in its shadow. Merdle's is one of the 'very few secret pockets', hence the 'counting-houses' and banks. Each of the millions of doors Arthur passes may or may not contain the information he is looking for. And there is no way of telling which doors will yield results. As in the gothic castle, the seeker after truth is both shut out by and also shut within the city.

Two of the key characteristics of the Sublime as defined by Edmund Burke that had been so crucial to the gothic castle have now been extended to the metropolis. Gothic novels presented villains who used the 'Vastness' or 'Greatness of dimension'[11] of their buildings to assert their power over the observing eye of character and reader and to impress them by terror with the futility of looking into their affairs.[12] Dickens's metropolitan gothic presents a confining space greater than the largest citadel. As far as the eye can see in the panorama given, it has swallowed up the entire outside world. There is nowhere to escape to from a city whose boundaries are beyond the visible horizon on every side and which gives the illusion of being entirely within the concealer's control.

The city's vastness, however, is more than matched by its 'Obscurity'.[13] Throughout this long paragraph, the city deliberately excludes the light of the open countryside and the shadows seem to be a means of enforcing repressive claustrophobia. A considerable part of the city has been structured to exclude a healthful light, because such light would bring buried guilt to the surface. Thirteen years earlier, *Martin Chuzzlewit* had noted the absence of daylight and breathable atmosphere in the metropolis:

> London ... hemmed Todgers's round, and hustled it, and crushed it, and stuck its brick and mortar elbows into it, and kept the air from it, and stood perpetually between it and the light ...
>
> (9 pp. 128–9)

The city is here personified as an oppressive bully, as though the capital were deliberately constructed by people with these characteristics in order to exclude its inhabitants from light and clean air.

In the later novel, this aspect of London becomes central to the novel's symbolic purpose. Darkness is no longer merely an aesthetic quality to produce a response: it is a barrier to the outside world that cuts off the source of life itself. The 'light of any day that dawned' therefore has an apocalyptic quality: it is the external threat resisted by the city's darkness, the inexorable movement towards closure, or uncovering secret things, contained within the narrative. As in the gothic novel, the projected 'day' is surely the day of narrative dénouement, a literary practice itself shaped by eighteenth-century Christian views of history as Providential, building inevitably towards a day of judgement from the perspective of which hidden things would become plain.[14] Indeed, the gothic concealers' increasingly desperate retreat to the refuge of the gothic shadow would rank them in the minds of Bible-literate readers against the apocalyptic light brought by Christ:

> For everyone that doeth evil hateth the light, neither
> cometh to the light, lest his deeds should be reproved
>
> (John 3:20)

In the discourse of the Gospels, however, it is the guarded-against eventuality of an inrush of light that itself holds the potential for granting new life to those trapped in the darkness, including those who have created it. Certainly the gothic villains' resistance to the forces of discovery is depicted as a perverse form of self-harm. In rejecting contact with the outside world to maintain their secrets, they have excluded both freedom and light, the source of life. Montoni ends beseiged in his castle and Manfred's life is crushed in his crumbling castle. There is little real sense, however, that they could be redeemed by contact with these positive forces, which would merely bring about their downfall if admitted earlier.

Dickens clearly found the gothic novel's re-figuration of the apocalyptic imagery of light and darkness extremely useful. However, he also adapted it somewhat to talk about more modern nineteenth-century strategies for precluding exposure to scrutiny. Religion erects the barriers to light in *Little Dorrit* and therefore Dickens seems especially keen in this novel to find a religious dimension to the admission of the light to counteract the pessimism implied in this.

Lack of light is presented in these novels as spiritually constricting and a rejection of a force potentially redemptive to these shrunken figures. Constantly retreating from it into their impregnable castles, the villains become imprisoned within them selves and are cut off from the outside world in an unwholesome state of atrophy. William Dorrit is safe from creditors and moral judgement in the Marshalsea, but he is a prisoner nevertheless and his sanity is eroded by the lie his life has become. Mrs Clennam chooses her self-confinement in her house and it leads to a slow, lingering death-in-life that is her downfall. Dickens emphasises that her change from 'old active habits' (*LD* I 3 p. 34) to virtual paralysis comes from a wilful desire to have as little as possible to do with the external world. With 'a grim kind of luxuriousness' she revels in her ignorance of what passes outside her door:

> All seasons are alike to me. ... I know nothing of summer and winter, shut up here.
>
> (I 3 p. 34)

This delight in her separateness from the outer world seems to be as much a factor in her limitation to a single room as her physical condition. The lack of fresh air caused by this locking of doors against the rest of the world erodes her health:

> There was a smell of black dye in the airless room, which the fire had been drawing out of the crape and stuff of the widow's dress for fifteen months, and out of the bier-like sofa for fifteen years.
>
> (I 3 p. 34)

This is an environment that feeds continually upon itself, without allowing any influx of life from outside.[15] The concealment necessary for the preservation of her self-image is strongly linked with physical and spiritual decay:

> The debilitated old house in the city, wrapped in its mantle of soot, and leaning heavily on the crutches that had partaken of its decay and worn out with it, never knew a healthy or a cheerful interval, let what would betide. If the sun ever touched it, it was but with a ray, and that was gone in half an hour; if the moonlight ever fell upon it, it was only to put a few patches on its doleful cloak, and make it look more wretched. ... as to street noises, the rumbling of wheels in the lane merely rushed in at the gateway in going past, and rushed out again. ... So with whistling, singing, talking, laughing and all pleasant human sounds.
>
> (I 15 p. 172)

The 'haunted house with a premature and preternatural darkness in it' (I 29 p. 337) not only excludes light, but it appears to contaminate even what light does reach it:

> all bad weather stood by it with a rare fidelity. ... and as to snow [a further covering], you should see it there for weeks, long after it

had changed from yellow to black, slowly weeping away its grimy life.

(I 15 p. 173)

The rusty 'iron railings' and buttresses 'overgrown with weeds' (I 3 p. 32) have excluded natural light altogether in order to preserve Mrs Clennam's isolation. In its place is the light of the fire, which 'shone sullenly all day, and sullenly all night' and 'was suppressed, like her, and preyed upon itself evenly and slowly' (I 15 p. 172).

As the novel's final chapters make clear, the light she is excluding is ultimately a religious light. Her ascetic doctrine that she is making reparation for her sins and even redemptively sharing the 'consequences of the original offence' (II 30 p. 756) gives her an immense pleasure in her confinement. She attributes the decay of her own body to the results of sin, seeing herself as 'justly infirm and righteously afflicted' (I 5 p. 45). Her theology is flawed because she chooses this form of self-sacrifice, which benefits nobody, rather than the self-sacrifice of genuine repentance. This would involve relinquishing her cherished hate and making amends to those she has wronged, bringing to light the connections of moral relationship long hidden by her religion: that she is not Arthur's mother, but that she *is* the person responsible for paying Amy Dorrit her inheritance. Such a state of stubborn self-imposed death, hiding one's own real accountability, precludes any hope of real regeneration. The fall of her decaying house is the only way the book could end, not because it is her punishment, but because it is what she has chosen. In Mrs Clennam's egocentric religion, Dickens depicts a state of mind that feeds only upon self, severing ties of relationship and responsibility to the outside world in order to enjoy a consuming sense of self-definition. Her rejection of 'The world' and 'its hollow vanities' is based upon a deadening absorption in herself (I 3 p. 34). Little Dorrit shows her that in cutting herself off from life to enjoy her own self-righteousness, Mrs Clennam has denied the essence of her Christian religion.

Dickens's city has been built by people in the grip of Mrs Clennam's religion to shield them from the light offered by Little Dorrit's form of Christianity. In this it retains the gothic interpretation of the light/dark symbolism of the Gospels, while adapting it for discussion of a culture determined by a blend of secular capitalism and latter-day religious Pharisaism. In its every locked door and dilapidated street, the decaying London of *Little Dorrit* reflects in a magnifying lens the self-absorbed, death-driven psychology of such individuals. Sunday is chosen for the introduction to London because it evokes the atmosphere of legalistic inactivity or paralysis that prevails in the house. The city is described in terms that will later be applied to the house: 'It was a Sunday evening in London, gloomy, close and stale', 'the inhabitants gasped for air' (I 3 p. 26). The narrator says of Arthur's father's room:

> Its close air was secret. The gloom, and must, and dust of the whole tenement, were secret.
>
> (II 10 p. 526)

London itself, shut up for Sunday, has severed all connection with anything outside itself, including even the 'unfamiliar animals', 'rare plants or flowers' and 'natural or artificial wonders of the ancient world' shown in the British Museum (I 3 p. 29). The result of this is mental and physical stultification, exemplified in the common lack of running water. People 'live so unwholesomely, that fair water put into their crowded rooms on Saturday night, would be corrupt on Sunday morning' (I 3 p. 29). Everything here has ceased to circulate freely. Even the Thames no longer seems to move from the country to the sea, maintaining a healthy, life-giving contact with the outside world:

> Through the heart of the town a deadly sewer ebbed and flowed, in the place of a fine fresh river.
>
> (I 3 p. 29)

Continually feeding upon itself, London becomes dirty, decayed and dead:

> In every thoroughfare, up almost every alley, and down almost every turning, some doleful bell was throbbing, jerking, tolling, as if the plague were in the city and the dead-carts were going round.
>
> (I 3 p. 29)

Dickens's reference to 'a Congregationless Church that seemed to be waiting for some adventurous Belzoni to dig it out and discover its history' (I 3 p. 31) emphasises that this society is already a ruined city.

Dickens constantly suggests that the reason for this is that the metropolis is populated – and indeed governed – by numerous Mrs Clennams, neurotically creating a total environment where human connections may be lost, so as to wallow in introspective self-righteousness. Dickens is careful to show that the closing of doors to places of recreation and refreshment on Sunday is really a way of withholding what is due to the working classes. He ironically asks:

> what secular want could the million or so of human beings whose daily labour, six days in the week, lay among the [airless buildings and streets] from the sweet sameness of which they had no escape between the cradle and the grave – what secular want could they possibly have upon their seventh day? Clearly they could want nothing but a stringent policeman.
>
> (LD I 3 p. 29)

The implication is that the Sabbatarian legislators owe the workers the ability to enjoy rest on this of all days, but that their solipsistic, ascetic Puritanism conceals their obligations so that they may revel in self-righteousness.

If the house gives symbolic expression to Mrs Clennam's concealing urges, then London expresses the effects upon society of being governed by such urges. A supposedly liberating faith has turned the whole city into a prison:

> Everything was bolted and barred that could by possibility furnish relief to an overworked people.
>
> (I 3 p. 29)

Lionel Trilling has highlighted the universality of the theme of imprisonment in *Little Dorrit*,[16] but it is important to note that this comment upon the carceral effect of secrecy is inherited from the gothic house. Emily in *The Mysteries of Udolpho*, for example, recognises this use of the castle:

> As the carriage-wheels rolled heavily under the portcullis, Emily's heart sunk, and she seemed, as if she was going into her prison.
>
> (II 5 pp. 226–7)

Gothic villains typically try to lock the hero and heroine into the parts of the castle where the truth is rendered inaccessible. At the same time, they must not be allowed to leave the building, which represents the concealers' realm of control over what others know about their identity, with the knowledge they do have. Thus they are both shut out of and shut into the world of the villain's ego boundaries. Manfred's desire to marry Isabella in *The Castle of Otranto* is a desire to confine her to a role in the secret of the usurped house, by making her complicit with it.

When these attempts are so strongly resisted, the villains must resort to literal imprisonment. Mrs Clennam imprisons Arthur in some of the dark places of her own home in an attempt to lock him into the secret of the house from his youth. These include an 'old dark closet, also with nothing in it of which he had been many a time the sole contents, in days of punishment, when he had regarded it as the veritable entrance to that bourne to which the tract had found him galloping' (I 3 p. 72). Locked in a cupboard he pictures as the gateway to Hell, Arthur experiences the full force of a gothic horror updated to symbolise a religious climate that restricts people and excludes them from knowledge of its power over them by a culture of guilt.

Others, such as the Barnacles and Merdle, create an equally self-defined milieu by shutting the door of their houses to connections with the outside world. The accumulated unhealthy results of this in the totality of London may be seen as Arthur loses himself among the 'Parasite little tenements' around Park Lane:

> Ricketty dwellings of undoubted fashion, but of a capacity to hold nothing comfortably except a dismal smell, looked like the last result of the great mansions' breeding in-and-in; and, where their little supplementary bows and balconies were supported on thin iron columns, seemed to be scrofulously resting upon crutches. ... On the door-steps there were ... butlers, solitary men of recluse demeanour, each of whom appeared distrustful of all other butlers. ... wicked little grooms in the tightest fitting garments, with twists in their legs answering to the twists in their minds, hung about in pairs, chewing straw and exchanging fraudulent secrets.
>
> (I 27 pp. 316–17)

Of course this recalls the 'half-dozen gigantic crutches' upon which Mrs Clennam's rotten house is 'Propped up' (I 3 p. 71). Such artificial systems of support for house and city show that the egocentric worlds of those responsible for them are also vulnerable to decay. They evoke Mrs Clennam's physical degeneration and suggest the wasting self-destructiveness of the attitudes that have formed London's ethos. Like Mrs Clennam, the builders, inhabitants and masters of these Park Lane houses, and of the sunlight-excluding city as a whole, have created for themselves an entirely self-referential world, out of sheer self-love and refusal to acknowledge necessary connections with the human race. Dickens's terrifying cityscapes graphically show that its logical result is inbred destruction.

III. The Adelphi

Showing the darkness of a whole society requires not just a single house, but an enormous metropolis. On her night away from home, Little Dorrit is startled when she sees 'a moving shadow among the street lamps' and the dangers she faces include 'homeless people, lying coiled up in nooks ... drunkards ... slinking men, whistling and signing to one another at bye corners, or running away at full speed' and a prostitute, all lurking in 'the dark vapour on the river' (I 14 pp. 166–9). Henry Mayhew catalogues very many of these dwellers in darkness, claiming that in 1857, the year of *Little Dorrit*'s publication, 8600 prostitutes were known to the police, with up to ten times that number possibly working.[17] One has only to think back to Fagin slinking about 'like some loathsome reptile, engendered in the slime and darkness through which he moved' (*OT* 19 pp. 120–1), to grasp the connection between the city's obscurity and criminality. Concealment is a moral issue for Dickens and the habitual tendency to hide in *Little Dorrit* reflects a fear of more than the police, who are absent from the novel, set, as it is, before the Metropolitan Police Act (1829). There is a sense, however, in which Dickens's real concealers are those who cause the deprivation that forces people to such local manifestations of criminality. Often it seems that there is an affiliation of gothic-style villains organising London so that the guilty secret behind its poverty should remain unapprehended. One particular dark corner of Dickens's London will repay detailed examination because it returns attention to the social aspect of what is deliberately concealed in the metropolis.

The Adelphi was a part of London that Dickens often re-visited in fact and fiction. The young David Copperfield is fascinated by it, recalling,

> I was fond of wandering about the Adelphi, because it was a myste-
> rious place, with those dark arches.
>
> (*DC* 11 p. 138)

It was an area near the Strand, itself so-called because of its original adjacency to the Thames, where wharves of the poorest character were built upon in 1768, without, one imagines, any permission sought from the users of the area. These muddy areas were enclosed in even greater darkness than before by streets of housing for the wealthy erected above them by two brothers named Adams, after whom the imposing edifice was named. This expression of their personality was supported upon a series of subterranean arches, which became a haunt for homeless people. It is almost certainly the setting for the third panel of Augustus Egg's series *Past and Present*, a scene of destitution typical of the area's image.[18] By the 1860s one Victorian reminisced of the arches that

> no sane person would have ventured to explore them without an armed escort.[19]

Darkness has been created by one group of citizens building their house on the exploitation of another displaced group: a guilty secret, like Mrs Clennam's, in the cellar.

Dickens describes the Adelphi as a particularly effective place for the keeping of secrets. Its structure, like that of the city as a whole, restricts access to information by means of numerous barriers. As well as the thick vertical barrier between rich and poor, there is a horizontal barrier between the subterranean part of the Adelphi and the outside world. What is said within cannot be heard in the surrounding streets. Entering it effects:

> a sudden pause in that place to the roar of the great thoroughfare. The many sounds become so deadened that the change is like putting cotton in the ears, or having the head thickly muffled.
>
> (II 9 p. 514)

This is of course a characteristic feature of Mrs Clennam's house too:

> As to street noises, the rumbling of wheels in the lane merely rushed in at the gateway in going past, and rushed out again. ... So with whistling, singing, talking, laughing, and all pleasant human sounds.
>
> (I 15 p. 172)

Flintwinch takes full advantage of this by having his secret conference with his brother about the codicil in its most soundproof recess (I 4 p. 14). The layout of the house is used to draw a veil over his transactions. When his wife does overhear him, he enforces this exclusion from perception of what is happening by force. Constantly threatened with physical suffering, Affery is so scared that she starts to impose a veil upon herself, throwing her apron over her face 'lest she should see something' (I 15 p. 182). The experience of being a pedestrian in the Adelphi is compared to being prevented from hearing by violent actions such as the thrusting of cotton into the ears and the muffling of the head. It suggests that those who control the city use such places to bully people into giving up their search for knowledge.

The atmosphere of the Adelphi excludes light as well as sound. The obscurity of the spot, like Mrs Clennam's house, seems to defeat any attempts to illuminate it. The 'street-lamps, blurred by the foggy air' (*LD* II 9 p. 513) reproduce on a larger scale the obstacles to clear vision used to aid the concealment in Mrs Clennam's residence, where 'the ceilings were so fantastically clouded by smoke and dust, that old women might have told fortunes in them, better than in grouts of tea; ... heaps of soot ... eddied about in little dusky whirlwinds when the doors were opened ... cobwebs ... fur and fungus' (I 5 p. 54). Mr Flintwinch adds personally to these unwholesome, impenetrable clouds by his tobacco smoke and Dickens merges this with the smoke of the whole city, extending one environment into the other yet again:

> The smoke came crookedly out of Mr Flintwinch's mouth, as if it circulated through the whole of his wry figure and came back by his wry throat, before coming forth to mingle with the smoke from the crooked chimneys and the mists from the crooked river.
>
> (II 23 p. 660)

As the next chapter will discuss, *Bleak House* had already explored the chilling neo-gothic possibilities of dirty air spreading to permeate the city and obscuring truth about society. *Little Dorrit*'s concentration of it in the subterranean portion of the Adelphi, however, reads like a deliberately fostered environment, a storehouse of smog, in which it is almost to be expected that something is being hidden. The exclusion of free-flowing air and water necessary for this has created an environment of deathly paralysis:

> nothing moving on the stream but waterman's wherries and coal-lighters. Long and broad tiers of the latter, moored fast in the mud as if they were never to move again, made the shore funereal and silent after dark; and kept what little water movement there was, far out towards mid-stream.
>
> (II 9 p. 514)

Those who live in London's underside are forced not only into darkness, but also into the concealer's own state of atrophy.

The Adelphi echoes the equally funereal atmosphere of Sabbatarian London but mainly focuses on the commercial rather than the religious aspect of the problem. The secret Clennam overhears here relates to the property owner Casby's domain (*LD* II 9). Casby owns large areas of London, but his outward benevolence is later exposed when it emerges that his greed has forced up rents to a level that reduces his tenants to poverty. Plornish is entirely deceived, accepting Casby's public image of generosity at face value. As he tries to unravel 'the tangled skein of his affairs', his bafflement about his plight involves him in a mystery as profound as the main plot:

> They was all hard up there. ... Well, he couldn't say how it was; he didn't know as anybody *could* say how it was; ... He could tell you who suffered, but he couldn't tell you whose fault it was.
>
> (I 12 p. 136)

To the reader, however, it is quite clear whose fault it is. Casby is denying the poor their rights, while feigning virtue as surely as Mrs Clennam is denying Little Dorrit what she owes to her under a cloak of righteousness. Bleeding Heart Yard is the squalid underside to the splendid edifice of his public persona, just as the respectable mansions of the Adelphi conceal the darkness and poverty they have exacerbated.

Little Dorrit presents a London built by various overlapping individuals and groups aiming to establish control over the city at the expense of the confused population in this way. Whereas Casby's bid for domination of the metropolis comes through property ownership, the Barnacles exert their grip over the city by their administration of it. They are protecting their own dynasty's image of indispensability to society by making it impossible for the people they exploit to investigate their affairs. Arthur soon learns how difficult they can make it for those who 'want to know, you know' (II 10, p. 108). Dickens represents its efficiency at keeping out the uninitiated by embodying its frightening bureaucracy in the complex internal design of the building:

> Numbers of people were lost in the Circumlocution Office ... and never re-appeared in the light of day.
>
> (II 10 pp. 101–2)

Here again, London's even more complex structure is built to project the ego boundaries of people like Casby, the Barnacles and Merdle, but that structure must hide the social suffering lurking at its foundation as the Adelphi did.

On this level, then, the metropolis of *Little Dorrit* is ultimately hiding its own social interconnectedness, the fact that the poverty lower down the system is actually caused by the negligence, greed and inactivity of those further up. Certainly the novel insists that, despite the best efforts of these concealers, this knowledge cannot remain hidden forever. Just as Mrs Clennam's secret must emerge and the house that embodies her public persona must crumble, so Dickens warns that the secret of social exploitation must emerge and the exploiters' power must collapse. This is described in terms that evoke the fall of the respectable upper housing of London because of the rottenness of the squalid caverns upon which it is built:

> look to the rats young and old, all ye Barnacles, for before God they are eating away our foundations, and will bring the roofs on our heads!
>
> (I 14 p. 208)[20]

The Adelphi summarises within its small area the novel's city, with its sense of a respectable London built over an exploited hidden zone. It shows what must be repressed for the city's sense of itself to remain intact.

Dickens had dwelt at greater length upon the Adelphi in *David Copperfield*, where his sense of the spot as emblematic of the two Londons neatly juxtaposed is clearly visible. David visits the world beneath in the days of his unhappy childhood. Later, in his prosperity, he comes to live in the houses above ground, just as Dickens did in the 1830s, and shows a keen awareness of the difference between the two adjacent worlds:

> I turned my face to the Adelphi, pondering on the old days when I used to roam about its subterranean arches, and on the happy changes which had brought me to the surface.
>
> (*DC* 23 p. 303)

Copperfield has moved from the labyrinth below in which he had been exploited and kept in ignorance to inclusion in the world of the establishment above. On the whole, this is presented as a positive move, brought about by a combination of Providential favour and David's own hard work. *David Copperfield* does not place the same emphasis on the corrupt social structure of London as *Little Dorrit*. Nevertheless, the reader does register in the hero's brooding reflections here a slight, conflicting sense of unease that in belonging to this upper London, he is participating in and perpetuating the system that kept those like his younger self in the dark.

It is interesting that there is part of David Copperfield's own past to be found in the underside of the city. Although there is no strong sense that he himself wishes to hide his former poverty, the real novelist, upon whom his experiences are based, kept his formative years in this part of London well hidden. He concealed them from public knowledge until after his death and did not even tell his children about them. It is not easy to say why he did so. Dickens, the genuinely active reformer, can hardly be accused of having exploited the poor to get to his position. Nevertheless, perhaps he retained an understandable, if irrational, sense of guilt regarding those who remained poor when he returned to his middle-class world. It is even possible that part of him felt that he had exploited those with whom he had come into contact during these years in representing them in the fiction that had made his name. He had even borrowed – or stolen – some of their names, such as that of Bob Fagin, who worked beside him in Warren's Blacking Warehouse.[21] His position as the dominant novelist of London certainly depended upon the experiential resources gained from this dark underworld. Perhaps Dickens's reluctance to talk about this period may also be due to a constant temptation to criminality enforced by his poverty. In his private memorandum to Forster, he said:

I know that, but for the mercy of God, I might easily have been, for any care that was taken of me, a little robber or a little vagabond.[22]

While this may not have led him to illegal actions, it is possible that guilt for this unrealised criminal potential may have remained with him. This is mere speculation, but it suggests how Dickens could depict so convincingly characters like William Dorrit who wish to keep their past hidden and the other concealers who use London to obscure the secrets about their past contained within it. It also suggests how the metropolis may have developed in Dickens's mind into a symbolic environment that protects the ego boundaries of the powerful by making the actions of the past invisible. If the Adelphi draws attention to the sociological motivation for the city's network of concealments, for Dickens it also resonates with ontological reasons for hiding. It seems to remind him that for some, a sense of self-defined identity or public image may depend upon keeping the secrets of one's origins and background out of sight.

IV. The self-revealing veil

For all London's effectiveness in keeping such secrets hidden in *Little Dorrit*, it paradoxically signals that an act of concealment is taking place. In another characteristic inherited from the gothic castle, the very existence of a veil implies that something is hidden behind. Commenting on a house in *Doctor Grimshawe's Secret* (1861), Nathaniel Hawthorne's biographer, H. H. Hoeltje, makes a passing remark which shows how fully he understands the relationship between these two symbolic forms inherited from the gothic castle, the house in the American tale of terror and the city in English Victorian fiction:

> This old mansion had that delightful intricacy that can never be contrived, never be attained by any design, but is the happy result of many builders, many designs, many ages – *a house to go astray in, as in a city*, and come to unexpected places, a house of dark passages and antique stairways where one might meet someone who might have a word of destiny to say to the wanderer. It was a dim, twilight place ... as if some strange vast mysterious truth long searched for was about to be revealed; a sense of something to come: an opening of doors, a drawing away of veils.[23]

The phrase I have italicised here clearly depends on the sort of city Dickens has constructed in his novels. To evoke the sense of searching for the mystery, Hawthorne's house must be too large to comprehend at a single effort. The 'delightful intricacy' necessary is the result of the work of many architects with conflicting aims. This is more powerfully achieved in a whole city where buildings of many centuries abut each other apparently at random. London is therefore readier for this use than a city with a more recent 'grid-iron' plan such as Manchester. Dickens keeps whisking the reader from Bleeding Heart Yard to Covent Garden to the Marshalsea to Harley Street, which recreates the miscellaneous nature of the city as perceived by the person lost in it. Certainly there is room for readers to 'go astray in' and the point is that they should.

Such mysterious environments provoke the imagination into speculation. Gothic architecture takes the shadow created by its projection into account as part of its design. The imagination is forced into action because so much is left to it. The vast scale of the gothic building also stimulates wonderment and fresh thought because the whole cannot be comprehended at a single glance. This is certainly true of the architecture of Mrs Clennam's house. Two people as different in temperament as Arthur Clennam and William Dorrit are both impressed at this level by the appearance of the house. For Clennam:

> It always affected his imagination as wrathful, mysterious, and sad; and his imagination was sufficiently impressible to see the whole neighbourhood under some tinge of its dark shadow.
>
> (II 10 p. 526)

Here is Dorrit's reaction:

> So powerfully was his imagination impressed by it, that when his driver stopped, after having asked the way more than once, and said to the best of his belief this was the gateway they wanted, Mr Dorrit stood hesitating, with the coach-door in his hand, half afraid of the dark look of the place.
>
> (II 17 p. 602)

The very fortifications against investigation stimulate the curiosity that leads to investigation. How much truer of the city! In the case of the Adelphi, the 'stoppage' that the place causes to Clennam's progress itself provokes awareness of its secret:

> a train of coal-waggons toiling up from the wharves at the river-side, brought him to a stand-still. He had been walking quickly, and going with some current of thought, and the sudden check given to both operations caused him to look freshly about him. ...
>
> (II 9 p. 513–14)

Attempts to obstruct the searcher's movement towards truth only serve to arouse his or her curiosity and stimulate observant thought. From this perspective, London's mimesis of the novel's structure here, and that of the haunted house, seems more even-handed, facilitating both the concealment and the discovery it denies.

Sometimes this leads to outlandish misconceptions, which nevertheless helps the searcher to arrive at the truth that underlies these apparently foolish ideas. This can be seen, for example, in Dickens's often parodic dialogue with another gothic convention carried over from the haunted house into the metropolitan landscape, that of the ghost. Ghosts are re-emergences from the dead, from the world that ought to remain buried. Mrs Snagsby's servants in *Bleak House* believe they are seeing and hearing otherworldly phenomena because of the atmosphere of secrecy and suspicion. This leads to the creation in their minds of yet another haunted house:

> Mrs Snagsby is so perpetually on the alert, that the house becomes ghostly with creaking boards and rustling garments. The 'prentices think somebody may have been murdered there, in bygone times. Guster holds ... that there is buried money underneath the cellar, guarded by an old man with a white beard, who cannot get out for seven thousand years, because he said the Lord's Prayer backwards.
>
> (*BH* 25 p. 408)

When one is responsible for the secrecy oneself, these imagined hauntings become more acute because it is mixed with a guilty fear of discovery. In Mr Krook's very urban haunted house, Mr Guppy notes that

> One disagreeable result of whispering is, that it seems to evoke an atmosphere of silence, haunted by the ghosts of sound – strange cracks and tickings, the rustling of garments that have no substance in them. ... the air is full of these phantoms ...

In his terror, he exclaims, 'This is a horrible house' (32 pp. 514–6). While these characters are mocked for their idle speculations, however, they tease the reader into engagement with the secrets really being kept behind the veils of which they are so keenly aware.

Similarly, since, in *Little Dorrit*, all is unknown to Affery, the origins of that unknown may conceivably be superhuman rather than human. She originally speculates that Arthur's mother is buried in the house and afterwards that:

> she haunts the house, then. Who else rustles about it, making signals by dropping dust so softly? Who else comes and goes, and marks the walls with long crooked touches when we are all a-bed?
>
> (II 30 p. 765)

And in a sense she is correct, or, as Dickens puts it:

> The mystery of the noises was out now; Affery, like greater people, had always been right in her facts, and always wrong in the theories she deduced from them.
>
> (II 31 p. 772)

Certainly there are no actual ghosts, but the past does keep turning up in the form of the evidence of wrong done. Furthermore, Little Dorrit herself in her 'dark corner' (I 3 p. 35) is a species of ghost. Her presence is a constant reminder to Mrs Clennam that she is concealing what is owed to her and of the past that she has otherwise succeeded in burying. It is the girl's mysterious appearance in the house that provokes Clennam to get to the bottom of the secret. As with Dickens's most traditional haunted house, Chesney Wold in *Bleak House*, with its mysterious Ghost's Walk, the supernatural is the imperfectly understood evidence of an equally distressing human secret. Esther Summerson displays a profound understanding of how gothic works when she says:

> there was a dreadful truth in the legend of the Ghost's Walk; that it was I, who was to bring calamity upon the stately house; and that my warning feet were haunting it even then.
>
> (*BH* 36 p. 586)

Shame does not come upon the family because a real ghost walks there, but because a flesh and blood illegitimate daughter walks the earth as a result of past misdeeds.

When such ghosts are proven to be human rather than supernatural phenomena in novels such as *The Mysteries of Udolpho*, Radcliffe and her followers attributed the re-appearances of truth they represent to an equally supernatural Providence. Kate Ferguson Ellis summarises this aspect of the Radcliffean novel, saying, 'The clues provided by superstition are ... present to strengthen [the heroine's] command over her imagination and at the same time to alert her to the need to penetrate below the surface of certain phenomena which, when subject to the probe of reason, provide guidance that is simultaneously "natural" and divine but not, finally, terrifying'. She cites the parallel example of Clara Reeve, whose *The Old English Baron* concludes with an assurance that its apparently coincidental discoveries demonstrate, 'the over-ruling hand of Providence, and the certainty of RETRIBUTION'[24] Dickens's houses seem organised, like the haunted houses of the earlier gothic fiction they draw upon, to prevent the Providential force mimed by the narrative from bringing the concealers' guilt to light.

In the haunted house proper, evidence of misdeeds appears in ways made even more unpredictable by its very suppression. Dickens's London is a place where figures from the past, whether it be Esther,

Alice Marwood or Magwitch, can re-emerge unsettlingly at any moment. It is, in Baudelaire's phrase, a

> Fourmillante cité, cité pleine de rêves,
> Où le spectre en plein jour raccroche le passant!
>
> ... swarming city, city full of dreams,
> where ghosts accost the passers-by in broad daylight!
>
> ('Les Sept Vieillards' ll. 1–2)[25]

As well as these human ghosts, the new visual stimuli of the city lead to strange supernatural suggestions that cause people to apprehend a truth underlying them. We have seen how the distortion of street lighting in the city reflects the obscuring of truths by concealing groups and individuals. Those who are searching for the sociological reasons for their poverty or for ontological information about their origins and identity find their way thwarted at every turn by the city's refusal to let them see anything clearly. Nevertheless, the blurred light of London produces strange phantasmagoria that actually stimulate the exploited characters to wonder what is to be seen there, transmuting the physical into the supernatural. Little Dorrit, for example, 'through the dark vapour on the river; had seen little spots of lighted water where the bridge lamps were reflected, shining like demon eyes, with a terrible fascination in them for guilt and misery' (I 14 p. 169). The difficulties of vision cause the observer to speculate that the secret hidden in the mist may actually be motivated by external evil powers.

Misery, like fear, is a feeling that distorts facts out of recognition in Dickens and presents them in another light. Fanny's bitter anger and selfish tears create another river with similar results:

> Waters of vexation filled her eyes; and they had the effect of making the famous Mr Merdle, in going down the street, appear to leap, and waltz, and gyrate, as if he were possessed of several Devils.
>
> (II 24 p. 683)

Although the devils have no existence outside the mind of the person caught up in the concealing atmosphere, the distortions of clear vision can paradoxically reveal a strange truth to him or her. Merdle, in his destructive deception, *is* a devil, although it takes Fanny's emotion to show her that. His web of deception in the city, by which he protects his public persona from those who would see behind it, is presented as motivated, if not directly empowered, by Satan. Those who uphold Merdle's secret are described as evil and 'would have done better to worship the Devil point-blank' (II 26 p. 691). His followers, 'the high priests of this worship' (II 12 p. 539), behave like a cult informed by a diabolical deity. The distortion of the phenomena of the streets by both waters, the Thames and the tears, seems paradoxically to reveal the truth about them, although the evil is rather societal then supernatural.

Reading the layout and peculiar climatic conditions of the city as a dialogue with the gothic's reconfiguration of spiritual symbolism is, however, perhaps an approach stimulated as much by *The Waste Land* as by *Little Dorrit* itself. Eliot's London is certainly rendered 'Unreal' by 'the brown fog of a winter dawn' (ll. 60–1) that frustrates any kind of authoritative revelation or self-knowledge. At the end its 'Falling towers' are linked with the collapsing gothic castle of Otranto, which segue into Dracula's castle and the *fin-de-siécle* gothic revival:

And bats with baby faces in the violet light
[recalling the 'violet hour' of the city at dusk in line 15]
Whistled, and beat their wings
And crawled head downward down a blackened wall
And upside down in air were towers
Tolling reminiscent bells that kept the hours
And voices singing out of empty cisterns and exhausted wells

(ll. 373–84)

The collapse of this house may signal the end of the city of unrealities and the heralding in of 'the city over the mountains' (l. 371), but it may not. Eliot conscripts the gothic castle into his discussion of symbols that dramatise the doomed unrealities human beings construct to exclude a reality that may or may not exist in the first place. This is bound to affect our reading of the gothic castle itself. His practice of fusing it with contemporary London, which he sees as the defining unreality of modern metropolitan culture, necessarily casts a strong backward shadow over earlier texts that also explore the links between house and city. This approach is especially fruitful when applied to *Little Dorrit* since the gothic-evoking haunted house and city clearly do engage with spiritual issues, standing, at least some of the time, for the religious thinking that restricts so many in the novel. To read it through the lens of Eliot's poem shows a text in nuanced engagement with its literary predecessors, allying contemporary religion, not its opponents, with the symbols of darkness and apocalyptic collapse. Indeed in fusing the London closed on the Sabbath with both the ethos of commercialism and the haunted castle, Dickens makes the neo-Puritan rhetoric of his times the key unreality that sustains his society. The novel may evoke the gothic too casually to constitute a sustained search for a narrative decorum governing the limits of humankind's power to resist uncomfortable truths about themselves. In any case there are too many other narrative styles constantly at work alongside. Nevertheless, its London, with its multitudes of suppressed but insistent ghosts, expresses a hope more generally that narratives of escape from the terrors of obscurity may ultimately ring true.

3

'A great (and dirty) city': London's Dirt and the Terrors of Obscurity

From *Dombey and Son* onwards, the city's filth comes to replace and update the gothic mechanisms of castle walls and ghosts in Dickens. That dirt can function in this way when required, however, speaks volumes about the language in which contemporary debate on sanitary reform was expressed. Indeed, whether overt or covert, religious elements can be seen throughout a range of discourses that address the theme of dirt in the Victorian era. Throughout his work, Dickens both reflects and interrogates many of these. In his modes of representing the disease-ridden parts of London, polemical factors compete with generic factors, secular discourses with religious discourses and, in terms of style, journalistic realism vies with neo-gothicism and anticipations of surrealism. In the perception of Dickens and his contemporaries, there were various types of obscurity and death created by London's dirt, requiring various forms of revelation and regeneration as an antidote to them.

I. The physical and moral effects of dirt

Dickens's interest in sanitary reform is well documented.[1] His brother-in-law, Henry Austin, was chief inspector to the General Board of Health and had been influential in forming the novelist's interest in these issues. In the 1840s, 30,000 inhabitants of London were without water.[2] Proper sanitation was a luxury enjoyed by the few and, in addition to the human excrement in the streets, overpowering quantities of dung were generated by cattle being driven to Smithfield and other markets. As late as 1900, two hundred people were employed to remove manure from the streets of the single parish of St Pancras.[3] Since the sewers were not constructed until 1858 and completed only in 1865, much of this seeped through into the water table, putting all London at risk. Overcrowding increased the risk of contagion. Between 1847 and 1848, 50,000 people died from influenza in London alone. Nationally, typhoid caused twice as many fatalities in the large towns as in the country.[4] Outbreaks of cholera were a constant feature of life in the capital and between 1845 and 1856 more than seven hundred works were published on the subject, most tracing the origins of the disease to the polluted atmosphere in which the poor of London lived.[5] Alarmed by this, Dickens joined the Health of Towns Association in early 1848 and was active with Austin in founding the Metropolitan Sanitary Association in 1850.

The discussion of London's sanitary problems in the forty-seventh chapter of *Dombey and Son*, then, contributes to a large body of contemporary published work and to a public debate in which Dickens was personally engaged. Nevertheless, when he prefaces his forty-seventh chapter, to which the whole novel has been building up, with three pages on the slums, it is not, as Humphry House claims:

> a curiously sudden, inept and passionate piece of propaganda for Public Health, ludicrously detached from the theme and mood of the novel.[6]

Instead, urban dirt and the need for its removal are introduced to illustrate the larger social, ontological and spiritual implications of the culture that has produced Dombey. As we shall see, in this brief passage, Dickens develops some of the symbolic potentialities of the problem of London's dirt that become essential to the whole method of *Bleak House*.

Dombey and Son's excursion into the adverse moral effects created by London's slums justifies itself as an analogy for the development of the Dombeys' pride in a commercial culture. Dickens for the first time invites the reader to identify with Dombey, explaining his character in terms of his circumstances:

> Coop any son or daughter of our mighty mother within narrow range, and bind the prisoner to one idea, and foster it by servile worship of it on the part of the few timid or designing people standing round, and what is Nature to the willing captive who has never risen up upon the wings of a free mind ...
>
> (47 p. 619)

Using the slums as an illustration already understood by the public, the passage is offered as an inquiry into 'what Nature is, and how men work to change her, and whether, in the enforced distinctions so produced, it is not natural to be unnatural' (47 p. 619).

The effects of environment are figured in the metaphorical representation of London as the breeding ground of twisted, unhealthy
vegetable life, whose filthy situation no longer allows it to draw upon
the divine source of life:

> Vainly attempt to think of any simple plant, or flower, or wholesome
> weed, that, set in this foetid bed, could have its natural growth, or
> put its little leaves forth to the sun as GOD designed it.
>
> (47 p. 619)

For an example of what is naturally produced in these circumstances,
Dickens chooses this 'ghastly child, with stunted form and wicked face'
(47 p. 619) – that is, displaying both physical and moral deformity.

Dickens's portrait of such slumflowers also enhances the reader's
perception of Florence, whose name connects her with them. The long
survival of her virtue in her own unwholesome environment seems
especially remarkable in the face of the other blighted-plant children,
whose difficulties illustrate the inevitability of the collapse of this
most precious of all blooms, who suffers from 'hopes that were
withered and tendernesses [Dombey] had frozen'. Ultimately, 'even
the patient trust that was in her, could not survive the daily blight of
such experience' (47 p. 621). Realising after he brutally strikes her that
her father cannot be won round to loving her, Florence leaves the
house altogether. The whole chapter depends upon making this
process convincing. 'The change, if it may be called one' (47 p. 621)
must not be too sudden or sharp in case Florence's early hope will
seem superficial,[7] yet it must be definite and understood by the reader
if the plot is to progress. By linking Dombey's house to the filthy surroundings of London's poor children through the image of the flower
struggling to grow in hostile conditions, Dickens achieves both ends
with great subtlety.

The flower grown in slum soil recurs in a speech to the Metropolitan
Sanitary Association on 10 May 1851:

> no one can estimate the amount of mischief which is grown in dirt ...
> either in its physical or in its moral results ...[8]

Squalor is a self-perpetuating source of two types of harm. Likewise in
Dombey and Son the 'polluted air' is 'poisonous to health and life' as a
whole and creates an environment where 'Vice and Fever propagate
together' (*DS* 47 p. 619). When every impression registered by the brain

is a signal of threatening physical destruction, moral degradation will inevitably develop:

> Breathe the polluted air, foul with every impurity that is poisonous to health and life; and have every sense ... sickened and disgusted, and made a channel by which misery and death alone can enter.
>
> (47 p. 619)

By sensory means, polluted air poisons minds as well as bodies. Dickens argues that seeing, hearing, smelling, touching and tasting nothing that is beautiful gives people nothing in their surroundings to indicate that there are values to aspire towards. If society will leave its members in such a state, they are unlikely to develop the belief in love that motivates the highest virtues.

Ruskin diagnosed the same condition in *Fiction, Fair and Foul*, which begins with a description of the dilapidation brought to Croxted Lane with its recent urbanisation, including a rather Dickensian list of 'every unclean thing that can ... rot or rust in damp'.[9] Once green, open and uncultivated (and therefore natural), the area is now characterised by decay and decomposition. This is, however, chiefly reprehensible because of the adverse moral effects such sights have upon the viewer. Constant contemplation of the 'forms of filth, and modes of ruin' of their physical surroundings, Ruskin argues, induces a comparable state of 'mental ruin'[10] in the inhabitants. Like those in *Dombey and Son*, who breathe 'polluted air' and cease to believe in anything other than 'misery and death', the inhabitants of Croxted Lane find that

> The power of all surroundings over them for evil; the incapacity of their own minds to refuse the *pollution* ... brings every law of *healthy existence* into question with them ... [which will] degrade the conscience, into sullen incredulity of all sunshine outside the *dunghill*, or breeze beyond the wafting of its impurity ...[11]

My emphasis suggest that the city's dirt, for Ruskin as for Dickens, was opposed to a concept of 'nature' whose twin components were morality and good health. Ruskin's chapter on 'Purity' in *Modern Painters* proposes that the idea is associated with the 'vital and energetic connection amongst [an object's] particles', while 'foulness is essentially associated with dissolution and death'.[12] Ultimately, Ruskin considers cleanness part of God's character because it is 'expressive of that constant presence and energising of the Deity by which all things live and move, and have their being'.[13] 'Impurity' attaches fundamentally 'to conditions of matter in which its various elements are placed in a relation incapable of healthy or proper operation; and most distinctly to conditions in which the negation of vital or energetic action is most evident'. Metropolitan filth is therefore to be abhorred because those living in squalor would not apprehend the truths of God's vitality that Ruskin saw at work in nature.

In making the city's squalid regions his metaphor for a climate of distorted nature where the unnatural is produced naturally, Dickens demonstrates a commitment to such assumptions about the relationship between nature, life and moral purity. But, as with any evocation of nature, both the writers' definitions imply ideological assumptions about which forms of relationship between human beings are 'natural'. This is shown by the porousness of literal and metaphorical definitions of impurity in the campaign for sanitary reform of which Dickens's writing formed a part. One of the 'unnatural' traits of the downtrodden classes mentioned in *Dombey and Son* is that of 'losing and confounding all distinctions between good and evil' (47 p. 619). Dirt is about distinctions. Mary Douglas, in *Purity and Danger*, argues that the whole concept involves judgements about the value of matter, what is and is not presentable and where it may or may not be touched. For example, a live fish is quite clean in a river, but dirty on a wedding dress:

> Dirt is the by-product of a systematic ordering and classification of matter, in so far as ordering involves rejecting inappropriate elements. This idea of dirt takes us straight into the field of symbolism and promises a link-up with more obviously symbolic systems of purity.[14]

The concept depends upon ideas about how the universe, and its microcosm, society, are held together which govern the rules of tribes and religions regarding which foods, animals, people or forms of sexual activity are considered clean or unclean. If it becomes impossible for individuals to understand how they are defined in relation to the rest of the things that combine to form the universe, then their sense of proper behaviour towards them will be threatened.

The motives of the Victorian sanitary reformers reflect this conception of hygiene. For them, the keeping apart of elements that did not belong together, for the preservation of the body, was closely associated with the keeping apart of people that did not belong together, for the preservation of a sound society. Overcrowding made it impossible not only to keep contaminating matter away from areas of food preparation, but also to maintain separate male and female sleeping accommodation.

Behaviour the reformers labelled 'dirty' was widespread as people became inured to sleeping with many partners. The Canon of Durham, pronounced to Chadwick that

> It shocks every feeling of propriety to think that in a room, and within such a space as I have been describing, civilised beings should be herding together without a decent separation of age and sex.[15]

Writing in 1855, R. Bickersteth put the same argument in terms that conceive physical and moral squalor as aspects of the same problem:

> There are tens of thousands in this metropolis whose physical condition is a positive bar to the practice of morality. Talk of morality amongst people who herd ... together with no regard to age or sex, in one narrow confined apartment! You might as well talk of cleanliness in a sty, or of limpid purity in a cess pool.[16]

Victorian reformers, often unconsciously, frequently used dirt as a moral metaphor. Their conceptions of which relationships between people were and were not acceptable, if the moral principles of healthy life were to be maintained, were reflected in the separation of objects contained in the ideology of dirt.

The classification of clean and dirty matter in Douglas's view reflects not only a structure of relationships between human beings, but also of relationships between mankind and the rest of the universe and sometimes ultimately with its creator. If for any reason humanity's sense of place in the hierarchy is upset, chaos will result – not merely the moral chaos already considered, but ontological chaos for the individual and society. To prevent this from happening at the most fundamental level, peoples come to regard those things that endanger their worldview as unclean. Contact with them defiles and must be avoided.

In her second chapter, Douglas takes the familiar example of the abominations of Leviticus. Those animals that do not fit into their categories – a scheme which she works hard to impose upon Leviticus – are pronounced untouchable:

> holiness requires that individuals shall conform to the class to which they belong. And holiness requires that different classes of things shall not be confused ... the dietary laws would have been like signs which at every turn inspired meditation on the oneness, purity and completeness of God.[17]

For the Levites, the world existed and was held in shape simply because of the holiness and pure goodness of God and his utter abhorrence of evil. What defined them as human beings was their relationship with this God, which required a similar intolerance of all that was not holy or clean. The principle behind their rules was God's much-repeated commandment: 'Be holy; for I am holy' (Leviticus 11:44 and elsewhere). Their law shaped a society that constantly reinforced this fact, by dividing almost every object and activity into categories of clean and unclean. Ruskin's post-Romantic conception of purity shares this association of cleanness with the divine nature (or perhaps rather with the divine in nature) and uncleanness as a corrupting distortion of it. The Levitical laws were interpreted differently in an article which Dickens published on 20 October 1860 in *All the Year Round* entitled 'Sanitary Science', which stated quite bluntly, 'Many of the Levitical laws are sanitary laws'.[18] In other words, unclean things were simply those that would have an adverse effect upon the digestion because difficult to store and likely to decay in a hot climate, contaminating the other foods with which they came into contact. Nevertheless, the two discourses in dialogue here are not as different as they may at first appear. *Dombey and Son's* depiction of the slum as an environment where the unnatural naturally becomes natural seems to indicate a religious and ideological dimension implicated deep in the apparently simple call to preserve life implicated in his sanitary reform. Perhaps this dimension to the question explains Dickens's religious choice of language as he describes the contaminating effects of London's fog in *Bleak House*:

> where it rolls defiled among the tiers of shipping, and the waterside pollutions of a great (and dirty) city.
>
> (1 p. 13)

The sanitary laws he advocated may unconsciously have been Levitical laws.

Esther Summerson's anxieties about dirt in *Bleak House* are based on the lack of proper distinctions. Her disapproving list of things found in Mrs Jellyby's cupboard is truly haphazard including: 'bits of mouldy pie, sour bottles, Mrs Jellyby's caps, letters, tea, forks, odd boots and shoes of children, firewood, wafers', and numerous other objects which do not ordinarily belong together (30 p. 480). This house is clearly a microcosm of the London at the beginning of the novel. Esther notes that 'no domestic object which was capable of collecting dirt, from a dear child's knee to the door-plate, was without as much dirt as could well accumulate upon it' (30 p. 479). The other narrator describes 'mud, sticking ... tenaciously to the pavement, and accumulating at compound interest' (1 p. 11). Pedestrians blend with 'tens of thousands of other foot passengers' and dogs are 'undistinguishable in mire' (1 p. 13). One simply cannot tell what anything is. Esther's own reaction to this scene shows that it disturbs her perceptions of the universe. London, she says, has 'the dirtiest and darkest streets that ever were seen in the world (I thought), and in such a distracting state of confusion that I wondered how the people kept their senses' (*BH* 3 p. 42).

Even names, the means by which human beings grasp the identities of themselves and the distinct objects in the surrounding world, become meaningless in this environment. Dickens informs the reader that 'few people are known in Tom-all-Alone's by any Christian sign' (*BH* 22 p. 358). Chadwick quotes a police inspector who comments on this phenomenon in the dirtiest tenements of Glasgow:

> The fact is ... they really have no names. Within this range of buildings I have no doubt I should be able to find a thousand children who have no names whatever, or only nicknames, like dogs.[19]

While this lack of nomenclature may simply reflect an understandable reluctance on the part of Glaswegian children to give their names to 'the polis', Chadwick's concern is that it makes such human beings indistinguishable from each other.

In Dickens, it also means that they cannot be differentiated from the animals around them. In the early fiction, Fagin's squalid environment makes him an amphibious creature 'like some loathsome reptile, engendered in the slime and darkness through which he moved' (*OT* 19 p. 121), to be shunned for its lack of conformity to definable categories. *Bleak House* is populated by a whole 'crowd of foul existence that crawls in and out of gaps in walls and boards; and coils itself to sleep, in maggot numbers' (16 pp. 256–7). Jo, a fully realised version of *Dombey and Son's* slum child as flower, is also ranked with the animals:

> native ignorance, the growth of English soil and climate, sink his immortal nature lower than the beasts that perish.
>
> (47 p. 724)

He can 'see the horses, dogs, and cattle, go by me, and to know that in ignorance I belong to them' (16 p. 258). Even this impression is too optimistic, however. There can be no sense of belonging in the nameless mire, even to the canine world:

> He is not of the same order of things [as George], not of the same place in creation. He is of no order and no place; neither of the beasts, nor of humanity.
>
> (47 p. 724)

London's dirt threatens the whole structure of the universe and must therefore be cleared away. In the meantime, 'Jo, and the other lower animals, get on in the unintelligible mess as they can' (16 p. 258).

The regressive slime that pollutes the city confounds not only contemporary species, but also those of all ages:

> it would not be wonderful to meet a Megalosaurus, forty feet long or so, waddling like an elephantine lizard up Holborn Hill.
>
> (1 p. 13)

Each day the crowds add 'new deposits to the crust upon crust of mud', suggesting a surreal juxtaposition of various geological eras, all visible at once. This is disconcerting for the same reasons as those that terrify Henry Knight, in Thomas Hardy's *A Pair of Blue Eyes*, as he hangs from the cliff, imagining all the layers of life fossilised within it.[20] So irrelevant are distinctions here that the spot is even known as 'the Cliff without a Name'.[21] He risks having his particular identity as a human being eroded and of merging into an indiscriminate mass of animal life. Dickens locates the threat to the distinction human beings apprehend between themselves and other living organisms not in the strata of the coastal rock, but in the dehumanising environment of the metropolis.

Such anxieties became a characteristic feature of Victorian thinking about the city. As notions of inheritable evolution developed, the parallel concept of degeneration emerged. The thought that a significant proportion of the British population might not be progressing in the direction of the surviving fittest or even that adaptation for survival in these new conditions might require them to shed distinguishing human traits, was horrifying. Contemporaries were not slow to identify this section of the community as the "waste" products of the struggle for survival. William Greenslade sums up contemporary concern about the habitat that made for this apparent proliferation of the unfit:

> The post-Darwinian city was imagined not merely as a city of moral darkness and of outcasts. Here were tracts of new degenerate energies, menageries of sub-races of men and women. ... So far from entailing extinction, these creatures of the biologically degenerate underground were the tenacious, perverse, and ambiguous fit/unfit, with an appropriately dark future ahead of them.[22]

Bleak House, written six years before the publication of *The Origin of Species*, is not, of course, a post-Darwinian novel, yet its city already engages with these concerns. George Levine has argued eloquently for reading Dickens's fiction as a response to an altering Victorian worldview to which Darwin contributed.[23] Gillian Beer even credits Dickens's plots with providing a model for Darwin's ordering of his thoughts in their emphasis on apparently chaotic profusion of detail which proves ultimately resolvable to relationships of descent and competition for survival.[24] It is not, then, anachronistic to read that novel's fascinated revulsion for the dirt, as a yearning for a clear sense of humanity differentiated from animal life. The philosophical basis for such categorisation was becoming increasingly slippery.

For readers, aware of these geological and biological theories, urban squalor profoundly threatened the all-important distinction between rational humanity and the irrational animal world. These slum areas were unclean primarily because their existence undermined the whole worldview of Victorian humanists. Their removal was necessitated by a moral obligation to support the framework of the universe – at least as an environment habitable by human beings. This, of course, is directly comparable to those duties felt by earlier societies to exclude certain anomalous things from the sanctified zones that represented how the world ought to be organised – or even to exterminate them altogether. In the new religion of secular progressivism, a sacred duty to protect the pure remained. Francis Galton, for example, portrayed the need to stem the tide of degeneration and to clear away the conditions that led to it as more than a question of social improvement. In his *Inquiries into the Human Faculty*, he wrote, 'Man has already furthered his evolution very considerably ... but he has not yet risen to the conviction that it is his religious duty to do so deliberately and systematically'.[25] A general concealment of the principles of healthy life was still in operation in modern London, which was dragging human beings back to the animal nature from which they had evolved, dissolving their identity and leading to the death of the species. It was necessary to resist this by creating living conditions that facilitated the upward development of humanity.

Nothing less than the salvation of humanity, not from Hell, but from regression and extinction was being called for in the campaign for cleaning up London and Galton correctly identifies this aim as a religious one. Dickens was more keenly aware than most of this nascent dimension to the contemporary cry for sanitary reform, whether from secular or Christian voice, recognising that a key aim of attempts to restore cleanness is to avert ontological chaos. Therefore he requires specifically religious vocabulary and symbolism to describe the compulsion to implement them.

II. Eliminating dirt from the discourse

One option available to the rationalist confronted with the problem of the filthy metropolis was to sweep the dirt out of sight. A disturbing consequence of this was the conceptualisation of the long-term poor and unemployed as the residuum, or waste matter, in the process of mankind's evolution. The only solution was totally to eliminate such contaminating matter from London. The words of Samuel Smith, a writer in the *Contemporary Review* in 1885, sound chilling in the light of twentieth-century history, but arose quite naturally from this way of thinking about people and dirt:

> While the flower of the population emigrate, the residuum stays, corrupting and being corrupted, like the sewage of the metropolis which remained floating at the mouth of the Thames last summer, because there was not scour sufficient to propel it into the sea.[26]

More than forty years earlier, Engels noted this tendency to push the slum dwellers out of sight, if not yet out of existence. He records a Manchester built by the middle classes with radial roads fronted by beautiful houses so that they could cross the whole city without even seeing the slums that lay behind:

> The town itself is peculiarly built, so that someone can live in it for years and travel into it and out of it daily without ever coming into contact with a working class quarter or even with workers. ... I have

never elsewhere seen a concealment of such fine sensibility of everything that might offend the eyes and nerves of the middle classes.[27]

Dickens too is aware of this Podsnappian exclusion of the working classes from visibility and refuses to participate in it:

dainty delicacy living in the next street, stops her ears, and lisps 'I don't believe it!

(p. 619)

This personified figure enacts a withdrawal from society into a self-deluding concealment of her duty of care to her neighbour. The passage returns to the plot by showing that the selfishness that perpetuates the slums reflects the broken father–daughter relationship between Dombey and Florence as another product of a sick money-centred environment. London is in the hands of people as neurotically anxious to conceal their dependence on the poorer classes as Dombey is to conceal his obligation to the Toodleses or to Florence. While the reader is invited to identify with Dombey as a victim of his environment, like the urchin child, he is also associated with those who cause such conditions. Failure to care for the needs of others is

a perversion of nature in their own contracted sympathies ... as great, and yet as natural in its development when once begun, as the lowest degradation known.

(47 p. 620)

Dickens boldly equates passive callousness on the part of respectable people who create slum conditions with the more obvious moral outrages committed by those who live in them. Unhealthy regions of London are 'the scenes of *our* too long neglect' (47 p. 620, emphasis added). Dickens's texts may share the horror at the implications of such places and their inhabitants shown in ideologies (be they religious, aesthetic or scientific) of the healthy and natural. Paradoxically, however, the categorisation of people into clean and dirty by which such ideologies sought to reintroduce clarity is presented with keen insight as frequently resulting in a villainous concealment in its own right. The desire to eliminate the people produced in the slums from representation and even from existence can be a catalyst, not a solution, to the problem.

Whether the impulse is journalistic or poetic, Dickens wished to make the physical and moral infection in the air visible in *Dombey and Son*:

if the noxious particles that rise from vitiated air, were palpable to the sight, we should see them lowering in a dense black cloud above such haunts, and rolling slowly on to corrupt the better portions of a town. But if the moral pestilence that rises with them, and, in the eternal laws of outraged Nature, is inseparable from them, could be made discernible too, how terrible the revelation!

(DS 47 p. 619)

As well as such an imaginary 'colouring in' of harmful air particles, a second fantastic suggestion is offered of how a revelation might be achieved, that of the

good spirit who would take the house-tops off ... and show a Christian people what dark shapes issue from amidst their homes ...

(47 p. 620)[28]

Dombey too must be made to see the results of his selfish neglect and this is included in the general apocalypse heralded by the spirit, an event which anticipates the 'day that dawned' dreaded by the secret-keepers of *Little Dorrit's* London:

But no such day had ever dawned on Mr Dombey, or his wife

(47 p. 739)

The main plot makes the results of egocentrism visible as the dirt in the social comment makes the sources of disease and socio-moral dysfunction visible. Dombey's apocalyptic realisation that he has created an environment in which his children could not live transfers the emotions involved in awakening to the need for social reform back to the domestic context where such emotions could be readily understood by Victorian readers.

In *Bleak House*, dirt – and in particular, dirty air – is not used simply as an illustration, but as a fully realised part of the novel's ethos and theme. An entire city in the advanced stages of decay, made filthy by the miasma proliferating from Tom-all-Alone's, provides the bewildering opening of this novel. In 1853, when *Bleak House* was published, the Smoke Nuisance Abatement (Metropolis) Act put London's filthy air high on the public agenda. Although this act proved largely unsuccessful, applying solely to London's small number of factories, rather than the densely packed homes and workshops wherein the problem originated, Dickens was able to turn the problem of contaminated air into a symbol that would immediately strike a chord with many of his readers.

In Chapter 1, the High Court of Chancery rather than Tom-all-Alone's is the focus for London's dirt. The two are immediately linked by the aside: 'This desirable property is in Chancery, of course' (16 p. 257). The area might have been clean and habitable had the parties involved not been squabbling so stubbornly there. The polluted fog functions most obviously to reflect the obstructions to clarity cherished by the court. The miasma that obscures vision and endangers health in the slum is a by-product of the same concealing cloud, which prevents any movement to rescue Tom-all-Alone's. The shift from literal to metaphorical use of dirt here is almost seamless. It is difficult to tell when 'fog' and 'mud' stop being applied to the external conditions around the court and when they begin to describe the complexity of the court's procedures. Similarly, the layer of dust around Tulkinghorn's home evokes that metaphorical dust which 'the law ... may scatter, on occasion, in the eyes of the laity' (22 p.352). Dirt reflects deliberate mystification for corrupt ends.

Krook, with his ironic title of Lord Chancellor and his 'liking for rust and must and cobwebs' (5 p. 70), represents the whole system in his desire to amass information for personal gain and then to conceal it from others. Despite the preface's insistence upon the factual possibility of spontaneous combustion, Krook's departure is dictated solely by symbolic aptness. He dies

> the death of all Lord Chancellors in all Courts. ... inborn, inbred, engendered in the corrupted humours of the vicious body itself, and that only – Spontaneous Combustion ...
>
> (32 p. 519)

Concealment has brought its own nemesis. The dust he has used to hide the documents he possesses has formed an unwholesome environment which destroys him, just as other exclusions of truth, light and air in Dickens lead ultimately to destruction. He is a warning to others. Snagsby fears he will end up like Krook, destroyed through unwise involvement in secrets:

> a party to some mysterious secret, without knowing what it is. And it is the fearful peculiarity of this condition that, at any hour of his daily life, at any opening of the shop-door, at any pull of the bell, at any entrance of a messenger, or any delivery of a letter, the secret may take air and fire, explode, and blow up ...
>
> (25 p. 407)

Yet, disturbingly, the harm does not stop with Krook himself. His internal substances merge with the fog that clouds the view from Jobling and Guppy's window, making it still darker, dirtier and more impenetrable. The 'stagnant, sickening oil, with some natural repulsion in it that makes them both shudder', so 'offensive to the touch and sight, and more offensive to the smell' (32 p. 516), horrifies the reader too. In the fog of *Bleak House*, dripping with such matter as this, Dickens has found a terrifying way to make the 'vitiated air' of *Dombey and Son* truly 'palpable to the sight'.

III. Ghosts and dirty air

Dickens's representation of dirt, however, was also motivated by generic considerations that interact with the political, anthropological and religious reasons already considered. Contemporary understanding of its effects allowed it to replace the gothic ghost as the evidence of repressed truth in a way more terrifying to nineteenth-century readers because it is more immediate to their daily experience. This is especially so when Dickens engages with the question of culpability for urban squalor.

Bleak House describes the 'mighty speech-making there has been, both in and out of Parliament' as a generator of dust (46 pp. 708–10). Various political, religious and social factions caused delays to sanitary reform by arguing about the means whenever the subject was raised. London's general lack of cleanliness is referable to a selfish reluctance to act, like Mrs Jellyby's devotion to the African mission, which literally produces filth at home by allowing her to evade her responsibility there. The neglect and inaction of Parliament create a miasmic smokescreen that allows the wealthier classes to evade their responsibility, masking a lack of will to provide a real solution as deceitful and unproductive as the endless talk in Chancery.

Dickens envisages the movement of polluted air across the capital, carrying fever into the middle-class parts of town, as the just wages of such greed and apathy. Not only is it dangerous to cross from the clean to the dirty zones of London, but the fatal air from the dirty zones threatens to invade the purer districts. Miasmic theory of disease contagion was widespread in Dickens's lifetime. Bacteriology developed only in the 1870s, after his death, and water-borne contagion, the largest cause of disease transmission in London, was not established as a fact until 1848, the year when *Dombey and Son* appeared. In that novel, the movement of disease-carrying air through London is used as an analogy for the immorality generated in the slums spreading across class boundaries in its effects. As people born there lose the ability to respond to distinct ideas of good and evil, their crimes affect the wealthier further afield. In this way, 'depravity' will 'blight the innocent and spread contagion among the pure'. Now the children of the rich as well as of the poor have become flowers of evil. The gardener responsible for the condition of these plants is then shown to be none other than the middle-class reader:

> where we generate disease to strike our children down ... there also we breed, by the same certain process, infancy that knows no innocence, youth without modesty or shame ...
>
> (47 p. 620)

The image of the rich man maliciously destroying those who turn out to be his own children is a characteristically gothic restating of the Biblical moral of wrong returning upon the sinner's head. Here it reinforces the link with the main plot. Dombey will certainly strike Florence in this chapter, but surely he cannot be said to strike down his own darling boy? And yet his determination to create an atmosphere in his house that will stifle Florence's insistence on the value of love, affection and domestic comfort makes it a place where Paul, who cannot fit the mould into which Dombey would press him, simply cannot live. The claustrophobic atmosphere of this one house is now reflected in the polluted air of all London, driving home the message that circumstances that create poverty of environment are ultimately a curse upon those who cause them.

Dirt, then, is not only the result of a social crime, but it is the evidence of that crime asserting itself in a form that refuses to go away. It has replaced the ghost of gothic fiction as that which insists on the concealer's culpability and brings him or her to judgement. *Bleak House* makes this connection explicit, the miasma spreading from the slums, represented by Tom-all-Alone's, to infect the areas inhabited by the negligent legislators responsible for their squalor. He underlines this chain of cause and effect by personifying the slum as 'Tom', exacting retribution:

> But he has his revenge. Even the winds are his messengers, and they serve him in these hours of darkness.
>
> (*BH* 46 p. 710)

This language from Psalm 104[29] even suggests divine appointment of such vengeance. Earlier, Nemo's burial in the ridiculously full city churchyard prompts another scriptural allusion, this time from 1 Corinthians 15:42:

> here, they lower our dear brother down a foot or two: here, sow him in corruption, to be raised in corruption: an avenging ghost at many a sick-bedside ...
>
> (11 p. 180)

The spread of fever denies the Christian belief in resurrection from the dead, which had formed such a solemn part of the imagery of transformative regeneration in *Dombey and Son* and in Dickens's private correspondence.[30] Its statement that the human body is 'sown in corruption; it is raised in incorruption', reasserts itself in this distorted form. The language of sowing and reaping is conflated with that other biblical axiom, 'whatsoever a man soweth, that shall he also reap' (Galatians 6:7 and elsewhere). The recurrent cultivation metaphor blends immorality with disease in the account of what is grown in London.

> There is not a drop of Tom's corrupted blood but propagates infection and contagion somewhere. ... There is not an atom of Tom's slime, not a cubic inch of any pestilential gas in which he lives, not one obscenity or degradation about him, ... but shall work its retribution ...
>
> (46 p. 710)

Gothic ghosts are victims who refuse to stay buried; urban dirt now bears their numinous accusing properties.

Polluted air, the damage done by the greedy and selfish, is not confined then to areas like Tom-all-Alone's, but affects all life in London. Many Victorian attempts to deal with the problem failed through a conservative fear of the centralised action that was needed. Fever, after all, did not respect borough boundaries, as Dickens pointed out in a speech to the Metropolitan Sanitary Association on 6 February 1850:

> With regard to the objectors on the principle of self-government, and that what was done in the next Parish was no business of theirs, he should begin to think there was something in it when he found any court or street keeping its disease within its own bounds, or any parish keeping to itself its own fever or its own smallpox, just as it maintained its own beadles and its own fire engine.

Dickens made the same point more concisely in a later speech to the Association on 10 May 1851, remarking that 'The air from Gin Lane will be carried, when the wind is Easterly, into May Fair'.[31] Piecemeal legislation was inadequate. Everyone who lived in London was responsible collectively for dealing with this problem, as the fiction states so forcefully. According to Raymond Williams, for Dickens, what is really concealed in the city is the social truth of mutual interdependence within a total system:

> the fog ... keeps us from seeing each other clearly and from seeing the relation between ourselves and our actions, ourselves and others'.[32]

It hides the utter indivisibility of London as a social ecosystem – yet this is what it paradoxically insists upon.

As F. S. Schwarzbach puts it in his article, '*Bleak House*: The Social Pathology of Urban Life':

> The much celebrated opening description – of a city mired in mud and clouded in fog – seems to present disconnected phenomena, but in fact nothing could be further from the truth. For most of the mud, made up of dirt, rubbish ... and raw sewage, ends in the Thames and then oozes downstream to the Essex marshes. There it rots and festers, soon producing infectious effluvia that are blown by the raw East wind back over the city. *This* is the stuff of the novel's dense fog, a fog that spreads disease wherever it is inhaled – which is to say, as the novel insists, *everywhere*. ... To say, then, as often has been said, that the mud and fog are *symbols* of social malaise is to miss the point entirely: Dickens is pointing to a literal economy of filth and disease that functions not as symbol but as fact to poison the very air his readers breathe, according to scientific laws as inexorable as those of gravity.[33]

Dickens uses a physical reality recognised by the medical authorities of the time to exemplify, rather than to provide a metaphor for, the revelation of an unavoidable system of social relationships created by an attempt to conceal it, figured elsewhere, and in a different mode, by the gothic imagery. While Dickens the reformer here uses the conceptual apparatus of his familiar gothic forms to make his political point, Dickens the novelist was drawing on contemporary understanding of sanitary reform to provide an updated figure for the tension between concealment and revelation in his plots. Sometimes, as we have seen, the two are combined. Seven years after the publication of *Bleak House*, Dickens revisited the theme of the haunted passage in an article in *All the Year Round* entitled 'Sanitary Science'. The reality behind the phantom is conceived here, however, not as the living evidence of past misdeeds, but as disease-carrying effluvia, improperly disposed of:

> there are many houses in Great Britain which have inherited evil reputations; there is a 'ghost's room,' or a 'ghost's corridor,' ... The true ghost's walk is, however, in the basement ... Your only exorcist is the sanitary engineer.[34]

Whether or not Dickens wrote the piece himself, the writer has grasped the imaginative link between contaminating dirt, ghosts and guilty secrets that creates the thematic unity of the novel from which the phrase 'ghost's walk' is drawn. The supposed apparitions in *Bleak House* and *Little Dorrit* are created by the re-emergence of suppressed truth and, as in the gothic texts, only disappear once that truth has been brought out into the open. Nevertheless, such spectres are merely imagined by the characters, whereas dirt fulfils a similar symbolic purpose, but is given a much more literal existence.

IV. Jo and Esther: Compulsive cleaners

Jo reflects Esther's situation as dirty ghost. Constantly moved on by the authorities, he is himself part of the dirt that must be swept away. That the sole aim of this filthy creature's existence should be to keep an area clean is then especially poignant. The one thing he knows is 'that it's hard to keep the mud off the crossing in dirty weather, and harder still to live by doing it' (16 p. 256). Likewise, because Esther has not been born in the proper sphere of wedlock, she must be swept out of sight of decent folk. Miss Barbary tells Jarndyce that she had 'blotted out all trace of her existence' and that, like Jo, 'she would be left entirely friendless, nameless, and unknown' (17 p. 276). Here she also resembles her father, who in a 'foul and filthy' room (10 p. 165), redolent of opium fumes, 'established his pretensions to his name by becoming indeed No one' (11 p. 167). Nemo is personally dirty, his beard 'ragged ... and grown, like the scum and mist around him, in neglect' (10 p. 165). He provides an objective correlative for human nature as defiled in the eyes of religious categorisation.

Esther too must decay in hiding until her life has been forgotten. Her resemblance to her mother in her obscure London surroundings constantly threatens to reveal the fornication that has generated her. In a gothic novel, she might have featured as a ghost. Just as the dirt threatens to become 'an avenging ghost', bringing disease to those responsible for it (11 p. 180), so Esther's existence brings the downfall of those who categorise her as dirty. She becomes 'the dreadful truth in the legend of the Ghost's Walk ... who was to bring calamity upon the stately house' (36 p. 586). It is, therefore, singularly appropriate within the novel's symbolic economy that when Lady Dedlock's past is exposed, she finally comes to embrace what she has formerly concealed, acknowledging Nemo's grave in the slums where he has first metaphorically and now literally been buried. Such areas function like the cellars of a gothic haunted house, where all that has stood in the way of a developing ideology of progress lie concealed – and from which it may reassert its existence.

In an article called 'Underground London', Dickens casually compares society's structures for dealing with criminals to its developing structures for dealing with dirt:

> Sewage ... is very much like our convicts; everybody wants to get rid of it, and no one consents to have it.[35]

However necessary prisons might be, Dickens finds such displacement of the problem by re-categorisation inadequate (and in some cases morally bankrupt) to the problem of reasserting a living human identity. In Esther, Dickens seeks a different approach to the ontological and spiritual issues raised by the problem of London's deadly squalor – one that can deal with its dehumanising aspects without itself dehumanising. Her response to being told she is 'dirty' is exactly the opposite from her father's. Exemplifying Mary Douglas's definition of 'dirt avoidance' as 'a creative movement, an attempt to relate form to function, to make unity of experience', she creates a universe where she has the moral and ontological place denied her by Miss Barbary.[36]

Esther's pursuit of her mother is a search for her own origins which requires a confrontation with open eyes of London's dirt and the burying ground, which in their various ways represent the process of hiding. Bucket guides her through London's 'slimy' areas, such as Limehouse Hole, 'which the wind from the river ... did not purify' (57 p. 868). As the chase nears its conclusion, in a graveyard which is 'hemmed in by filthy houses ... on whose walls a thick humidity broke out like a disease' (59 p. 913), the dirty environment takes on a human significance to Esther's troubled mind:

the wet housetops, the clogged and bursting gutters and water-spouts. ... the stained house fronts put on human shapes and looked at me [so that] the unreal things were more substantial than the real.

(59 p. 913)

The dirt of this unreal city disrupts Esther's sense of reality, yet she emerges from these scenes with a clear sense of her and her mother's place in the drama that has unfolded.

Esther gains the power to pull the lives around her out of the fog. Jarndyce and Ada feel 'that wherever Dame Durden went, there was sunshine and summer air' (30 p. 486). She transmits the sense of truth and purity that is the antidote to London's poisonous air but is such order in Dickens an efficacious yet artificial construct or a reflection of spiritual principles that govern the novels' universe? Dickens elsewhere rhetorically proclaimed that clean air would allow revelation of a Christ who was invisible through the man-made dirt of London. Assuming the voice of a slum dweller responding to an outraged moralist, he exclaimed in a speech to the Metropolitan Sanitary Association:

give me my first glimpse of Heaven through a little of its light and air ... help me to be clean ... and, Teacher, then I'll hear, you know how willingly, of Him whose thoughts were so much with the Poor.[37]

Little Dorrit also equates Heaven with clean air. Edwin B. Barnett, in 'Little Dorrit and the Disease of Modern Life',[38] usefully traces how the claustrophobic atmosphere of London on a Sunday afternoon, sets the tone for the whole novel, much as the climate of the opening paragraphs does in *Bleak House*. We have considered how the dust-clouds within Mrs Clennam's house and the city's fog, which expands their symbolic meaning, represent an attempt to restrict the visibility of truth in the manner of the gothic haunted house. Perhaps, however, this concealment is paradoxically an attempt to reduce an untidy universe to a tidy order – *her* order. At any rate, the fall of her house leads above all to the clearing of the air. Amy Dorrit reveals the goodness that the soiled environment of London renders invisible, showing that moral distinctions and perception of one's place in an interdependent universe do indeed have value.[39]

Ultimately the framework of the universe that dirt threatens for Dickens has as its root an idea of collective responsibility and love. This is why the novelist still found a value in the person of Jesus, although he did not believe in the inspiration of the Bible. Alice's death in *Dombey and Son* suggests that he read Christ's socially inclusive caring life as a different sort of answer to the problem of dirtiness than the solution offered by Mrs Barbary and Mrs Clennam in His name. The gospels are:

> the blessed history, in which the blind lame palsied beggar, the criminal, the woman *stained* with shame, the *shunned* of all our dainty clay, has each a portion, that no human pride, indifference, or sophistry ... can take away ...
>
> (*DS* 58 p. 785, my italics)

In other words, the genuine follower of Christ must acknowledge the dirty as human beings, rather than eliminating them from sight. Dickens's stories and symbolic environments show concepts of dirtiness formed by people who exclude as dirty those who do not fit into their self-centred conceptions of how the world ought to be. Because they have power, the institutions of the city reflect their exclusions. Clarifiers such as Florence, Esther and Little Dorrit expose the narrowness of such conceptions. Dirt must still be cleared away but the judgement must be made on proper criteria. Dickens's characters must ultimately find a comprehensive order for themselves in the chaos of London's dirt. Then they can even help those responsible for their degradation to confront their own equally dirty origins in redeeming love.

Underpinning these narratives of transcendence, through love, of a spoiled origin is the Christianity that partially shaped the general cultural climate of the Britain in which Dickens grew up. Its vocabulary of escape from humanity's deathbound uncleanness, however, is treated with scepticism as well as trust. Chadband reads Jo's confusion and decaying physical state as a result of his having been born into original sin and feels that a lengthy sermon about this doctrine may set him straight:

> O running stream of sparkling joy
> To be a soaring human boy!

and do you cool yourself in that stream now, my young friend? No. Why do you not cool yourself in that stream now? Because you are in a state of darkness, because you are in a state of obscurity, because you are in a state of sinfulness, because you are in a state of bondage.

(*BH*, 19 pp. 313–14)

Although Dickens uses this language ironically, Chadband's statements are true – otherwise there would be no point to the revelations sought in *Bleak House*. The darkness takes objective form in the 'red and violet-tinted smoke' that comes between him and 'the great Cross on the summit of St Paul's Cathedral', which he feels to be 'the crowning confusion of the great, confused city' (p. 315). The implication is that the cross, 'that sacred emblem', holds the answer to the darkness and bondage which Jo's life in the mud and smog impose upon him, but that these metropolitan conditions prevent him from apprehending it. In its own architecture, the city contains the regenerating information he needs, but other aspects of the city conceal it from his view.

Dickens does not read the cross in terms of conventional theology as compensation for original sin. For Dickens, there is no original sin *per se*, but there are originators, transgressive 'parents', who cover their relationships of responsibility to enjoy selfish pleasure and leave the people whose identities they have shaped in the process, to deal with the results as they may. In labelling Jo's state as primarily one of 'sinfulness', Chadband is like those mentioned in *Dombey and Son*, who behold another slum child and 'hold forth on its natural sinfulness, and lament its being, so early, far away from Heaven' (47 p. 619). The narrator invites them to think about how the squalid urban environment has made the development of healthy morality almost impossible for such boys and girls, who have 'been conceived, and born, and bred, in Hell' (p. 619). The atmosphere in which they live predisposes them to wickedness. They have been born into an artificially generated original sin, a collective transgression of society that leads to each individual born into it committing further transgressions with grim inevitability. Dickens aimed to shock his Evangelical readers into feeling that their negligence might be a form of man-made foreordination to a lost eternity. Such assertions had serious implications. If souls were really prevented from living righteously because of their environment, and the middle classes failed to do what was in their power to help, then they must also be held responsible for their damnation.

The obscured cross does, however, seem to represent a more vaguely defined self-sacrificing love that will restore relationships between people and with God. Chadband, unlike Jo, is intellectually equipped to read this story of ultimate altruism in the Bible and in the architecture of the city.

It is in his power to declare God's relationship of selfless love to Jo by showing His grace and kindness in action. Instead, his self-important and incomprehensible sermon merely condemns him as a sinner. The sterile Christianity he offers can only label people as wicked, having lost its power to enlighten and transform because its practitioners fail to reflect the selfless giving of Calvary. In blocking the message of the cross, he has contributed to the confusing smog. Such people have obscured the primary symbol of their faith, making the restored relationship between people and God that it offers 'so far out of ... reach' (p. 315).

The Chadbands of the world are thus complicit in a villainous concealment in condemning the Jos for living in a situation created by their own inactivity. Jo's inability to orient himself towards the city's crosses restates the futility at the inquest of his swearing on a Bible of whose contents he is entirely ignorant. Ultimately, Woodcourt, not Chadband, goes furthest towards explaining the cross in terms he can understand, by demonstrating the relationship of love in practical kindness.[40] Even he, however, can only go so far. Jo finds the words of the Lord's Prayer 'wery good' (47 p. 734) and thus akin to the 'wery good' generosity of Mr Nemo (11 p. 178), who turns out to be the father of another lost child. Woodcourt, repeating the first line of that prayer, seeks to reveal Jo's relationship as a child to one common father, but whether he succeeds or not is left chillingly ambiguous. To Jo, the words seem merely disconnected phrases. His question, 'Is there any light a comin?' (47 pp. 733–4), contrasts pathetically with Paul Dombey's confident vision of 'The light about the head' of Christ (*DS* 16 p. 225).[41]

Previous generations have evaded their responsibilities as have contemporaries who ought to stand *in loco parentis* to Jo including the king, lords, 'Right Reverends and Wrong Reverends' and 'men and women, born with Heavenly compassion in your hearts' appealed to at Jo's death (47 p. 734). Consequently, Jo perpetuates the infection spreading from their mistakes, passing on the smallpox that deforms Esther. His sense of guilt about this leads him for the first time to consider his relationship with the world. His proposed method of rectifying this is very telling. If Mr Snagsby could somehow 'write out, wery large so that anyone could see it anywheres, as that I wos wery truly hearty sorry that I done it', then Woodcourt, along with the rest of the world, would 'be able to forgive me in his mind. If the writin could be made to say it wery large, he might' (47 p. 731). In his illiteracy, he has been denied access to vital information contained in such public writing, the language of the city. It is also where the Christian message is contained, in harmony with the message contained in the city's architecture. Woodcourt and

Snagsby's attempt to re-integrate him into loving relationships has allowed him some limited understanding of that message. By putting his own repentance in writing, he will be able to participate for the first time in the revelation of truth encoded in the city.

To Dickens, then, there is something more involved in the system of connections concealed by some and discovered by others, than simple co-operation for mutual benefit on utilitarian grounds. I substantially agree with Ephraim Sicher's summary of what Dickens is recommending as 'an ethics of capitalism based on mutual responsibility and benevolence fuelled by an imaginative sympathy for the city's outcasts'.[42] I would however wish to remember that the truth of fatherhood and fraternity amongst men is, to Dickens, the religious truth potentially communicated by the cross and the Lord's Prayer, so determinedly shrouded by the metropolitan smog. Equally, the truth the urban squalor of *Dombey and Son* is said to conceal is that mankind is 'one family' with 'one Father' (47 p. 620). Those who have failed to care for succeeding generations have transgressed not only a social principle, but also the same principle of divine familial love that makes Dombey's refusal to care for Florence so horrifying.

Florence constantly seeks to break through Dombey's self-absorbed attitude with a revelation of such love. Dombey's vision of his daughter and his dead wife clasped in 'clear depths of tenderness and truth ... while he stood on the bank above them, looking down a mere spectator – not a sharer with them – quite shut out' is 'a revelation' to him of 'something secret in his breast, of the nature of which he was hardly informed himself' (3 p. 31). The secret, that his self-referential world is inadequate and that he ultimately needs to be part of the network of love relationships, is insupportable to him. In his perverse urge to conceal it, he frantically asks, 'what was there he could interpose between himself and it?' (20 p. 278) In the following novels, and in Chapter 47 of this particular novel, characters like Dombey find something large enough to interpose between themselves and revelation of the love relationships they ought to be participating in – namely, London.

Florence's message then is linked to the message of the cross in *Bleak House*. The 'strange ethereal light that seemed to rest upon her head' (47 p. 620) is the same that rested upon Christ's head in little Paul's vision of the embrace of his mother – a human parental love relationship, integrated with the love relationship with the Everlasting Father in which it originates. The vision of a mother's embrace that was so unbearable to Dombey brings peace of mind to Paul. In *Bleak House*, the Chancery Court, Parliament and Chadband, with their parental position in society, can no more tolerate this revelation than Dombey can and, literally and metaphorically, generate the fog to hide it. Most of Dickens's heroines, including Agnes Wickfield, Esther Summerson, Little Dorrit and Lizzie Hexham, exist, like Florence, to reveal relationships of love that are part of a network of such relationships stemming from God's love for his children. This leads Alexander Welsh to say that 'novelists are hinting at ... much more than a person in a heroine like Little Dorrit. They are invoking something more nearly divine',[43] perhaps what his chapter heading calls 'The Spirit of Love and Truth'. These virtues, Welsh argues, became increasingly abstract over the course of the Victorian era, rather than expressions of the divine character seen in the connections between men and women. Welsh sees the relationships of familial love, localised in the hearth, as fortified places to flee to from London's deathly climate. These novels are products of an increasingly secular age in offering salvation from the city's destruction not in the visions of the afterlife they occasionally invoke, but in 'the firesides and family circles that are defended against the surrounding city'.[44]

As I have argued, however, Dickens retains a positive belief in the divine origin of the family inherent in the discourse he drew upon to motivate a religious readership. The hearth and its relationships are no defensive zone to retreat into, shutting out the outer world. This, after all, is Dombey's fantasy with his 'double door of gold' (20 p. 275). Rather they are the bases from which such relationships can spread positively outwards into the city, converting its inhabitants to their proper relations with each other. The local family circles show what is possible for the whole human society if they will restore their familial love for one another. The forces that conceal social inter-relatedness are ranged against a Divine power that adds sacred status to human brotherhood. To be complicit in hushing the matter over is to take sides against Him.

Dennis Walder says that Dickens 'believed in a conception of conversion which did not primarily involve an acceptance of Christ or the sinfulness of man, but which did involve spiritual transformation affirming a new consciousness of oneself and one's place in the universe'.[45] The personal compulsions to abstract oneself from the network that fascinated Dickens, however, may be sinful in the sense that they are not merely resistant to social principles or to the demands of ontological well-being, but to the love of God itself. Certainly the 'spiritual transformation' brought about in Mrs Clennam when Little Dorrit tries to awaken her to 'consciousness' of her 'place in the universe' which she has denied for so long presents itself to the heroine primarily as a religious realisation. The older woman is invited to 'remember later and better days' of the New Covenant between God and human beings and to emulate Christ, 'following Him' in the task of forgiveness (II 31 p. 770). When Mrs Clennam is given strength for one last attempt at an unselfish action, the house that has embodied her secrecy falls down. At first it seems as though the result will be further obscurity as the spectators are 'Deafened by the noise, stifled, choked, and blinded by the dust', but the end result is transcendent clarity:

> The dust storm, driving between them and the placid sky, parted for a moment and showed them the stars.
>
> (II 31 p. 771)

As she considers this, the cityscape outside changes before her, so that

> The vista of street and bridge was plain to see, and the sky was serene and beautiful. ... numbers were walking for air.
>
> (II 31 p. 771)

The suffocating London of Arthur's first Sunday back at home, which, in its prohibition of enjoyment, shared in the Puritanical atmosphere of the house, seems to have been demolished. As they watch, 'the clear steeples of the many churches looked as if they had advanced out of the murk that usually enshrouded them and come much nearer' (pp. 771–2). The city, then, has the message of Little Dorrit's theology built into it, even if it simultaneously creates the 'murk' that conceals it. The rays of sunlight that illuminate the renewed cityscape following the triumph of her New Testament thinking are 'signs of the blessed later covenant of peace and hope that changed the crown of thorns into a glory' (p. 771). Even though Dickens is not specific about why or how the new covenant supersedes the old, the thorns, symbolic of Adam's curse (Genesis 3:18), have been transformed in this moment of revelation into a symbol of eternal life in a way that is embodied in the entire metropolis. *Little Dorrit* suggests a direct remedy to Jo's situation, unable, as he is, to see the city's Christian revelation through the obscuring smog. A partial transformation like this happens in the earlier novel when Woodcourt performs an act of love in securing lodgings and medical help for Jo and 'the high church spires ... are so near and clear in the morning light that the city itself seems renewed by rest' (47 p. 719). This is exactly opposite to the effect of the encounter with Chadband: the crosses are now visible, resolving themselves into a more meaningful vista for Jo.

London's power to generate dirt has been considered primarily in its gothic aspect. It functions in the novels as a means of obscuring information that the characters must uncover as the plot progresses and as a modernised version of the ghost whereby what has been buried or suppressed returns in distorted and dangerous form. As we have seen, however, this generic use of dirt interacts with other modes of representation including the journalistic realism needed to point the political message and the competing ontological and religious implications of dirt and cleanliness inherent in the discourses surrounding sanitary reform. The interaction between these ways of accounting for London's dirt is what makes it so compelling. In all three novels considered and the surrounding speeches and journalism, Dickens interrogates the religious vocabulary of dirt and cleansing he finds himself using to stimulate a nominally Christian readership into engagement with the problem. He expresses concern about the contribution its rigid categorisations can make to the problem, yet also finds it meaningful in exemplifying the obstructions that must be cleared away to make visible cherished family and societal values.

What is certain, however, is that these uses of London press it into the services of concealment. London's enormous size and complexity – and the bewildering effect it had on contemporaries as a distinctively modern phenomenon – makes it easy to understand why Dickens should so often use it to block the progress towards dénouement in his novels. His awareness that the city could assume that function within the novel's structure, elsewhere performed by the gothic castle, had stimulated him to ask how far London could figure the interesting psychological and religious territories gothic writers had used that symbol to explore. While he focused on the effectiveness by which individuals can be kept from knowledge by the city's vastness, he was also able to carry forward the genre's ambiguity about whether all such concealment was ultimately doomed, destined to collapse in on itself. *Dombey and Son's* rooftop-removing 'good spirit' must destroy the city to restore clarity, Mrs Clennam's house and by extension the city that extrapolates it must fall down before the air becomes clear. Nevertheless, at other times even within these same novels, Dickens seems to present London's mechanisms entirely differently. The inscrutable processes of the capital militate against the concealers to bring to light information that works towards the resolution of the plot. This suggests a more optimistic account of metropolitan modernity that conflicts with the pessimism inherent in the gothic mode. The following chapters deal with aspects of the city's institutions that generally assist the narrative's task of disclosing concealed information – and which allow Dickens to explore ideas of how truth is to be arrived at.

4
'Angel and devil by turns': The Detective Figure in *Bleak House*

The burying ground emerged from the previous chapter as one of the key microcosms of *Bleak House*'s London. It is the place where evidence of past transgression may be buried in the thickest of the city's mud, although, in the form of diseased air at least, unwelcome consequences may come of its artificially generated obscurity. London's bulging graveyards are full of unfathomable secrets, spreading their corruption from unseen sources. With its dirty fog and labyrinthine structure, all London has become a burying ground, a theme developed in the even more gothic world of *Little Dorrit*. The 'secrets of the lonely church-vaults, where the people who had hoarded and secreted in iron coffers were in their turn similarly hoarded, not yet at rest from doing harm' are prominent in the landscape of innumerable accumulated secrets that is London to Arthur Clennam (II 10 p. 526). At its centre, Mrs Clennam's house has a cellar 'like a sort of coffin in compartments' and a 'bier-like sofa' (I 3 p. 33) which serves to bury her own secret, the codicil. William Dorrit dreams about the house functioning literally as a tomb for 'the body of the missing Blandois, now buried in a cellar and now bricked up in a wall' (II 17 p. 608). The novel, however, is permeated by unease that, even here, nothing can stay buried:

> The clouds were flying fast, the wind was ... rushing round and round a confined adjacent churchyard as if it had a mind to blow the dead citizens out of their graves. The low thunder, muttering in all quarters of the sky at once, seemed to threaten vengeance for this attempted desecration, and to mutter, 'Let them rest! Let them rest!'
>
> (I 29 p. 337)

91

Individuals such as Mrs Clennam fear exhumation of what has been buried. The wind picking over the churchyard bones seems continuous with *Dombey and Son*'s good spirit and the ghost of Tom rising to retribution, especially the latter with its profane parody of Christian resurrection. In this book, the good spirit, not content with merely removing the roof, exposes the secrets of Mrs Clennam's house by overturning it altogether. It is paradoxical that the revitalising discovery of the secret should be the very thing that leads to the falling of the house and the death of the concealer, yet this has always been a hallmark of gothic fiction. Once the metaphorical foundations of Montoni's rule in *The Castle of Otranto* have been proven false, the whole edifice that externalises his power and conceals his crime crumbles. It happens suddenly, however, with no preparation in the early chapters. When Dickens takes up the image, the whole work builds up to it.

This fear of resurrection cannot fail to remind the reader familiar with *The Waste Land* of the wind that blows over London's deadest land threatening a fearful resurrection in that poem. Here the rejuvenating wind that sweeps through the Valley of Dry Bones in Ezekiel 37, refashioning Israel's dead into a powerful army, is recast as a thoroughly malevolent force:

> But at my back in a cold blast I hear
> The rattle of the bones, and chuckle spread from ear to ear.
>
> (ll. 185–6)[1]

Resurrection from this metropolitan venue for 'The Burial of the Dead' is no longer to be welcomed like its Biblical counterpart. Modern people have become comfortable in this state of death-in-life, kept warm by winter (l. 4). Eliot's poem casts a shadow backward over Dickens's London. The response is subjective, but it suggests the question of whether the churchyard winds in *Bleak House* and *Little Dorrit* may also be read as supplying evidence about the appetite for resurrection in his community. This may not have formed part of his conscious agenda. Nevertheless, we have clearly seen an engagement with the Christian texts of resurrection in the neo-gothic treatment of graveyard contamination. Ezekiel's wind, dreaded, if present at all, in *The Waste Land*, is the Holy Spirit. *Dombey and Son* longs at least for a 'good spirit', but would settle for visible air particles. *Bleak House* offers only a grim parody of the revivifying wind, which resurrects only Tom's corruption and death and carries them to bring about further death. Even in the passage quoted from *Little Dorrit*, the wind seems able to exhume but not to revive and many would consider it a mercy if it did not. Nevertheless, there is an apocalyptic quality about all three that suggests a movement towards an unveiling of truth that is harmonious with the drive towards discovery inherent in the teleological structure of the novel.

In Dickens resurrection day is frequently a day to be feared. Even David Copperfield is terrified by 'how Lazarus was raised up from the dead', explaining:

> And I am so frightened that they are afterwards obliged to take me out of bed, and show me the quiet churchyard out of the bedroom-window, with the dead all lying in their graves at rest.
>
> (2 p. 12)

Peter Ackroyd deduces from the evidence of the novelist's own child-hood fears a recurrence of 'the idea of the dead coming alive, the horror of being pursued'.[2] Dickens's urbanites fear resurrection not because they have settled for sterility, as in Eliot, but because they fear the discovery of knowledge about themselves it would bring. Burying is primarily concealment of information about themselves and their connection with others. April is the cruellest month for Dickens's characters because the regeneration threatened by the resurrecting wind will reveal to the world what has been carefully buried. Even those innocent figures whose lives are buried with this knowledge, such as Arthur Clennam and Esther, are apprehensive about digging too deeply into the burying ground and hesitate to emerge from it into newness of life. Nevertheless, there are forces inherent in the organisation of the city that function in certain of Dickens's novels as a breath of fresh air, blowing through the burying ground. They are not always benign. They are in no way a comfortable presence, either to concealers or to searchers. They are, however, powerful. They assist the narrative's movement towards denouement and they are essentially metropolitan. This chapter considers one of these, the detective police force, and the next moves on to another, the railway system. Among the many discourses informing their representation, we can ask how the inevitability with which they help the plot towards closure interacts with more traditional symbols of teleologically underscored revelation.

I. London and the detective

In the metropolitan detective, Dickens chose as a symbol of the forces of revelation a figure that had long been established within the popular consciousness.[3] In 1749, the Bow Street Runners were founded. Dickens satirised them for their self-importance and inefficiency in Blathers and Duff in *Oliver Twist*, but they were the beginnings of an organised detective force. Later, in 1798, the Thames Police came into being, also undertaking investigative work. As the names of these early forces suggest, crime and its discovery were associated with the capital: a popular impression consolidated by Peel's Metropolitan Police Act of 1829. Other areas were not given legislation for a further ten years.[4] The name of Scotland Yard, its headquarters, became broadly synonymous with the Police Force, further fixing the link with London in the public mind. Originally, the area of London covered by the force was similar to the county of London but was extended to outlying towns and villages in 1840 to make flight more difficult.[5] Small wonder, then, that Bucket and his task seem an integral part of the London of *Bleak House*.

The detective force itself was not officially founded until 1842, although there had been some plain-clothes policemen since 1829. Dickens's imagination was captured immediately by this new force, apparently far more organised than anything that had preceded it. On 13 July 1850, *Household Words* published a piece by Dickens's subeditor, W. H. Wills, called 'The Modern Science of Thief-taking',[6] which claims that by this stage, there were 42 investigative officers working for Scotland Yard. So impressed was his employer with this that he invited many of the plain-clothes men to a party held in the magazine's offices. An account of this appeared in the article, 'A "Detective" Police Party' (27 July 1850).[7] Sergeant Thornton became 'Sgt. Dornton', Sergeant Shaw became 'Sgt. Straw', Sergeant Whicher, 'Sgt. Witchem' and so on. 'Inspector Wield', or Inspector Field, had much to do with Dickens. He was employed by the author to prevent trouble at the opening night of one of his friend Edward Bulwer-Lytton's plays. 'Three "Detective" Anecdotes' followed (14 September 1850)[8], and finally Field took Dickens on a hunt around the slums of St Giles, leading to the third article, 'On Duty With Inspector Field' (14 June 1851).[9] He spoke of them in glowing terms:

> the Detective Force ... is so well chosen and trained, proceeds so systematically and quietly, does its business in such a workman-like manner, and is always so calmly and steadily engaged in the service of the public, that the public really do not know enough of it, to know a tithe of its usefulness.[10]

The appeal to Dickens's imagination, visible throughout the *Household Words* articles, of these striking figures, serving society below the level of its notice or even its trust, helps to explain the character of the fascination Bucket exerts in the fiction over characters such as Mr Snagsby and Esther herself.

II. Bucket as seen by Snagsby and Esther

Snagsby's tour of Tom-all-Alone's in Chapter 22 of *Bleak House* closely resembles Dickens's wanderings around the slum-infested area of St Giles's in 'On Duty with Inspector Field'. Dickens was evidently proud of a friend who had access to and understanding of such areas and took great satisfaction in telling Bulwer-Lytton that Field 'is quite devoted to me'.[11] This delight in friendship with the detective bursts out in the fiction when Bucket rather oddly tells Smallweed that he loves Snagsby 'like a brother' (54 p. 823). Dickens places into the mouth of Bucket the statement of personal affection borne by the investigator to the man whom he has initiated into the secrets of London that he boasted of with regard to Field. Since Dickens seems to identify Snagsby's relationship with the detective with his own, the reasons for the law stationer's fascination with him provide some clues for Dickens's personal interest in the figure of the detective (see Figure 2).

The law stationer is introduced as 'rather a meditative and poetical man' with a yearning to find some hidden meaning in the city – perhaps the kind of person Dickens imagined enjoying his own novels of urban secrets. Before he even meets Bucket, he speculates that his own mundane environment houses buried artefacts with a story to tell, commenting that

> there were old times once, and that you'd find a stone coffin or two, now, under that chapel, he'll be bound, if you was to dig for it.
>
> (10 p. 158)

By means of this taste for romantic secrets, Bucket establishes a firm grip upon Snagsby's life. He is associated with what is hidden in London in the mind of the fanciful man. Dickens remarks:

> Tom-all-Alone's and Lincoln's Inn Fields persist in harnessing themselves, a pair of ungovernable coursers, to the chariot of Mr Snagsby's imagination; and Mr Bucket drives ...
>
> (25 p. 406)

Similarly, in the article, Field comes immediately from the 'elder world' of the British Museum,[12] whetting the reader's appetite for an introduction to the unknown. This of course was a role that Dickens himself delighted in. At the beginning of his career, he takes obvious pleasure in whisking Oliver Twist and the reader through a list of bewildering names of obscure London streets and areas (*OT* 8 p. 102), and this becomes a hallmark of his style. Bucket, moreover, is able to show the mysterious meanings whose presence not far beneath the surface of metropolitan life is suspected by the urbanite. Like Shakespeare's Prospero, Bucket conjures up visions and makes them vanish. The Police are his familiar spirits and they evaporate at the touch of his magical stick or wand (22 pp. 357–8). Perhaps the novelist saw in this figure a modern emblem of his own art. Snagsby not only reflects Dickens in his relationship to Field, but he also represents the wondering reader in relation to Dickens. Bucket, therefore, plays a crucial role in the novel as the author's representative. In making the revelations upon which its plot depends with near omniscience and calculated timing, he seems to personify the narrative scheme.

Throughout the Victorian era, the reading public sought authors who could guide them into uncharted territory in this way. London's slums certainly presented themselves to the middle-class imagination as *terra incognita*. With some of Snagsby's romantic appetite for what was buried beneath the familiar side of the city, they devoured the work of writers who could take them into this world. It was not only authors of fiction, however, that supplied this demand. Henry Mayhew's *Life and Labour of the London Poor* (1851–2) had given a gripping and detailed account of the lives of the very poorest in society. In 1890, William Booth published *In Darkest England and the Way Out*[13] and Peter Keating's anthology about Victorian urban poverty sums up the titles of the works contained within it: *Into Unknown England*.[14] Poorer areas of London were seen as a foreign continent full of savages and much of the delight evident in Dickens's articles is at being admitted by the detective into this environment. 'The Detective Police' shows Dickens's fascination with the detective's ability to infiltrate cabals and alien environments, such as the butcher's shop gang penetrated by Mith. The responses of Dickens and Snagsby suggest that desire to be initiated into mystery in general stems primarily from a craving for excitement and 'exotic' new experience.

Yet there is more to it than this. Booth and his contemporaries fed popular curiosity, but they aimed at provoking a deeper response. They wanted the revelation of the hidden London they provided to awaken their readers to their obligation to do something about the situation of the poor. This is also true of Dickens's detective-led journeys into the slums. Characteristically, in 'On Duty with Inspector Field' the real revelation this access to the city's dark underside permits is the suffering caused by insanitary conditions:

> How many people may there be in London, who, if we had brought them deviously and blindfold to this street, fifty paces from the Station House, and within call of St. Giles's church, would know it for a not remote part of the city in which their lives are passed? How many, who amidst this compound of sickening smells, these heapsof filth, these tumbling houses, with all their vile contents, animate and inanimate, slimily overflowing into the black road, would believe that they breathe *this* air?[15]

The crucial discovery that middle-class Londoners 'breathe *this* air' essentially means that they are part of the same environmental system as the inhabitants of St Giles's, and the impurities there are finding their way into the atmosphere in which they live themselves. Thus the police inspector does the work of *Dombey and Son's* 'good spirit who would take the house-tops off' to expose the disease spreading from within (*DS* 47 p. 620) and uncovers a social truth. This may not be the information Field is intentionally detecting, but it is the truth his findings make known to Dickens. Bucket, too, can hardly be credited with a social conscience, but the effect of what he shows to Snagsby is to awaken the law stationer's sense of his relationship of obligation to the poor. Dickens emphasises the absolutely foreign nature of this area amid the familiar city in almost identical terms to those of the *Household Words* article. Snagsby walks down a

> villainous street, undrained, unventilated, deep in black mud and corrupt water ... reeking with such smells and sights that he, who has lived in London all his life, can scarce believe his senses. ... heaps of ruins ... streets and courts so infamous that Mr Snagsby sickens in body and mind, and feels as if he were going, every moment deeper down, into the infernal gulf.
>
> (22 p. 358)

In his capacity as a guide, Bucket is a mysterious conductor through an urban hell, comparable to Virgil in Dante's *Inferno*. Indeed, Dickens treats Bucket as if he were taking Snagsby on a spiritual quest through the underworld, where his perceptions of the framework of reality are totally dissolved. There is an unreal visionary character to this expedition. What is seen is barely tangible:

> the crowd ... hovers round the three visitors, like a dream of horrible faces, and fades away up alleys and into ruins, and behind walls; and with occasional cries and shrill whistles of warning, thenceforth flits about them until they leave the place.
>
> (22 p. 358)

Again:

> the crowd, like a concourse of imprisoned demons, turns back, yelling, and is seen no more.
>
> (22 p. 358)

Perhaps it is the visit to Parnell's grave in the cemetery passage in James Joyce's *Ulysses*[16] casting a long backward shadow, but the culmination of Snagsby's visit in the graveyard to which Jo has conducted Lady Dedlock seems equally to signify that a trip to Hades is being made. Certainly both relocations of the encounter with death and its horrors to the modern city engage with the question of what value there can be in exposure to death and its horrors in the absence of an established mythological narrative of journey. As the vision of Hades draws to a close, the narrator remarks:

> By the noisome ways through which they descended into that pit, they gradually emerge from it ...
>
> (22 p. 358)

The experience has left Snagsby initially 'confused by the events of the evening' and 'doubtful of the reality of the streets through which he goes' (p. 365). Although he has been overwhelmed by his encounter with the realm of death, however, he has been helped towards a new way of understanding his relationship with the whole city, as seen in his direct involvement with Jo's problem. Afterwards, London's everyday regions feel more real and substantial as a result of the journey:

> Through the clearer and fresher streets, never so clear and fresh to Mr Snagsby's mind as now, they walk and ride ...
>
> (22 p. 362)

Bucket has taken Snagsby through the realm of death and evil to a clearer understanding of his place in the cosmos. Such a semi-mystical journey, early in the novel, with the aid of Bucket, suggests something of the way the institutions of the city may offer revelation through an experience of that same city's confusing disorientation and restored life through descent into death.

Snagsby's attitude to Bucket paves the way for Esther's. The two characters are closely linked in the novel's thematic structure. Mrs Snagsby's efforts to discover the 'fact' that Esther and her husband are having an affair and that Jo is the result parody Esther's search for her own origins and clearance from inherited guilt. When she announces 'It is as clear as crystal that Mr Snagsby is that boy's father' (25 p. 409), the reader is reminded of Mr Snagsby's interest in Old Holborn Brook flowing *underneath* the city 'as clear as crystial [*sic*]' (10 p. 158). Both are thirsty for an insight into this subterranean river that will show them the truth about their environment. Like Snagsby and Dickens, Esther is proud of the detective's compliments and respect (59 p. 902) and Snagsby's journey prepares the reader for her vision in the city, again culminating in a graveyard, which is the real focus of the book.

Whereas the stationer is driven by Bucket in a metaphorical chariot of imagination, Esther's carriage is more tangible. The speed imposed by the detective blurs an already confused city, reflecting the confusion in Esther's mind and adding to the phantasmal character of the experience:

> We rattled with great rapidity through such a labyrinth of streets, that I soon lost all idea where we were.
>
> (57 p. 868)

All is surreal and Esther underlines this by repeating:

> I was far from sure that I was not in a dream. ... And still it was like the horror of a dream.
>
> (57 pp. 868–9)

Like Snagsby earlier in the novel, Esther is taken into an area of the city where her perceptions of the framework of reality have become utterly dissolved. Completely disorientated, she feels that she has entered the world of death. Once more, London's slums are the layered circles of Hell and Bucket is the guide:

> we appeared to seek out the narrowest and worst streets in London. Whenever I saw him directing the driver, I was prepared for our descending into a deeper complication of such streets, and we never failed to do so.
>
> (59 p. 903)

Meanwhile, the Thames at night, so often associated with death, resembles the underground rivers of mythology. Esther remarks that 'we had crossed and re-crossed the river' (57 p. 868), so that she does not know which side she is on, and adds 'The river had a fearful look, so overcast and secret ... so deathlike and mysterious' (57 p. 870). Limehouse Hole, with its 'FOUND DROWNED' notices and 'slimy' corpses, serves as a reminder of the universal presence of death. Real things are distorted in the surface of the Thames, so that, for example, carriage lamps become what Esther fears to see, 'a face, rising out of the dreaded water', like the lost souls coming up to meet Dante's narrator. Ultimately, she arrives at the very lowest circle, the city burial ground and its

> heaps of dishonored [*sic*] graves and stones, hemmed in by filthy houses, with a few dull lights in their windows, and on whose walls a thick humidity broke out like a disease.
>
> (59 p. 903)

Here she finally confronts her dead mother, as Aeneas and Ulysses confront their dead fathers. Like them she re-emerges from her vision of death with a fuller understanding of the significance of her life. The scene provides a point of closure in the book, the updated descent into Hell apparently achieving a purpose as satisfactory within the story as these classical archetypes.

The pursuit has been not only a search for Lady Dedlock's physical body, but a deeper ontological inquiry into Esther's own identity. What kind of inheritance has she been bequeathed by her mother and what position is she to assume in relation to her past and present? From the moment Tulkinghorn is killed, the question becomes not merely 'Who killed Tulkinghorn?' but 'Is Esther's mother guilty?' The reader at this point thinks he or she knows who the murderer is and is watching a process of inevitable capture, as in the case of Nadgett and Jonas in *Martin Chuzzlewit*. Something more complicated is happening here, however. For six chapters, Bucket dominates the action, unexpectedly proving that she is not. This is even more a relief to Esther than it would be to most people under the circumstances. For most of her life she has been told that her mother has made a transgression and that she has inherited her shame. Bucket's discovery of Lady Dedlock's innocence of murder exonerates her from a crime that would have consolidated her role as a guilty figure. Esther may be the daughter of a fornicator, but she is not the daughter of a murderess. Moreover, Esther's resemblance to her has not been the cause, accidental or otherwise, of the killing of

Tulkinghorn. She is thus still able to say, 'I was as innocent of my birth, as a queen of hers; and that before my Heavenly Father I should not be punished for birth, nor a queen rewarded for it' (p. 587). Bucket's search through London, with Esther, to find her mother is a way of dramatising the quest to find and validate Esther's origins that has already been enacted by the solving of the mystery. The finding of her body allows Esther to confront what has happened and acknowledge her relationship with her mother in a way that would not have been possible in life. It is a more formalised version of Lady Dedlock's earlier disclosure of identity to Esther in Chapter 36, which constitutes an acknowledgement of her motherhood and true connection with humanity. Esther tells her that her 'heart overflowed with love for her, that it was natural love' (p. 579). In return, she hears that Lady Dedlock 'loved me ... with a mother's love' (p. 580).

Bucket has demonstrated to Esther that her origins have not led to her existence compounding this 'original sin' by turning sexual transgression into murder. Instead, her unconditional love and forgiveness of her mother have helped to restore correct relationships between people. Although he is not officially interested in ontological and spiritual mysteries, this is what his factual discoveries solve in real terms for Esther. Dickens makes sure the reader associates his inexorable powers of discovery with it by bringing the crucial documents concerning her parentage into his hands where their power for harm is neutralised. This is cemented when he is placed in the driving seat in the search for the body. Having apprehended the truth about her origins and reversed the effect of the original concealment through restored love, Esther can at length move towards shaping a rightly informed sense of her own identity. Ultimately she must do this for herself, but, both to her and the reader, Bucket has valuably demonstrated that discovery of truth is possible.

III. Bucket and Christ

It is significant that it is Bucket and not Chadband, with all his emphasis on 'Terewth', who achieves this. Since the detective is assuming something of the preacher's rôle, Dickens is extremely interested in how such a modern and determinedly unsentimental institution as the Metropolitan Police force will perform this function. Bucket and his men do, in effect, guide Esther through her experience like a secular Providence, carefully controlling the pace at which she discovers the truth with her well-being in mind. He is constantly credited with powers of deity such as omniscience and even omnipresence. Jo believes him to be 'in all manner of places, all at wunst' (46 p. 717), the narrator refers to him as 'a homely Jupiter' (54 p. 837) and his name even replaces God's in a phrase like 'Mr Bucket only knows whom' (25 p. 407). His freedom from the general laws of physics even allows him to stage resurrections of a kind:

> Time and place cannot bind Mr Bucket. Like man in the abstract, he is here to-day and gone to-morrow – but, very unlike man indeed, he is here again the next day.
>
> (53 p. 803)

The policeman's initial introduction as 'a person ... who was not there when [Snagsby] came in, and has not since entered by the door or by either of the windows' (22 p. 35) recalls the risen Christ's entry into the upper room:

> when the doors were shut where the disciples were assembled for fear of the Jews, came Jesus and stood in the midst ...
>
> (John 20:19)

Like the disciples who 'supposed that they had seen a spirit' (Luke 24:37), Snagsby considers this a 'ghostly manner of appearing' (22 p. 355).

As an Evangelical twenty-first century reader with critical habits trained by the intervening practices of Modernism, it is tempting to make too much of these echoes of the Gospel narratives. Nevertheless, they do offer the fascinating possibility that Dickens's detective force provides evidence about the issues involved for a mid-Victorian writer in evoking the trustworthy and benign revealer, external to the self, inherited from the Christian tradition. His detective demonstrably does some of the work of apocalyptic revelation assigned to Jesus Christ in Christian narratives of history. The reader is therefore bound to compare how far the police bring about meaningful resolution in the universe of the novel with the revelation promised in more overtly religious teleology.

Indeed the force of these metaphorical associations with Christ comes mainly from his rôle as the ultimate revealer of mysteries to his disciples.[17] Of course the specific mysteries unveiled by these two figures differ enormously. Bucket has no power to display the eternal purposes of God in redeeming the human race, nor is he interested in doing so. Nevertheless, to those who trust him in a comparable way, he allows another set of ontological insights about the system of interrelationships that obtain between human beings, despite the best efforts of men and women to conceal them. As well as doing this for Snagsby in a social capacity, he is able to confirm Esther's true identity and to guide her through dissolution of that identity to a newly reconstituted role in the world. Bucket moreover demands a declaration of faith and trust from his followers before he can open the initiate's eyes to what is hidden in the city. His repeated question, 'you know me, my dear; now, don't you?', receives the response, 'he was far more capable than I of deciding what we ought to do' (57 p. 885). Although Esther cannot understand why they are pursuing Jenny, she allows herself to be guided by him. On her journey, she says, 'I felt a confidence in his sagacity which reassured me' (57 p. 868). Placing her own necessary vigilance and alertness under a confidence in him much as she would in Providence is the key to Esther's discovery of her particular mystery.

As far as the guilty are concerned, however, his function in the narrative replaces that of Christ rather in his power to bring about an apocalyptic dénouement, fully realised at the Second Coming, when the dead are raised:

> Therefore judge nothing before the time, until the Lord come, who both will bring to light the hidden things of darkness, and will make manifest the counsels of the hearts ...
>
> (1 Corinthians 4:5)

The Biblical resurrection is to be feared by the unjust since their buried guilt will be exhumed with their physical bodies. We are not always comfortable with what will be disclosed. Bucket, then, is Godlike primarily because his power brings the criminal to judgement and allows no hiding place.

Furthermore, Bucket's power is not to be understood by ordinary mortals. Dickens never allows the reader to enter into the intellectual process of deduction by which the detective solves the mystery. Here, the author's interest is very different from that which created Dupin or later detectives such as Sherlock Holmes. Nevertheless, Bucket represents another of Edgar Allan Poe's fundamental concerns, the compulsion to keep things hidden and the force with which things burst into the open. Early fiction by Boz that Poe praised included 'The Black Veil', a story about a mother whose son turns out to have been hanged, 'A Madman's Manuscript' in Chapter 11 of The Pickwick Papers, and 'The Clock Case' in the third number of Master Humphrey's Clock. Here, a man buries the 'dreadful secret' of a murdered boy underneath a chair from which he presides over a banquet, but bloodhounds leap over the wall and uncover the body, causing his guests to exclaim, 'There is some foul mystery here!' In these stories, the opposite of burial is detection and there is no remorse on the part of the concealer – only a dread of discovery. The last is reminiscent of Poe's 'The Tell-Tale Heart', in which the killer entertains the police where the corpse is concealed until the uncannny beating of the dead man's heart forces him to give himself away. Similarly, when Jonas Chuzzlewit fears capture in a later novel, he 'heard his own heart beating Murder, Murder, Murder, in the bed' (*MC* 47 p. 725). In the works of both writers, the plot is consistently motivated by the tension between a neurotic impulse to conceal and a force inexorably pushing truth into the open.

Had Poe lived until 1853, he would have found in Bucket the ultimate embodiment of this force that irresistibly brings the truth into the open. It is this same power that appears to interest Dickens about Field. Whereas Wills's article emphasises Witchem's ability to deduce facts from details as tiny as a lost button alongside his curious personal authority over individual criminals, the detective in Dickens's piece makes no brilliant mental connections. He merely strolls around St Giles's, perfectly at ease in the maze, until he ultimately finds the criminal. Dickens is fascinated by the respect and subservience commanded by the detective. He notes:

> Every thief here, cowers before him, like a schoolboy before his schoolmaster. All watch him, all answer when addressed, all laugh at his jokes, all seek to propitiate him.[18]

Equally, in the slum, 'everybody seemed to know and defer to' Bucket (57 p. 869). In middle-class London, however, he is not so universally recognised (although equally authoritative) and Snagsby 'is quite in the dark as to who Mr Bucket may be' (22 p. 355). Nevertheless, both Field and Bucket can interfere in any circle once the moment is right without fear of resistance:

> let Inspector Field have a mind to pick out one thief here, and take him ... and all Rat's Castle shall be stricken with paralysis, and not a finger move against him, as he fits the handcuffs on!

Bucket has the same confidence in himself that Dickens invests in Field:

> 'Do you see this hand, and do you think that *I* don't know the right time to stretch it out, and put it on the arm that fired that shot?'

Such is the dread power of the man, and so terribly evident it is
that he makes no idle boast, that Mr Smallweed begins to apologise.

(54 p. 825)

The characters fully believe in this omnipotence. Sir Leicester Dedlock
feels that he can hide nothing from him – not even his gout, thinking
that 'Mr Bucket palpably knows all about it' (54 p. 817). Dedlock perceives him as an embodiment of Providence, whom nothing can take by
surprise and whose attitude to any mystery is that of one having made
skilful calculations as to correct timing:

From the expression of his face, he might be a famous whist-player ...
with the game in his hand, but with a high reputation involved in
playing his hand out to the last card, in a masterly way. ... 'I don't
suppose there's a move on the board that would surprise *me*' ...

(54 pp. 816–18)

Solving the crime becomes almost a foregone conclusion.
Characteristically in *Household Words*, Dickens pauses to empathise with
the criminal:

And to know that I *must* be stopped, come what will. To know that
I am no match for this individual energy and keenness, or this organised and steady system.

Bucket's significance is that he represents a system that can classify things
in their correct relationship to each other, even in a vast metropolis.
He has the power of God, whose discoveries cannot be resisted, over
man, making revelations at just the right moment. Most importantly,
these are powers which the novelist also holds. Bucket personifies the
narrative drive towards discovery inherent in the story, irresistibly dis-
pensing an even-handed justice operating by inscrutable methods.

To the ordinary person, the city itself is actually designed to be
impenetrable and to conceal its secrets. 'On Duty with Inspector Field'
evokes this magical environment:

Come across the street, here, and entering by a little shop, and yard,
examine these intricate passages and doors, contrived for escape,
flapping and counter-flapping like the lids of conjurer's boxes.

Dickens builds his description of the city as the ultimate means by
which secrecy may be preserved and then demolishes it with 'But what

avail they?' Field's power is emphasised because even the obscurest zones of London are transparent to him.

For Field is the ultimate conjuror. Indeed the police seem to rely on the city's bewildering complexity to preserve the mystery necessary to their profession quite as much as do the criminals. Their highly organised code of secret signals and hidden paths through the city make them a clarifying element in London's framework that works both with and against the capital's disorienting dirt and complexity. Dickens compares them with the priests of the ancient mystery religions who offered revelation by supernatural means in referring to them as 'The Augurs of the Detective Temple' (53 p. 803) and the comparison of function seems stronger than the half-ironic contrast of form. Like the priests of the Orphic mystery, which promised a vision of the underworld, they are the guardians of hidden knowledge, guiding their initiates through a bewildering mimesis of death towards a revelation that brings new life. To those on the inside, it is through precisely the means of anonymous city routine that truth is revealed. Bucket says:

> I've communicated with Mrs Bucket, in the baker's loaves and in the milk ...
>
> (54 p. 834)

Commonplace items like these can be the means through which important secrets are communicated. The complexity of the city's routine obscures truth but also excites anticipation that it is about to emerge.

In *Martin Chuzzlewit*'s Mr Nadgett, the author had already managed a figure like the similarly named Bucket, merging invisibly with the metropolitan routine to bring the concealer to observation:

> Jonas sometimes saw him in the street, hovering in the outer office, waiting at the door for the man who never came ... but he would as soon have thought of the cross upon the top of St Paul's Cathedral taking note of what he did, or slowly winding a great net about his feet, as of Nadgett's being engaged in such an occupation.
>
> (38 p. 587)

J. Hillis Miller has commented extensively on the link between this man and his urban environment, with its separation of 'public role and private self'.[19] Strikingly, both Nadgett and Bucket are in league with as well as opposed to the city in their task of unearthing truth. Like Field, they represent the other, non-labyrinthine, side of the city – its revelatory aspect, which is charted in police records and controlled by an efficient system with knowledge catalogued and at its fingertips.

Nadgett is certainly perceived by Jonas as a man elevated by his unaccountable knowledge to supernatural status. His adversary is described as his 'pursuing Fate' (*MC* 38 p. 597) and as 'Another of the phantom forms of this terrific Truth!' (51 p. 783) Both Nadgett and Bucket are semi-allegorical figures who embody the city's forces that drive truth into the open. Nevertheless, their roles are not identical. In the earlier novel, the focus is upon the fugitive and his fear, with Nadgett remaining in the shadows. *Bleak House* focuses upon the pursuer, leaving his quarry out of sight until caught, as in the modern detective story, allowing for suspense and surprise regarding the murderer's identity. Furthermore, Bucket has a duty to make his revelation and does so gladly. When Nadgett tells Tigg, 'It almost takes away any pleasure I may have had in this inquiry even to make it known to you' (38 p. 590), he sounds more like Tulkinghorn, who enjoys his secrets as 'old wine' (22 p. 352).

Bucket may be seen on the one hand as the antithesis of Tulkinghorn, one man's *raison d'être* being to acquire power over others by keeping secrets and the other's being to unravel them and to proclaim them for the good of society. Tulkinghorn shows what happens when secret knowledge is gained and then concealed for self-advancement. Although he discovers hidden connections between people, he merely accumulates them and restricts the flow of information about them, instead of proclaiming them. His keen enjoyment of his job comes from exclusively 'being master of the mysteries of great houses' (36 p. 581) and denying his social duty to use his knowledge to benefit others. That such an attitude is a deathbound withdrawal from the principles of life is shown – first, as a warning, in Krook's explosion – and then in the murder that comes to him because he has become involved in one secret too many. The motives of Tulkinghorn and Bucket for involvement – anti-social and social respectively – must, Dickens claims, be carefully separated. Both men are present in the chariot of Snagsby's imagination, Bucket as driver, Tulkinghorn as passenger (25 p. 406). When Mrs Snagsby attempts to make selfish capital out of Esther's secret, Bucket returns to this image, showing the dangers created when the Tulkinghorn attitude is allowed to assume the driving seat:

> Mr Tulkinghorn, deceased, he held all these horses in his hand, and could have drove 'em his own way, I haven't a doubt; but he was fetched off the box head-foremost, and now they have got their legs

over the traces, and are all dragging and pulling their own ways. So it is, and such is life.

(54 p. 829)

Mrs Snagsby, he warns, will also get herself into difficulties if she tries to emulate Tulkinghorn in using what she knows – or thinks she knows – about Esther to exert a power over the Dedlock family.

On the other hand, however, the two characters are closely linked. Tulkinghorn himself calls Bucket to help him to trace Jo and the two speak with surprising confidentiality. Bucket solves Tulkinghorn's murder and the connection between the two is underlined at the funeral. Dickens writes of the 'Contrast ... between Mr Tulkinghorn shut up in his dark carriage, and Mr Bucket shut up in *his*' (53 p. 805). Although Bucket and Tulkinghorn represent apparently opposed attitudes to secrets, there is a disturbing sense that they are co-operating as parts of a whole system. Their ambiguous relationship is microcosmic of the ambiguous relationship between the detective force and the Chancery Court in *Bleak House* upon which D. A. Miller comments in *The Novel and the Police*. Miller contends that although the police investigator stands for pushing conclusions into the open as quickly as possible, the detective 'serves a particular ideological function within this system and not against it'.[20] Institutions like Chancery depend upon preserving the spurious hope that a revelation can be arrived at and the tidy resolution at the end of the detective story is one way of achieving this. In this way, the police exist to provide an authoritative gratification of the desire for clarity – as long as that clarity can be safely contained within a system that depends upon withholding vital information from the powerless, while leading them to believe that it can ultimately be obtained.

Certainly, Dickens conveys an uneasy sense that Bucket is rather upholding the Chancery Court than resisting its tendency to obscure justice. His arrest of Gridley renders his role more ambivalent, despite his affable tone and anxiousness for the older man's welfare. George is afterwards disposed to think of Bucket as a 'rum customer' (47 p. 722) and links him with the oppression imposed upon him by Tulkinghorn, of whom he says:

I know the man; and know him to have been in communication with Bucket ... He has got a power over me ...

(47 pp. 726–7)

Lady Dedlock too views Tulkinghorn as having the power and omnipresence attributed by others to Bucket, describing him as 'Always at hand. Haunting every place. No relief or security from him for a moment' (48 p. 737). The use the manipulative lawyer makes of these powers casts doubt upon the detective's right to hold them. Indeed, there is a chill feeling that Bucket is only a hair's breadth from being Tulkinghorn. These two characters pave the way for the still more ambiguous figure of Jaggers in *Great Expectations*, who loves to establish power over others with enormous potential for good and evil, but who is the working manifestation of Providence in the novel, keeping secrets until the crucial moments of revelation.

This is harmonious with Miller's claims that the structure of the novel as a form is itself like Chancery, expecting its readers to wait for a final judgement that may or may not come. The role of the detective plot is, in this analysis, to generate a feeling that the closure implicitly promised in the Victorian novel has been granted.[21] Thus the narrative form, as personified in Bucket, leads the reader to expect that closure and revelation of social relationships must inevitably come, and trains the reader 'in the sensibilty for inhabiting the new bureaucratic, administrative structures' of the time.[22] F. S. Schwarzbach extends Miller's Foucauldian analysis to another aspect of the city, which we have also considered in some depth. In '*Bleak House* – The Social Pathology of Urban Life', he opposes the clarity brought by Bucket to the confusion of London's dirt and disease rather than to the Chancery Court. The desire to clear away the dirt and to show the connections upon which the city as a system is based is linked to Bucket's own revelations of interrelationships between Londoners. Schwarzbach raises the idea, however, that revelation as a concept, encoded within the discourse of sanitary reform and police work, is repressive. The task of clearing the fog – whether literally or metaphorically, as in the case of the police force, who eliminate obscurity to organise London into a comprehensive system of reliable information – means exposing the poor to 'the gaze of the powerful at the powerless'.[23] No doubt the yearning in *Dombey and Son* for 'a good spirit who would take the house-tops off' (*DS* 47 p. 620), of which Bucket is a partial fulfilment, may constitute an example of this potentially repressive aspect of social revelation. Dickens is credited, in Schwarzbach's article, with registering his uneasiness about this aspect in the poor characters who resist examination and in Bucket's own ambivalence:

> Dickens does not fail to point toward the ways in which Bucket, well-intentioned though he may be, acts as agent for the very political and social institutions the novel so forcefully attacks.

Like Miller, he suggests hidden concerns on Dickens's part that the detective police – and indeed the very desire for revealed social interconnections beneath a confusing environment that creates their function in the novel – keep institutions like the Chancery Court in business.

Dickens does indeed point intelligently to the limitations of the revelation Bucket can provide, including his complicity with the confusing system he symbolically opposes. The clarity with which he sees London may assist the poor by revealing social connections to the latently generous, such as Mr Snagsby; it may aid Esther in her journey towards ontological and spiritual revelation. Nevertheless, it may also be used to keep people, such as Gridley, imprisoned within the confusing city institutions. The end result is not, however, a discrediting of the notion of revelation *per se*, as the work of Miller and Schwarzbach may suggest. Instead, the partial success of Bucket's work and of the detective plot in general show Esther and the reader that an affirming revelation is possible, but the limitations of that success show with equal certainty that full revelation is to be sought outside the flawed systems these represent. As the final section of this chapter will show, the wider scheme in which the detective plot encourages trust is not political or administrative, but spiritual and Providential.

IV. The other Christ in *Bleak House*

Bucket's awe-inspiring power to bring to light buried connections and his numerous comparisons to Christ suggest that the force he represents – the police force – will at last make the obscured message of the cross visible to Jo. At the same time as Dickens builds up this image of the Christlike Bucket, representing all that penetrates the novel's cross-concealing fog, however, he skilfully highlights the factors that implicate him with it. Indeed, the detective's power comes at least in part from the deadly forces that keep it in place. Readers of *The Waste Land* are familiar with the tantalising presence of the hooded 'third who walks always beside you', who may or may not be Christ, walking through the city with the Emmaus road disciples. Presumably He is about to grant an opening of their eyes to the truth of his resurrection (Luke 24:31) that is never unambiguously narrated in the poem. The mysterious figure of the detective, with his supernatural abilities and benevolence on the one hand and his limitations and alignments with institutional concealment on the other, constitutes Dickens's re-examination of whether the risen Christ can be truly re-figured in this secular, surveillant and complicated modern world.

Woven into the supernatural aspect of Bucket's personality there is the other facet of the ghostly guide, quite at home in the underworld, in charge of occult powers, equally associated with supernatural evil as with supernatural good. Bucket's forefinger is said to be a 'familiar demon' (53 p. 803) with the power to whisper information, increase sensory powers and charm the guilty towards destruction. Sir Leicester Dedlock perceives it as 'the cruel finger that is probing the life-blood of his heart' (54 p. 821). At the revelation of the murder mystery, Hortense curiously calls Bucket 'my angel' (54 p. 830) and his role as apocalyptic angel has already been discussed. When he unexpectedly discovers her guilt, she also exclaims, 'you are a devil!' Bucket replies with some amusement, 'Angel and devil by turns, eh?' (54 p. 837) – and this is just what this elusive character is.

For Bucket is only presented as Godlike from the implied viewpoint of other characters. The narrator is aware of limitations to his power beyond any moral or social deficiencies. Hortense alone of all the people he meets recognises this and draws it to the reader's attention, saying to Bucket upon his solving the case, 'You are very spiritual'. This strange choice of word recalls her previous 'Angel' and reinforces Bucket as supernatural revealer. She then punctures this by asking:

> But can you res-tore him back to life? ... Can you make a honorable lady of Her?
>
> (54 p. 837)

Even Bucket seems lost for words and his 'Not exactly' and 'Don't be so malicious' sound rather feeble. He can discover transgressions, but is powerless to reverse their effects. In the face of death, Bucket is impotent. Although he catches Gridley, he cannot apprehend him because he dies, and even his stock-in-trade cajolery achieves nothing:

> You want excitement, you know, to keep *you* up; that's what *you* want.
>
> (24 p. 405)

Equally, Lady Dedlock is found dead and Bucket arrives at the limit of his powers. It almost seems that he really represents that other force that inevitably catches up with everyone: not merely justice, but death itself. He may be a revealer, but Dickens pointedly shows his inability to provide the full resurrection that accompanies revelation in the Christian scheme. Although Bucket is the most tangible personification of emergent truth in the story, he only points to the need for a more complete figure if exhumation is to be converted into genuine resurrection.

Having established Bucket's power and his centrality to the book's Providential aesthetic, Dickens registers much unease about the detective's role. We have considered the writer's own proto-Foucauldian suspicions that he – and indeed the detective novel in general – exists to increase our dependence upon the surveillant state. Indeed, to Dickens that the individual subject ceaselessly becomes the object of investigation is one of the key phenomena of metropolitan life. The detective's power to stand for a Christian Providence is compromised by his connection with the state corruption that has created Tom-all-Alone's, his fluid identity and the lies that he tells to extract his information. The *deus ex machina*, who should manifest divinely ordained order, is deeply ambivalent, suggesting an anxiety that Providential order external to the novel may share this moral ambivalence. He can supply revelation but not regeneration; justice, but not mercy.

Bucket's weaknesses as investigator, however, makes the reader aware of Woodcourt's explicitly Christian altruism as a more dependable guide for Esther. The contrasts between the two men in their role as guides to the city show Dickens's readiness to allow interplay between various conceptions of whether or not revelation may yet be credited to benign Providential decree. For Woodcourt, and not Bucket alone, is present with Esther on her journey through London. Indeed his sudden appearance at this stage of the search for Lady Dedlock is hard to explain, except as a signal to the reader that he is going to at least complement the rôle that has been played by Bucket. Ultimately it is the doctor who shows Esther her true identity and guides her to the place prepared for her in the world. The second time the detective appears in the novel, he is in disguise as a physician (24 p. 401), immediately establishing a link between the two characters. They share between them the role of guide through Hell and both are equally conversant with Tom-all-Alone's. Woodcourt is observant and vigilant, like the Inspector:

> Attracted by curiosity, he often pauses and looks about him, up and down the miserable byways. Nor is he merely curious, for in his bright dark eye there is compassionate interest; and as he looks here and there, he seems to understand such wretchedness, and to have studied it before.
>
> (46 pp. 710–11)

Woodcourt has penetrated the slum in a way that even Bucket has not. He achieves this through genuine care and love, coming to that environment to help people and not to seek information or to capture them.

It is the same key that helps him to understand Esther's mystery – to feel for Esther's real self despite the fragmented personality imposed upon her by her shame before society (represented by her mother), by the countless names and roles given to her by others, and by her own self-deprecating attitude. He is the genuinely Christlike figure who shows the way, whose existence is suggested but never fully realised by Bucket's messianic qualities. For Woodcourt, power is not something to be had for its own sake, yet he has it nevertheless:

Allan restrains the woman, merely by a quiet gesture, but effectually.

(46 p. 715)

There is a religious dimension to his mission as he transports Jo from this underworld to an environment where he is equipped to transcend death. Jo's appreciation that the Lord's Prayer is 'wery good' (47 p. 734) seems very little[24] and there are severe limitations faced by Woodcourt also, yet he still seems more powerful in the face of death than Bucket. In the lives of the individuals with whom he has come into contact, he has succeeded at least partially in clearing the fog that surrounds the cross. He has potently revealed by example the interlocking system of love relationships expressing God's existence as a Father to His children.

Esther is more effectively rescued from her confusion than Jo and trusts Woodcourt as a guide even more than she does Bucket. Her language echoes that of religious devotion: 'I owe it all to him. ... everything I do in life for his sake' (67 p. 989). Just as Esther puts aside the veil of hair covering her mother's face (59 p. 915), Woodcourt, having led her there, closes the book by allowing Esther to see her own face:

do you ever look in the glass ... don't you know that you are prettier than you ever were?

(67 p. 989)

Esther seems close to accepting this revelation at the end. Her husband, unlike everyone else in the book, helps her to find her own identity, by truthful means, without imposing his own version of it upon her. Here, he stands in contrast even to Mr Jarndyce, who tries to shape her identity by giving her names. Woodcourt tends to avoid these, although admittedly Esther is known as 'the doctor's wife' and presumably becomes 'Mrs Woodcourt' (67 p. 988). Jarndyce has his own ideas that marriage to him is what is best for Esther and, in his goodness, retracts these when he perceives that she really loves Woodcourt. Even then his deceptive means of leading her to the doctor's new home – also called Bleak House – in the belief that she is going to oversee domestic arrangements seems somewhat manipulative. Such behaviour may have its origins in the conventions of Romantic comedy, but the reader cannot but compare it unfavourably with Woodcourt's direct and truthful manner of speaking to her. Whereas Esther learns Jarndyce's plans through his circumlocutory phrases and elaborate schemes of dénouement, she says:

> When Mr Woodcourt spoke to me ... I learned in a moment that he loved me.
>
> (61 p. 937)

This truthfulness and respect for the integrity of Esther's own identity is what makes the revelation he provides so superior to that offered by Bucket. For a revealer of truth, the latter tells a lot of lies. His identity is certainly very fluid. Like Nadgett, who 'carried contradictory cards, in some of which he called himself a coal-merchant, in others a wine-merchant, in others a commission-agent, in others a collector, in others an accountant: as if he really didn't know the secret himself' (*MC* 27 p. 408), Bucket has an uncle in law stationery (22 p. 356), an aunt in Chelsea and a whole family in service, including a father who progressed from page to steward before retiring to become an innkeeper (53 pp. 813–14). He is also the friend of a sculptor (p. 812) and of a musician who requires a second-hand cello (49). The Bagnets do not think this chameleon adaptability an admirable quality (52 p. 798). He is a master of disguise. The narrator records, amongst others, his disguise as a doctor:

> the physician stopped, and, taking off his hat, appeared to vanish by magic, and to leave another and quite a different man in his place.
>
> (24 p. 401)

'Three Detective Anecdotes' suggests that this theatrical element to detective work appealed strongly to Dickens, himself a keen actor. Witchem boasts that he has pretended to know the identity of criminals he meets so that they will think they are passing on no new information to them. On one occasion he mentions having told two suspects, 'I know you both very well' and then interrupts his story to tell the audience, 'I'd never seen or heard of 'em in all my life'. Bucket similarly claims false knowledge of people to obtain genuine knowledge. Dickens recognised that much of Field's knowledge must be imaginary, cheerfully telling Wills that 'CHARLEY FIELD is of course an evasive humbug'.[25] Bucket even claims to be able to read Sir Leicester Dedlock's mind when he is paralysed, but Dickens's irony suggests that the baronet might not really be saying, 'Take 'em for expenses':

> The velocity and certainty of Mr Bucket's interpretation on all these heads is little short of miraculous.
>
> (56 p. 860)

Bucket goes further still, however. Not only does he claim spurious knowledge to gain confessions, but he moulds the characters and actions of others by making them believe what he 'knows'. Thus the naive Snagsby is told:

> You're a man of the world, you know, and a man of business, and a man of sense.
>
> (22 p. 356)

Later, he adds, 'you're a man it's of no use pumping; that's what *you* are' (22 p. 365). Bucket has given him a new identity – but only by telling him that he is what he patently is not. After such a conversation, the narrator tellingly remarks:

> 'Then here's your hat,' returns his new friend, quite as intimate with it as if he had made it.
>
> (22 p. 357)

A transferral has taken place here. Bucket is even more intimate with Snagsby than with his hat and he really has made him in his new role of worldly-wise keeper of secrets. Esther also notices this habit of mind, observing him 'addressing people whom he had never beheld before, as old acquaintances' (57 p. 881). She does not seem to suspect, however, that the compliments she so cherishes, such as 'You're a pattern, you know, that's what you are' (59 p. 902), might be a further application of his customary technique.

Woodcourt, by contrast, bases his remarks solely upon behaviour he has seen in Esther and which the reader can readily verify. When he makes his revelations to Esther, unswerving candour is the hallmark of his speech:

> I heard his voice thrill with his belief that what he said was true.
>
> (61 p. 937)

Woodcourt has the life-restoring power even Bucket lacks because he adheres strictly to truth. He holds the key to restoring a sense of social interconnectedness because his actions are guaranteed by faithfulness to the relationships of divine love. Woodcourt always addresses people as they are and not in the role in which he wants to keep them. Dickens remarks on

> A habit in him of speaking to the poor, and of avoiding patronage or condescension, or childishness (which is the favourite device, many people deeming it quite a subtlety to talk to them like little spelling books) ...
>
> (46 p. 711)

Here he is most unlike Bucket, whose 'Well, well ... you train him respectable, and he'll be a comfort to you, and look after you in your old age, you know' sounds remarkably hollow (22 p. 361).

The detective police, then, go some considerable way towards making credible belief that mysterious forces are to be trusted in clarifying the ontological mysteries of identity and origin. Although his aims are more prosaic, Bucket's revelations intersect with those ontological revelations that need to be given to a heroine in a novel of self-discovery. The likely effect upon the reader is the illusion that this knowledge has been released as part of the same capably and benignly managed process. He is able in some sense to show Esther the way out of guilt inherited from her ancestry and shows the layers of meaning possible in the apparently confused city. As fundamental a part of the city's inscrutable routine as the manufacture of the smog, the detective force gives a comforting impression in this and other novels[26] that the world is under the control of guardians who can bring about justice and penetrate to the heart of truth. They combine an awesome control over secrets with a fitting sense of duty within the social system. This modern metropolitan reality in effect provides the author, still working in an essentially teleological Providential aesthetic, with a powerful new figure for the clarifying impulse in his own narrative. Dickens, however, is careful to point to his moral ambiguity and the boundaries to his representational effectiveness, which help the reader to see how Woodcourt, less obviously striking, quietly reveals the mystery to Esther in a way that is genuinely regenerative as well as revelatory. Through his gentle method of combined love and truth, he brings the connections between people, which are manifestations of divine love, to light with a power as assured and confident as that figured in the novel by the Metropolitan Detective

Force. In the light of Modernist interrogation of symbols, we may regard the ambiguous presence of Bucket as voicing an unphrased question in Dickens's mind about whether guides to the truth may be trusted in this new cultural environment. Bucket's successes seem to indicate that he answered this question with a qualified affirmative in *Bleak House*. Bucket's failures, on the other hand, and his need to be complemented by Woodcourt suggest that the secular forces of modernity have not exactly replaced religion by fulfilling its function. Rather they provide a powerful new objective correlative for a Providence expressed through the love of human beings that is quite consistent with Dickens's version of Christianity.

5
'A road of ashes': London's Railway and the Providential Timetable

The railway in *Dombey and Son,* which so radically redefines the London lifestyle, is a good case study for exploring how readers assemble symbolic interpretations of Dickens's novels. Susan R. Horton chooses this very example to caution against the common critical assumption that recurrent items in a novel are to be read as forming a symbolic unity:

> The railroad that kills Carker ... is representative of moral judgement. The railroad passing through Staggs's Gardens is representative of industrial progress and change. But there is no fair way to connect the symbol of industrial progress with the symbol of moral judgement and be anything but nonsensical.[1]

Even if the railway signifies symbolically at one point, in other words, it should not be assumed that its function elsewhere is either symbolic or symbolic in a way essentially related to it.[2]

Horton's frustration is understandable. For example, in *Dickens: from Pickwick to Dombey*, Steven Marcus, commenting on Chapter 15, categorically states, 'In *Dombey and Son* the railroad is the great symbol of social transformation'.[3] By Chapter 55, however, 'The railroad has here become one of the great forces of Nemesis at work in the novel'. This is a lot of work for one image to do. How can one signifier stand for both narrative justice and technologically enabled social transformation? Horton would probably answer that the former use is casual and metaphorical. Trains do not exist to punish the wicked. Dickens simply uses them to do so in Carker's case, finding them particularly apt because certain aspects of their nature (their speed, power and operation to a fixed timetable) lend themselves to illustrating rhetorical points about the irrevocable consequences of human acts. The latter

Augustus Egg, *Past and Present III*

William Frith, *The Railway Station*

'Taking the Census in the Arches of the Adelphi',
Illustrated Times, xii, 1861 (British Library)

Portrait of Inspector Field, *Illustrated Times*, 2nd Feb 1856

John Cooke Bourne (British Library), 'Construction
of the Euston Arch, London, October 1837'

function is more synecdochic: the railways actually effected physical changes to London's landscape and they are therefore able to represent change generally. Both uses are independent and suggested by their local context, although the railway's presence for the one purpose in the novel may have brought it readily to the author's mind for the other.

To seek any more fundamental connection, in spite of Horton's warning, one might suggest that Dickens was able to use the railways for both purposes because it was itself essentially linked with both signified concepts simultaneously. This seems unlikely, however, since Carker is not being punished for resisting social transformation. It would appear more fruitful to look for a dialogue of some kind between these signified concepts, not primarily connected with the railway, and to argue that Dickens grasped it imaginatively and illustrated it symbolically. This would read the use of the railway for both purposes as evidence that the novel is interested in precisely what connections may exist between industrial progress and a morally teleological universe. Marcus's confidence that 'Dickens ... always tended to regard social change as created by man', without any external agency necessarily governing the process, prevents him from exploring this means of uniting these symbolic uses of the railway. Nevertheless, Dickens was writing for readers whose certainties about their place in a universal narrative were increasingly eroding. Many already questioned a Christian view of history heading inexorably from creation towards an endpoint of rewards and punishments. The question of where scientific discoveries and technological innovation could fit into such a narrative was an urgent matter, as was the question of whether social and moral progress was guaranteed by any kind of narrative, be it religious or secular. Perhaps, however, these big questions are ours as much as the Victorians' and meditation on the contrast between these representations of the railways, enforced by modern critical habits and this particular study's theological interest, brings them sharply into focus. Whether or not Dickens systematically linked his depictions of the changes brought to Camden Town with his portrayal of Carker's destruction, the railway's presence at both points raises issues important to contemporaries and to us.

Horton's assertion, then, that various local imperatives govern each representation of the railway may be safely accepted. Numerous discourses affected discussion of the railway and the interplay between them influenced Dickens at different points in the novel in different ways. Nevertheless this chapter does aim to trace some connections between these radically different functions of the rail infrastructure and its impact on London without being entirely nonsensical.

I. The railway and death

The railway has (literally) its most significant impact on the novel's plot at Carker's death. Famously providing the first depiction of a rail accident in English fiction, Dickens is representing an exciting contemporary phenomenon. Connecting death with the railways would not require a symbolic imagination for Victorian readers. Even at the opening of the first passenger line, the Liverpool and Manchester, in 1830, William Huskisson, the President of the Board of Trade and a politician notoriously proud of Britain's rail development, was struck down and killed by the Rocket.[4] By 1842, it was felt necessary to introduce an inspectorate by Act of Parliament to reduce the risks involved to passengers, yet accidents such as the derailment of the engine 'Hecla', which killed eight people on Christmas Eve, in 1841, continued. In 1865, Dickens was himself involved in the Staplehurst disaster, in which ten people were killed. Unsurprisingly anxieties about safety continued long after Dickens's death.[5]

Carker's unexplained supernatural premonitions of the railway, however, suggest that it is operating at the level of symbolism as well as reportage. Throughout his flight, the manager feels 'Some other terror ... quite removed from this of being pursued. ... like Death upon the wing':

> a trembling of the ground, – a rush and sweep of something through the air ... He shrunk, as if to let the thing go by. It was not gone, it never had been there, yet what a startling horror it had left behind.
>
> (55 pp. 731–2)

Carker is astonished when he encounters a precise physical embodiment of the sensation at the junction:

> For now, indeed, it was no fancy. The ground shook, the house rattled, the fierce impetuous rush was in the air! He felt it come up, and go darting by; and even when he had hurried to the window, and saw what it was, he stood, shrinking from it, as if it were not safe to look.
>
> (55 p. 741)

The train is not merely the arbitrarily chosen instrument of the villain's comeuppance. Even Carker sees something in its inflexible movement and destructive power that answers to his growing awareness that the inevitable consequences of his actions in the novel's just universe are coming upon him. The 'fierce fire dropping glowing coals' (55 p. 741) evokes Hell itself and the accident's aftermath is inspired by the visitations of Yahweh's wrath in the Old Testament:

> others drove some dogs away that sniffed upon the road, and soaked his blood up, with a train of ashes.
>
> (55 p. 743)

This recalls, for example, the complete destruction visited upon Ahab and Jezebel:

> In the place where dogs licked the blood of Naboth shall dogs lick thy blood. ... The dogs shall eat Jezebel by the wall of Jezreel ... And they went to bury her: but they found no more of her than the skull, and the feet, and the palms of her hands.
>
> (1 Kings 21:19, 23; 2 Kings 9:35)

Dickens's prose moves Carker to his death with the steam engine's own compulsive velocity until judgement comes to pass as surely as the word of the Lord.

Dickens's private remarks may have dismissed what he perceived as the vengeful God of the Old Testament. His novels, however, often suggest a sense of justice actually informed by the concept of a God whose punishment of the guilty is irrevocably guaranteed. Carker reflects upon the 'irresistible bearing' of his mechanised avenger and thinks 'what a cruel power and might it had' (55 pp. 741–2). Each train that passes provides a foretaste of his doom and, as always in Dickens, the condemned man is fascinated by what awaits him. In the space of one short chapter, he becomes 'irresistibly attracted' (55 p. 741) to the trains and considers what it would be 'To see the great wheels slowly turning, and to think of being run down and crushed!' The regularity and power of these revolutions extrapolate Longfellow's image of Divine justice as destructive wheels operating to a strict, inexorable rhythm:

> Though the mills of God grind slowly,
> Yet they grind exceeding small.[6]

A. O. J. Cockshut feels that the episode is an ambitious failure on Dickens's part, claiming that 'It would need a much stronger and more persuasive sense of Divine Providence than Dickens could rise to, to convince us of the artistic rightness of this semi-miraculous intervention'.[7] We have seen, however, that Dickens at least claimed a firm personal belief in Providence.[8] Perhaps, therefore, rather than a failure to convey this to the reader, the factors that make the railway problematic in this role should be read as Dickens's response to the ambiguities of belief in a teleological world in a technological age. Moreover, it is not clear that the sense of predetermined doom is an artistic failure. It does not emerge out of a vacuum in Chapter 55, but is prepared for throughout the novel, prompting uneasy questions about how events are predetermined in its world. The ominous hints carried by the railway from its very first appearance in the novel intensify the sense of premonition. Toodles's occupation is seen as a threat to the life of little Paul:

> 'A choker!' said Miss Tox, quite aghast.
> 'Stoker,' said the man. 'Steamingin.'
> 'Oh-h! Yes!' returned Miss Tox, looking thoughtfully at him, and seeming still to have but a very imperfect understanding of his meaning.
>
> (2 p. 16)

Paul's nurse is married to this man whose chest is affected by 'ashes' (p. 17), the first of many places in the novel where the leftovers of rail travel suggest human remains. For Dombey and his entourage here, the railway deepens anxieties that contact with such working-class people may contaminate and ultimately kill Paul. From the beginning, the child's death is written into the logic of the novel's plot as clearly as Carker's is. For the reader, the child's death is immediately preceded by the completion of the London-Birmingham Railway through Camden Town. When Dombey rides on that line with Toodles himself on the footplate, his thoughts unsurprisingly connect the locomotive with the predetermined loss of his son:

> The very speed at which the train was whirled along, mocked the swift course of the young life that had been borne away so steadily and so inexorably to its fore-doomed end. The power that forced itself upon its iron way – its own – defiant of all paths and roads, piercing through the heart of every obstacle, and dragging living creatures of all classes, ages, and degrees behind it, was a type of the triumphant monster, Death.
>
> (20 p. 275)

Even Dombey perceives that the train may be interpreted symbolically, comparing the fixedness of the route and the certainty of mankind's fate. The train's speed underlines the impossibility of recalling the past. Through the window, Dombey sees the buildings that represent other men's aspirations rapidly disappearing into the perspective:

> great works ... fall like a beam of shadow an inch broad, upon the eye, and then are lost.
>
> (20 p. 276)

Division of passengers into first, second and third classes (Euston even had three separate entrances for them) does not alter the fact that all travel to the same destination. To Dombey, this underlines the solemn truth, earlier conceded to Paul, 'that money, though a very potent spirit, never to be disparaged on any account whatever, could not keep people alive whose time was come to die' (8 p. 94).

Although Dombey is on the train, he too seems to be running from it. Paul's death, which the train figures so vividly for Dombey, is the death of his own identity, summarised in the words 'Dombey and Son'. Carker's flight is the more terrible to the reader because Dombey has already shown what it is like to fear the train instinctively as a bringer of death against which there is no defence. In turn, Carker's inability to flee the train suggests that Dombey's own desperate attempts to shore up his house and pass it on to a new son are heading for utter destruction. Indeed, as his marriage and business collapse and creditors strip his house, he is as much 'a broken man' (58 p. 776) spiritually as Carker is physically, and he wanders 'through the despoiled house like a ghost' (59 p. 798). The impact that has been expected from the beginning comes with tremendous power and Dombey is on the point of completing the image by killing himself outright when Florence intervenes. Perhaps the train is a 'remorseless monster' to Carker's master because he is subconsciously aware of a judgement to come upon him for the wrong he remorselessly persists in doing Florence by ignoring her love in favour of his obsession.

In this respect, *Dombey and Son* is more typical of Dickens's novels than *Bleak House*. That novel, as considered in the previous chapter, focuses upon the agent of nemesis, the metropolitan police force, whereas Hortense and Lady Dedlock remain out of sight during the pursuit. Here another new metropolitan institution becomes both means and metaphor of the consequences of a character's actions inevitably catching up with him. As so often, particularly in the early fiction, we are given the perspective of the fugitive. Such characters, usually murderers, such as Bill Sikes or Jonas Chuzzlewit, fear revelation of the facts they have worked so hard to conceal above even capture or execution. Carker is another character in this tradition, but his intense 'visionary terror' (*DS* 55 p. 731) is different because it does not exist solely within his own mind. There is hardly a character in *Dombey and Son* who is not conscious of it at some level. Psychoanalysts may wish to read Carker and Dombey's interpretations of the train-as-nemesis as typifying a purely internal but irresistible return of the repressed. Carker's proleptic visions, however, with their suggestions that there may actually be an overarching supernatural justice bringing exposure and retribution for wickedness, show Dickens exploring his religious as well as his psychological interests and allowing a fascinating interplay between the two.

II. The railway and truth

The clearest demonstration that the railway signifies differently at different stages in the novel is perhaps the different metaphorical applications drawn from it by the characters themselves. Whereas Dombey sees a more negative metaphor in the steam engine, Toodles, whose living it provides, uses it to illustrate the need for openness and honesty to his children:

> wotever you're up to in a honest way, it's my opinion as you can't do better than be open. If you find yourselves in cuttings or in tunnels, don't you play no secret games. Keep your whistles going, and let's know where you are.
>
> (38 p. 512)

This is a purely casual figure of speech, its charm being the novelty of a man using the apparently unpoetic materials of his quotidian life to communicate such supposedly timeless wisdom. Nevertheless, Dombey's fear of the train is not entirely unconnected with his fear of the Toodles – and in particular with their openness, signified by the railway here. If contact with this class of persons represents a potential source of contamination to his son during Paul's life, the contact with Toodles enforced by his rail journey breeds especial class repugnance after his death. Dombey is outraged when he presumes to share in his grief by wearing black in his cap:

> To think that he dared to enter ... into the trial and disappointment of a proud gentleman's secret heart! To think that this lost child ... with

whom he was to have shut out all the world as with a double door of gold, should have let in such a herd ...

(20 p. 275)

The declaration of his inner life to the world – especially to the working classes – and the connection with him implied by the action is utterly abhorrent to him. Determined to be the untouchable public character of his own creation, this 'strange apparition that was not to be accosted or understood' (3 p. 25) refuses to admit anyone into his private world.

Perhaps this association between the trains and public scrutiny reveals a particular interest on the part of Dickens, the journalist and recent editor of the *Daily News*, in the speed with which information could be communicated in the railway age. In 1838, a Travelling Post Office between Birmingham and Liverpool came into being, allowing faster mail delivery.[9] Newspapers were also able to receive reports far more quickly than in horse-drawn days. Dickens, knowing at first hand the importance of being the first to publish news as soon after it happened as possible, eagerly welcomed this.[10] Thanks to rail distribution, affairs reported from London in the *Daily News* could still be current by the time they reached Glasgow, making national newspapers a possibility at last. This function of the railways is also registered in the text when Dombey agonises about the number of those with access to the emerging news of the break-up of his marriage and business:

> When he is shut up in his room at night, it is in his house, outside it, audible in footsteps on the pavement, visible in print upon the table, steaming to and fro on railroads and in ships; restless and busy everywhere, with nothing else but him.
>
> (51 p. 682)[11]

Indeed Dombey's fate was gradually unfolded to the readers of the novel by means of rail transport as the monthly numbers were distributed. As part of 'the World' Dombey may not exclude, readers are made to participate directly in the story. By making the means by which the product reaches them part of the ruthless scheme that enforces Dombey's connections with the wider world, the novel encourages participation in the market that shapes technology.

D. A. Miller's Foucauldian analysis of the police[12] seems even more applicable to the railways. In giving concrete form to the narrative's metaphors for a truth that brings death to the concealer, the railway engine fulfils a similar function to Bucket's. Just as *Bleak House* shows a London systematised by the police and the *Household Words* articles suggest an infallible network of information circulating into Scotland Yard, so *Dombey and Son* depicts another highly organised system governing London with information passing endlessly out of it into the country at large. One of the marvels of the age was the almost instantaneous communication of messages by the telegraph wires, which invariably accompanied the railway tracks from 1839. Dickens refers to the politicians, who 'sent on messages before by the electric telegraph, to say that they were coming' (15 p. 218). What appealed most strongly to the Victorian imagination about this device, however, was its usefulness in the apprehension of fugitives. In 1896, John Pendleton wrote:

> it has checked many a forger in his flight from his dupes and the Assize Court, and more than one murderer trying to travel beyond the memory of his victim, and the uncomfortable sensation that is inseparable from the hangman's touch.[13]

A similarly inescapable force apprehends Carker, even if, in contrast to the police force, railway technology serves narrative rather than social justice. *The Novel and the Police* claims that through the detective plot, readers of serialised fiction develop unquestioning faith in the commercial apparatus by which the text is produced and distributed, so that the final clarifying instalment will reward their patience.[14] Dickens's self-referential allusion to the distribution of printed matter here implicates the reader much more directly in Dombey's downfall, insisting on his or her position as part of a surveillant society at the centre of the panopticon.

Dickens clearly felt that the exposure of hidden things to public scrutiny was an important function of the written word. The 'good spirit' longed for in Chapter 47, 'who would take the house-tops off ... and show a Christian people what dark shapes issue from amidst their homes' (47 p. 620), clearly states his own aspiration in representing, for example, slum conditions or neglect of domestic virtues.[15] However painful to accept, the revelation to 'the World' of the failure of Dombey's values is consistent with the novel's project of displaying to a vast readership the dark shapes that can issue from homes and here Dickens acknowledges the railway's rôle in this process. When modern communications bring knowledge of his collapse to 'The World', his discomfort about the contact with Toodles enforced by the railways seem fulfilled. His attempts to conceal the truth about himself, even from himself, are therefore still more desperate than Carker's flight from the train. A figure of speech in the third chapter eerily links the two men by prefiguring the accident:

> perhaps, unlearned as [Mrs Toodles] was, she could have brought a dawning knowledge home to Mr Dombey at that early day, which would not then have struck him in the end like lightning.
>
> (3 p. 29)

The associations between the railway and truth present in Toodles' advice and in the comment on rail-empowered distribution of newspapers may arise from local imperatives from the novelist's perspective, but both illustrate the novel's commitment to portraying the revelation of repressed truth as just and inescapable.

This is why Dombey's rail journey causes him to think not only of death, but also 'to think of this face of Florence' (p. 277). His daughter understands the spiritual vacuum at the centre of Dombey's personality and has the power to reveal it. Her father feels:

> As if she held the clue to something secret in his breast, of the nature of which he was hardly informed himself. As if she had an innate knowledge of one jarring and discordant string within him, and her very breath could sound it.
>
> (3 p. 31)

Most obviously, her resemblance to the lost child continually reminds Dombey of his shattered hopes. She is the useless female child remaining to him in place of his much-meditated posterity. In seeking to extend a relationship of love to him, she emphasises the effects of his materialistic repression of his need to give and receive love. His pride cannot deal with this clarity that constantly threatens to burst into his world. Admission of error would mercilessly undermine the protective ego barriers and structures of personality that he has used to define his identity. Moreover, since Florence encourages Paul to embrace a different set of values from his father's, she kills him as an actor in Dombey's scheme. Thus he transfers the blame for the boy's death onto her young shoulders, perceiving her as the originator of his destruction, when in fact she is merely the agent showing its inevitability to him and urging him to confront it at its real source. This is, of course, exactly the distinction that Dombey fails to make

with regard to the railway and the city slums he is compelled to see
through the carriage windows:

> it is never in his thoughts that the monster who has brought him there
> has let the light of day in on these things: not made or caused them.
>
> (20 p. 277)

His connection of the train with Florence's face, then, demonstrates
how monstrous her revelation of his hollowness is to him.

When Florence reveals to Edith the truth about herself, she is described
as the ultimate agent of discovery: 'My better angel!' (61 p. 824). Her
father, however, cannot accept her in this rôle and the reader is told that
he 'rejected the angel, and took up with the tormenting spirit' (20 p. 278).
This same dual nature can be seen in his perception of her representative
in his thoughts, the railway. Despite its link with the work of the revealing angel, he chooses to see it as a 'triumphant monster', a 'remorseless
monster' and an 'indomitable monster' (20 pp. 275–6). Carker also views
the trains as 'approaching monsters' and each one is 'another Devil' (55
p. 741). Like Bucket, Florence and her powerful co-symbol may be
described as 'Angel and devil by turns' (*BH* 54 p. 837) by those who fear
the identity-dissolving truth they bring. Dickens's apparent sympathy
with Dombey's pain here registers unease with the panoptical project of
his journalism of discovery, potentially assisted by the new technology,
but here at any rate, the choice to interpret it negatively is presented as
a matter of flawed human perspective.

The following chapter fuses Florence with the railway again in its
metaphors describing Dombey's state of mind during his courtship of
Edith. Here he aims to generate another Son and resume his dream, but he
is also determined to shut out the light of Florence in so doing. The music
his fiancée sings 'tamed the monster of the iron road, and made it less
inexorable' (21 p. 291) until she unwittingly takes up the tune sung by
Florence to her dying brother. Even his second marriage cannot shut out
the truth taught by Florence and suggested to him afresh by the railway. It
only adds another carriage to the train of defeat heading towards him:

> Their pride ... made their marriage way a road of ashes.
>
> (47 p. 618)

The metaphor again merges the connotations of the railway as bringer
of death and of ontologically fatal truth about himself.

Alexander Welsh has justly observed that 'For some reason the chapter [in which Dombey travels to Birmingham] has attracted more readers

interested in railroading than in allegory or the death of Paul. Neglected altogether is the part Florence plays in the journey – or the part played by Florence's face, which becomes increasingly prominent as the pulsating engine of death fades from the foreground'.[16] Thirty-five years later this is still largely the case.[17] Welsh addresses the problem by emphasising the duality inherent in the quasi-religious function of the Victorian heroine in pointing the male protagonist to a home beyond the grave, while insisting that he must pass through the experience of death to reach it:[18]

> The famous railway journey demonstrates the availability to the Victorian imagination of two angels of death, a saving angel as well as a destroying angel ...[19]

It is indeed striking that the essential characteristic of Dickens's heroines – their uncompromising declaration of truth – should in this passage be explicitly compared to a machine of such terrifying destructiveness. Welsh perceptively reads the train as evidence that transcendent revelation cannot come without a death that it is human nature to fear. Indeed, the revelation of new life Florence offers cannot be realised unless Dombey's old worldview is smashed to atoms.

If the novel's insistence on guaranteed emergence of clarity encourages readers to trust the economic and institutional structures that its production depends on, as in the Foucauldian reading advanced above, it achieves this through its embodiments of irrepressible truth such as Florence and, on occasions, the railway. Welsh's reading reminds us that the unlikely connection between the function of the railway and the heroine may teach us something about nineteenth-century conceptions of whatever spiritual revelation was necessary or available for mankind's salvation. Meeting his challenge to discuss this passage in its religious context will require placing the trains within their context as part of a whole metropolis. For the depiction of London's transformation by railway culture opens up the novel's blend of anxieties about whether anything guarantees this revelation of truth to a hungry public gaze – and about whether its effects will be ultimately destructive or redemptive.

III. The railway and time

So far I have mainly discussed the railway as a symbol of moral judgement, whether in the form of death or exposure. When we consider the railway's crucial rôle in re-shaping London life, however, its other key function, that of representing industrial and social change, becomes more prominent. Dombey's journey to Birmingham dramatises his internal fears, but also registers profound unease about a new way of life and relationship between metropolis and country. This extends key concerns expressed in the descriptions of Staggs's Gardens before and after the construction of the railway in Chapters 6 and 15 respectively. Nevertheless, our reading experience of the one aspect influences our reading experience of the other. It is the very interplay created by the ambivalence of the railway's representative function that suggests most about the ideas concerning the presence or absence of divine revelation available to the nineteenth-century mind – and to ours through the experience of reading Dickens.

Perhaps the most far-reaching change to London brought by the railway in Dickens's account is the revolution in the concept of time they effected.[20] Accurate measurement of time is one of the novel's recurring motives. Cuttle's admiration of Solomon Gills's science reaches its peak when he imagines his ability to make a timepiece:

> I suppose he could make a clock if he tried? ... And it would go! ... Lord, how that clock would go!
>
> (4 p. 44)

Gills himself is fiercely proud of the 'tremendous chronometer in his fob, rather than doubt which precious possession, he would have believed in a conspiracy against it on the part of all the clocks and watches in the City, and even of the very Sun itself' (4 p. 37). Just such a conspiracy seems to appear, however, nine chapters later:

> There was even railway time observed in clocks, as if the sun itself had given in.
>
> (15 p. 218)

The railway has replaced the natural world as the reference point for the rhythms that hold the universe together, governing every movement of the modern capital. People 'with watches in their hands' must catch their trains on time and plot their motions accordingly. Since the rail networks connected far-flung parts of the country, chaos would have resulted if they had not observed the same time from beginning to end of their routes. Captain Melhuish of the Board of Trade recommended that all railway clocks should be standardised to London time in 1840[21] and by 1880, legislation had eradicated local times in favour of Greenwich Mean Time.[22]

This was not observed universally until radio brought it conveniently into the home, but it is significant that a single framework of time makes the city a unified whole in this novel and that the railway forces this change. Gills reflects sorrowfully upon this new timetable, which seems so different from the old system of time that he has observed:

> I have fallen behind the time, and am too old to catch it again. Even the noise it makes a long way ahead, confuses me.
>
> (4 p. 42)

As the plot unfolds, however, it becomes obvious that the disjunction between railway time and that observed by Gills's chronometer is only apparent. It is 'The relentless chronometer', for example, not the City clocks, that 'announced that Walter must turn his back upon the Wooden Midshipman' (19 p. 266). Eventually, Sol's apparently hopeless investments pay off and it is revealed that instead of being behind the time, he is 'a little before it, and had to wait the fullness of the time and the design'(62 p. 830). This suggests that there is in the world of the novel a timetable governing the events of human lives as well as the movements of the trains. The vagaries of supply and demand here seem to be underwritten by a Providence that rewards the good. The changes that so bewilder Gills militate in his favour and his apparently hollow statement, 'We are men of business. We belong to the City' (4 p. 91), proves true. The London of the railway age works to their good and the chronometer tallies with Bradshaw after all.

Captain Cuttle's watch, however, with its accompanying instructions to 'Put it back half an hour every morning, and about another quarter towards the arternoon, and it's a watch that'll do you credit' (19 p. 266) does not keep railway time. Murray Baumgarten tries to reconcile the two types of time by saying:

> Dickens was able to hope that the punctuality so important for the new railroad civilization would be informed by the personal ease of Cap'n Cuttle, for he was still part of a transitional era.[23]

Cuttle's own hopes, however, represent the ordinary person hopelessly confused by the contradiction between actual events and the articles of his personal faith – that Walter will become the head of the company and achieve greatness. This is identical with Dombey's plan, but for the crucial fact that Walter, whom he describes as 'a'most a son of mine' (17 p. 230), has supplanted Paul. Like Dombey, the Captain must see this dream receive its 'death-shock' (32 p. 447) in the process of the real design before a new and truer version of it can arise. Cuttle constantly tries to impose his own Providential scheme for realising the story he has devised for Walter. His efforts at secret manipulation of events prolong the mystery, his removal from Brig Place preventing his reception of the explanatory letters. In this most fatalistic of Dickens's novels, the hands of the clock may not be put forward or back at will in the way the Captain recommends.

Cuttle provides a comic parallel to Dombey's need to learn this lesson. The businessman seeks to accelerate time, in order to enjoy the onto-logical fulfilment of being the Dombey in Dombey and Son the sooner. At Paul's birth, his watch is 'running a race' with the doctor's (1 p. 10) and the reader is told 'how long Paul's childish life had been to him, and how his hopes were set upon a later stage of his existence' (11 p. 139). The artificial system of education by which Dombey intends to accelerate time causes boys to learn with unnatural rapidity and then to die intellectually. Blimber's clock, with its refrain of 'how, is, my, lit, tle, friend!' (11 p. 145), fascinates Paul because it is a reminder to him of where the time is really leading him, like the rhythmic song of the waves. The more Dombey rushes Paul through his childhood, the more he hastens his death. Paul would prefer to hold time back, saying 'I had rather be a child'. The journey in Chapter 20 depends upon reading the railway as a concrete expression of the irrevocable passage of time – and of time operating to an incomprehensible new rhythm – established in Chapter 15.

Dombey and Son updates Dickens's immediately preceding fiction in terms of its conception of what makes London tick. The paragraphs in *Master Humphrey's Clock* between the end of *The Old Curiosity Shop* and the beginning of *Barnaby Rudge* had seen the clock of St Paul's as the heart of the city's identity:

> marking that ... it ... regulated the progress of the life around, the fancy came upon me that this was London's Heart, and that when it should cease to beat, the city would be no more.

Master Humphrey meditates upon its 'indomitable working', represent-ing time as an unstoppable machine whose task is inexorably to bring punishment:

> as if its business were to crush the seconds as they came trooping on, and remorselessly to clear a path before the Day of Judgement.[24]

By 1848, Dickens has organised his London as an emblem of human life, governed by the mighty force of time, around the still more 'remorseless' and 'indomitable monster' that is the train (20 p. 276). *Dombey and Son's* renewed London has a new 'heart', another machine whose symbolic function later emphasises the countdown to moral judgement:

> To and from the heart of this great change, all day and night, throbbing currents rushed and returned incessantly like its life's blood.
>
> (15 p. 218)

The station is the heart not only of the city, but also of the 'great change' that characterises the metropolis.[25] Sending and receiving trains around the clock, it 'produced a fermentation in the place that was always in action'. Perceptively, Dickens describes how the whole ethos of the modern city is designed to facilitate rapid movement:

> The very houses seemed disposed to pack up and take trips.
>
> (15 p. 218)

London becomes a centre for people and goods to come into and move around in, never staying too fixedly in one place – sometimes to be shipped overseas, sometimes to another part of the city. The city's blood, that is to say its life, is the 'Crowds of people and mountains of goods, departing and arriving scores upon scores of times in every four-and-twenty hours'.

Before the advent of the Underground, most people did not move around London itself by rail, but by horse-drawn methods.[26] Often, however, the routes of the omnibuses were between the rail termini, as names like 'the King's Crosses', 'The Great Northerns' and 'The Paddingtons' testify.[27] Cabs also benefited as the need to arrive at the platform on time increased.[28] Dickens's comment on the 'railway hackney-coach and cab-stands; railway omnibuses' (15 p. 214) reports a fuller and faster city following the advent of rail travel. The constantly circulating crowd, apparently random but governed by elliptical and constantly intersecting patterns, has a positive role to play in the later chapters of *Dombey and Son* in stimulating Florence to a wider engagement with life outside her father's house and these early glimpses of the external world show the railway taking a firm hand in forming its character.[29]

When Ruskin takes up this figure of speech one year later in *The Seven Lamps of Architecture*, the railway again makes London the heart of the country. The social change it represents here, however, is not progress. Instead, the movement is symptomatic of 'the ceaseless fever of ... life':

> along the iron veins that traverse the frame of our country, beat and flow the fiery pulses of its exertion, hotter and faster every hour. All vitality is concentrated through those throbbing arteries into the central cities; the country is passed over like a green sea by narrow bridges, and we are thrown back in continually closer crowds upon the city gates.[30]

Ruskin also sees the railway as essentially metropolitan, but to him, there is something diseased about the pace involved and it leads only to the countryside becoming marginalised. Both writers respond to the emerging phenomenon with an identical metaphor but Ruskin's reaction to the scene resembles Dombey's. Dickens uses the metaphor to invest the novel's backdrop with a symbolic suggestion of healthy rhythms of social circulation.

In a single sentence, Dickens captures the conflicting senses of, on the one hand, predictable mechanical order and, on the other, of incomprehensible alien mystery that the steam engines simultaneously presented to the early Victorians:

> Night and day the conquering engines rumbled at their distant work, or, advancing smoothly to their journey's end, and gliding like tame dragons into the allotted corners grooved out to the inch for their reception, stood bubbling and trembling there, making the walls quake, as if they were dilating with the secret knowledge of great powers yet unsuspected in them, and strong purposes not yet achieved.
>
> (15 p. 219)

This newly imposed order is both reassuring and dangerous, displaying the profound ambiguities that existed in the nineteenth-century imagination concerning both the railways and Providential notions of history. If the trains are 'tame', they are 'dragons' nevertheless and even in the station yard they threaten destruction to their shelter, as they vibrate with potential energy. Nevertheless, a higher power is controlling them with astonishing precision. Their journeys are planned out 'to the inch'. Dickens impresses the reader with the 'great powers' and 'strong purposes' he has in store for these engines with authorial foresight of Carker's doom.

Dombey and Son delights in the tension between the bewildering variety and apparent randomness of the ever-changing railway world and the reassuring, if vast, overall plan, whose workings give a powerful sense of purpose to it all. The Staggs's Gardens passages themselves seem carefully planned to invest the railways with a sense of carefully planned purpose, which will confirm their function as nemesis later in the novel. On the most prosaic level, it is the London and Birmingham timetable that states when the engines embark on their journeys. On the other hand, the schedule planners did not set out to kill Carker at 4 a.m. precisely. Rather it is the author himself who holds the trains back, champing at the bit, until the correct moment for their mission arrived.

Of course the structuring power of a plot tending towards inevitability is built into the whole genre of the novel, whether it reflects a Christian-influenced worldview or not. This may be traced to its emulation of dramatic form. The concept of poetic justice is at least as old as Aristotle's *Poetics*, if Thomas Rymer coined the English term. *Nemesis* may be brought about in tragedy, for example, without necessarily intending good either to the individual or to society. Nevertheless, even here, Aristotle's insistence on the relationship between *nemesis* and *hamartia* in true tragedy seems to be about ameliorating a sense of the gods' injustice and reinforcing the eternal principles on which society should be governed. If *Pilgrim's Progress* provides the point of departure for prose narrative with a sense of ordered events in a Christian Providential outlook, even John Bunyan was working from a long-established tradition of literary justice. While some novels in the centuries that followed sought directly to inculcate trust in Providential ordering of events, others saw such optimism in conflict with the ideas inherent in the genres in which they were writing. New ways of considering the narrative of history as natural theology made such tensions even more complicated. Damrosch[31] charts this process in eighteenth-century fiction, but it is particularly marked in the dark patterns of inevitability with which the gothic novel brings about the collapse of the villain's schemes. As we have seen, the rhythms governing the concealing aspects of Dickens's city are heavily influenced by this particular genre, even affecting his representation of scientific and social theories of sanitary reform. The eerie premonitions of Carker's demise in the train-yard, the apocalyptic language of Staggs's Gardens and Dombey's transmogrification of the engines into indomitable monsters gothicise his discussion of economic and technological phenomena and bring complex gothic attitudes towards inevitability with them. As the gothic evolved into melodrama in the popular theatre and fiction of

Dickens's time, an increasingly stagy dramatisation of poetic justice came to be expected. George Levine reads the artificiality of nineteenth-century poetic justice as evidence of a lack of confidence in its real existence in the face of first geological and then biological theories that undermined teleological notions of history. Responding to Harland Nelson's argument that Dickens's plotting shows more faith in divine justice than that of Wilkie Collins,[32] he comments 'Dickens still uses chance to project a world governed by a great designer, even if he often has difficulty in doing so. ... the self consciously less episodic and more thematically coherent later novels use mysterious and apparently inexplicable details for the sake of human significance'.[33] Nevertheless he is compelled to add a footnote emphasising Dickens's half-acknowledged doubts in this formulation:

> But the strain to make the harmony is evident in the great novels and the ways of Providence or of natural theology are often challenged by the methods designed to affirm them.[34]

The letter in which Dickens states most directly his profound conviction that the writer's judgement of the timing of a fictional apprehension only shadowed an actual Providential scheme is to Collins himself. This suggests that Dickens was confirming the religious agenda to the aspect of his own practise that coincided most nearly with the methods of melodrama. In 1848, the unstoppable momentum and accurate system of control required by the railway seems to allow Dickens to present teleology convincingly as an aspect of the modern age.[35] The fear this arouses in the imagination of those in awe of it allow him to explore anxieties carried over from alternative generic traditions and contemporary doubt while firmly maintaining his central point about a benign and unified monotheistic design.

In presenting the railway terminus as potentially inspiring reverent confidence in a benign overall plan, Dickens's representation of the railway terminus seems closer to G. K. Chesterton's view than Ruskin's. Chesterton, claiming not so much that the commercial and mechanical had replaced the religious in the nineteenth-century imagination, but that in them the religious had found a new way to manifest itself, said of the London terminus:

> It has many of the characteristics of a great ecclesiastical building; it has vast arches, void spaces, coloured lights, and, above all, it has recurrence or ritual.[36]

Likewise, Gautier called the stations 'These cathedrals of the new humanity'.[37] Such an alignment goes some way towards justifying Ruskin's much-quoted accusation that Dickens was 'a pure modernist' and 'leader of the steam-whistle party'. By the turn of the century, A. W. Ward recognised this aspect of his aesthetic more positively:

> Dickens had a strong sense of what I may call the poetry of the railway train.[38]

Ruskin would not have acknowledged that such a thing existed. Dickens, however, depicts a positive, exhilarating change that could push towards discovery of a new identity in relation to the rest of the world. This inexorable metropolitan force embodied Dickens's hope that his society was being taken onwards to a transforming apprehension of divinely appointed love relationships by means of technological and moral progress happening concurrently. By investing these awesome vehicles with such qualities, symbolically linking them to the powerful revelation of love offered by Florence, he elevated them to the Sublime.

If, however, the railway may be read as an appropriate figure for the workings of divine justice, then this must have been a terrifying force to contemporaries – especially since, unlike the detective police, the trains' unalterable mechanism was tempered with no human or humanising dimension. One of the most chilling sentences in the whole of Dickens's fiction is the uncompromising, matter-of-fact statement of the station waiter:

> Express comes through at four, Sir. – It don't stop.
>
> (55 p. 742)

Yet the same 'design' (whether of the author or of God) determines both that the train is speeding through the rural station at just the moment Carker stumbles on to the track and that Gills's investments mature on Walter's return. Does some kind of Providence benignly underscore or overrule the market forces that control the stock market? If so, the novel promotes an optimistic view of capitalist London, in the wake of the railways, as belonging to a stage in the narrative of progress, even while its presentation of this narrative as impersonal and ruthless militates against full endorsement of this view. Certainly, the railway technology emerging from the market controlling Gills's investments seems to bring beneficial order to London itself out of apparent chaos in what turns out to be a carefully laid plan. For this, however, we must turn not to Chapter 55, but to Chapters 6 and 15.

IV. The railway and the city

In moulding London's time, rail travel reshaped the character of metropolitan life. The two chapters set in Camden Town show the railway taking a more tangible part in shaping the London environment. The novel's first portrait of Staggs's Gardens describes nothing less than the destruction of a neighbourhood. In fact immense damage to the capital was caused as more and more railways drove their way through. By 1867, more than 50,000 inhabitants of London had been forced to move from their homes. In 1866 alone, the Midland Railway Company demolished 4000 working-class homes to reach St Pancras, displacing 32,000 inhabitants.[39] Even the dead were disrupted as a cemetery had to be flattened and the bodies reburied.[40] Legislation providing new homes for their breathing counterparts did not come until 1885.

Perhaps the most striking feature of London under construction was the incompleteness of the landscape:

> Everywhere were bridges that led nowhere; thoroughfares that were wholly impassable; Babel towers of chimneys, wanting half their height; ... fragments of unfinished walls and arches, ... wildernesses of bricks, and giant forms of cranes, and tripods straddling above nothing ... a hundred thousand shapes and substances of incompleteness, wildly mingled out of their places ... unintelligible as any dream.
>
> (6 p. 65)

The sublime scale of this fragmentation is admirably captured by the illustration of the construction of the Euston Arch in Figure 3 and Dickens's evocation befits the railway that later reduces Carker to 'mutilated fragments' (55 p. 743). At the other end of the line, the narrative suggests that the train has collided with Birmingham, causing a destruction of the city as complete as the destruction of Carker's body:

> Everything around is blackened. There are dark pools of water, muddy lanes, and miserable habitations far below. There are jagged walls and falling houses close at hand, and through the battered roofs and broken windows, wretched rooms are seen, where want and fever hide themselves in many wretched shapes, while smoke, and crowded gables, and distorted chimneys, and deformity of brick and mortar penning up deformity of mind and body, choke the murky distance.
>
> (20 pp. 276–7)

Dombey interprets the effects of social change in terms that suggest some kind of apocalyptic judgement has fallen upon Birmingham:

It was the journey's fitting end, and might have been the end of everything; it was so ruinous and dreary.

(20 p. 277)

This is not only the end of the line, but the end of the world. The railway supposedly heralded in the age of a new civilisation, yet we see here the shattered remains of one.[41] While these cities are not being punished for their actions, the sublime scale of these scenes prepares the reader for the terror of Carker's doom. More immediately, Dombey links the mutilated West-Midlands environment (inevitably recalling the descriptions of Camden Town five chapters previously) with the collapse Dombey and Son is heading for after the death of Paul. The destructive effects of the whole process that creates railways, and not just the destructive potential of individual trains, participate in representing nemesis.

Echoing the subjective views of the dwellers of Staggs's Gardens, Chapter 6 gives little indication that the railway will ever benefit anyone:

Nothing was the better for it, or thought of being so.

(6 p. 66)

Critics who cite these passages as evidence that Dickens 'painted a horrified picture of the impact of the railways on London in *Dombey and Son*'[42] seem to ignore Chapter 15, which shows the fruits of this upheaval. 'The miserable waste ground' with its 'rotten' buildings and 'refuse-matter' has been replaced by 'palaces' and opulent 'warehouses, crammed with rich goods and costly merchandise'. Weary 'streets that had stopped disheartened in the mud and wagon-ruts' have gone and an immense energy has come. This is the first sign in the novel that breakdown may lead to reformation, providing hope that the landscape of destruction might only be evidence of work in progress towards connection and community. Although the change brought by the railway has destroyed the identity of Camden Town, rendering it unrecognisable even to its former inhabitants, this metaphorical death has brought a 'wholesome' new identity. Dickens's statement that 'from the very core of all this dire disorder, [the railway] trailed smoothly away, upon its mighty course of civilisation and improvement' (6 p. 65) initially sounds ironic, but turns out to be accurate.

The building of the railways really did transform London. The destruction of adjacent streets exposed the deprivation of slum areas to public view, prompting middle-class will for change. Engels describes this process as it took place in Manchester in *The Condition of the Working Class in England* in 1844:

> ... immediately under the railway bridge there exists a court that in point of filth and horror far surpasses all the others – just because it was formerly so shut up, so hidden and secluded that it could not be reached without considerable difficulty. I thought I knew this entire district thoroughly, but even I would never have found it myself without the breach made here by the railway viaduct.[43]

Dickens's brother-in-law, Henry Austin, whose lifelong work for sanitary reform stimulated the novelist's own, was among those shocked into action by his experience of the London-Blackwall line in the 1830s.

The railway, then, actualised the 'good spirit who would take the house-tops off ... and show a Christian people what dark shapes issue from amidst their homes' (47 p. 620), performing the work of the written word. Industrial progress exposed the long suppressed truth that the network of connections between human beings had gone awry. The reader can see this process directly in the novel. Dombey's journey has 'let the light of day in on these things' (20 p. 277), making him uncomfortably aware of the living conditions of the poor, just as it had for Austin and Engels.

As well as raising awareness of social problems, however, the railways actively destroyed many slums, forcing the people to move to other areas. Of course this only led to people being made homeless at first but it encouraged the move outwards towards the more salubrious and carefully planned suburban districts. This at least was how the predominantly middle-class newspapers reported the situation. *The Times* said, on 2 March 1861, that the destruction caused by the building of the lines, 'though attended with the present inconvenience of disturbing the occupants, is ultimately of unmixed advantage, by driving them into new and better tenements in the suburbs'.[44]

London's history may in fact be mythologised in terms of catastrophic disasters, which ultimately regenerated the urban environment and transformed the cityscape. To Dickens the paradigm was the Great Fire of London in 1666 which cleared some of the most disease-ridden slums, arresting the spread of the plague and leading to the building of

Christopher Wren's fine churches. His assessment in *A Child's History of England* is one of apocalyptic destruction and positive transformation:

> This was a terrible visitation at the time, and occasioned great loss and suffering to the two hundred thousand burnt-out people. ... But the fire was a great blessing to the city afterwards, for it arose from its ruins very much improved – built more regularly, more widely, more clearly and carefully, and therefore much more healthily. It might be far more healthy than it is, but that there are some people in it still – even now, at this time, nearly two hundred years later – so selfish, so pig-headed, and so ignorant, that I doubt if even another Great Fire would warm them up to do their duty.
>
> (p. 395)

Three years earlier in *Dombey and Son*, he had imagined just that. This time the disaster that demolishes the capital is a 'great earthquake' (6 p. 65) that precipitates the replacement of the 'carcasses of ragged tenements' with wholesome new ones which have 'sprung into existence'. The *Child's History* foregrounds both urban planning and the divine planning responsible for the blessing equally. If anything, the former seems like a function of the latter, but there is a warning that although Providence may give human beings the opportunity to provide for others through the advanced means available to them, it is not absolutely guaranteed. Duty must play its part if this opportunity is not to be wasted. *Dombey and Son* transmits the same message, the imagery's inherent sense of a railway timetable in harmony with the narrative's Providential timetable conflicting with the plot's insistence on the real possibilities of misinterpreting that timetable or of trying to ignore it altogether.

In the face of the upbeat outcome to Staggs's Gardens, then, what are we to make of the inhabitants' initial resistance? To Terry Eagleton, Dickens was reflecting the ambivalence of his class. The book's treatment of the railway 'affirms bourgeois industrial progress at the same time as it protests gloomily against it on behalf of the petty bourgeoisie it dooms to obsolescence'.[45] In this Marxist reading, Dickens encourages the cohesion brought to society by such forces and sees them as part of a benign narrative of history.[46] At the same time, he also appears to regret the passing of the old order's picturesque chaos, sensing that market forces of this sort could leave behind humanising qualities he values. Certainly the Gardeners' attitude, regarding their home as 'a sacred grove not to be withered by Railroads' (6 p. 66) is portrayed as a Romantic abhorrence at industrial spoiling of nature's holiness. Dickens's free indirect discourse here even quotes Wordsworth's objections in 'On the Projected Kendal and Windermere Railway'. Dickens clearly approves of their devotion to the natural values of home, but satirises their attitude: they are not defending the Lake District, but a dreary suburban street. In the event, their homes are decidedly improved, rewarding the confidence of the Toodles, who provide the reason for both visits to this area and are the novel's contrast to the Dombeys as a functioning family. Dickens unexpectedly seems to have sided with the utilitarians Wordsworth blames for railway construction in his backyard.

The Staggs's Gardeners' resistance evaporates as soon as the prosperity arrives. While their regret in Chapter 6 has some poignancy, their eager embrace of change in Chapter 15 is exhilarating. Dickens turns to the vocabulary of Christian conversion to portray this mass change of heart and the resultant change of identity, personifying Camden Town as a convert, who has been through the death of self and emerged in newness of life. It has become 'wise and penitent' (p. 218). The joke, of course, is that the transformation is as complete as that claimed by religious converts, but without their acknowledgement of previous scepticism, which has vanished with apparently miraculous speed and been replaced by evangelistic zeal for the new order. While this is evoked ironically, it hints that the much-resisted breakdown of the old can lead to regeneration at an individual level. What is done for the city symbolises what can be done for Dombey. His attitude to the railway parallels the Staggs's Gardeners'. Although Dickens describes Birmingham as a 'scene of transition', Dombey prefers to characterise it as 'a ruin and a picture of decay, instead of hopeful change, and promise of better things' (20 p. 277). Likewise the truth shown by Florence's love offers the dynamic of regeneration but Dombey can only see the destruction that embracing this would bring to the world of 'Dombey and Son'. His connection with his daughter is thus left in a broken state, like the half-finished roads and 'bridges that led nowhere' of Camden Town, merging with the approaching wreckage of his dream. He too must become 'wise and penitent' and the change of heart which Dickens worked so hard to justify in the Preface is the only thing that can save him.

April seems to be the cruellest month for both Dombey and the inhabitants of London. T. S. Eliot's paradox that 'winter kept us warm' (*The Waste Land*, 1. 4) seems especially appropriate to Dombey whose coldness shields him from exposure to the painful sunshine of Florence's love and the opportunity for life and growth it offers. Indeed, it is hard for modern readers to read this transformation of Camden Town's 'miserable waste ground' (*DS* 15 p. 218) without their reading practices being influenced at some level by knowledge of *The Waste Land*. In that poem, written seventy-four years later, Londoners require yet resist a spiritual regeneration. They have cut off relationships of love, choosing instead a sterile, self-absorbed world of business routine and meaningless sex. Their need is figured by connecting their individual corruption with a decaying, rat-infested city, which is in turn connected with the archetypal imagery of the dessert. Eliot's broader spiritual indictments hardly fit the reactionary chimney-sweeper and his cronies. Nevertheless, familiarity with the poem may confirm a tendency to carry forward the vocabulary of the waste ground in Staggs's Gardens to the general panorama of London corrupt from East to West provided by the good spirit in Chapter 47. Perhaps developing Dickens's technique in *Little Dorrit*, Eliot explores the link between the city and the gothic haunted house as emblems for the denial of life-giving connections.[47] While Staggs's Gardens is too homely to be gothic, its fragmentary cityscape anticipates the apocalyptic conclusion to Eliot's poem. This is especially the case with its inversion of traditional symbols of time:

> And upside down in air were towers
> Tolling reminiscent bells that kept the hours

(ll. 372–84)[48]

The bells are reminiscent of those of St Mary Woolnoth in 'The Burial of the Dead', which chimed 'With a dead sound on the final stroke of nine' (l. 68). Like so many of Dickens's novels, this poem is concerned with the failure of the traditional symbols of Christianity including church architecture to sound out a message of life in the city. Eliot's time-keeping church bells cannot signal a point on the timeline of history, moving towards regeneration of all things, but are themselves part of the general deadness. At the end, the skyline collapses altogether with only the chapel visible.

This final section achingly suggests the possibility of regeneration, but the only sign that this London has been transformed in a comparable way to that of *Dombey and Son* is the question 'What is the city over the mountains' (l. 371). Whether such a New Jerusalem will descend or not, Eliot's quester is looking for it, like Abraham, who 'looked for a city which hath foundations, whose builder and maker is God' (Hebrews 11:10).

The poem not only pointed to an unwholesome contemporary European culture tending towards mass destruction, but also captured a search for spiritual regeneration that Eliot believed was timeless. His depiction of London's destruction as an inevitable consequence of society's withdrawal from meaningful interaction with others resonated with meaning for those who saw the towers falling in the Blitz.[49] The poem's tormenting hope that this falling might be the decisive step towards building a renewed society with a renewed spirituality was read again with enthusiasm by a generation that sought to re-build the post-war world along different lines.[50] Eliot's vision of contemporary London as a metropolis yearning to become a glorious heavenly city, yet resisting it, is surely indebted to the apocalyptic language Dickens and his contemporaries applied, often opportunistically, to social reform. By causing us to re-think the connections that may obtain between the various usages of its recurring images, it, in turn, empowers us to return to Dickens's novels and to assemble a reading of them as texts that, consciously or unconsciously, address modern spiritual concerns at the profoundest level.

Nevertheless, Dickens is much more optimistic about the possibility of revelation and renewal than Eliot in his early poems. He is also more prepared to define this supernatural revelation in his account of social care as the manifestation of the love of the Christian God. This is especially true of the more overtly religious transformed cityscape witnessed by the heroine in *Little Dorrit* and by Mrs Clennam, following the fall of her house and theology. The extension of this collapse into the apocalyptic transformation of London dominates the novel's climax. Once the secrets upon which its city is built are brought out into the open, the destruction it is so obviously tending towards occurs. First the financial fall of Merdle's business house is represented as the fall of the city it overshadows. Since men and women throughout London's boundaries have invested in the house, which contains society in microcosm, this adds up to the fall of the entire metropolis, crushing the inhabitants beneath its weight. Bar and Physician:

> looked round upon the immense city, and said, If all those hundreds and thousands of beggared people who were yet asleep, could only know, as they two spoke, the ruin that impended over them, what a fearful cry against one miserable soul would go up to Heaven!
>
> (II 25 p. 689)

As the dust from Merdle's tumbling city settles, the author progresses to the final fall, which provides a concrete image of it. Dickens's magnificent rumbling tone captures perfectly the complicated rhythms of an intricate edifice tumbling to the ground:

> it heaved, surged outward, trembled asunder in fifty places, collapsed, and fell. ... As they looked up, wildly crying for help, the great pile of chimneys which was then alone left standing like a tower in a whirlwind, rocked, broke, and hailed itself down upon the heap of ruin, as if every tumbling fragment were intent upon burying the crushed wretch deeper.
>
> (II 31 p. 772)

This moment is the focal point of the book, not only because it gives meaning to its other crumbling structures, but also because it is at this point of death that regeneration can occur. Mrs Clennam steps out of her old self-referential world and finds herself in a new environment where familial relationships are fully realised again and men and women apprehend their connections of love with one another:

> People stood and sat at their doors, playing with children and enjoying the evening ...
>
> (p. 771)

As in *Dombey and Son*, the panorama's chief characteristic is a healthy lifestyle with a suggestion of unobscured Christian duty. Little Dorrit's encouragement of Mrs Clennam to see Christianity in its true perspective is reflected for the reader in the beautiful change in the city that results from such a radical overturning of the metropolitan order:[51]

> It was one of those summer evenings when there is no greater darkness than a long twilight. ... The smoke that rose into the sky had lost its dingy hue and taken a brightness upon it. The beauties of the sunset had not faded from the long light films of cloud that lay at peace in the horizon. From a radiant centre, over the whole length and breadth of the tranquil firmament, great shoots of light streamed among the early stars, like signs of the blessed later covenant of peace and hope that changed the crown of thorns into a glory.
>
> (p. 771)

The perpetually bright twilight of the reformed London seems a direct allusion to John's eternal metropolis in Revelation:

> And the city had no need of the sun, neither of the moon, to shine in it: for the glory of God did lighten it, and the lamb is the light thereof. And the nations of them which are saved shall walk in the light of it ...
>
> (Revelation 21:23–5)

This leads Dennis Walder to conclude that 'There is no more profound or original expression of the religious aspect of Dickens's imagination than *Little Dorrit*'.[52] If Dickens wants his Heaven on earth, it is nonetheless a Heaven defined by the genuine divine love that exists between its inhabitants.

Little Dorrit's city is unquestionably changed. Although the Circumlocution Office remains, Merdle and Casby are gone and the dominance of the Puritanical elite has faded. Nevertheless the cityscape looks different only from a subjective point of view privileged by the author.[53] The ending itself is far from triumphal, concluding with London's decidedly untransformed crowds making their 'usual' uproar. The transformation of the cityscape in *Dombey and Son* is physical and much more tangible. Although the methodology is different, it again reflects what happens to an individual bound within the confines of a house when his world is smashed to atoms by revelation of a profound truth and then built anew by the same force. Dickens perceived a potent emblem of this force in the speed and strength of the railway trains and in the irreversible alterations they effected in London. The words that herald the arrival of the New Jerusalem, 'Behold, I make all things new' (Revelation 21:5) could be pronounced by the chairman of the railway. John's vision, like Dickens's, was one of a perfect urban environment in which Christian principles of love for God and for one's brothers and sisters shaped the ethos. It is no accident that 'churches' still have their place in the new cityscape of Staggs's Gardens:

> Bridges that had led to nothing, led to villas, gardens, churches, healthy public walks.
>
> (15 p. 218)

As in John's version, Dickens describes the complete destruction of the current order as absolutely necessary for the emergence of the new city. Whereas John considered the realisation of this vision to be in the future, after the return of Christ, however, Dickens presents this trans-forming application of Christ's standards as realisable now. Like Blake, he seeks to build this New Jerusalem in England's green and pleasant land. As in the account of the great fire in the *Child's History*, divine planning has provided an opportunity for human planning and provision. If the ultimately positive depiction of the railways is representative of the spirit of the age, Dickens is optimistic about that spirit because it is 'a good spirit' making known a system of love relationships according to a timetable of Providential progress.

In *Dombey and Son*, the railway is one of three flowing forces integral to the presentation of the city that potentially provide a sense of direction and purpose. Having considered the railway, it is time to deal with the other two, as they appear in Dickens's fiction, namely the river and the crowd itself.

6

'The secrets of the river': The Thames within London

'Dickens's earliest attempt to pull a novel together by repeating a "symbol" seems to be *Dombey and Son*',[1] says John Carey at the beginning of his section on Dickens's 'symbols' – and attempt implies failure. If so, both the attempt and the limitations the 'symbol' faces are surely significant in the context of this study. Carey's inverted commas indicate that he considers the word misleading. Objects in Dickens's world, he insists, are 'intensely themselves, not signs for something else'.[2] His scepticism about attempts to find a coherent meaning in the image of the river, good for each time it is used, anticipate Susan Horton's suspicions of symbolic readings of the railway in the same novel.[3] Carey does not blame over-interpretative critics for such readings, however, but Dickens himself, who perpetually comments on the image's transcendental meaning, leaving little doubt that it is to be read symbolically as evoking Victorian Christian iconography.

I began this book with Edgar Johnson's remark that 'The Thames of *Our Mutual Friend* is the same river that flows through [Eliot's] waste land, a river sweating tar and waste, bearing a flotsam of debris in its muddy waters'. Both texts, Johnson implies, are concerned with the failure of the traditional symbol of the river to be a regenerative force in the face of the modern city's sterile life:

> Once a symbol of the renewal of life, the waters themselves are sullied with the muck of the dustheaps infecting their purity in loathsome solution[4]

In the fragmented world of Eliot's poem, the eastward flow of the Thames is all that supplies any linear direction. The river itself is felt to be bearing the quester towards a sea of death, the crucial motif being the shipwreck of 'Phlebas the Phoenician' (l. 312). The quotations from Ariel's song in *The Tempest* that prefigure this leave the reader expecting that something valuable may arise out of such apparent destruction:

> Those are pearls that were his eyes. Look!
>
> (l. 48)

Such transformation, however, is never unambiguously granted. London here is a symbolic as well as a real environment, a place in which to be both physically and spiritually lost on the quest for revelation and renewal. It constantly pushes towards its mid point, the river, and the resurrection that may or may not emerge from it. Helen Williams suggests two interesting possibilities here: one that Eliot finds the river inadequate as a spiritual signifier and the other that the problem is rather the quester's perspective:

> Perhaps the river is a lost source of natural vitality and no longer the right medium for the quester's search. As the spring stirring of life inspired fear, so perhaps the terrors of drowning are to be endured despite fear.[5]

Dombey and Son is equally interested in examining whether the river symbol, in its context at the heart of a commercial metropolis, can mean in the powerful religious ways it did previously. Dickens is more committed to making it do so at this earlier stage in his career, tending to shoe-horn it into significance and this may explain *Our Mutual Friend*'s greater effectiveness in its handling of the river. Representation of the chilling ambiguities in whatever religious truths it might be intended to evoke is largely left to the image of the railway.

This chapter charts the development of Dickens's use of the Thames to explore themes of transformation between *Dombey and Son* and *Our Mutual Friend*, showing that the author refined his symbolic method in response to the very problems Carey identifies. Without assuming that the river's function is always primarily symbolic – or always symbolic in the same way, it explores the dialogue between the various treatments of the river motif in the four novels discussed, illustrating a wide range of responses to the religious issues implied in its use. The particular focus, of course, is on how the river's symbolic functions interact with those of the city through which it flows.

I. *Dombey and Son*

Roselee Robison considers the river to be 'the most complex symbol in all Dickens's novels'[6] since it can represent diametrically opposed things, such as corruption and death on the one hand, and innocence and rebirth on the other. Such variety suggests that Dickens is doing something more sophisticated than merely 'repeating a "symbol"'. Conveying such a tangled mass of referents to the reader, however, without damaging the immediacy of the vehicle, the realism that Carey so admires becomes almost impossible.

As Robison perceptively remarks, the river in *Dombey and Son* is generally a conceptual rather than a directly experienced phenomenon, manifesting itself primarily within young Paul's imagination. Nevertheless, the child's rather abstract river is also the actual Thames of London:

> His fancy had a strange tendency to wander to the river, which he knew was flowing through the great city ...
>
> (*DS* 16 p. 220)

A. O. J. Cockshut attributes its success to the fact that London is a port.[7] The river provides the livelihood of all the maritime characters and is central to Mr Dombey's trade. He is seen 'walking in the Docks, looking at his ships' (4 p. 46) while Walter carries out his business at the river (6 pp. 76–7). The first chapter introduces Dombey's conception of it:

> Rivers and seas were formed to float their ships ...
>
> (1 p. 2)

Almost immediately, however, a different perspective of the river rolling towards the ocean emerges, as Mrs Dombey is said to have 'drifted out upon the dark and unknown sea that rolls round all the world' (1 p. 11). The first statement is not metaphorical. It comes from a character confident that he understands the real world and how it behaves. The second is a totally abstract comment from a narrator whose sea can be known with no such certainty. From this point onwards, it becomes increasingly clear that the novel will be about the tension between a limited apprehension of such things as rivers and seas and a wider one which understands what it is about them that makes such metaphors meaningful.

Some feel that the Thames and its flow to the sea have a hidden message to convey and some, such as the dying Mrs Skewton, do not.

Although 'the waves are hoarse with repetition of their mystery', their 'speech is dark and gloomy to her'. Other narrow-minded characters are said to be 'deaf to the waves' (41 pp. 560–1), yet Mr Toots 'hears the requiem of little Dombey on the waters' which occasionally 'whisper a kind thought to him' (pp. 554–5). Meanwhile it is a matter of urgency to Paul to know, 'What the Waves were always saying'. In this neo-Romantic world, only semi-delirious children and holy idiots intuitively grasp that there is a comforting message contained in the water, allowing Dickens to associate images with themes without the necessity for rational exposition.

Within this novel's symbolic scheme, the river only has significance in so far as it is connected to the sea. At his mother's deathbed, the ocean's properties of being 'dark', 'unknown' and inevitably omnipresent ('rolls round all the world') associate it with death. Paul applies these same qualities to the river that leads to the sea:

> he thought how black it was, and how deep it would look, reflecting the host of stars – and more than all, how steadily it rolled away to meet the sea'
>
> (16 pp. 220–1)

Paul learns to read the river and sea as the narrator conceptualises them, taking him 'towards that invisible region, far away' (8 p. 111). The river's goal is death, but also transcendence afterwards. When he dies, he has a vision of his dead mother and the welcoming arms of Jesus, telling Florence, that 'the motion of the boat upon the stream was lulling him to rest. ... Now the boat was out at sea' (16 p. 224–5). The link between the river, the unfolding narrative and the Providential ordering of events is frequently confirmed in the narrator's incidental metaphor:

> Through a whole year, the winds and clouds had come and gone; the ceaseless work of Time had been performed, in storm and sunshine. Through a whole year, the tides of human chance and change had set in their allotted courses.
>
> (58 p. 773)

The river, then, emphasises the same themes of the inexorable passage of time towards death as the 'throbbing currents' of the railway (15 p. 218), which acts as a stylised version of it.[8] Indeed the vision of eternity beyond is conceived in terms of a restoration of familial relationships emanating from a divine source desirable in the present consistent with the glimpses of the New Jerusalem characteristic of Dickens's transformed cityscapes. Such confidence in the river's capacity to bear reassuring religious meaning differs from *The Waste Land*'s constant questioning of whether this stagnant stream can still offer any comforting narrative. Dickens's acceptance of the river's benevolent rôle as symbol of narrative time bringing about transformations is, however, by no means unconflicted. Paul's imagination, for example, acts upon the Thames to produce a surreal terror. He initially tries to slow down its flow because, at some subconscious level, he perceives that death is at the end of it:

> His only trouble was, the swift and rapid river. He felt forced, sometimes, to try to stop it – to stem it with his childish hands – or choke its way with sand – and when he saw it coming on, resistless, he cried out!
>
> (16 p. 220)

Walter Gay, moreover, in his archetypal rôle as the drowned man of this text, reminds us that real dangers exist at sea. Although his shipwreck is not narrated directly, the descriptions of death on the high seas he so cherishes eerily prefigure his own experience and provide a vivid image for the novel's others metaphorical references to the sea. The name of the wrecked ship, *The Son and Heir*, a title given to Paul (11 p. 139), unites the unlikely figures of Dombey and Cuttle. The latter's initial reluctance to face up to the change of outlook on the world required when his plans for Walter are devastated complements Dombey's deeper failure to come to terms with the loss of his son and decline of his firm. Nevertheless, these are merely painful experiences on the road to a regeneration that the novel unambiguously grants. Dombey pictures his wife's death in Florence's arms as a river showing him 'clear depths of tenderness and truth' into which he cannot bring himself to plunge. Left 'on the bank above them ... quite shut out' (3 p. 83), he is the most reluctant character in the novel to enter into any kind of death by water comparable to that of his fellow merchant, Phlebas. Julian Moynahan makes this connection as he famously mocks the volume of tears shed by Florence.

> For Dombey at this point the sharing of love seems a death by water. To be saved from his own stoniness he must leap from the bark and dissolve his proud self in his daughter's tears. ... Florence wants to get Dombey's head down on the pillow where she can drown him in a dissolving love.[9]

Dombey's surrender to love is tied to the motifs of drowning and re-emergence that permeate the novel. As Paul ceased to struggle against the course of the river and the Providentially ordained course of time it represents, so, at last, does his father. When his business collapses and his house is compared to a wrecked ship (58 p. 773), Florence enters bearing a new Paul, in the form of her own child by Walter, to replace the one he has just surrendered.

Florence too comes to identify the brokenness of her aspirations with Walter's fate, realising that she is 'left like the sole survivor on a lonely shore from the wreck of a great vessel' (48 p. 638). Dreaming of her father dead and never having loved her, she sees the river and hears Paul's voice exclaiming that the river holds better things ahead:

It is running on, Floy! It has never stopped! You are moving with it!

(35 p. 488)

In the fatalistic, but ultimately optimistic world of this novel at least, with the renunciation of one's own aims, surrendered visions are given back. This principle is the point of Cuttle's morbid repetition of the question, 'Drownded, An't he?' in Chapter 49.

Florence has always been invested with an innate ability to soothe the terrors of the river:

But a word from Florence, who was always at his side, restored him to himself ...

(16 p. 293)

At Fulham, where the literal and metaphorical rivers meet explicitly for the first and only time in the novel, she finally grasps the connection between the 'current flowing on to rest' and 'the darker river rippling at her feet ... which her brother had so often said was bearing him away' (24 p. 340). Here she sees a reversal of her own situation – a father unap-preciated by his 'impatient' daughter, at work upon a broken boat, sug-gesting that, unlike Dombey, he has learned the lesson of the flowing stream. He recognises that he will not always have his daughter with him and so loves her while he can. Florence carries the meaning she apprehends here into adulthood, where she will finally teach her father what may be heard in the speech of the waves.

Decoding such an unspoken significance in a symbol is one of the means by which the reader imaginatively participates in Dombey's dis-covery of a mysterious truth. The conflicting levels of meaning in the waves suggested by the narrator challenge the reader to decide what they *are* always saying. Yet a certain vagueness of definition also suggests that investing this traditional symbol with a clear meaning in the metropolitan age is problematic. Carey is correct that Dickens's symbols are more effective when permitted to speak for themselves as realistically portrayed objects than when he underlines them with paragraphs of moralistic gloss that ultimately fail to clarify. When the narrator tries to explain verbally what the waves have actually been saying, their voice is less powerful than when they have been simply described. They are made to speak of

> love, eternal and illimitable, not bounded by the confines of this world, or by the end of time, but ranging still, beyond the sea, beyond the sky, to the invisible country far away!
>
> (57 p. 773)

This is less clearly defined than the image it sets out to explain, suggesting that the Christian theology of eternal love with which Dickens is at pains to invest his symbol is also nebulous. The reader remains as much at a loss as Paul himself to explain 'why the sea should make me think of my Mama that's dead' (12 p. 217). She dies far from the sea and Paul is unaware of the narratorial figure of speech that connects them. Carey's objection to Dickens's 'making metaphysical noises about his stage properties, instead of letting the objects ... exist for themselves'[10] could be sustained here, but fault found with the commentary does not deny the potency of the symbols themselves.

II. *Little Dorrit*

In *Little Dorrit* the river is a much more visible part of the environment in which the characters live, whether gazed upon by Amy at Southwark Bridge or by Arthur at Twickenham. The latter at least still tends to interpret it metaphorically, seeing the inevitable passage of time embodied in its unalterable course:

> He softly opened his window, and looked out upon the serene river. Year after year so much allowance for the drifting of the ferry-boat, so many miles an hour the flowing of the stream. ... And he thought – who has not thought for a moment, sometimes – that it might be better to flow away monotonously, like the river, and

to compound for its insensibility to happiness with its insensibility to pain.

(I 16 pp. 194–7)

Here, however, the death by water called for by the Thames seems more like suicide. Clennam sees the order underlying it as indifferent and the river beckons to oblivion rather than Heaven.

When Arthur later launches the rose petals given to him by Pet onto the river and watches them floating towards 'the eternal seas' (I 28 p. 320), he is consigning them too to oblivion. They represent neo-adolescent fantasies and aspirations that must now be forgotten in a surrender of immature hopes similar to those made in *Dombey and Son*. While the river promises no reward for such renunciation and plays no part towards providing it at the level of plot, its description at this point at least suggests peace and order:

> the little green islands in the river, the beds of rushes, the water-lillies floating on the surface of the stream, the distant voices in boats borne musically towards him on the ripple of the water and the evening air, were all expressive of rest.
>
> (p. 325)

Clennam's direct response to the stimulus of an immediately present Thames suggests, more powerfully than pages of *Dombey*-style authorial commentary upon an absent symbol, that the river contains lessons of renunciation and surrender to a Providential plan. This in turn creates a firmer sense that these truths are part of the intrinsic laws of the novel's world. The narrator emphasises the inseparable unity of the river's reflection of reality and the reality itself:

> Between the real landscape and its shadow in the water, there was no division; both were so untroubled and clear, and, while so fraught with solemn mystery of life and death, so hopefully re-assuring to the gazer's soothed heart, because so tenderly and mercifully beautiful.
>
> (p. 326)

The river is still conveying a 'solemn mystery', then, but here it is in complete unity with the rest of the novel's world, which it organically reflects.

Mostly, however, *Little Dorrit* privileges the bare passage of time amongst the river's traditional messages over the motif of baptismal rebirth it conveys in *Dombey and Son*. Indeed with its 'silent warehouses and wharves' (I 3 p. 31), it functions as a place of gothic burial rather than resurrection, collaborating in the general concealment of Mrs Clennam and her ilk. Its aspect seems unrelentingly obscure and confused from Southwark Bridge, where 'the wilderness of masts on the river and the wilderness of steeples on the shore' are 'indistinctly mixed together in the stormy haze' (I 9 p. 94). The river seems to leave it to other natural phenomena with traditional symbolic associations, such as the wind, to suggest the continued presence of life in Dickens's London as it moves towards the transformation of its cityscape.[11]

Little Dorrit subsumes the Thames not into the abstract symbol of the sea, but into the concrete symbol of the city, making it the defining equator between North and South London:

> the secrets of the river, as it rolled its turbid tide between two frowning wildernesses of secrets
>
> (*LD* II 10 p. 526)

From nowhere else is there such a sense of being surrounded by the capital. This is consolidated in Dickens's journalism of this period. As the Uncommercial Traveller puts it, 'The very shadow of the immensity of London seemed to lie oppressively on the river.'[12] 'Down with the Tide', written four years before *Little Dorrit*, sees the river as an extension of London's impenetrable labyrinth:

> the tiers of shipping, whose many hulls, lying close together, rose out of the water like black streets.[13]

Therefore the Thames has as great a capacity for hiding incriminating things as the darkest slum: 'River thieves can always get rid of stolen property in a moment by dropping it overboard'. 'On Duty with Inspector Field' portrays the author as fascinated with these mysteries, but adds that, to such keepers of information as the detective, even these things are well known:

> *He* does not trouble his head as I do, about the river at night. *He* does not care for its creeping, black and silent, on our right there, ... hiding strange things in its mud.[14]

Equally, when Dickens launches into the embryonic version of the *Little Dorrit* passage noted above, the Thames Police officer merely coughs in boredom. The river in passages like these sides decidedly with the city's bewildering dirt, attempting to hide guilt, unacknowledged obligations and severed relationships. It is ranged against the figure of the detective, who, in the form of Field or Bucket seems able to penetrate even the obscurities of the Thames. This is quite consistent with the more modest form of transcendence on offer in *Little Dorrit* whereby transformation of the cityscape into Christian altruism is subjective, if not less real for that. The Thames can sink things into oblivion, whether for good or ill, but mature renunciation to its waters is its own hard-won reward. The more muted world of this novel suppresses its traditional function of speaking about any glorious country on the other side.

III. Great Expectations

In *Signs for the Times*, Chris Brooks highlights an advance in Dickens's symbolic method by contrasting the river in *Dombey and Son* with the fog in *Bleak House*:

> In the earlier novels, the river ... symbolises personal time: the river is also, within the conventions of realism, real. Symbolic mediation – the sign standing between us and what is signified – and realist immediacy, forcefully held in the same entity, do not surrender their basic natures. They form, in effect, an amalgam. But in *Bleak House* fog cannot be said to symbolise opacity as the river symbolises personal time. It is precisely because the river is not, *in itself*, an instance of the operation of personal time that the mediatory nature of symbolism still obtains, while its presence in a realist medium gives its emblematic meaning immediacy. Fog, however, is, *in itself*, opaque: that is, connotation and denotation, metaphoric meaning and realist meaning are not amalgamated but synthesised.[15]

Dombey and Son's presentation of the Thames is almost entirely mediatory and only rarely realistic. While its stronger physical presence in *Little Dorrit* allows it to do whatever symbolic work is required of it more economically, however, it still appears rather to belong to Brooks's amalgam than to his 'synthesis' since the link between tenor and vehicle is only thematic. When connoting the burial of secrets, however, it moves closer to the method of realistic exemplification. The Thames actually does have secrets buried in it, although none of the major secrets of the story itself are found there. Brooks, however, could have pointed to the Thames in Dickens's final two novels for his contrast with the methods at work in the river of the earlier fiction. Here, Dickens gives it an inherent fitness for its symbolic connotation still more authoritative than that given to the fog in *Bleak House* by incorporating it into the plot itself.

In *Great Expectations*, the Thames provides a constant link between Pip's London self and his suppressed past on the 'low leaden line' that is the edge of the Thames estuary (I 1 p. 4). Out of this environment, the menacing convict arises to threaten the boy and from it he re-surfaces upon his return from Australia. It is also, however, his attempted means of escape. The threat of inexorably re-emerging truths is thus brilliantly connected with the struggle to conceal them again by means of Pip's plan to hide Magwitch in the river from the boggy margins of which he first emerged.

Wemmick neatly summarises one of the river's functions in Dickens's world in a metaphor about Jaggers's somewhat dangerous ability to hide knowledge:

> A river's its natural depth, and he's his natural depth.
>
> (II 6 p. 205)

Depth implies inaccessibility and obscurity and Jaggers exploits the complexities of his London world to prevent truth from emerging. The lawyer's whole manner of speech aims at the concealment of all facts – even innocuous ones. Even in casual conversation, the Thames is a constant reminder that secrets are being kept.

When Pip becomes a concealer of secrets in his own right, the landscape of the river-city uniquely suits his purposes. Chinks's Basin is difficult enough for him to find, let alone a pursuer, surrounded as it is by a multiplicity of unknown names. Furthermore, the river's debris and hazards demand great skill from anyone seeking to navigate it:

> avoiding rusty chain-cables frayed hempen hawsers and bobbing buoys, sinking for the moment floating broken baskets, scattering floating chips of wood and shaving, cleaving floating scum of coal ...
>
> (III 15 p. 432)

Impossibly huge figureheads decorate the ships in this surreal nightmare obstacle course. Many participles suggest continual movement:

> hammers going in ship-builders' yards, saws going at timber, clashing engines going at things unknown, pumps going in leaky ships, capstans going ...
>
> (III 15 p. 432)

Magwitch's hiding place, however, is filled with half-personified after-effects of such activity:

> rusty anchors blindly biting into the ground ... a series of wooden frames ... that looked like superannuated haymaking rakes which had grown old and lost most of their teeth.
>
> (III 17 p. 372)

As in *Little Dorrit*, the cityscape points out the life-denying effects of concealment.

The widespread images of decrepitude and disability suggest loss of power on a societal scale. Indeed London resembles nothing more than a multiple shipwreck:

> stranded ships repairing in dry docks ... old hulls of ships in course of being knocked to pieces ... ooze and slime and other dregs of tide.
>
> (p. 371)

Pip the storyteller has already chosen the image of the shipwreck to express the death of his hopes regarding Estella:

> I began fully to know how wrecked I was, and how the ship in which I had sailed was gone to pieces.
>
> (II 20 p. 320)

This vessel in which he has put his confidence is his identity as Miss Havisham's adopted son, groomed to marry the adopted daughter. The discovery that no such person ever existed is as devastating to his hopes as the sinking of *The Son and Heir* to Cuttle's ambition for Walter as Dombey's adopted son, scheduled to marry the boss's daughter. Although Gay's shipwreck is more literal, it takes place offstage. In this novel, where Pip's downfall is explored directly, London's omnipresent decomposing ships magnify the image that figures it on to a huge urban context. The riverscape echoes his surrender to the utter collapse of the futile self-enclosed world he has chosen in place of his true connections with home and family. *The Waste Land* follows Dickens in making the shipwreck a key image for the whole capital, a huge and fragmented environment to evoke the experience of being utterly lost and broken.

There is no shortage of actual deaths on the Thames. Some meet a violent end in the river. Others throw the bodies of their murdered victims there. The form of death most readily associated with the

Thames, however, is suicide. Examples abound of the river exerting a deathbound attraction for men and women, especially fallen women. Nancy feels that she must eventually 'spring into the tide' (*OT* 46 p. 316). Martha in *David Copperfield* exclaims, 'It haunts me day and night.' The scenery on its banks as she prepares to jump resembles the ship-wreck seen by Pip:

> carcases of houses [which had] rotted away [and] rusty iron monsters of steam-boilers, wheels, cranks, pipes, furnaces, paddles, anchors, diving-bells, windmill-sails, and I know not what strange objects ...
>
> (p. 580)

Resting in peace is unlikely for those who throw themselves into this hellish world. Objects have 'the appearance of vainly trying to hide themselves', echoing the individual's desire to be forgotten in eternal oblivion. Suicide in the Thames is a self-imposed death by water with no prospect of or desire for regeneration, yet which denies a satisfying end to disgrace. Pip's submergence of himself and Magwitch (who is responsible for originating his London self as Pip the gentleman) in this deathly landscape may be a suicide in this tradition.

Nevertheless, as in *Dombey and Son* and *Little Dorrit*, the river itself is still sometimes required to act as a somewhat fatalistic embodiment of the certainty of the narrative, bringing about events at a predetermined time. Pip initially feels that it is inevitably transporting Magwitch out of urban imprisonment:

> the moving river itself – the road that ran with us, seeming to sym-pathize with us, animate us, and encourage us on – freshened me with new hope.
>
> (*GE* III 15 p. 431)

There follows a list of far away locations for which the surrounding ship-ping is bound, including 'Rotterdam' and 'Hamburg', suggesting that this traveller too should be able to escape. Whereas, however, Paul Dombey's visionary river travels towards a sea of love and release, the Thames, as it affects young Pip's imagination, flows towards confine-ment and imprisonment. He pictures himself 'drifting down the river on a strong springtide, to the Hulks' (I 2 p. 15). This dream is actualised many years later with the failure of Magwitch's flight. Nowhere in Dickens's fiction is the capability for the Thames to stand for escape to transcendence or even a future of freedom so ambiguous. Pip's negative view of its course contrasts strikingly with the more optimistic perspective of Herbert, who

> had sometimes said to me that he found it pleasant to stand at one of our windows after dark, when the tide was running down, and to think it was flowing, with everything it bore, towards Clara. But I thought with dread that it was flowing towards Magwitch, and that any black mark on its surface might be his pursuers, going swiftly, silently, and surely, to take him.
>
> (III 7 p. 378)

As the River Police catch up with the fugitives, Pip's perspective is proven correct. The Thames was only 'seeming to sympathise' after all. Although release may be striven for and suggested, in this darker novel, it is not to be found.

Here the river has an advantage over the railway as an emblem of fate and the narrative force: it has a tide that can suddenly turn. One minute it supports the travellers, the next they must fight against it. Pip himself uses the river metaphorically to describe the events of the chase:

> we returned towards the setting sun we had yesterday left behind us, and ... the stream of our hopes seemed all running back.
>
> (III 15 p. 443)

This turns out to be literally true, the tides ultimately preventing Magwitch's escape. Now the river actually determines events and consequently shapes the plot. It is not only *like* the passage of time, it *is* the passage of time – and it is running out:

> I was a thinking through my smoke just then, that we can no more see to the bottom of the next few hours, than we can see to the bottom of this river what I catches hold of. Nor yet we can't no more hold their tide than I can hold this. And it's run through my fingers and gone, you see!
>
> (III 15 p. 434)

Magwitch here shows an understanding of both aspects of the river's function in the novel, its impenetrability and its irresistibility. Its significance is so forcefully apprehended that the characters in the story fashion metaphors from it as a natural way of discussing their world.

Both the message and the method of the river symbolism in *Great Expectations* are very different from that in *Dombey and Son*. If there has been a death by water in the Eliotian sense in the later novel, it is displaced on to Magwitch, who is submerged in his struggle with Compeyson and dies shortly afterwards. With this would-be father figure gone, Pip must refashion his identity as Jo's 'son' after all. He must emulate his brother-in-law's example of achieving selfhood through generous spirited love and conscientious effort, rather than having it conferred upon him from outside. Initially he seeks to make of Biddy a personal heroine to play the part of Florence Dombey or Little Dorrit in pointing the way to the renewed system of relationships through marital love. This is ultimately denied to him. At the end it is highly ambiguous whether he finds such a figure in the reformed Estella. *Great Expectations* seems determined to confront the possibility that the surrendered dreams will *not* be returned after the death by water.

IV. *Our Mutual Friend*

Dickens's final completed novel returns to *Dombey and Son*'s willingness to invest the river with transformative significance. Here not one man, but two go through a death by water experience and find resurrection into a new life with the aid of women who love them disinterestedly. It is not merely a re-statement of the earlier novel's determined optimism about what the river image says to mankind. Dickens has adapted the refinements of symbolic method explored in the intervening books. The lesson learned in *Little Dorrit* of making the Thames central to a whole metropolis of gothic secrecy influences its representation here. The tactic in *Great Expectations* of incorporating the symbolic environment directly into the plot is also crucial to *Our Mutual Friend*. Furthermore, Dickens rigorously examines the river's failures to signify in a religious way as well as its successes, consciously interacting with numerous modes of representing it from different discourses.

   Our Mutual Friend has plenty to say about the river but it is a filthy river. 'The golden water ... on the wall' of *Dombey and Son* (24 p. 340) is absent from Jenny Wren's visitations of the supernatural community, which constitute *Our Mutual Friend*'s equivalent to Paul Dombey's visions. The uncompromising unpleasantness of the Thames seems to suggest not only that Dickens has done with this method altogether, but that the chilly world below the sheltered environment of Pubsey's roof mocks any striving after transcendence.

   In placing this river at the imaginative centre of his London, Dickens anticipates the method and themes of *The Waste Land*. Both writers use the polluted but still flowing river to diagnose a whole society in need of renewal, let down even by its traditional symbols of regeneration. Sometimes this has the effect of elevating the modern capital to participation in a timeless scheme, but mostly the grimness of the subject matter hints that the mythic archetypes are now impotent, if they ever had any power at all. The resistance of the Thames to signification in this novel is especially visible when considered in dialogue with the confident adoption of London's river to invest it with religious meaning in the earlier fiction. As Adrian Poole says in his introduction to the Penguin Classics edition, in this truly post-Darwinian novel:

> There is a quickened curiosity about the force of biblical tales and the credibility of their teachings. Indeed one of the most fraught questions about this novel is the status of its religious allusions and associations. Are they living or dead? Or are they, like so much else in this fictional world, suspended between the two?[16]

Having identified these similarities of concern and method, it is tempting to see in, say, Gaffer Hexham another modernised Fisher king or Ferdinand, Prince of Naples:

> fishing in the dull canal
> On a winter evening round behind the gashouse
> Musing upon the king my brother's wreck
>
> (ll. 189–91)

We might read him as another metropolitan quester unconsciously echoing mythic archetypes and proving by his seediness their inadequacy for the modern age. This, however, is to apply the terms of criticism on T. S. Eliot to a writer unfamiliar with Frazerian anthropology. Yet Dickens's Thames was interacting with one religious symbol whose meaning was vigorously contested in his society at the time of writing – that of Christian baptism.

When Gaffer drowns, he is said to be 'baptized unto Death' (I 14 p. 175). Carey indignantly calls this 'a misrememberance of Paul's phrase in *Romans* about being baptized into Christ's death' and denounces the whole baptism/re-emergence theme as a 'similar, and similarly unfortunate bid for religious significance' as the theme of self-sacrifice in *A Tale of Two Cities*.[17] Yet Dickens has not drastically misquoted the wording of Romans 6:3–4:

> Know ye not, that so many of us as were baptized into Jesus Christ were baptized into his death?

> Therefore we are buried with him by baptism into death: that like as Christ was raised up from the dead by the glory of the Father, even so we also should walk in newness of life.

Early Christians' baptism signified the death of their old way of life, which they identified with Christ's death on behalf of their old sinful self. Their re-emergence from the water signified the beginning of a new eternal life commencing with their salvation and made possible by Christ's resurrection. While Sicher reads his passage optimistically, saying 'This allusion to a passage central to the baptismal rite might hint that Hexham ... too might not be beyond the reach of atonement',[18] the contrast between the rite and the metropolitan reality that evokes it seems too great to be much more than ironic. Just as Eliot quotes ironically, for example from Spenser, to highlight the tawdriness of today's Thames in contrast to its past significance, so Dickens's (mis?) quotes biblical water imagery to ironic effect. The phrase is part of the mocking call of the winds:

> Was it you, thus baptized unto death, with these flying impurities now flung upon your face?
>
> *Our Mutual Friend* (I 14 p. 175)

Gaffer's immersion in such filthy water makes a nonsense of any hope that it can represent any form of cleansing or a spiritual death from which one can emerge into newness of life.

When Rogue Riderhood is almost killed by the steamboat, undefined baptismal associations give his daughter hope that his death by water will have a renewing and converting effect:

> some vague idea that the old evil is drowned out of him, and that if he should happily come back to resume his occupation of the empty form that lies upon the bed, his spirit will be altered.
>
> (III 3 p. 441)

Unfortunately, however, it is the 'low, bad, unimpressible face' that is 'coming up from the depths of the river, or what other depths, to the surface again' (III 3 p. 441) and he is reluctantly reborn into the same oldness of life. Although the Thames suggests a resurrection archetype to Pleasant Riderhood, the text cruelly denies its availability.

Other Biblical references casually allude to themes of submergence and resurrection. Charley Hexham says of the man he believes to be John Harmon, 'If Lazarus was only half as far gone, that was the greatest of all the miracles' (I 3 p. 28). Charley then relates the body to

'Pharaoh's multitude, that were drowned in the Red Sea'. Wrayburn's surprise that the boy is conversant with such phrases and that he applies them to the sordid events at Limehouse draws attention very markedly to these allusions. Readers familiar with their Bibles, however, would remember that although the Egyptians were drowned in the waters, as Gaffer has been in the Thames, the Israelites passed through triumphantly. Paul explicitly reads this as a type of the experience now symbolised in believer's baptism:

> All our fathers ... passed through the sea; And were all baptized unto Moses
>
> (1 Corinthians 10:2)

Are modern human beings too far gone for great miracles as in Charley's analysis? If such allusions are not debased by being put into the boy's mouth, but are startling hints of the scriptural positives that go along with these negatives, how does Dickens propose to restore their potency and relevance to the nineteenth-century urbanite?

Interestingly, in a letter to Walter Savage Landor in 1841, Dickens said that the 'realities had gone out of the ceremony' of baptism and that its chief function was now social.[19] It is hard to know what realities Dickens considered baptism once to have had and why he felt it had lost them. His remark and the baptismal dimension to his imagery must be understood in the context of lively public debate amongst Christians on the significance of the ritual during the mid-Victorian era. Tractarians and other High Church Anglicans saw the sacrament itself as the time when God's grace regenerated the sinner. Evangelicals saw it as merely an outward symbol of an inner change that had already taken place in a believer. Many felt that the radical alteration of the ceremony in the traditional churches into the form of infant sprinkling before conversion robbed it of its signifying power on two counts. Firstly, its changed form emphasised only the secondary element of cleansing, whereas immersion baptism also emphasised the primary aspect of burial, new life and hope of resurrection. Secondly, the relationship between sign and reality had been altered. A baby had not yet experienced any such change as that which gives the act significance in the writings of Paul and some would never experience this as a personal reality to the end of their days. They were especially concerned that the statement that babies became 'partakers of the Divine Nature' on the strength of this action was gravely misleading about salvation. Those of the less defined Broad Church grouping within the Church of England tended to see mankind in general as redeemed irrespective of belief and viewed baptism of whatever type as a re-enactment of Christ's divine cleansing at Calvary.

Anglican clergymen who agreed with Evangelical doctrine somewhat uncomfortably justified their requirement to perform christenings by claiming them as a hopeful hypothesis of a new birth the child would come to experience. If they challenged the Established Church's position directly, they could experience strong resistance from the bishops. This prompted Dickens's most substantial direct contribution to the public debate on baptism. When the episcopal appointment of an Evangelical Anglican clergyman, George Gorham, was opposed because he taught that regeneration did not come through the ceremony but by faith, Dickens published a piece entitled 'The Three Kingdoms', expressing the strongest support for him in the *Household Narrative of Current Events*. The writer's condemnation is directed towards the Church's intolerance of a different view and the implication that only Anglican baptism could guarantee regeneration. Nevertheless, that Dickens published an article so uncharacteristically and unreservedly sympathetic to an Evangelical's position suggests that to him whatever power baptism had resided in what it could represent rather than in the ritual itself.

The only baptism depicted at any length in Dickens's novels is little Paul's in *Dombey and Son*, which is more like a funeral. Although this is a christening, the writer takes the trouble to invest it with meanings of death and surrender more readily associated with immersion baptism, because these themes are associated with water in this novel. Tellingly, in order to make him aware that he is going through a symbolic burial, Paul has to be given the superimposed reactions of a much older man. Upon being brought into the church, he 'might have asked with Hamlet "into my grave?" so chill and earthy was the place' (5 p. 58). Mr Dombey, however, is completely oblivious to this significance:

> It might have been well for Mr Dombey, if he had thought of his own dignity a little less; and had thought of the great origin and purpose of the ceremony in which he took so formal and so stiff a part, a little more.
>
> (5 p. 60)

This sentence was inserted after Forster suggested that readers might see the chapter as a mockery of Christening *per se*,[20] but it does indicate that the ritual has something to convey to Dombey if he were willing to hear it.

His refusal to listen is continuous in Dickens's imaginative vision with his inability to hear what the waves are always saying. While Gaffer's 'baptism' is so called by an ironical narrator, it suggests an inaccessible meaning to those who are present. Eugene has an inexplicable sensation of *déja vu* in reverse, as though it were his own body floating in the Thames. He exclaims, 'I feel as if I had been half drowned' (I 13 p. 166), as he will be later on. This lends an air of preordained inevitability to the events of the fourth book. In *The Waste Land*, the host of verbal echoes of Madame Sosostris's warning to 'fear death by water' (ll. 43–55)[21] offers the tantalising suggestion that all may be happening to some supernaturally underwritten narrative plan and that each person's experience may have a meaning intelligible in terms of universal archetypes. For Wrayburn, the river can suggest only that death by water is terrifyingly inevitable. In this anthropomorphic world, even the ships have a 'fell intention' and the depth markers seem to say, 'That's to drown *you* in, my dears':

> Not a lumbering black barge, with its cracked and blistered side impending over them, but seemed to suck at the river with a thirst for sucking them under. And everything so vaunted the spoiling influences of water ... that the after-consequences of being crushed, sucked under, and drawn down, looked as ugly to the imagination as the main event.
>
> (I 14 p. 173)

No possibility of re-emergence is suggested and any transformation by this river will not be into anything positive. When the Thames can evoke death so effectively, there is less need to evoke the sea and the lack of flow alone threatens to make the river seem more stagnant than in previous novels.

The surrounding cityscape offers Dickens's characteristic blend of gothic decay and social comment. Here London's deathbound collapse is presented at its most hopeless:

> Very little life was to be seen on either bank, windows and doors were shut, and the staring black and white letters upon wharves and warehouses 'looked,' said Eugene to Mortimer, 'like inscriptions over the graves of dead businesses.'
>
> (pp. 172–3)

Likewise, Gaffer's home is a mill that has fallen out of use and now has 'a look of decomposition' (I 3 p. 31). East London – especially that part of it whose life is organised around the river – is clearly in need of economic regeneration at least. The river holds a particular attraction for the hopelessly poor, crying:

> Come to me, come to me! ... I am the Relieving Officer appointed by eternal ordinance to do my work; ... death in my arms is peacefuller than among the pauper-wards.
>
> (III 8 p. 497)

Again death by water here seems rather suicidal than baptismal.

If poverty, as riverborne traders failed to make a living, is one reason why life on the Thames is so precarious in these passages, another is the attendant evil of dirt. Because the river contained so much contaminated matter, the risk of disease to those living nearby was enormous. The social reformer in Dickens had been outraged by the pitiful conditions of riverside areas in these years – especially as the Board of Health had seen fit to flush the sewers into the Thames in 1849. One letter complains of the resultant 'offensive smells ... of a most head-and-stomach distracting nature'.[22] Rotherhithe is described as 'a dark corner, river-washed and otherwise not washed at all' (I 3 p. 30). As we have seen, dirt led very naturally to criminality in the minds of Victorian reformers. Moreover, human beings have been flushed from the rest of the city to Rotherhithe

> where accumulated scum of humanity seemed to be washed from higher grounds, like so much moral sewage, and to be pausing until its own weight forced it over the bank and sunk it in the river.
>
> (I 3 p. 30)

Dickens has to an extent adopted the language of the doomed residuum favoured by post-Darwinian humanists, but his phrases here raise uncomfortable questions about how this criminality with its self-destructive tendencies has been generated. The daily life of even the most respectable parts of London seem to create this sewage filling the Thames as a natural outcome of their selfish way of life. Reluctant to take responsibility for this, they, like the Board, flush it out of sight, where it festers in an unnatural concentration.

Dickens had addressed this in *David Copperfield* where Martha stands in a similar landscape and the narrator observes that it looked 'as if it had gradually decomposed into that nightmare condition, out of the overflowings of the polluted stream' (*DC* 47 p. 580). She is seen as 'part of the refuse' and tends (until rescued by the forgiving confidence reposed in her by David and Mr Peggotty) towards flushing herself into the river. Indeed, she sees in its urban dirtiness a metaphor for her own history:

> It comes from country places, where there was once no harm in it – and it creeps through the dismal streets, defiled and miserable – and it goes away, like my life, to a great sea, that is always troubled – and I feel that I must go with it!
>
> (47 p. 581)

The river, standing as always for the inevitable passage of time towards death, is not benign, nor merely indifferent as in *Little Dorrit*, but decisively harmful. It represents the process by which a person passes from innocence to experience. Dickens often personifies it as having a 'cradle' in the countryside and a 'grave' in the sea and as 'acquiring ... various experience' as it passes through the contaminating city in between.[23] *Our Mutual Friend* demonstrates its continued commitment to this view of the metropolitan river, saying of the Surrey and Berkshire reaches:

> In those pleasant little towns on Thames, you may hear the fall of the water over the weirs ... and from the bridge you may see the young river, dimpled like a young child, playfully gliding away among the trees, unpolluted by the defilements that lie in wait for it on its course, and as yet out of hearing of the deep summons of the sea.
>
> (III 8 p. 497)

There is nothing particularly original in this literary commonplace, which promotes the simplistic city-is-bad and country-is-good scheme of the earlier novel. Dickens's representation of these defilements once the river reaches London is, however, tremendously powerful. The Thames now becomes a force as powerful as the fog in *Bleak House* to blur all proper categories of things. It washes over the surrounding city eroding distinction as it goes, even between 'vessels that seemed to have got ashore, and houses that seemed to have got afloat' (I 3 p. 30).

If these waters are unlikely to signify regeneration, there is also little indication that they can offer revelation. The metropolis of this book is an ideal place for keeping secrets, a disorienting place that sucks its inhabitants into a bewildering river where human beings become objects without identity and everything is robbed of its context. Bradley Headstone is one among many who seeks to use the river's opacity to bury information about his guilt and thus becomes one of Dickens's last urban concealers. The muddy river is ranged against the figure of the detective here and shows a city divided between its geography and its institutions. Ironically, however, the Thames shows the duality associated throughout Dickens with all forms of dirt and gothic veiling – it can be exploited by the concealer, but can also undermine him. Indeed, Bradley becomes terrified of what the river will wash up. In a novel which begins with the unnerving trade of converting what is buried in the river into monetary value there is always the risk that evidence buried in one place will be washed up into unwelcome hands at another. It seems, then, that the river can at least resume its role as agent of narrative justice, even if, for Bradley, at any rate, this is far from benign.

It would be interesting to know how exactly Mayhew would have classified 'waterside characters' like Riderhood and Hexham. He certainly gives a full account of the mudlarks, who scoured the waters for fuel and lost goods to sell to the poor. Gaffer only extends this principle a little in making money from the retrieval of corpses. He is a skilled fisherman, trawling the depths for shoals that only he understands:

> there was no clue to what he looked for, but he looked for something, with a most intent and searching gaze.
>
> (p. 13)

When his own corpse must be fished out of the river, his role is taken over by Mr Inspector, allying him with one of the few clarifying forces in the novel. He is also at pains to stress that the river can transform dead matter into something of value. Sicher comments on this link established between the two characters, claiming them as a metaphor for the novelist's role in retrieving metropolitan phenomena from de-individuating death so that it may again signify meaningfully:

> This secular resurrection restores the body to meaning as semantic sign in the plot and in the city's necropolis.[24]

Personifying it as 'your oldest friend', Gaffer defensively tells Lizzie of a kind of sea change its touch has effected:

> The very fire that warmed you when you were a babby, was picked out of the river alongside the coal barges. The very basket that you

slept in, the tide washed ashore. The very rockers that I put it upon to make a cradle of it, I cut out of a piece of wood that drifted from some ship or another.

(I 1 p. 15)

Extraordinarily, sodden city debris can be turned into a fire or 'meat and drink'. That this should be obtainable from the decaying human flesh and rubbish of the Thames sickens Lizzie. Like most other Londoners, she and her father must sustain life without being overwhelmed by disgust at their means of doing so. Their livelihood capitalises on the deaths and losses of others and the same is true in less obvious ways of other urbanites in the novel, whose every advantage comes from the disadvantage of another. Mr Venus, London's premier 'Articulator of human bones' (I 7 p. 89), provides a further example of the city's desperate attempts to re-animate the dead in trade.[25] He appears to be the closest thing in this novel to the revivifying wind, providing T. S. Eliot's 'rattle of the bones', if not the 'chuckle spread from ear to ear' (l. 186). His raw materials are found 'down at the water-side' (III 7 p. 492). As in *The Waste Land*, there are some Londoners who yearn to represent a resurrecting power that the city is too shabby and decayed to be part of. In spite of his down to earth nature, Gaffer's fishing for corpses is symptomatic of a desire to invest the Thames with meaning.

To all appearances, however, Gaffer belongs firmly to the world of death rather than new life. He resembles the corpses he finds, 'Half savage as the man showed, with no covering on his matted head' (I 1 p. 13). Even his boat is 'Allied to the bottom of the river rather than the surface, by reason of the slime and ooze with which it was covered' (I 1 p. 13). His daughter's horror at the work threatens to undermine belief in its value, as do Riderhood's constant accusations. The lack of value placed upon his own body at its retrieval seems to be the final proof that the dirty river of this metropolis cannot bear even the modest significance he seeks to attach to it.

And yet the dredging of the body in the first chapter does represent a sort of rebirth. Although it is not really his own corpse, John Harmon's supposed death allows him to re-evaluate the life he has inherited from his father, with its fortune acquired from the dustheaps and loveless automatic marriage to Bella. Taking advantage of the confusion he resolves to be dead and to begin anew: 'So John Harmon died ... and John Rokesmith was born' (II 13 p. 366). The difficulty of this process is figured not only by his struggle to escape from the river, but also by his disorientation in the complex labyrinth of the metropolis during which he recounts this experience:

> He tried a new direction, but made nothing of it; walls, dark doorways, flights of stairs and rooms, were too abundant. And, like most people so puzzled, he again and again described a circle, and found himself at the point from which he had begun.
>
> (II 13 p. 359)

Dickens blends the death by water image with the larger motif of being lost in London. Having undergone such an experience, the crucial question of the novel then becomes 'John Harmon is dead. Should John Harmon come to life?' It is only when he resumes his own identity as John Harmon, married to Bella and having received the inheritance after all, that the transformation becomes obvious. As in *Dombey and Son*, the surrendered dream is returned – but is very different in the light of a changed personality. The same could be said of Bella, whose materialistic dreams are destroyed with Harmon's supposed drowning and restored to her once she is capable of correctly valuing them. The self-conscious artificiality of Boffin acting as *deus ex machina* to embody the narrative and bring her to this point, however, seems to underline a suspicion of the improbability of a teleological scheme while it cheerfully dramatises its desirability.

This plot, however, is not merely a reassuring repetition of a classic archetype, but a searching exploration of how the individual may fit into the exchange-based mechanism of the city without losing individual moral agency. As Ephraim Sicher puts it, 'the major symbolic patterns of this novel place [Harmon's] staged death and "resurrection" in a mythical mode that nonetheless loses none of its contemporary social relevance, not least for the question of moral and personal identity in the city'.[26] As the story progresses, these events become a precursor to the even more striking transformation of Eugene Wrayburn from idle *flaneur* to a responsible gentleman. This is the book's real focus and Eugene's death by water is directly described as part of the present action of the plot. He too realises that the life handed down from his 'Respected Father' is worthless, but does not know with what to replace it. His own death by water is the turning point for him as he realises who he is, what his long buried values are and how he truly relates to those around him (which only Twemlow in the whole of 'Society' seems to grasp with him). The use to which Lizzie puts her knowledge of her father's trade as she fishes him out of the river finally validates Hexham's sense of its value. It was in those distasteful urban waters that she learned the skills that enable her to pull Eugene from the Thames further upstream, so that she can at last exclaim:

> Now, merciful Heaven be thanked for that old time, enabling me, without a wasted moment, to have got the boat afloat again, and to row back against the stream!
>
> (IV 6 p. 684)

A transformation of the cityscape of a very different sort has occurred. What had seemed grimy, cheerless and deathly in the activities of London is actually a divine gift for the restoration of life.

Lizzie's act of retrieval from the waters here is presented as bearing a religious significance as she seeks to sanctify her skills to a dependable higher power. Unusually in Dickens, we are given the wording of her prayer, 'help my humble hands, Lord God, to raise it from death and restore it' (IV 6 p. 683), and, once she has retrieved it, she adds:

> And grant, O Blessed Lord God, that through poor me he may be raised from death, and preserved ...
>
> (p. 684)

She sees the salvation she brings as a Divine action by human hands, revealing the symbolic significance of a drowning in the river: the death and burial of self-interest and the surrender to saving love. This exemplifies J. Hillis Miller's remark that 'Though they do not express orthodox Christian doctrine, Dickens's novels are religious in that they demand the regeneration of man and society through contact with something transcending the merely human'.[27]

Eugene's struggle to regain consciousness is figured as an essential part of his death by water. Initially, he is 'insensible, if not virtually dead' (IV 6 p. 683). Lizzie nurses him through the 'frequent rising of a drowning man from the deep' (IV 10 p. 721) in a scene that recalls the dying Paul in *Dombey and Son* in the symbolic work it requires the Thames to do:

> A darkened and hushed room; the river outside the windows flowing on to the vast ocean ...
>
> (IV 10 p. 717)

Florence-like, Lizzie's 'presence and her touch upon his breast or face' (p. 721) is able to restore him to consciousness. Again the dying person is taught to confide in an angel figure revealing a Providential scheme of drowning and transcendence beyond.[28] Lizzie herself has learned the value of surrender in the call to 'Come up and be dead!' (II 5 p. 280) even in the heart of the busy city and now she creates a similarly tranquil environment for Wrayburn.

She does not nurse him back to his old life, but to a radically altered one. Her patience – developed in her years as a waterman's daughter in London – prepares her for this moment when she can rescue Eugene not merely from these depths of the river, but also from the depths of his former indolent and egocentric nature. Eugene's first act upon coming to himself is to urge Lightwood to let his enemy escape, fearing that Headstone's arrest will reveal facts that could harm Lizzie. In a manner paralleling Christian theology, his baptism and its accompanying experience has killed his old identity and recreated him in the character of his saviour. Although Dickens never publicly identifies Christ's death with his own in this redemptive way, the Christian disciple's rebirth in the personality of Christ seems to have struck a chord in his imagination.

Interestingly, the 'sure touch of her old practised hand' (IV 6 p. 683) provides the same image as T. S. Eliot chooses to represent surrender to the controlling power of love:

> *Damyata*: the boat responded
> Gaily, to the hand expert with sail and oar
> The sea was calm, your heart would have responded
> Gaily, when invited, beating obedient
> To controlling hands
>
> (ll. 418–22)[29]

In the boat now floating upon the formerly submerging waters, Eliot has captured perfectly the effects of the yearned-for surrender to a resurrecting power that has been lost in a London environment where people settle for a sterile world without it. Because of the vessel's submission to careful steering, it may sail purposefully on the river rather than being wrecked in it. Critical tradition has been quick to see this control as that of divine love operating in human relationships, which has been ignored in the London world. George Williamson, for example, reads the phrase 'beating obedient' (l. 421) as a 'response of the heart ... to the will' as distinct from the 'blood shaking' it (l. 402) in response to physical lust, meeting 'the conditions of ascent to higher love ... which would relieve [the Wastelanders'] anguish. These commands have all been violated in the Waste Land'.[30]

Strangely, Eliot's critics have tended to assume an inherent transcendental meaning in the use of the image in *The Waste Land*, but Dickens's have not tended to read Lizzie's expert hand as a religious symbol. Perhaps this is because it has a localised narrative context in the novel, whereas in the poem the image is isolated in a fragment of the interpretation of the Thunder's sibyllic utterance. Perhaps also the overtly didactic purpose causes us to focus on the human example rather than the divine assistance. Moreover, whereas *The Waste Land* mainly focuses on the surrender of the drowned man as a model for imitation, *Our Mutual Friend* invites the reader to emulate the controller, Lizzie, as well as the responder to control, Eugene Wrayburn.

Nevertheless, as earlier chapters have considered, Dickens did not necessarily make fine distinctions between human care for brothers and sisters and the 'higher love'. Rather he considered practical action on behalf of one's neighbour in need a direct expression of God's love to his children manifesting itself in the world. Equally, acknowledgement of dependence upon others is transformative in novels such as *Dombey and Son* and *Little Dorrit*. In situating his symbolic river of death and renewal at the heart of the London environment in which the majority of his readers lived, Dickens highlighted the need for such love-transformed life immediately in their own circumstances. Investing Lizzie's triumphant redeeming act in such overtly religious terminology in this one place in the novel at least, he also shows his sense of its availability.

It is, at any rate, available to some. Many drown in this novel within a very small geographical area, giving the novel a claustrophobic unity of vision. John Harmon, the sailor mistaken for him, Gaffer Hexham, Rogue Riderhood (twice!), Bradley Headstone and Eugene Wrayburn all go under the same river. Not all of them re-emerge. Unlike Wrayburn, Riderhood is unaffected by Gaffer's baptism or the dangers he passes through at the paddles of the steamboat, mistakenly believing that the outward form of having drowned is all-sufficient and 'that him as has been brought out o' drowning, can never be drowned' (IV 1 p. 623). Such premonitions seem to be tests of whether the characters will read the meaning potentially present in the river and respond to the ubiquitous warning. Such revelation must accompany the death by water if it is to be at all regenerative. For some a baptismal immersion in the Thames

is an empty symbol, for others it is a vital one. A. O. J. Cockshut toys
with an Anglo-Catholic reading:

> It is hard to resist the idea that the river has a sacramental, baptismal
> character. It is a mystery bringing salvation or damnation as it is
> received worthily or unworthily.[31]

He ultimately distances himself from this, mainly because of Dickens's
impatience with High Church teaching. The reading is also subject to
question in that for all its potency, the novel insists that the symbol is
just that – a symbol. It is not so much preparation for or reaction to the
immersion in the Thames itself that determines the character's regeneration or lack of it, but whether or not there is an actual process of
change already taking place in the character for re-emergence to signify.
The presence or absence of a signified behind the signifier is all. Perhaps
coming from a different religious background, Karen Hattaway draws
from this the radically different conclusion that

> the distinction he makes in *Our Mutual Friend* between baptismal
> immersions that are renewing experiences and those that are not
> indicates clearly his partial acceptance of the Evangelical notion that
> ritual did not always imply spiritual awakening.[32]

Although in his horror of dogmatism Dickens may not have accepted
the teaching of adult-baptising Evangelicals, imaginatively he seems to
have agreed with their view that the symbol is only powerful if representative of a prior change of heart. The references to baptism contribute to a sense of supernatural marvel associated with the genuine
rebirths. Eliot may have given more systematic thought to the question
of how the individual may experience regenerative baptism in *The
Waste Land*, but Dickens's use and urbanisation of the symbol in *Our
Mutual Friend* is no less deliberate.

This is why Limehouse Hole becomes the great imaginative centre of
London in Dickens's later work, as Euston Station is its 'heart' in *Dombey
and Son* (15 p. 218), generating the rhythms that bring about surrender
to death and emerging clarity within that novel's symbolic scheme.
Here it is that innumerable bodies are 'FOUND DROWNED' (*LD* I 3
p. 31). Although most remain undeniably dead, many are pulled out of
the waters at this spot. Bucket immediately looks for Lady Dedlock here
(*BH* 57 pp. 868–9), but for her it is too late for resurrection. Limehouse
concentrates the range of meanings contained in the river symbol and

makes them central to the economic, sociological and symbolic scheme of London. It can serve as the deepest point of London's hopelessness, as the place where long-concealed information will finally wash up for scrutiny or as the venue for the beginnings of new lives. Like London as a whole, it can serve the wider narrative by burying information and washing it up in unpredictable ways. It leads characters towards onto-logical bewilderment and death, but the experience of immersion in both is sometimes a revitalising experience. Throughout his fiction, Dickens has looked to the Thames to invest his texts with (often vague) transcendental meaning according to the imperatives of the plot and his fluctuating attitudes to the religious ideas traditionally discussed in terms of water imagery. The yearning for the river to retain such signif-icance is nowhere more powerful, however, than in the final novels in which he is prepared to look the possibility that this meaning may no longer be present steadily in the face.

7

'A dream of demon heads and savage eyes': Dickens's Metropolitan Crowd

Dickens's London has emerged from this study as conflicted between resistance to and embodiment of the narrative's general movement towards closure. Some of its institutions, like the detective police, push uncompromisingly towards a conclusive revelation of truth in contrast with other elements of city life, such as its layout and its dirt that hide information and threaten dissolution and death. Such suggestions of narrative justice embedded in the city's structure are themselves frighteningly ambiguous. In the case of the railway too, the distributor of truth is the agent of death, suggesting a hope that Providential justice is compatible with technological progress – but also a fear that it may simply be an impersonal and secularised form of fate after all. Other forces, such as the river, are even more ambiguous, as instrumental in burying facts as in washing them up for public scrutiny. London's crowds, however, constitute a third moving force in Dickens's city. They are constantly described in terms that evoke the generally adjacent Thames, suggesting that some of the river's work of exploring the power of religious symbolism in a modern context may also be discernible in the flow of the crowd. Like the river, it serves different functions at different times and therefore reflects a wide range of attitudes to the larger religious and ontological concerns raised by Dickens's treatments of London.

This chapter begins with a comparison of this symbolic juxtaposition in *Dombey and Son* with its significance in *The Waste Land*. It then turns its attention to the exploration of the crowd in Dickens's earlier fiction such as *Oliver Twist* and *Barnaby Rudge*, where the properties that qualify the crowd for its symbolic burdens later are in the process of development.[1] More ambiguous still than the Thames, it is made of the very people of London and thus it is the most representative microsymbol within the vast macrosymbol of his metropolis.

I. The crowd and the river

In *The Waste Land* the movement of the populace seems to take over
from the river as emblem of the irresistible journey towards death:

> A crowd *flowed* over London Bridge, so many
> I had not thought death had undone so many ...
> (ll. 62–3, my italics)[2]

This more modern stream, however, has none of the river's regenerative
potential.

Eliot's crowd is a product of a rigidly ordered commercial metropolis
and is governed strictly by time as it circulates around the city:

> Flowed up the hill and down King William Street,
> To where Saint Mary Woolnoth kept the hours
> With a dead sound on the final stroke of nine.
> (ll. 66–8)

To be in this crowd is a form of living death. Eliot's notes refer the reader
to the 'woeful city' of the *Inferno*, where the narrator says, 'I saw people
at the shore of a great river' (III 70). Here, those who have chosen neither good nor evil exist in an eternal state of eerie no-man's-land
between death and life:

> These have no hope of death, and their blind life is so abject that
> they are envious of every other lot.
> (III 46–8)[3]

For Dante, as for Eliot, only those who participate in the moral scheme
can be said to live and thus he calls his sufferers 'These wretches who
never were alive'. Therefore, their punishment for being 'neither rebel-
lious nor faithful to God' (III 39) is to exist for eternity in this state.[4] Eliot
recasts this environment as contemporary London, a society that is dead,
but stubbornly refuses to acknowledge the fact in decent burial. It has
ended up in this state, like the hideous Sybil of Cumae in the epigraph,
conscious but impotent and imprisoned.

Whereas, however, the river is a moving force through the stagnant
city, taking the quester through the city in a definite direction, to a point
where resurrection might occur, its updated counterpart, the crowd seems
unable to share its signifying function. Madame Sosostris sees only 'crowds

of people, walking round in a ring' (l. 56), rather than upon a purposeful course. The lessons of surrender and renewal offered by the Thames are neither taught nor learned by the metropolitan multitudes. To be immersed in them is to surrender identity. There is no question that such a loss may lead to the discovery of a new and vibrant identity.

Dickens too is interested in the crossover between what the flowing river has traditionally represented and what the flowing crowd of commercial London can represent. In *Dombey and Son*, where so much use is made of the river symbol, Dickens recognises the crowd's role in evoking whatever the river may convey to metropolitan minds. It is the blended and incoherent sound of the crowd's motion past Paul Dombey's window that causes him to think directly of the Thames and its ceaseless message:

> By little and little, he got tired of the bustle of the day, the noise of carriages and carts, and people passing and re-passing; and would fall asleep, or be troubled with a restless and uneasy sense again – the child could hardly tell whether this were in his sleeping or his waking moments – of that rushing river.

(DS 16 p. 221)

The throng is another flowing force, moving according to a still more mysterious rhythm of its own and bringing to Paul's mind the other reminder that the plot is taking him inevitably towards a fixed goal.

In *The Old Curiosity Shop*, Dickens had already imagined the anxious hallucinations of the urban invalid as he registers the sounds of the incessant movement on the streets:

> Think of a sick man in such a place as Saint Martin's court, listening to the footsteps, and in the midst of pain and weariness obliged, despite himself (as though it were a task he must perform) to detect the child's step from the man's ... the dull heel of the sauntering outcast from the quick tread of an expectant pleasure seeker – think of the hum and noise being always present to his senses, and of the stream of life that will not stop, pouring on, on, on, through all his restless dreams.

(1 p. 6)

In his delirium, the man is led by the crowd to think of the river and his own journey towards death. Even 'the crowds for ever passing and repassing on the bridges' make this association between the slow, inevitable movement of the river towards the sea and their own towards decease:

> looking listlessly down upon the water with some vague idea that by-and-by it runs between green banks which grow wider and wider until at last it joins the broad vast sea.

(1 p. 6)

Some among them find the river's promise of oblivion attractive, feeling that 'to smoke and lounge away one's life ... in a dull, slow sluggish barge, must be happiness unalloyed'. They recall 'that drowning was not a hard death, but of all means of suicide the easiest and best'.

The sick man, however, has Paul Dombey's sense of the inexplicable and eternal task imposed upon him of being 'forced, sometimes, to try to stop [the river] ... or choke its way with sand' (DS 16 p. 221). This manifests itself in a desire to resist the process of disappearance into the flow of the crowd. Each footstep must retain its individual significance for him, whereas the rapidity and jumble of the streets would turn it into mere 'hum and noise'. His insistence upon the separate identity of each pedestrian seems like an obsessive last-minute attempt to assert his own perpetually diminishing identity, a refusal to surrender to the dissolving currents of the crowd, which this passage implies would bring an end to his suffering. This, however, only keeps him in a state of artificial living death that brings no peace, 'as if he were condemned to lie dead but conscious, in a noisy churchyard, and had no hope of rest for centuries to come'. Thus when he calls the crowd a 'stream of life', Master Humphrey means rather a stream of death-in-life that may be understood as an earlier account of Eliot's deadened concourse that yet refuses to surrender to death. Here Dickens seems to share Eliot's pessimism about the effects of immersion in this modernised tide. The crowd threatens to function only as an objective correlative for modernity's de-individuating effects upon the spirit. The contrast of this 'stream of life' with the accompanying river seems to point up its failure to signify potential re-emergence.

When, however, the phrase recurs in *Dombey and Son*, the crowd more accurately lives up to this title. In a chapter entitled 'The Thunderbolt', Florence's view of herself as a daughter capable of winning her father's love is cruelly shattered as Dombey strikes her. Leaving the house and, implicitly, this conception of her identity, she steps into the bewildering anonymity of the crowd. We have seen how Florence identifies her lost and broken identity at this point with Walter's shipwreck.[5] In the earlier fiction, the crowd evokes the same sensation in Little Nell and her grandfather, who are presented as 'feeling amidst the crowd a solitude which has no parallel but in the thirst of the shipwrecked mariner' (*OCS* 44 p. 338). Florence's shipwreck, however, seems to afford her an opportunity to begin afresh. Her senses are ultimately aroused rather than deadened by the dissolution of identity she undergoes. She is

> *carried onward in a stream of life* setting that way, and flowing, indifferently, past marts and mansions, prisons, churches, market-places, wealth, poverty, good, and evil, *like the broad river, side by side with it*, awakened from its dreams of rushes, willows, and green moss, and rolling on, turbid and troubled, among the works and cares of men, to the deep sea.
>
> (48 p. 639, my italics)

The movement of London's people here conveys both aspects of the river symbol it accompanies, death and transcendent new life. Just as the river is 'awakened from its dreams', immersion in its human counterpart has the effect of 'recalling her in some degree to herself' (48 p. 638). Her childhood experience of being lost in the London crowds (Chapter 6) had been merely frightening. Nevertheless, it provided experience of a world outside the closed environment of Dombey's house, allowing her to be defined in other ways and bringing her into meaningful contact with others, most notably Walter. In this later scene, the crowd is permitted the river's potential to signify baptismally impossible in *The Old Curiosity Shop* and later in *The Waste Land*. The experience of immersing herself in the city's crowd acts as a more tangible version of her brother's surrender to the imagined Thames. Governed by time as rigidly as the flow of the river, as may be seen in a phrase like 'It is half-past five o'clock. ... and the human tide is still rolling westward' (4 p. 38), London's crowds seem compatible with the novel's more directly symbolic agents of teleological narrative, the river and the railway. The multitudes, moving to and from work at set hours and hurrying to reach their stations on time, follow a compatible timetable. Allowing herself to be borne along by the time-bound crowd is liberating to Florence. It suggests a yielding to an incomprehensible plan of transformation of her identity and ambitions akin to Paul's surrender to the current of the river.

The crowd's importance to the symbolic patterns of Dickens's city did not begin in 1848, however. Both *Oliver Twist* and *Barnaby Rudge* deal with the dissolution and re-discovery of self in the urban concourse. Both engage with sophistication and complexity with its conflicting functions as both agent and opponent of narrative revelation. While these earlier novels tend to emphasise the crowd's de-individuating effects, they also allow Florence's hope that people may emerge from their immersion in the throng with a transformed sense of identity and of relation to human society as a whole. Indeed, Dickens's ability to turn London's crowd into an ambivalent symbol of his hopes and anxieties about the individual's relationship to society in his mature work may be traced to his perceptions about its operation in these two novels.

II. The crowd and loss of identity

That London was a crowded city in Dickens's time scarcely requires demonstration. Its population had risen from 500,000 in 1660 to 1,250,000 in 1820.[6] The figures for the intervening years suggest that the rate of growth accelerated in the years of the Industrial Revolution. In 1700 there were 575 000 inhabitants. By 1801 this had risen to 900,000 and George Rudé estimates a population of 2,000,000 for 1850.[7] London's area did not expand at the same rate to accommodate this influx and over the course of the nineteenth century, London's population density doubled.[8] Since Dickens was writing at a time when the capital's streets were crowded to an unprecedented and discernibly increasing extent, it is natural that this should be a major preoccupation in his work.

Both of the earlier novels under discussion have protagonists who come from outside London to add one more unit to the multitude. Like the influx in real life, Barnaby is fleeing rural poverty, mostly for his mother's sake. Stagg the pickpocket encourages him to associate the multitudes with gold, which, he informs him, is 'not in solitary places like those you pass your time in, but in crowds, and where there's noise and rattle' (46 p. 428). The density of the population attracts his mother to London, not for economic reasons, but because she hopes 'by plunging into the crowd, to rid herself of her terrible pursuer' (*BR* 47 p. 440). Oliver Twist dreams of 'London! – that great large place! – nobody – not even Mr Bumble – could ever find him there!' (8 p. 44). The industrial town offers a similar consolation to Little Nell, who says:

> we are lost in the crowd and hurry of this place, and if any cruel people should pursue us, they could surely never trace us further. There's comfort in that.
>
> (*OCS* 44 p. 340)

Such expectations could only be entertained of a city that was on its way to becoming, in the words of Joseph Conrad's *The Secret Agent*:

> a monstrous town more populous than some continents [with] darkness enough to bury five millions of lives.[9]

Burial here relates to the possibility of absolute erasure of identity in such an environment. Conrad's word suggests that London's vast population is an enormous weight, crushing all who hide there. Dickens is equally ready to depict the dream of anonymity turned bad. His crowd blurs personal contexts, rendering the emotions of individuals insignificant. Little Nell and her grandfather feel this way about Birmingham:

> They were but an atom, here, in a mountain heap of misery, the very sight of which increased their hopelessness and suffering.
>
> (*OCS* 44 p. 339)

London, with its greater population, decontextualises grief all the more. Seeing it from afar, the 'stragglers who came wandering into London' in *Dombey and Son* speculate that 'their misery there would be but as a drop of water in the sea, or as a grain of sea-sand on the shore' (*DS* 33 p. 462). This is the London in which Florence has been lost. Such cold, homogenising dissolution seems to offer little hope that true identity can be revealed here.

Dickens seems to suggest that the city's commercial character is ultimately responsible for the loss of identity that takes place in its crowds. As people come to be regarded as part of a system, an animate resource necessary for the operation of the commercial machine, the sheer numbers involved make them as faceless and indistinguishable from the commodities themselves. *Oliver Twist* paints a vivid picture of human beings in Smithfield as penned in as the animals they deal in. The market, in all senses of the word, erodes distinctions between men and things, a characteristic concern of Dickens, and it is the packedness of the place that leads to this perception. As soon as Oliver enters London, he is conscious that children who live there have become the 'stock in trade' of the shops that shelter them (8 p. 49). Later, in Jacob's Island, 'the visitor' finds himself

> Jostling with unemployed labourers of the lowest class, ballast-heavers, coal-whippers, brazen women, ragged children, and the very raff and refuse of the river ...
>
> (50 p. 338)

Such people, representing so many labour hours, are heaped up like the 'great piles of merchandise from the stacks of warehouses' they live among (50 p. 338). Already the ground is prepared for the more modern sensibility of Tigg Montague's demonstration in *Martin Chuzzlewit*, complete with 'printed calculations', of the number of people in the 'crowded street' outside the window who may be expected to insure themselves at the office (27 p. 444). Equally, in *Hard Times*, people are reduced to 'figures in a soom' (II 5 p. 182). The crowd, with their lack of individuality and aptness to be conceptualised in statistical form, becomes a symbol of the commercial mechanism whereby people can be reduced to monetary relationships.

A telling simile in *Little Dorrit* connects the removal of personal distinctions in the business-dominated concourse and another great dissolver of vital differentiation:

> What the mud had been doing with itself, or where it came from, who could say? But it seemed to collect in a moment, as a crowd will, and in five minutes to have splashed all the sons and daughters of Adam.
>
> (I 3 p. 31)

Dickens is mainly providing socio-economic commentary here, but he also connects this with the ontological issues involved in loss of identity raised in his discussion of London's dirt. The confused conglomeration of matter that is urban mud is compared to the crowd as a bringing together of particles belonging to categories that ought to remain separate.[10] The crowd further jumbles disparate elements, concealing the true nature of society and one's place in it. Both create an urban environment that vividly figures the confusion of the individual as to his or her identity in relation to the rest of humanity. However, just as London's dirt challenges Jo and Esther to tidy it up and re-assess their relation to the world, so the confusion of the crowd leads Florence, Oliver and others to re-evaluate their identity more accurately.

Dickens develops a concept of the polluted crowd spontaneously generating itself around the activity of the city, much as the Elizabethans believed that flies spontaneously generated themselves around excrement. *Oliver Twist* describes 'heaps of children ... crawling in and out at the doors' (8 p. 49) and Tom-all-Alone's is said to be inhabited by 'a swarm of misery' and 'vermin parasites':

> a crowd of foul existence that crawls in and out of gaps in walls and boards; and coils itself to sleep, in maggot numbers ... fetching and carrying fever...
>
> (*BH* 16 pp. 256–7)

The density of this environment is as significant as its dirtiness in establishing London as a place resisting attempts to categorise ontological phenomena. Many contemporary social reformers felt that both dirt and overcrowding contributed to the criminal mentality. Besides the difficulty of maintaining proper hygiene, the enforced intimate contact between people in such places was seen as diminishing a proper sense of distinctions between people. Their horror about the implications for social relationships is echoed in *The Old Curiosity Shop*, which speaks of 'dense and squalid masses where social decency is lost, or rather never found' (38 p. 293). Likewise Dickens is clearly disturbed by the lack even of gender distinctions in the 'assemblage of heads' in the Three Cripples:

> as the eye grew more accustomed to the scene, the spectator gradually became aware of the presence of a numerous company, male and female, crowded round a long table. ... with every mark and stamp of their sex utterly beaten out, and presenting but one loathsome blank of profligacy and crime ...
>
> (26 p. 164)

In *Oliver Twist*, this dirty, amoral – if not essentially wicked – crowd spills out on to the streets of London, where its resistance to classification overwhelmingly conceals knowledge of the individual's true identity.

III. Destruction and the mob

With its tendency to confuse right and wrong, the metropolitan crowd easily becomes a mob in these two early novels. While *A Tale of Two Cities* demonstrates Dickens's continuing fascination with this transition, *Barnaby Rudge* is the work that most fully allows the reader to participate in the experience of the mob and to explore it from within. The Gordon Riots of 1780 protested against the 1778 Catholic Relief Act, which removed restrictions upon Roman Catholics, such as the prohibition of land inheritance for members of that religion and arbitrary imprisonment for their priests and teachers.[11] Although the march to Parliament on Friday, 2 June was initially peaceful, chaos broke loose and several peers were assaulted. Over the next six days, Catholic chapels and the homes and businesses of suspected Papists were ransacked. Various prisons including Newgate were stormed to release those taken captive in the ensuing struggle with the authorities. Although Dickens remained largely faithful to his major historical sources[12] in terms of reported speech and incident, he did not intend simply to reproduce what actually happened. In one letter, he exclaims, 'I think I can make a better riot than Lord George Gordon did.'[13] The differences between the documented events of the uprising and their presentation in *Barnaby Rudge* are worth considering because they show what Dickens regarded as 'better' for his symbolic purposes.

Most obviously, Dickens entirely omitted certain important episodes from the story, including the unsuccessful attacks upon the Bank and Pay Office. Nor does he mention the severe conduct of magistrate John Wilkes, formerly a popular radical demagogue who had been imprisoned by the government himself. When John Landseer pointed out this omission, Dickens replied:

> No man in the crowd who was pressed and trodden here and there, saw Wilkes ... or anything but a great mass of magistrates, rioters, and soldiery, all mixed up together.[14]

Details like this are only important to historians and commentators. To recreate the impressions registered by the uncritical participants, individual figures must melt into the blur of the action. Nothing could be admitted to the narrative that would interrupt the power of the urban crowd once unleashed. As they are swept along in the action of the riots, even the main characters disconcertingly slip from their place at the forefront of the narrative. Dickens explained this technique in a letter to John Landseer:

> a broad, bold, hurried effect must be produced, or the reader instead of being forced and driven along by imaginary crowds will find himself dawdling very uncomfortably through the town ... my object has been to convey an idea of multitudes, violence, and fury; and even to lose my own dramatis personae in the throng ...

London is to be directly experienced as a bewildering place where all personality must be subsumed in the corporate and fundamentally different group identity. Conversely, however, the same persons who are lost in the group contribute significantly, but subtly, to the reader's understanding of the whole. As A. O. J. Cockshut observes:

> Our knowledge of the thoughts and personality of three or four people in the crowd imperceptibly modifies our view of the crowd itself.[15]

Barnaby's naïvety and irrationality, Hugh's bestiality and Sim's reactionary meanness become characteristics of the rioters generally. The extent to which the individual shapes the mob and that to which the mob changes the actions and attitudes of the individual is of vital importance in this novel.

A more subtle difference is that the poverty and criminality that characterise Dickens's mob throughout do not accord with the findings of modern historians. George Rudé points out that of 160 tried at the Old Bailey and Surrey Assizes, 76 were wage earners and only 11 were labourers, quoting a witness in T. B. Howell's *A Complete Collection of State Trials* who describes the participants as 'the better sort of tradesmen; they were all well-dressed decent sort of people'.[16] Dickens had this book in his library at Gadshill and must have consciously chosen to make the crowd poorer and more criminal so that he could portray mass violence as arising organically from the urban atmosphere:

> composed for the most part of the very scum and refuse of London, whose growth was fostered by bad criminal laws, bad prison regulations, and the worst conceivable police ...
>
> (*BR* 49 p. 453)

Again, Dickens connects the city's crowd and dirt as symptomatic of the collapse of proper social relationships and for this reason he depicts the untidiest of the great unwashed as the dominant element in the riots.

Rudé's figures, however, include only those who were actually arrested. Many more than 160 were involved in the riots themselves. The respectable Protestant citizens who held initial prominence in the early stages of the march soon attracted drunken idlers and those bent on looting victims and their properties. Christopher Hibbert asserts that the mob that smashed the Duke Street chapel was composed of 'hundreds of street boys and prostitutes, drunks, pickpockets and rowdies', despite the fact that 'All thirteen men arrested' for the disruption 'were gainfully employed'.[17]

Dickens's point, however, is not that upstanding working men were absent, but that these distinctions of class and occupation, which usually separate people and regulate behaviour, become irrelevant in this situation. In the excitement of the commotion, even the most orderly become part of the 'scum and refuse':

> sober workmen ... were seen to cast down their baskets of tools and become rioters in an instant; mere boys on errands did the like.
>
> (53 p. 484)

Similarly, when another crowd pursues Oliver, they quickly divest themselves of all distinguishing factors:

> the butcher throws down his tray, the baker his basket ... the school-boy his marbles ...
>
> (*OT* 10 p. 116)

Dickens observes the rioters' tendency to surrender their individuality to the corporate identity, matching Hibbert's account of individuals 'losing their identities in a fusing welter of destruction'.[18]

More generally, psychologists have written a great deal about the process of 'de-individuation' that takes place once a person becomes part of a large group of people.[19] Perhaps the earliest to tackle this issue was Gustave Le Bon, whose politically reactionary book, *The Crowd: A Study of the Popular Mind*, first published in France in 1895, exemplifies theoretical thinking on the matter during the nineteenth century. Le Bon claims that a large group becomes a single entity different from any individual within it:

> A collective mind is formed ... It forms a single being, and is subjected to *the law of the mental unity of crowds*.[20]

His central idea is that in a crowd people are governed by reason less than usual because their brains are overwhelmed with more sensual impressions than they have power to register simultaneously. They are therefore more susceptible to irrational suggestions and less capable of making accurate judgements, so that the collective identity reflects a much lower level of human development:

> By the mere fact that he forms part of an organised crowd, a man descends several rungs in the ladder of civilisation. Isolated, he may be a cultivated individual; in a crowd, he is a barbarian – that is, a creature acting by instinct. ... among the special characteristics of crowds there are several – such as impulsiveness, irritability, incapacity to reason, the absence of judgement and of the critical spirit, the exaggeration of the sentiments, and others besides – which are almost always observed in beings belonging to inferior forms of evolution – in women, savages and children, for instance.[21]

Late nineteenth-century fears of regression were clearly evoked by the numbers of urban people as much as by urban living conditions.

Although Dickens does not particularly single out women as Le Bon does, he had also described the behaviour of the mob in terms of children, savages, and others whose minds he perceived as guided more by basic instinct than 'rational' Western adults. The riot scenes of *Barnaby Rudge* bluntly demonstrate that 'The great mass never reasoned or thought at all, but were stimulated by their own headlong passions' (53 pp. 483–4). Equally, when the Maypole Inn is attacked in *Barnaby Rudge*, 'the mob quickened their pace; shouting and whooping like savages' (54 p. 495). To appeal to the crowd, the mass manipulator must, according to Le Bon and Dickens before him, draw on mankind's simplest emotions and impulses. How to stir the response of a large number of people was evidently a question of some importance to a novelist who had to cater for a large readership with varying tastes and degrees of literacy. As Cockshut points out,[22] he later became a kind of agitator at the public readings. His most noticeable diversion from the historical Gordon Riots is the inclusion of Gashford, a fictitious demagogue, whose techniques accord with those recommended by Le Bon. Like the psychologist, he points back to prehistoric times to find the key to spurring a vast assemblage of people into action:

> To surround anything ... with an air of mystery, is to invest it with a secret charm, and power of attraction which to the crowd is irresistible. False priests, false prophets, false doctors ... veiling their proceedings in mystery, have always addressed themselves at an immense advantage to the popular credulity. ... Curiosity is, and has been from the creation of the world, a master-passion. To awaken it, to gratify it by slight degrees ... is to establish the surest hold that can be had ... on the unthinking portion of mankind.
>
> (*BR* 37 p. 347)

The great concentration of bored people in the capital, unhappy in dreary routine-based jobs – and of course many more with no prospect of the employment they came there to seek – makes London's crowd particular vulnerable to such stimulation:

> A mob is usually a creature of very mysterious existence, particularly in a large city ... where there must always be a large number of idle and profligate persons.
>
> (52 p. 475)

The idleness of Dickens's crowd is shown by their regarding throwing stones at Haredale as an 'amusement' (43 p. 410) and burning Catholic property as a 'Sunday evening's recreation' (52 p. 482).

Contemporary social commentators describe many like him in accounting for the mounting attraction to the city among rural labourers.
H. Llewellyn Smith, a contributor to Charles Booth's *Life and Labour of
the People in London* writes of

> the contagion of numbers, the sense of something going on ... all, in
> short, that makes the difference between the Mile End Fair on a
> Saturday night, and a dark and muddy country lane ... with nothing
> to do.[23]

In contrast with his mother's search for oblivion in the crowd, Barnaby
is chiefly drawn into the mob by excitement at Stagg's description of life
among its ranks and the activity that it proves to offer:

> Forgetful of all other things in the ecstasy of the moment, his face
> flushed and his eyes sparkling with delight, heedless of the weight of
> the great banner he carried, and mindful only of its flashing in the
> sun and rustling in the summer breeze, on he went, proud, happy,
> elated past all telling ...
>
> (49 p. 450)

Once such people are in the city, the crowd may be easily stimulated to
gratify these expectations.

Another basic instinct that is seen to stimulate the mob powerfully is
fear of those outside the group and Gashford exploits this repeatedly.
The narrator sets the products of reason, 'Truth and Common Sense' in
opposition to the anxiety evoked by a list of bloody deeds which the
Catholics allegedly intend to perpetrate:

> when terrors and alarms which no man understood were perpetually
> broached ... then the mania spread indeed, and the body, still
> increasing every day, grew forty-thousand strong.
>
> (37 pp. 347–8)

Gordon's speech has patriotism as its keynote. This becomes tribal
hatred once it is disseminated among the mob. Only when he suggests
that the crowd might 'wade in blood' do they throw up their hats and
cheer (35 p. 339). The breaking down of distinctions between individuals within the mob is counterbalanced by an intense distinction between
themselves and individuals outside that group. United not in love, but
in hatred, the mob is the very opposite of society. In such a condition,

the London crowd seems least able to reveal the regenerating connections between people that immersion in the 'stream of life' achieves in *Dombey and Son.*

Of course for these antisocial instincts to be given free rein to this extent, the calculations of morality, self-interest and fear of punishment that normally restrict them in a civilised society must be powerfully overcome. Le Bon proposes that since they have become indistinguishable, they subconsciously assume that they cannot be held individually accountable:

> the individual forming part of a crowd acquires, solely from numerical considerations, a sentiment of invincible power which allows him to yield to instincts which, had he been alone, he would perforce have kept under restraint. He will be the less disposed to check himself from the consideration that, a crowd being anonymous, and in consequence irresponsible, the sentiment of responsibility which always controls individuals disappears entirely.[24]

In *Barnaby Rudge* too, 'the sense of having gone too far to be forgiven, held the timid together no less than the bold. ... at the worst, they were too many to be all punished' (*BR* 53 p. 483). Dickens makes powerful symbolic use of the thinking on de-individuation in the crowd that was emerging in the mid-nineteenth century to amplify the loss of points of reference that render them individuals accountable to an interconnected society in the metropolitan environment. The crowd is as much an 'unintelligible mess' as that in which 'Jo, and the other lower animals, get on' (16 p. 258) in *Bleak House*. The network of love relationships between people, which this book has posited as the central mystery to be revealed to the initiated in Dickens's fiction, is at its most obscured in this environment.

Oliver Twist, struggling to cope with the sensory impressions he receives in a packed Smithfield Market (21 pp. 135–6), provides a practical example of this. Dickens shows how the crowd steadily forms in the course of the morning and the confusion is seen to increase with it. At first, the streets are 'noiseless and empty', but soon there are 'a few scattered people'. The arriving workers seem half-asleep and still in a somnambulistic, subconscious state, 'straggling' and 'trudging' rather than walking. The crowd is unclean and the dirt and pea-soupers are partially animal in character:

> The ground was covered, nearly ankle-deep, with filth and mire; and a thick steam, perpetually rising from the reeking bodies of the cattle, and mingling with the fog ...
>
> (21 p. 135)

The 'unbroken concourse of people' itself is composed of 'unwashed, unshaven, squalid, and dirty figures constantly running to and fro'. Soon disparate social classes become inextricably mixed:

> Countrymen, butchers, drovers ... and vagabonds of every low grade, were mingled together in a dense mass ...
>
> (21 p. 136)

This is taken to extremes when, in the 'hideous and discordant din that resounded from every corner of the market', human and animal noise is blended quite indiscriminately, including, 'the whistling of drovers, the barking of dogs, the bellowing and plunging of oxen'. There is no rest here, but eternal movement. One sentence has nineteen verbs ending in '-ing', suggesting constant activity (21 pp. 135–6). The people are as packed in as the animals in the urban marketplace and it is no wonder when they later behave like them. When Oliver is pursued in Chapter 10, the mixture of noises is conveyed again by fast active present participles abutting each other without pausing for conjunctions:

> tearing, yelling, screaming: knocking down ...
>
> (p. 59, following 1867 edition)

Similarly there is rapid polyphonic conversation without 'he saids' or indentation. The result of all this 'stunning and bewildering scene, which quite confounded the senses' (21 p. 136) is that Oliver becomes incapable of defining any of the things he registers here or of defining himself in relation to his surroundings. Questions of the boy's own identity are amplified by this atmosphere – especially his own confusion as to whether or not he will be subsumed within the collective criminal identity of Fagin's gang.

If, however, people become children, savages and even animals in Dickens's crowd, their suspension of rationality is still more fittingly linked to the insane. Although Barnaby is by no means to be understood as a typical crowd member, his lunatic enthusiasm within it seems to spread to the whole. Dickens observes, 'The whole great mass were mad' (64 p. 583) and later adds:

> In a word, a moral plague ran through the city. The noise, and hurry, and excitement, had for hundreds and hundreds an attraction they had no firmness to resist. The contagion spread like a dread fever: an infectious madness, as yet not near its height, seized on new victims every hour, and society began to tremble at their ravings.
>
> (53 p. 484)

The two images of mental illness and of bodily illness anticipate Le Bon's metaphors of unwholesomeness and death to represent the fundamentally antisocial aspect of the crowd's artificial society:

> In consequence of the purely destructive nature of their power, crowds act like those microbes which hasten the dissolution of enfeebled or dead bodies.[25]

Dickens's London is portrayed as suffering a kind of decay as one individual after another loses his or her separate identity in collective violence.

At the attack upon the prison, however, Dickens goes one further and compares the rioters to evil spirits, bearing out Lord Gordon's anxieties that his Association of 'godly men and true' is really a godless mob of 'devils' (35 p. 338). Dickens presents the connection between flames, the natural habitat of demons, and the demonic energy of the crowd:

> The more the fire crackled and raged, the wilder and more cruel the men grew; as though moving in that element they became fiends, and changed their earthly nature for the qualities that give delight in hell.
>
> (55 p. 507)

Not only does this resemble Hell, but it also realises hellish values. At the destruction of the distillery, phrases like 'this hideous lake' and 'liquid fire' echo Dante and Milton (cf. *Paradise Lost* I 228–9). The growth of the fire at the prison is built up in an apparently interminable series of 'when' clauses, suggesting the inexorable growth of the flames. Finally, as if the narrator has run out of breath in his excitement, the 'then' clause bursts in, revealing that the power of the crowd has been growing in proportion:

> then the mob began to join the whirl ... with loud yells, and shouts, and clamour, such as happily is seldom heard ...
>
> (64 p. 581)

Everywhere the mob goes there is an irrational and antisocial delight in destruction for its own sake. Before the assault upon Newgate, the rioters, 'rather than do nothing, tore up the pavement of the street, and did so with a haste and fury they could not have surpassed if that had been the jail' (64 p. 583). This even extends to destroying themselves, most notably at Haredale's distillery, where intoxication by the flames and by alcohol drives these savage people to a frenzied death. They danced, half in a mad triumph, and half in the agony of suffocation, until they fell, and steeped their corpses in the liquor that had killed them.

(68 p. 618)

Barnaby's search for consuming ecstasy at the expense of sustaining life is shared by the whole crowd and it is this vision that makes the boy flee such a metropolis:

with all he saw in this last glance fixed indelibly upon his mind, Barnaby hurried from the city which enclosed such horrors.

(68 p. 618)

The urban population is figured as in a state of gothic decay like the urban architecture with rotten foundations in *Little Dorrit*. Whereas T. S. Eliot's London crowd is compared to the amoral lost in Dante's *Inferno*, Dickens's mob members are both tormented sinners and devils. The chapters surrounding the burning of the prison are full of sounds that evoke the howling of lost souls, including, the 'dismal cries and wailings ... so full of agony and despair' (64 p. 582). Even the paint suffers as a result of the flames in reflection of the suffering of the mob members, 'swelling into boils, as it were from excess of torture' (p. 581). Equally the crowd that pursues Sikes consumes itself and undergoes hellish torments:

The cries and shrieks of those who were pressed almost to suffocation, or trampled down ... were dreadful

(*OT* 50 p. 346)

Dickens clearly understands the root of what he is describing. Crowd – or cread – existed as a verb long before it was a noun, meaning, in the Old English *Chronicle* (937), to press forward. The thought of pressure and discomfort remained the primary aspect as the word developed into its modern usage. Dickens says of this crowd's 'multitude of angry voices':

Of all the terrific yells that ever fell on mortal ears, none could exceed the cry of the infuriated throng.

(p. 344)

This invites comparison with those cries that fall upon the ears of the *im*mortal damned.

The presentation of the mob in Dickens's early fiction, discarding the civilising aspects of humanity in favour of the savage, bestial and demonic, makes the feeling behind developing contemporary theories of degeneration readily apparent. The residuum's unaccountable tendency to take mankind backwards in a corrupting journey towards death is terrifyingly visible, suggesting that nineteenth-century fear of degeneration was actually a fear of the deathbound and antisocial urges later discussed in terms of Freudian psychoanalysis. At any rate, Dickens's early heroes are those, such as Oliver Twist and Gabriel Varden, who can resist the crowd's pressure to forget the true connections that exist between people and stand up for civilised values. In *Oliver Twist*, people are 'not able to stand upright with the pressing of the mob (*OT* 50 p. 341). Nancy has to force her way through the concourse, 'elbowing the passengers from side to side' (39 p. 268), in order to do a good action, whereas the crowd assists good-naturedly when she does wrong (Chapter 15). Florence's surrender of identity is not allowed to go to this extent. Her baptism in the crowd releases her aims and desires without robbing her of her moral sense in this way. *Barnaby Rudge* and *Oliver Twist* explore the moral dangers of taking surrendered identity in the crowd too far in preparation for its more optimistic treatment in *Dombey and Son*.

IV. The mob and narrative design

Barnaby Rudge's powerful and much-read images of mob behaviour contributed to developing nineteenth-century conceptions of the urban masses across several discourses, consolidated at the end of the century in the writings of Le Bon. Both, however, are likely to have been influenced by the ideas of a work published early in the century, namely Thomas Carlyle's *The French Revolution*. Dickens himself owned the 1837 edition and the 1857 edition was in the Gadshill library at the time of his death. In a letter to John Forster, he claimed to have read 'that wonderful book the *French Revolution* [sic] again, for the 500th time'.[26] Carlyle presents the people in the crowd as abandoning rational modes of behaviour altogether as in *Oliver Twist* and *Barnaby Rudge*:

> Seven hundred thousand individuals, on the sudden, find all their old paths, old ways of acting and deciding, vanish from under their feet. ... madness rules the hour.[27]

People in *The French Revolution* frequently behave like animals. When the Parisians seize firearms in preparation for storming the Bastille, they are said to be '[m]ore ravenous than famishing lions over dead prey'.[28] Carlyle too feels that human beings return to a more primitive state in a crowd and are no longer governed by intellect, but by primal impulses. Nevertheless, his response had been more ambivalent. Le Bon's repugnance at the crowd is more likely to have been motivated by reactionary fear of democracy than by any insight into the moral effects of obscured social relationships between individuals. In *The French Revolution*, Carlyle also finds a kind of dignity and honesty in it:

> Great is the combined voice of men; the utterance of their *instincts*, which are truer than their *thoughts* ...[29]

The book paradoxically suggests that a kind of terrible justice is making use of these baser instincts of the populace. The key events it describes came to pass because of the animalistic and crazed actions of the masses. At the same time, however, Carlyle eagerly claims that the Revolution was an onward struggle towards liberation. This tension runs throughout the book[30] and it often seems that although the people in the crowd do not know what they are doing, the crowd itself is acting purposefully in achieving the necessary actions of the narrative of history.

In Dickens too, actions born of the irrational, ignorant destructive motives of the mob can drive the novels to the revelatory conclusions of their narratives. Like the railway and, to a greater extent, the river, the crowd can function, where necessary, to assist the concealer or to bring destruction on him or her. As well as burying distinct personalities into an indiscriminate mass, the crowd can also unearth them mercilessly, whether this is desired by the subject or not. Consequently, it plays a crucial part throughout Dickens's fiction in the city's task of exploring the enduring validity of figures of teleology available in the modern world. Even in *Oliver Twist* and *Barnaby Rudge*, the crowd performs the revelatory and regenerative aspects of London's work, as it does for Florence in *Dombey and Son*. If indeed the crowds are governed by an author greater than themselves, creating progress through destruction and a mixture of good and ill motives, Dickens seems to share Carlyle's ambivalent mixture of disgust at popular uprising and conception of it as the voice of the narrative of history. The question to be addressed here is whether Dickens's portrayal retains the Providential apocalyptic language Carlyle borrows to describe the crowd as an expression of secular historical forces.

The crowd in the earlier fiction is not connected to the river and the sea in anything resembling the formal scheme of symbolism employed in *Dombey and Son*. Nevertheless occasional metaphor sometimes draws parallels that make the reader compare their range of meanings. For example, a simile in *Burnaby Rudge* captures the mystery of many smaller units being absorbed into a much more powerful whole in which they cannot be traced:[31]

> Each party swelled as it went along, like rivers as they roll towards the sea ...
>
> (53 p. 484)

Like the river, this is both a place where complete dissolution of the self is possible and where facts may be buried. Individuals in Dickens such as Oliver Twist never know which other selves have allowed themselves to be dissolved in the crowd and what relationship they may have to them:

> Assembling and dispersing with equal suddenness, it is as difficult to follow to its various sources as the sea itself; nor does the parallel stop here, for the ocean is not more fickle and uncertain, more terrible when roused, more unreasonable, or more cruel.
>
> (52 p. 475)

If this river is assuming any of the river's traditional symbolic function, it conveys a very impersonal view of a flow towards dissolution of identity and ultimately death.

Mrs Rudge and Oliver are not seeking any form of resurrection from the experience, but rather resemble figures like Martha in *David Copperfield*, who simply wish to drown themselves in the river and be wiped out altogether. Passages like this show that the stream of people into which they wish to plunge themselves is not heading towards a restful oblivion, but to an ongoing death-in-life.

Just as the river can wash up objects and facts as easily as it can bury them in water, however, so the enforced contact brought about by the pressures of the crowd can unpredictably bring related people together as efficiently as it can mask the relationship between them. Jonathan Raban comments that London in the early nineteenth century was the optimal size for this double function:

> A city of less than two millions was big – plenty big enough for people to disappear into it without a trace for years at a time. It was also small enough to ensure that chance meetings, coincidences, would continually happen in it, unexpectedly and out of context.[32]

The density of the city's population made it possible that the secret of one's origins may be within arm's length only waiting to be discovered. Mr Pancks in *Little Dorrit* observes of Miss Wade:

> I expect ... I know as much about her, as she knows about herself. She is somebody's child – anybody's – nobody's. Put her in a room in London here with any six people old enough to be her parents, and her parents may be there for anything she knows. They may be in any house she sees, they may be in any churchyard she passes, she may run against 'em in any street, she may make chance acquaintances of 'em at any time; and never know it.
>
> (II 9 p. 584)

The author was as fascinated as Meagles by this potential for mystery in the urban concourse. In the same chapter the crowd manifests such a connection, rather than concealing it, jostling Arthur Clennam into contact with the missing Tattycoram and Blandois, who are 'so near to him that he could have touched them by stretching out his arm' (II 9 p. 585).

Elsewhere, Brownlow, from whose robbery Oliver Twist flees proves to be a figure who will assume parental responsibility for him. The crowd, upon which the act of pick-pocketing depends, functions as a means of bringing together people who would otherwise be separated geographically in London by their apparent social status. The force that brings them together and through which this more uncomplicatedly Providential narrative re-asserts relationships of familial love is the very crowd that elsewhere denies the connections between people. In this novel, even those most desperate to retain their status as anonymous members of the crowd may not do so forever. The crowd, like the river, has a tide, and once it has turned, there is no way back. Once Sikes's guilt threatens to single him out as a murderer, he seeks a baptism within it that will enable him to conceal his identity. At a rural outbreak of fire, Sikes, 'flying from memory and himself, plunged into the thickest of the throng' (48 p. 328). For a while he succeeds and even finds this experience as regenerative as Florence does:

> There were people there – men and women – light, bustle. It was like new life to him.
>
> (48 p. 328)

Dickens himself found a vivifying escape from anxieties in the anonymity of the crowd, telling Forster, 'I don't seem to be able to lose my spectres unless I can lose them in crowds'.[33] But the 'new life' sought by Sikes as he surrenders his identity to dissolution in the concourse is more akin to the anonymity sought by Mrs Rudge and Oliver than that enjoyed by Florence. It does not give him a new identity as an individual in relation to other individuals, but instead marks a choice of perpetual dissolution of that identity and results in a fearful death-in-life.

Sikes hopes to keep his identity buried in a multitude of people, but he is not prepared for the exhumation of his identity that the metropolitan crowd moves on to bring about, eventually singling him out and pressing towards his capture. Ultimately, he cannot accept the genuine resurrection offered by the crowd to characters in the later fiction because in Dickens regeneration is always the product of a terrifying revelation about oneself, as Dombey, Mrs Clennam, Pip and others discover. As the tide of the crowd changes direction, he finds himself isolated upon an 'Island', which he, as 'the visitor' can only reach with some difficulty, 'through a maze of ... narrow, and muddy streets, thronged by the roughest and poorest of water-side people' (50 p. 338). This large body of people soon recognises and pursues him. When even his fellow criminals side with the crowd, his alienation and exposure is complete.

Rudge senior is another person who feels that he is 'one man against the whole united concourse'. His consciousness of his crime excludes him from groups inside and outside the prison:

> The other prisoners were a host, hiding and sheltering each other – a crowd like that without the walls.
>
> (65 p. 585)

Not permitted the protection which membership of the mob affords, he too is forced into the role of individual:

> In all ... the great pest-house of the capital, he stood alone, marked and singled out by his great guilt, a Lucifer among the devils.
>
> (65 p. 585)

Thus the crowd can hold terrors for those marked out by extraordinary vice as well as extraordinary virtue. The same city and the same crowd that provides a haven of anonymity for other evildoers now turns and points directly to him.

If the mob is animalistic and guided by instincts, Dickens has a particular sort of animal and a particular sort of instinct in mind. In an explanation that forms the *raison d'être* of the crowd in *Oliver Twist*, the narrator comments:

> There is a passion *for hunting something* deeply implanted in the human breast.
>
> (10 p. 116)

Here Dickens makes explicit an important part of the English conception of large groups of people. The word 'rabble', according to the *Oxford English Dictionary*, initially denoted a pack of hunting dogs, and is not found describing a human group until 1513. Those who pursue Oliver are responding to such an urge to track down a common prey together that seems to belong to the bestial world as much as to the human. The reader's compassion for the innocent victim in these scenes prepares the ground for the magnificent extension of sympathy to Sikes, the guilty victim, when it is his turn to be pursued. In Chapter 50, the power of the crowd in its hunting aspect is first described second-hand, so that it has already acquired a sense of terror when it finally appears. Chitling tells Sikes of how at Fagin's arrest they behaved like wild beasts:

> I can see 'em now ... the people jumping up, one behind another, and snarling with their teeth and making at him ... the women ... swore they'd tear his heart out!
>
> (p. 341)

Later, at his trial, people are impossibly packed in, so that 'Inquisitive and eager eyes peered from every inch of space'. They are prying into his secrets and suggest the company he has in his cell the night before, namely the spirits of

> all the men he had known who had died upon the scaffold; some of them through his means ... he could hardly count them.
>
> (p. 360)

The mob that 'assailed him with opprobrious names, and screeched and hissed' (p. 360) externalises his inner demons of guilt. In the light of such events, the slow degrees by which the mob reveals its approaching presence are agonising to Sikes. First he hears 'the tramp of hurried footsteps' (p. 448), then, 'a loud huzzah burst from the crowd; giving the listener, for the first time, some adequate idea of its immense extent' (p. 344).

Finally they burst in, displaying many of their now expected characteristics. Carried along by their irrational instincts, they move 'with the ecstasy of madmen' (p. 345). Although they bring Sikes to justice as far as the plot is concerned, this is not their primary motivation. Their lack of a rational purpose is seen when the failure of Sikes's escape is applauded at the front and 'Those who were at too great a distance to know its meaning, took up the sound' (p. 345). Excitement and the fundamental urge to bring the hiding man into the open are shown to be absolutely irresistible.

In *Barnaby Rudge*, the people are again converted into hunting animals, 'wild and savage, like beasts at the sight of prey' (49 p. 454). Even Gabriel feels that they 'thirsted, like wild animals, for his blood'. Having established the crowd in terms of subhuman instinct, Dickens has invested it with the power needed for the scenes where Rudge is the running man to whom concealment in the mob is denied. He therefore attempts to hide in the darkest corners of Newgate, believing that the crowd that is coming to release him intends to treat him as dogs treat their quarry. They are the 'furious multitude' and he is terrified of the 'fury of the rabble'. Trying to make sense of the noises he hears, his imagination concludes that he is being specifically sought out for mob justice:

> It might be that the intelligence of his capture having been bruited abroad, they had come there purposely to drag him out and kill him in the street.
>
> (65 pp. 584–5)

The more tangible rabble, hunting down its prey and inflicting destruction, externalises the still more terrible 'hunt of spectres' that pursues him in his mind because of his guilt and fear. Such demons fill his brain as the crowd fills all the available space in London:

> here all space was full. The one pursuing voice was everywhere ...
>
> (55 p. 504)

This is why he is far more afraid of the crowd than of burning to death.

Dickens's later novels take up the predatory atmosphere of the urban crowd explored in these books. *Dombey and Son* obliquely returns to the theme of the crowd bursting into the cell of the imprisoned person, full of eyes staring into his secrets. Mr Dombey is tormented by the thought that the swarming people at the station have perceptive access into his inner world. He resents that the armband of mourning 'should have let in such a herd to insult him with their knowledge of his defeated hopes' (20 p. 275). After his separation from Edith, he, like Rudge, imagines that the vast numbers of people he encounters in London exist purely to expose him:

> The world. What the world thinks of him, how it looks at him, what it sees in him, and what it says – this is the haunting demon of his mind. It is everywhere where he is; and worse than that, it is every-where where he is not. ... he sees it pointing after him in the street; ... it goes beckoning and babbling among the crowd; ... restless and busy everywhere, with nothing else but him.
>
> (51 p. 682)

Paradoxically, the crowd may submerge identity or declare it and both outcomes are to be feared.

In *Little Dorrit*, the ashamed Nandy feels that he lives in 'a city of cats' (I 31 p. 413). These innumerable feline watchers of London symboli-cally amplify the power of Blandois, the unwelcome revealer of secrets whom Dickens explicitly compares to the 'many vagrant cats ... looking at him with eyes by no means unlike his own' (II 10 p. 527). This atmos-phere establishes the crowd as full of watchful eyes, inexorably gaining access to long hidden secrets, so that it comes to represent those to whom the secrets of all concealers must one day be exposed. Thus Mrs Clennam rightly feels 'as if she were environed by distracting thoughts, rather than by external humanity and observation' and fears 'the turbulent interruption of this multitude of staring faces into her cell of years' (*LD* II 31 p. 766).

Although it is the force that largely defines the character of the metropolis, the crowd is not in this aspect allied to the crooked streets of London that provide what shape it has, nor even to the clarity-reducing mud and fog to which Dickens compares it elsewhere in his fiction. Instead, it is connected to all in Dickens's city that inherently pushes truth into the open, most importantly in the context of the fleeing criminal, the Detective Police Force. This is why Rudge interprets it as a force of revelation that will bring him to execution:

> His guilty conscience instantly arrayed these men against himself, and brought the fear upon him that he would be singled out, and torn to pieces.
>
> (65 p. 584)

Although the mob's bestiality and irrationality are factors that aid concealment of identity and threaten to bury humanity in deathbound regression, then, they become the crucial motivators of revelation and enforcers of identity. Cockshut sees Dickens as in sympathy with the bloodthirsty mob justice that pursues Sikes, but realising that in the interests of orderly society, he cannot allow the crowd to execute it themselves. He therefore allows their wishes to be granted by an accident overruled by narrative justice. The picture in *A Tale of Two Cities* is rather more complicated – the crowd can be moved to right feeling, but may forget this instantly when under some new influence, as is the case with the status accorded to Dr Mannette's testimony.[34] This discomfort of the responsible social novelist with the fitness of the crowd to signify narrative justice is, however, also present and in conflict with the inclination of the imaginative artist to trust its power in the earlier novels. In this, the function of the crowd in these novels closely resembles that of the railway sytem in *Dombey and Son*. Both are represented as an integral part of the city's workings, both operate according to their own rules which are mysterious to the ordinary Londoner and both appear actively to bring about the catastrophe of the plot, while they are merely following their own inscrutable patterns. Indeed, Carker's fear of the train catching up with him and destroying him in a moment of exposure is a reworking of Sikes's flight from the crowd. Dickens uses both as agents of the teleological aspects of the narrative which reveal denied connections between people, punishing the wicked with death and the good with new life, yet both are deeply ambiguous manifestations of Providence, bringing about the desired revelations and resurrections with chillingly amoral motivation.

V. The regenerating crowd

As well as the potential to represent Providential justice and a scheme of revelation, the crowd in Dickens's London holds the promise of renewed life. Like the train in *Dombey and Son*, it is a force of metropolitan modernity that threatens death and destruction of identity, yet can bring a genuinely vibrant and healthy new life to those who can embrace the death of that old identity. Paradoxically, the crowd that is consistently described in terms of the regressive and deathbound in *Barnaby Rudge* revitalises the author, whose imaginative energy is restored once he starts to describe the activity of the rioters, as his well-known relish for the destruction he described may demonstrate:

> I have let all the prisoners out of Newgate, burnt down Lord Mansfield's, and played the very devil.[35]

Despite the crowd's criminality and evil and Dickens's genuine horror at the abandonment of social order, the novelist as Philip Collins points out[36] seems rather in sympathy with the mob than with the soldiers. Unlike Milton in Blake's famous phrase, he certainly does know that he is on the side of the devils he describes.

Throughout his private writings, Dickens shows that the life that characterises his fiction comes from his immersion as an author in the crowds of large cities. In a letter to Forster, he acknowledged his acute consciousness of dependence upon London for the production of vibrant art. He attributes his difficulty in writing in Switzerland to

> the absence of streets and numbers of figures. I can't express how much I want these. It seems as if they supplied something to my brain, which it cannot bear, when busy, to lose. ... a day in London sets me up again and starts me. But the toil and labour of writing, day after day, without that magic lantern, is IMMENSE!! ... *My* figures seem disposed to stagnate without crowds about them.[37]

Here the metropolitan masses are the solution to atrophy and death, rather than their cause. His daughter, Kate, further commented upon the artistic regeneration he found there:

> he would walk through the busy, noisy streets, which would act on him like a tonic and enable him to take up with new vigour the flagging interest of his story and breathe new life into its pages.[38]

Dickens longed to mingle with the crowd again during the writing of *Dombey and Son* because he felt it would provide a resurrection for his creativity. It is no wonder then that his character, Florence, experiences immersion in the urban concourse as revivifying after her deadening experiences.

The subject matter and form of Dickens's art capture the *flâneur's* excitement at being out in the metropolitan throng as strongly as do the drawings of Constantin Guys. From the beginning of his career, Dickens spells out to the reader the fact that the source of his imaginative energy will be the busy thoroughfares of London and displays an intolerance for anyone who cannot share such pleasures:

> we have not the slightest commiseration for the man who can take up his hat and stick, and walk from Covent–garden to St. Paul's

Churchyard, and back into the bargain, without deriving some amusement—we had almost said instruction—from his perambulation.

('Shops and their Tenants', *SBB* p.80)

The other *Sketches by Boz*, including 'Seven Dials' and 'Greenwich Fair', show immense enjoyment of the movement of people through the streets. Dickens brings the dialogue between positive and negative ways of experiencing the crowd directly into the symbolic framework of *Dombey and Son*. For Florence's response to the crowd as an agent of death *and* resurrection, Dickens has worked upon the early nineteenth-century view of the metropolitan masses summarised in the Lamb letter and developed in his own previous fiction. Equally, for Dombey's attitude in seeing the crowd as bringing death to a fixed identity, he has worked upon the response characterised by the earlier Wordsworth and explored in the more frightening aspects of the mob in *Oliver Twist* and *Barnaby Rudge*.

The same duality of response is shown as late as *Our Mutual Friend*. In this book, when the deadness of Wrayburn's old life is paramount, 'the faces of the people' on the streets are compared to the leaves and scraps of paper blown about by the wind which 'nibbled and pinched' both the human and inanimate debris of London (I 12 p. 147).[39] This is contrasted with another sort of metropolitan crowd, that of Paris, which is full of 'wonderful human ants' who are able to pick up the fragments of paper and assemble them into a meaningful whole. Indeed, the metaphor of ants suggests that they themselves are not an amorphous collection of fragments, but people in an organised society. In the later fiction, however, the Thames tends to take over the role of the crowd as the defining aspect of the metropolis, allowing, like the whole city of which it forms a part, an exploration of the ongoing validity of religious symbolism. In the early fiction, it is the crowd that ambiguously effects the concealments of the self-centred and despairing. It does the river's work of bringing death – or sometimes a baptismal death *and* revivification at the plot's predetermined moment to those elect few who can surrender to that death and emerge from it to walk in newness of life. Sometimes its failure to do so suggests a modern aesthetic not far from that on display in *Our Mutual Friend*, where the river/sea in this updated form cannot bring any true renewal, but only a hideous death-in-life, or which can only do so for some.

The very form of Dickens's writing about the irresistible surge of the crowd forces his readers to participate directly in the disorienting journey towards a possible point of closure it symbolises. Constant scene changes and polyphony of voice continually disorient them and force them to share the experience of submersion in London's population. Raymond Williams comments perceptively upon this identity of form and subject matter in Dickens's fiction:

> As we stand and look back at a Dickens novel the general movement we remember ... is a hurrying seemingly random passing of men and women, each heard in some fixed phrase, seen in some fixed expression: a way of seeing men and women that belongs to the street. ... But then as the action develops, unknown and unacknowledged relationships, profound and decisive connections, definite and committing recognitions ... are as it were forced into consciousness. These are the real and inevitable relationships and connections, the necessary recognitions and avowals of any human society. But they are of a kind that are obscured, complicated, mystified, by the sheer rush and noise and miscellaneity of this new and complex social order.[40]

This book has, of course, claimed that Dickens saw this revelation of connections as a divine operation. It brings the human being who will surrender an identity based upon concealment of relationships with others to a knowledge of his or her place within the larger scheme of things, the total human society, which develops organically out of mankind's relationship with the Father God. Like the river, Dickens's crowded prose carries reader and character towards a disconcerting burial of identity and then works inexorably towards a washing up of truth, a pointing towards the individual, and this is experienced vividly whenever Dickens describes the metropolitan multitude. Even at the moment when the unique style leaves readers most bewildered, the liveliness of the language and the incessant variety and motion of the crowd reinvigorates them and draws them forward to the story's conclusion.

The essential ambiguity of the crowd is its ability to lead both to concealment and revelation, both to death and resurrection, as the Providential mechanism of mystery requires. Its ability to represent and even to enact the revelations and concealments that must take place in the narrative/Providential design are characteristic of the function of the metropolis as a whole. Even to the characters in Dickens's novels, the idea of the one is inseparable from the other. For Noah Claypole, for example, the masses define London:

> he arrived at the Angel at Islington, where he wisely judged, from the crowd of passengers and number of vehicles, that London began in earnest.
>
> (OT 42 p. 286)

Equally their absence defines the country in *Oliver Twist*. The boy loves the churchyard because it is 'not crowded':

> Oliver, whose days had been spent among squalid crowds, and in the midst of noise and brawling, seemed to enter on a new existence there.
>
> (32 p. 210)

At the hanging in *Barnaby Rudge*, every available space in the capital is covered by a single, solid mass of people whose shape is identical to London's physical geography:

> Every window was now choked up with heads; the house-tops teemed with people – clinging to chimneys, peering over gable-ends, and holding on where the sudden loosening of any brick or stone would dash them down into the street. The church tower, the church roof, the church yard, the prison leads, the very water-spouts and lamp-posts – every inch of room – swarmed with human life.
>
> (77 p. 691)

For Bill Sikes too, the crowd is the essential part of the city, again assuming its structure:

> tiers and tiers of faces in every window; and cluster upon cluster of people clinging to every house-top. Each little bridge (and there were three in sight) bent beneath the weight of the crowd upon it.
>
> (*OT* 50 p. 346)

No wonder he feels 'as though the whole city had poured its population out to curse him' (50 p. 345). The crowd crystalises London's symbolic work of hinting at a scheme of teleological justice or of entirely obliterating ontological revelations of identity and more than any other of its features takes on the very shape and form of the metropolis.

Sometimes in Dickens, however, the city both is and is not co-terminous with the crowd and the two views simultaneously appear and clash violently, adding to the universal chaos. Within one paragraph in *Barnaby Rudge*, the mob both opposes London, conceived as its built environment of churches, houses and streets, and *is* London, conceived as the people who form the city. To some it seems 'as though it were the intention of the insurgents to wrap the city in a circle of flames', while to others, it seems 'as if all London were arrayed against them, and they stood alone against the town' (67 p. 606). With extraordinary flexibility, the throng that represents anarchy and savagery soon comes to stand for society and a kind of order. In one chapter, it is burning down Newgate Prison; in another, it is supporting the public hanging of the rioters. The 'roar' of those watching the execution (77 p. 691) closely resembles the roar of the disturbances. It is impossible to determine whether this mob baying for Hugh's blood is largely the same as that which followed him. This induces reflection and fear in readers' minds at how quickly they may be turned from love to hatred should they be too heavily influenced by pressure from the crowd and not by objective standards of morality. It also shows that the force that destroys society and the force that builds it again are unnervingly the same in Dickens's world.

In Chapter 77, in which Hugh and Dennis are hanged, Dickens is keenly aware of the contrast between the vibrancy of the city architecture – 'the roofs and upper stories ... the spires of city churches and the great cathedral dome' – and the focal point of the picture:

> in the midst of so much life, and hope, and renewal of existence, stood the terrible instrument of death.
>
> (p. 689)

The contrast between the people of London and their reason for congregating is even more startling. In this scene, all is cheerful bustle and the description closely resembles Florence's crowd as the 'stream of life' rather than that depicted earlier in *Barnaby Rudge* leaving destruction in its wake:

> Along the two main streets at either end of the cross-way, a living stream had now set in, rolling towards the marts of gain and business.
>
> (p. 689)

It is disconcerting to remember that at the 'centre' of this 'eager crowd' stands the gallows. *Oliver Twist* notes this dependency of the crowd's life-giving function upon its death-bringing aspect with great economy at Fagin's hanging. The penultimate chapter closes with the words:

> A great multitude had already assembled; ... the crowd were pushing, quarrelling, and joking. Everything told of life and animation, but one dark cluster of objects in the very centre of all – the black stage, the cross-beam, the rope, and all the hideous apparatus of death.
>
> (52 p. 364)

As always, the emergence of new life cannot come about without an experience of death. Vitalising revelation of connections between people cannot be fully made without the death of Fagin and his doctrine of 'take care of number one' (*OT* 48 p. 293). While this philosophy of 'mutual trust' (p. 294) promises to forge a society of sorts out of the crowd with which he is surrounded, it is the ultimate concealment of the true relationships between people because it is based upon self-interest and not upon love. This is why Dickens's London is structured in such a way that the life of the crowd depends upon the death of Fagin. It is why the rebirth of Staggs's Gardens depends upon the impact of the railway network so feared by Dombey and the self-absorbed philosophy he represents and why Eugene Wrayburn must break with his old way of life in a baptismal drowning in the Thames. The working of London in Dickens's fiction at its most optimistic symbolises the workings of a divinely ordained mystery which reveals, at just the right time, the regenerating network of familial connections with other human beings. This is presented as the antidote to the death and atrophy, which has come from mankind's self-absorbed concealment of those relationships. To those prepared to surrender to the death brought about by the old way of life, the revealing aspects of London can effect a transforming resurrection. The most disturbing thing about Dickens's fiction is that the mechanisms of the city that represents this process of mystery seem for the most part frighteningly amoral. The benign order that governs their behaviour is visible to the author and eventually to the reader, but not from the perspective of the characters. The crowd discovers Rudge, Sikes and Fagin and pushes towards the capture of these self-absorbed concealers, but ironically it may do so at the instigation of men like Gashford, following their own motives of concealment. In Dickens's novels the ambiguous behaviour of his created London emphasises the religious and secular attitudes in constant dialogue underlying his version of religious mystery. For him, it is the very force that buries truth fathoms deep, it is the antisocial, the deathbound, even the evil, that ultimately brings about the dénouement, that works towards the greater good, that brings new life and ultimately makes inevitable the benevolent revelation.

Conclusion: 'What is the city over the mountains'

A study that has made so much of the narrative drive towards discovery ought to reach a conclusion as decisive as one of Mr Bucket's denouements. The word itself suggests that revelation and the organising principle that goes with it will triumph over the bewildering mass of information that is Dickens's representation of London throughout his fiction. And indeed these are novels that celebrate the possibility of drawing conclusions. In them, Dickens characteristically delights in establishing connections between apparently random groupings of characters and events, revealing origins and relationships between human beings in the process.

Modern readers looking at the novels through the lens of *The Waste Land* may be tempted to read them as a symbolic poem in many parts – one which shows a slippery universe suggesting and withholding an order that would ultimately guarantee a progress towards revivifying revelation of meaning. Nevertheless, it has also become clear that any position of overview from which Dickens's London can be seen as a totality will necessarily be an artificial construct. The writer's depiction of London was determined by too many local imperatives across the thirty-seven years of his published career to be viewed as a coherent artistic whole with a single symbolic agenda. We have considered some of the political, generic and biographical factors that determined his modes of representing London alongside the instinct to use it as a vehicle for dramatising his religious vision – and his anxieties about it – that has formed the focus of this study. The complex interaction between these forces makes Dickens's work characteristic of how Victorian writers absorbed the unprecedented phenomenon of metropolitan London into their shifting ideologies.

211

It should not cause us to wonder that it triggered renewed reflection on how the individual relates to the whole universe (and indeed whether or not it could still be thought of as a totality) and that there should be a religious dimension to such reflection. Dickens unquestionably used London's sublime immensity to amplify the inner experiences of characters forced to engage with such enormous questions. Indeed, he played a crucial role in developing ways of perceiving the city and of writing about it that cause reflection on religious issues. That this was not always his primary consideration in introducing his depictions of metropolitan culture makes these texts all the more useful. The multiplicity of these functional motivations means that these texts are representative of a society making sense of new phenomena through a wide range of discourses, such as the religious, the political, the scientific and the philosophical, once held to be stable and unified and now increasingly bifurcating.

Panning back from the component aspects of London that each chapter has focused on, how does London as a totality interact with the traditional religious symbolic domain? We might want to think of Dickens's London as in contrast to Augustine's City of God (mediated, perhaps, through John Bunyan, and itself adapted from the books of Hebrews and Revelation). Alexander Welsh's *The City of Dickens* has already treated this theme comprehensively, identifying London as a social and spiritual problem with Augustine's earthly city, based on corrupt values and destined for destruction. The novelist presents London's cash culture as unheavenly in character because it is hostile to the principles of healthy life, which, according to Welsh, are to be found in familial relationships as expressed in the comfortable home:

> the problem that challenges the imagination of Dickens can be named ... the city of death. ... [H]is answer can be named the hearth.[1]

This account of Dickens's treatment of the city seems to ally him with the early Ruskin, conceiving London as evidence of a religious problem in society manifesting itself in social ills. Like Ruskin too, the solution seems to be the increasingly secular one of middle-class domesticity, albeit retaining the religious vocabulary and symbolic patterns used in discussion of the problem. London figures as a place to withdraw from to the hearth, if any kind of life and revelation of healthy relationships is to be achieved.

Retaining Dickens's vague early commitment to Romantic ideologies of nature, the country may offer an alternative destination in an escape to nature. *Oliver Twist* and *The Old Curiosity Shop* attempt to realise this, if somewhat imperfectly, and Ephraim Sicher sees Lizzie's upstream refuge at the paper mill in *Our Mutual Friend* as maintaining this binary paradigm of a paradise outside the city, otherwise glimpsed only in dreams. Sicher reads the mill as an economically productive rural society transforming waste into useful material like that of the 'wonderful human ants' in Paris that can turn the 'mysterious paper currency' of the city's rubbish to account (I 12 p.147), whose absence the narrator so sorely laments.[2] This, however, seems to set up 'Paris, where nothing is wasted' as an alternative vision of the possibilities of the city to embody a complex transformative system in a metropolitan context. Here there is none of the pejorative association of Wordsworth's description of London as a 'monstrous anthill on the plain' (*The Prelude*, Book VII, ll. 149–51): to the habitually tidy and active Dickens, this energy is an unambiguous urban positive. When the reader later sees the dolls' dressmaker and Mr Venus turning cast-off matter to economic account, Dickens seems to signal that such ants may exist in London after all, even if the novelist alone and not the organised structure of the anthill supplies the purposeful sense of order.

Such fluctuations obviously reflect the constantly changing perception of a public figure whose business kept him in regular contact with the experience of life in the capital. Indeed, during the writing of this novel, London was undergoing extensive reorganisation for the very purpose of hygienic disposal of its waste. Alongside the building of Bazlguette's sewer system, the Thames embankment and Underground railway were being constructed leading to a wholesale transformation of London's appearance. The progress of these and the difficulties encountered were a matter of public debate, influencing perceptions of the city's possibility of becoming an ordered and healthy environment and Dickens's correspondence shows him to have been more excited than otherwise at the prospect. The comment on the inability of London to deal with its waste paper, moreover, serves an artistic rather than a journalistic purpose within the novel's structure, contextualising the wastefulness of Wrayburn's life, which is the subject of their discussion in the chapter that follows. By contrast, Jenny Wren seems to suggest a hope (somewhat pathetically at first) during his pursuit of Lizzie that waste material can be turned into something of homely value. Mr Venus's more morbid attempts seem to mock at the hope while encouraging it more faintly.

If varying personal experiences and attitudes combine with local needs of plot to complicate the possibility of measuring London against the concept of the heavenly city, this is even more true in relation to the body of the work as a whole. We have thought a great deal of Dickens's London with its impenetrable fog and incomprehensible structure as an update of the symbol of the gothic haunted castle. Insofar as this allows a restatement of the religious attitudes implied in the late eighteenth-century texts for a different society, it seems very much a re-figuration of the earthly city. 'The City', whether as a geographical space or metonymy for the commercial system of exchange, provides a figurative structure under the control of individuals like Dombey, Merdle, the Barnacles or Mrs Clennam, who stand for what is wrong with its ethos. Its complicity with their power suggests that it has been constructed as a rejection of the true values of family and community in favour of an artificial selfishness doomed eventually to apocalyptic collapse. The tangle of impenetrable streets full of locked doors, the funereal Adelphi arches, the smothering fog and mud have all been seen consistently to create a symbolic environment which hides relationships and brings destruction to those who live there. The gothic symbolism here, however, is sometimes merely grafted on to lend force to a Carlylean analysis of a depersonalising society in a state of atrophy, borrowing its tendency to religious rhetoric with broadly secular content. Moreover, Dickens may have found the gothic template useful primarily for generic reasons, a brick and mortar structure, now even more impenetrable and bewildering, resisting the point of closure until the time determined by the narrative.

In fact, however, as we have seen at length, the situation is a satisfyingly complex mixture of these. The generic function of the gothically treated city seems to serve the needs of the social rhetoric, but the reverse is also true. The reader's agreement about the imminent collapse of society so constituted is sometimes assumed as a metaphorical way of amplifying the gothic inevitability on which the plot depends. Moreover, the pervasive gothic imagery that finds its way into the rhetoric of urban sanitary reform allows an imaginative opportunity to explore the possibility that those who exploit London's complexity are ranging themselves against supernatural values. Even when Dickens did abandon the plot to declaim purely on social issues, he tended to see social problems as manifestations of spiritual problems, although he clearly felt neither qualified nor inclined to label these with anthropological or theological specificity.

The obvious denial of familial relationships between Dombey and Florence because of commercial values characterises a whole society where commercial values conceal obligations of care. The resultant collapse of both individual and societal family is explicitly traced to human rejection of filial relationships with the universal Father. The city's dilapidation in *Dombey and Son*, *Bleak House* and *Little Dorrit* is literally caused by a suppressed understanding of the relationships that bind society together but is also symbolic of the self-destructive results of concealing such relationships in other unconnected cases. Mrs Clennam's abandonment of her relationship of responsibility to Little Dorrit is presented specifically in the dénouement as an exclusion of the principles of New Testament Christianity. *Bleak House* tackles the problems arising from London's ever-spreading disease more directly as an external reality with a social solution. Nevertheless, it also heightens our perception of the devastation caused to the main characters by obscuring relationships of care. When the miasma is seen concealing the cross of St Paul's, Dickens consciously emphasises the inseparability of the religious from the political and moral implications of such concealments. Dickens does not merely introduce crosses and church spires as evidence of the hypocrisy of an urban culture paying lip service to their message while denying it in the metropolitan culture they have produced. At certain points, which have been discussed, they emerge from the gloom and show possibilities of urban life resembling the heavenly rather then the earthly city. In *Dombey and Son* it seems on the one hand that London is irrevocably fallen and earthly in culture, producing only unredeemed humanity:

> when fields of grain shall spring up from the offal in the by-ways of our wicked cities, and roses bloom in the fat church-yards that they cherish; then we may look for natural humanity and find it growing from such seed.
>
> (47 p. 620)

The good spirit must tear it down altogether before 'men, delayed no more by stumbling blocks of their own making, which are but specks of dust upon the path between them and eternity, would ... apply themselves, like creatures of one common origin, owning one duty to the Father of one family, and tending to one common end, to make the world a better place!' (*DS* 47 p. 620) Nevertheless, as discussed in Chapter 5, the railways already seem to be granting this wish in the case of Camden Town. Dombey's firm may dominate the City, but the city is governed by forces neither he nor Carker understand. These forces of modernity are drafted into the service of the project to take the narrative forward. Invested early on with suggestion of ominous powers, they are involved in various ways in exposing Dombey's inner life to the public gaze and are chosen as the agent of nemesis for Carker. At the more literal level, they are involved in the economic regeneration and ordered reorganisation of the city.

Likewise the chaotic London of *Bleak House* from Esther's perspective, exploited by the Chancery Court and the novel's more private concealers, turns out to be legible to and in some degree under the control of the omnipresent, if not quite omniscient metropolitan police force. Bucket and his men seem to be able to organise London's mass of information into a whole scheme that the fog is powerless to obscure. They exist to reinforce relationships of responsibility between people and the inevitability of punishment for those who transgress them.

The important thing to note is that these forces of transformative modernity are not alien factors imposed upon the city from outside in the country. Nor are they emanations of a separate holy realm of the hearth. They are fundamentally metropolitan institutions as central to the fabric of Dickens's London as the fog and labyrinthine streets. Moments of faith in a Providentially endorsed Progress emerge when the new modes of social organisation inherent in the metropolis are represented as the solution rather than the problem. Since 1970s, critics have tended to favour Ruskin's analysis of Dickens as leader of the steam whistle party over Chesterton's nostalgic painter of the coaching days. Andrew Sanders calls the portrait of a society renewed by the construction of the railways a typical example of 'mid-Victorian optimism' that technology would inevitably bring social progress in spite of some initial disruption.[3] Dickens's social optimism is not uncomplicated, however. Rather, Dickens uses London to dramatise the tension between pessimistic and optimistic views of the relationship between social progress and an underwriting Providence. He thus projects a future where the revelatory metropolitan forces allow social relationships to be seen while also demonstrating that other developing social structures may equally continue to conceal them if not pursued with the right determination.

What does become clear is that the city's economy is not solely under the control of the concealing villains after all. Its incomprehensibly complex rhythms seem to generate apocalypses in one place while representing a society shored up against them at another, usually in the same novel. The irony of this would not have escaped Dickens who frequently comments on the larger power of the city over those who think its complexity serves their ends. Just as the gothic villain often finds himself frustrated by the castle that he has used to maintain his power, so Quilp is kept from his rescuers by the impenetrability of the yard he has cultivated. Tulkinghorn thinks he can read the secrets of the house-tops he walks beneath, but cannot hear their warning not to go home. Merdle seeks to manipulate society and the market and is equally capti-vated himself precisely because of his position. It seems likely then that the functions for which he co-opts the city as essentially conflicted (i.e. between concealment and discovery, deadening and revivification) can-not simply be seen as an accident arising from the varying local causes that necessitated them. It seems a deliberate development of the dra-matic irony inherent in the gothic.

This seems consonant with the apocalyptic discourse of the heavenly city itself. Dickens's characteristic transformed cityscapes seem to reflect attitudes towards this symbol that involve fluctuating degrees of accept-ance of its specifically Christian and supernatural elements. *Dombey and Son* (15 p. 318), *Bleak House* (47 p. 719), *Little Dorrit* (II 31 p. 771) and *Great Expectations* (II 14 p. 130) give glimpses of a regenerated city in which human relationships are restored. Especially when read together, the prominence of the crosses and church spires in these is striking. These have been built into the city's architecture all along and these scenes imply that the altruistic values of Calvary have now been revealed and acted upon. Jo sees the cross through the fog when Woodcourt charitably provides for his needs and teaches him by exam-ple about the Fatherhood of God, emphasised in the Lord's prayer. The new church-filled cityscape in which people visibly enjoy family life and social interaction in *Little Dorrit* is seen once Mrs Clennam has made restitution to the woman she has wronged. It is an embodiment of the New Testament values she has learned from Little Dorrit and is the direct opposite of the panorama of Sabbatarian London at the beginning of the story (I 3), which had embodied her old religious out-look. The old has collapsed with the house and the new has arisen, albeit from the subjective viewpoint of these characters privileged by the narrator. Ephraim Sicher comes close to the truth with his statement that 'the religious language of salvation sounds as a still small voice in the wilderness of a social discourse preoccupied with the administration of efficient sanitation and police control as the means to regulate epi-demic disease and class conflict'.[4] This is intended to suggest that this element to the rhetoric, while present, is mainly drowned out by more secular discursive aspects. It will be remembered, however, that Elijah found God's word, not in the more obviously apocalyptic wind, earth-quake or fire, but in the still small voice (1 Kings 19). We can surely accept the implication in this allusion that something of immense sig-nificance, to Dickens at least, is conveyed when he introduces directly

Christian rhetoric to his mechanism of urban reform. For although the city's workings create the cross-concealing fog, they also contain the message of Christ's self-sacrifice and eventually proclaim it to those with eyes to see it. London, then, becomes the New Jerusalem in the immediate future without the need for an actual Second Coming. Instead, the changes seem to be effected by the market forces of a mass consumer society, coupled mysteriously with individual acts of kindness rippling outwards into socially responsible government. Nevertheless, these are glimpses of an alternative city where the Christian relationships called for in the narrator's rhetoric are realised, with suggestions of a Providentially ordained apocalyptic destruction of the old order.

Recalling the apocalyptic element to the New Jerusalem image may resolve some of the ambiguities surrounding Dickens's representation of the city without oversimplifying them. Moments of optimism and despair about London's ability to embody the heavenly rather than earthly city, as it were, seem to have been genuine responses in their own right. The city's power to bring both destruction and assertion of individual identity in relation to others, however, becomes increasingly systematised in Dickens's representational style. Dickens's increasingly careful plotting depends upon a process of mystery carefully deferred yet consistently hinted at throughout. In dramatising this process, the city's absolute resistance to the clear communication of information is emphasised at some points and its unprecedented means of systematising information at others both provide useful figures. It must foreground the contradiction if this technique is to be successful.

This view of London itself as the means by which characters participate in an ambiguous scheme of concealment and revelation had been seen in the earlier fiction. In *Oliver Twist* and *Barnaby Rudge*, the defining aspect of city life is the crowd. Like the railway, the crowd enforces the novelist's programme of mystery. Some seek to exploit its natural tendency to blur individual identity and conceal relationships so as to obscure their own guilty relationships with others. Sikes and Rudge, however, find that the crowd in Dickens may turn and insist upon individual identity, hunting the guilty and exposing him or her to its multitude of eyes. Chapter 7 of the book also considered that these early novels portray immersion in the crowd as bringing a re-invigorating life as well as death and dissolution of human identity. When *Dombey and Son* takes up the motif, the crowd has become part of the railway-organised London, moved around by the trains and travelling along the pavement in time to catch them. Florence immerses herself in this crowd after 'The Thunderbolt' has struck in a burial of her old identity as Dombey's daughter. Almost immediately, she is re-vitalised by the 'stream of life' (48 p. 639) and enters into a new existence at the Wooden Midshipman as Walter's wife.

In Dickens's later fiction, however, it is the Thames that assumes the role played here by the crowd and the railway. Like them, it is the central feature of city life, exploited by the concealer, bringing death to all, but also washing up truth and bringing new life to those prepared to surrender to the death of identity which it enforces. In *Little Dorrit*, 'the two frowning wildernesses of secrets' of North and South London converge upon 'the secrets of the river' in the middle. Chapter 6 considered the gradual development of Dickens's use of the Thames to include both a sense that the river concentrates London's tension between burial and exhumation. Like the railway, the fixity of its route embodies such narrative programme of mystery as exists in this world and like the railway it can seem conflicted between representation as indifferent or as benevolent. *Our Mutual Friend* draws these threads together by sucking its major characters into the river, burying their old identities and allowing them to re-emerge with new ones. The city throughout Dickens's fiction has always been a place to be immersed in, whether this is felt through its labyrinthine network of streets, fog or crowds, so that the enforced loss of preconceived identity may lead to the emergence of a new, true and vibrant identity. In making submergence in the river the most palpable part of this metropolitan experience, *Our Mutual Friend* draws the reader's attention to what it really is: a baptism in the mysteries tradition. F. S. Schwarzbach's Pauline language in discussing this novel recognises the renunciation of a deathbound old self and the emergence of a new self that is figured in the immersions of the two male protagonists in the Thames. They have been 'drowning in the cash nexus, and they must die to it to escape it'.[5] An old identity and relationship to the world has gone and a new one has come in the best anthropocentric *Bildungsroman* tradition. In a world where the relationship between the individual and the forces that govern his or her immediate environment are now too complex to be understood, the city provides an unprecedented metaphor for what is to be hoped for such a narrative.

I have tended to discuss Dickens's London as existing in a realist medium at the level of plot, but transcending it. It functions as a recurring symbol, composed of many smaller symbols each of which individually interacts with related images in overlapping discourses and previous literary genres, but greater than the sum of its parts. It is a symbol rather than a metaphor or component of allegory. It allows for dialogic discussion with its antecedents and analogues in other literary genres and spheres of discourse. Through it, Dickens diagnoses annihilating concealment of identity and relationship to human society as the major failure of the modern metropolis to live up to the archetypes with which he brings the city and its elements into comparison. Elsewhere he seems able to update archetypes of the city as an eternally realised Christian vision or as a mark of more secular civilisation and progress to the realities of the vibrant modern metropolis without too much trouble. Sicher's remark on contradictions in Dickens's worldview increasingly flagged up in the fiction is particularly apt here:

> the dialogic discourse, far from distancing itself in despair at any stable meaning in an unredeemed world, does not preclude belief in another world beyond empirical verification and in a Creator to whom there is moral responsibility. On the contrary, it suggests the possibility of transcendence, as well as the consequences of blindness to it
>
> (p. 375)

At his most insightful, Dickens makes the character's experience of urban disorientation and alienation, which his prose style so skilfully replicates, part of a process that enforces revelation of real identities and relationships. Some are brought to recognise their dependence upon and obligation to a network of other people, immediately filial or conjugal, but spreading outwards to involve living as part of a whole society. Others, such as Florence Dombey or Esther Summerson, who already act towards others in an altruistic spirit, gain a sense of who they really are and their new life becomes a liberating enactment of that new identity. Dickens is keen in his mature fiction to question whether – and how – fiction may still embody a Providential scheme to lead people to such insights in the midst of a fragmenting heap of discourses. His constantly varying comments on the transforming power the structures and mechanisms of the city could signify (sometimes ironic, sometimes approving, sometimes both in equal measure) arise in any number of contexts. The moments when he is able to suggest an overview that makes use of the city's obstacles to clarity may be read as epiphanies of faith in modernity's compatibility with religiously optimistic ways of looking at the world.

The river and the crowds are microcosmic of the whole metropolis in potentially bringing both concealment and revelation, death and regeneration. Dickens's London consistently provides the mechanism by which a connection with the divine is concealed and then revealed at a preordained point of surrender to death, just as it was in the mystery religions. The complex of literary archetypes and images, violently recast in other contemporary fields of discourse, suggest a radical re-examination of the effectiveness of these for the world in which Dickens wrote.[6] Thus he created a new way of looking at the city that profoundly influenced the next generations of writers. It is directly re-examined, in T. S. Eliot's *The Waste Land*, which dramatises a modern yearning for the revelation and regeneration in a dying world addressed by Christianity and the mystery religions. As in Dickens, London militates against any such clarity by its dirt, decay, homogenising crowds and the river, which threatens to suck the quester into its mud. It is made clear that 'death had undone so many' (l. 63)[7] because people have perversely rejected real relationships, just as they do in Dickens's fiction. Lil's choice of sterility over motherhood, for example, in the form of 'them pills I took to bring it off' (l. 159),[8] is presented as the cause of her disintegration into a toothless state, resembling the 'dead mountain mouth of carious teeth that cannot spit' (l. 349). The characteristic Londoner, as in Dickens, lives in a perpetually decaying death-in-life which is figured in the decomposing metropolis that surrounds him or her. 'April is the cruellest month' for these people because they cannot tolerate contact with genuine regenerating forces. They have too strong a desire to keep their connections with the outside world buried and persist in their deathly, but never fully dead, existence. In this they demonstrate the same warped outlook diagnosed as characteristic of London society in *Our Mutual Friend*. Strangely, for example, Mortimer Lightwood says of Harmon Senior, 'He directs himself to be buried with certain eccentric ceremonies and precautions against his coming to life, with which I need not bore you' (I 2 p. 26). Generally burial customs are designed to provide for rather than to prevent resurrection, but in the London of these two works, people have chosen a self-enclosed culture that leads to death, and rejected the regenerative connections between people. At the same time they refuse to acknowledge that their chosen path leads ultimately to the destruction they have cut themselves off to protect. Thus they shore up their crumbling identities until the last possible moment and never make the surrender to death that can lead to resurrection, as John Harmon and Eugene Wrayburn ultimately do.

Yet like them, Eliot's poet/quester hopes that the city, with the Thames at its centre, may be taking those prepared to surrender to a baptismal 'death by water' to a revelation of spiritual life. Indeed, the city tantalisingly suggests that such is its purpose. The quester reads Ariel's song of transformation out of shipwreck from *The Tempest* in vibrant music from a public house and the promise of spiritual vitality in the city churches:

> 'This music crept by me upon the waters'
> And along the Strand, up Queen Victoria Street.
> O city, city, I can sometimes hear
> Beside a public bar in Lower Thames Street,
> The pleasant whining of a mandoline
> And a clatter and a chatter from within
> Where fishermen lounge at noon: where the walls
> Of Magnus Martyr hold
> Inexplicable splendour of Ionian white and gold
>
> (ll. 257–65)[9]

In the final section, the cityscape even seems to experience an apocalyptic destruction in the manner of that which befalls London in *Dombey and Son* in preparation for the emergence of new life. Although Eliot is less optimistic than Dickens that this collapse will precipitate the arrival of the New Jerusalem, his question 'What is the city over the mountains' (l. 371) keeps the hope in view. Like so many of Dickens's novels, this poem is concerned with the failure or success of the traditional symbols of Christianity to sound out a message of regenerative revelation in a modern urban context. *The Waste Land* is a song of hope that London may after all represent a Providential scheme of regenerative revelation through immersion in its deadening confusion as Dickens had encouraged the world to view it – and of despair that it may not be so – paralleling the doubts embedded in Dickens. The nineteenth-century novelist had thus opened up a way of perceiving the city and of writing about it symbolically as potentially a contemporary mechanism of a mysterious programme of spiritual regeneration. It is just as impossible to view the city in the same way after the creative energy of Dickens has taken hold of it, as it is for the Staggs's Gardeners in *Dombey and Son* after the impact of the railway stamps its own vision upon Camden Town.

To Raymond Williams, 'the true significance of the city' in Dickens's fiction is the simultaneous representation of 'the random and the systematic, the visible and the obscured'. London's forces of discovered social organisation, however, win out, so that the 'creation of consciousness – of recognitions and relationships – can then be seen as the purpose of Dickens's developed fiction'.[10] Thus to participate in the city's conflict of forces is a 'transforming social experience'.[11]

Notes

Introduction: 'A heap of broken images'

1. Most critics of *The Waste Land*, from Conrad Aiken's essay, 'An Anatomy of Melancholy' (reproduced in *T. S. Eliot, The Critical Heritage*, vol. I, pp. 156–7) have read the poem's city passages as the culmination of a series of symbols describing a state of spiritual aridity over many centuries. These earlier symbolic narratives usually imply a way to transform that condition through revelatory renewal. It is frequently debated whether or not Eliot's evocation of these images suggests, by ironic contrast, that the power of renewal inherent in these images is exhausted in the modern world. Summarising Cleanth Brooks's argument in '*The Waste Land*: An analysis' (*T. S. Eliot: A Study of His Writings in Several Hands* (London: Dennis Dobson, 1947), p. 21), A. D. Moody explains that each allusion 'only intensifies the failure to experience the rites of transformation, and emphasises the actuality of untransmuted nature. In his meeting with Mr Eugenides in the Unreal City there is again a lacerating sense of parody. The sodomite Smyrna merchant is not a carrier of the ancient mysteries ... only of dried currants' (*Thomas Stearns Eliot, Poet* (Cambridge: Cambridge University Press, 1979), p. 90). On the other hand, the music of the fishmen's bar and the splendour of Magnus Martyr suggest a transformed Thames-side urban life, leading Helen Gardener to read *The Waste Land* as an anticipation of Eliot's later embrace of a ritualistic form of Christianity (*The Art of T. S. Eliot* (London: Cresset, 1949)). Others have recognised the rich ambivalence of Eliot's use of this symbolism. Helen Williams suggests that a hinted series of (missed) moments for embracing the real 'remains to the reader's imagination ... a perpetual possibility' (*T. S. Eliot: The Waste Land* (London: Edward Arnold, 1973), pp. 40–3). Derek Traversi discusses 'the chief symbols which Eliot sought in his poem to impose on his "broken" material, in the absence of an accepted and common tradition', saying, 'The true importance of *The Waste Land* lies precisely in the refusal to simplify, to produce a final statement of belief which was not adequately based on experience as given in the course of the poem' (*The Longer Poems* (London: The Bodely Head, 1976), pp. 22, 44).
2. *Charles Dickens: His Tragedy and Triumph*, 2 vols (London: Hamish Hamilton, 1952), vol. II, pp. 1043–4.
3. '*Ulysses*, Order and Myth' in *The Dial* (November 1923), pp. 480–3, for example, recommends a consciously ritualistic approach for Modernist writers.
4. Michael Hollington gives a helpful summary of Dickens's playful comparisons with classical incident, usually to imply the inferiority of modern attempts to project heroism ('Classical myth and legend' in P. Schlicke (ed.), *Oxford Reader's Companion to Dickens* (Oxford: Oxford University Press, 1999), p. 110.).
5. See 'Hamlet as Orestes' in *The Classical Tradition in Poetry* (Cambridge, MA: Harvard University Press, 1927).

6. Perhaps the best-known example of such a mythical study of Dickens, although it does not seek to address the subject of the river, is Northrop Frye's essay 'Dickens and the Comedy of Humors' (re-printed in Harold Bloom (ed.), *Modern Critical Views* (New York: Chelsea House, 1987), pp. 71–91).
7. Oxford: Clarendon, 1994.
8. See ibid., pp. 22 ff.
9. *Collected Poems 1909–1962* (London: Faber, 1974), p. 65.
10. Ibid, pp. 80–1.
11. *The Imagination of Charles Dickens* (London: Collins, 1961), p. 183.
12. *Selected Essays* (London: Faber & Faber, 1951), p. 15.

1 'A revelation by which men are to guide themselves': Dickens and Christian Theology

1. London: George Allen & Unwin, 1981, p. 3.
2. Ibid., p. 179.
3. *Charles Dickens Resurrectionist* (London and Basingstoke: Macmillan, 1982), p. 62.
4. Ibid., p. 197.
5. *Dickens and the Broken Scripture* (Athens, GA: University of Georgia Press, 1985), p. 44.
6. Ibid., p. 90.
7. Alexander Welsh, *The City of Dickens* (Oxford: Oxford University Press, 1971), p. 74.
8. See, for example, ibid., pp. 83–4.
9. Walder, *Dickens and Religion* (London: George Allen and Unwin, 1981), p. xiii.
10. Quoted in ibid., p. 422.
11. To Jerrold, 3 May 1843, *Letters*, vol. III, p. 482.
12. Quoted in Walder, *Dickens and Religion*, p. 93.
13. Quoted in ibid., p. 35.
14. Quoted in Philip Collins, *Dickens Interviews and Recollections*, 2 vols (London and Basingstoke: Macmillan, 1981), vol. II, p. 340.
15. In December 1842, *The Christian Remembrancer* observed that 'His religion, whenever any is introduced, is for the most part such mere pagan sentimentalism, that we should have been better pleased by its absence' (quoted in H. House, *The Dickens World* (London: Oxford University Press, 1942), p. 113).
16. Quoted in Philip Collins, *Dickens Interviews and Recollections*, vol. II, p. 320.
17. This is discussed in Larson, *Dickens and the Broken Scripture* (Athens, GA: University of Georgia Press, 1985), pp. 202, 209–14.
18. 28 May 1861, *Letters*, vol. X, pp. 252–3.
19. *The Life of Our Lord* (London and Edinburgh: Morrison & Gibb, 1934), p. 14.
20. Ibid., p. 35.
21. To Felton, 2 March 1843, *Letters*, vol. III, pp. 455–6.
22. Had Dickens intended to publish it, he would undoubtedly have corrected these peculiarities of capitalisation.
23. *The Life of Our Lord*, pp. 124–7.
24. House, *The Dickens World*, p. 109.
25. Walder, *Dickens and Religion*, p. 174.

26. Larson, *Dickens and the Broken Scripture*, p. 319.
27. To de Cerjat, 28 May 1863, *Letters*, vol. X, p. 253.
28. To Forster, 13–14 October 1844, *Letters*, vol. IV, p. 207.
29. Larson, *Dickens and the Broken Scripture*, p. 320.
30. Most famously by Dorothy Van Ghent in 'The Dickens World: A View From Todgers's' (1950), George H. Ford and Lauriat Lane (eds), *The Dickens Critics* (Ithaca: NY: Cornell University Press, 1961), pp. 213–32.
31. To Forster, 19–21 September, *Letters*, vol. VI, p. 764.
32. House, *The Dickens World*, p. 112.
33. See M. Wheeler, *Heaven, Hell and the Victorians* (Cambridge: Cambridge University Press, 1994), p. 219.
34. House, *The Dickens World*, p. 112.
35. The other is at the deaths of children, which will be dealt with shortly.
36. Noah Claypole, Quilp's boy and the young Smallweeds seem hardly to belong to this category and represent a conflicting view of children.
37. Larson, *Dickens and the Broken Scripture*, p. 233.
38. Ibid., p. 234.
39. See also Barabara Hardy, 'The Change of Heart in Dickens's Novels', in *Victorian Studies*, vol. V (1961), pp. 49–67.
40. A phrase so important, it is included prominently in the manuscript number plan for this chapter.
41. *The Life of Our Lord*, p. 103.
42. Ibid., p. 123.
43. Forster, J. *The Life of Charles Dickens* (London: Dent, 1966), vol. II, p. 422.
44. *The Life of Our Lord*, p. 28.
45. To Forster, 8 Jan 1845.
46. Theologically speaking, Providentialism differs from Fatalism in that while the latter emphasises humanity's lack of control over events, it does not assume a guiding, benevolent intention.
47. To Wilkie Collins, 6 October 1859, *Letters*, vol. IX, p. 128, quoted in Mark Knight, '*Little Dorrit* and Providence', *Dickens Studies Annual*, vol. XXXII (2002), pp. 179–90.
48. 'Dickens and Social Ideas', in Michael Slater (ed.), *Dickens 1970* (London: Chapman & Hall, 1970), pp. 96–7.
49. New York: AMS Press, 2003.
50. Ibid., p. 332.
51. For the argument summarised here, see ibid., pp. 365–9.
52. Ibid., p. 346.
53. Ibid., p. 375.

2 'The debilitated old house in the city': London as Haunted House

1. David Jarret has comprehensively traced Mrs Clennam's house to its antecedents in the gothic castle in 'The Fall of the House of Clennam', *Dickensian*, vol. LXXIII (1977), pp. 155–61.
2. To John Forster, 18 March 1841, *The Letters of Charles Dickens* (Oxford: Clarendon Press, 1965–2002), vol. II, pp. 238–9.

3. See *The Letters of Charles Dickens*, vol. VII, p. 547.
4. See also *A Tale of Two Cities* (I 3).
5. *Love and Death in the American Novel* (Normal, IL: Dalkey, 1966), p. 132.
6. The question of whether the child is to be held responsible for the parent's originating sin is explored when Dickens treats the question of legitimate and illegitimate birth, most obviously in the case of Esther Summerson in *Bleak House*.
7. For Adam's desire for covering see *Paradise Lost*, Book IX, ll. 1067–98. For his fear of his descendants' curses, see X, ll. 720–41.
8. *Horror Fiction and the Protestant Tradition* (Basingstoke and London: Meredith, 1988).
9. Perhaps the most sustained discussion of the use of the haunted castle with Genesis is to be found in Kate Ferguson Ellis, *The Contested Castle* (Urbana and Chicago: University of Illinois Press, 1989), which reads these novels primarily as 'the Gothic revision of the myth of the fall' (p. 57), re-writing Milton's account for a society heavily dependent upon Female figures who could protect the Eden of the bourgeois home by their alertness and resistance to temptation.
10. For the ideas summarised here, see *The Closed Space* (Manchester and New York: Manchester University Press, 1990), pp. 75–87.
11. Burke, E. *A Philosophical Enquiry into the Origin of Our Ideas of the Sublime and the Beautiful*. Oxford: Oxford University Press, 1990, pp. 66–7.
12. For a concise summary of this use of the Sublime in the gothic novel, see Eve Kosofsky Sedgwick, *The Coherence of Gothic Conventions* (New York: Arno, 1980), pp. 28–9.
13. Burke, *A Philosophical Enquiry*, pp. 54–5.
14. See Leopold Damrosch Jr, *God's Plot and Man's Stories: Studies in the Fictional Imagination from Milton to Fielding*. Chicago and London: University of Chicago Press, 1985.
15. Miss Havisham in *Great Expectations* is a still more extreme re-working of Mrs Clennam.
16. 'Introduction' to Little Dorrit, re-printed in George H. Ford and Lauriat Lane Jr (eds) *The Dickens Critics* (Westport, CN: Greenwood, 1972), pp. 279–93.
17. *London Labour and the London Poor*, 4 vols (New York: Dover, 1968), vol. 1V, p. 213.
18. See Colour Plate 1 for this painting and Figure 1 for another contemporary image of life under the arches.
19. Quoted in R. Samuel, 'Comers and Goers', in H. J. Dyos and M. Wolff (eds) *The Victorian City*, 2 vols, (London and Boston: Routledge & Kegan Paul, 1973), vol. I, pp. 128–9.
20. Ephraim Sicher attributes such apostrophising of society's negligent administrators to warn that buried social injustice will cause the apocalyptic collapse of society to the influence of Thomas Carlyle and Thomas Macaulay's prose, which he sees as incorporating gothic narrative strategies into a conception of history (*Rereading the City, Rereading Dickens* (New York: AMS Press, 2003)), pp. 182–5.
21. Dickens records another borrowing of this person's name in a private record quoted in Forster, *The Life of Charles Dickens*, vol. I, p. 22.
22. Quoted in Forster, *The Life of Charles Dickens*, vol. I, p. 25.

23. *Inward Sky: The Mind and Heart of Nathaniel Hawthorne* (Durham, NC: Duke University Press, 1962), pp. 549–50.
24. H. H. Hoeltje, *Inward Sky*, pp. 119, 61.
25. *The Complete Verse*, Francis Scarfe (trans.), (London: Anvil, 1986), p. 179.

3 'A great (and dirty) city': London's Dirt and the Terrors of Obscurity

1. For a fuller summary of Dickens's involvement in this field than I give here, see Norris Pope's extensive entry on 'Public health, sanitation, and housing' in Paul Schlicke, *Oxford Reader's Companion to Dickens*, pp. 469–74.
2. A. S. Wohl, *Endangered Lives* (London: Dent, 1983), p. 62.
3. Ibid., p. 84.
4. Ibid., p. 128.
5. Ibid., p. 118.
6. House, *The Dickens World*, pp. 192–3.
7. Dickens's concern about whether it is possible for even his purest heroines to be corrupted by their environment lies at the bottom of the famous debate on Little Dorrit's 'speck'. I have relocated this debate in its metropolitan context in an article based on an earlier version of this chapter, 'Little Dorrit's "speck" and Florence's "daily blight": urban contamination and the Dickensian heroine' in *Dickens Studies Annual*, vol. XXIV, 2004.
8. K. J. Fielding, *The Speeches of Charles Dickens* (London: Oxford University Press, 1960), p. 128.
9. *The Works of Ruskin* (ed. E. T. Cook and A. Wedderburn), 39 vols (London: Geo Allen, 1908–1912), vol. XXXIV, p. 266.
10. Ibid., p. 268.
11. Ibid., p. 269.
12. Ibid., p. 132.
13. Ibid., p. 133.
14. *Purity and Danger* (London and New York: Routledge, 1984), p. 36.
15. *Report on the Sanitary Condition of the Labouring People* (Edinburgh: Edinburgh University Press, 1965), pp. 198–9.
16. Quoted in *Endangered Lives*, p. 7.
17. Douglas, *Purity and Danger*, pp. 54, 58.
18. *All The Year Round*, vol. IV (1860), p. 29.
19. E. Chadwick, pp. 198–9.
20. London and Basingstoke: Macmillan, 1975, p. 222.
21. Ibid., p. 218.
22. *Degeneration, Culture and the Novel* (Cambridge: Cambridge University Press, 1994), pp. 36, 38–9.
23. *Darwin and the Novelists* (London and Cambridge, MA: 1988), pp. 119–76. For Dickens's acceptance of contemporary geological and biological theories, see K. J. Fielding, 'science' in Schlicke, pp. 516–17).
24. *Darwin's Plots* (London: Routledge and Kegan Paul, 1983), pp. 46–8.
25. Quoted and discussed in *Degeneration, Culture and the Novel* (Cambridge: Cambridge University Press, 1994), p. 26.
26. Quoted in G. S. Jones, *Outcast London* (Oxford: Clarendon, 1971), p. 309.

27. Stephen Marcus, 'Reading the Illegible', in Dyos and Wolff, *The Victorian City*, vol. I, pp. 258–60.
28. The most immediate allusion here is to Alain René Lesage's evil spirit, Asmodeus, in *The Devil Upon Two Sticks*. (Athens, GA: University of Georgia Press).
29. This Psalm speaks of God '... who walketh upon the wings of the wind: Who maketh his angels spirits; his ministers a flaming fire' (v. 4).
30. See Chapter 1.
31. Fielding, *The Speeches of Charles Dickens*, p. 128.
32. *The Country and the City* (London: Chatto & Windus, 1973), p. 156.
33. In *Literature and Medicine*, vol. IX (1990), p. 95.
34. *All The Year Round*, vol. IV (1860), p. 31.
35. 'Underground London' in *All The Year Round*, vol. V (1860), p. 454.
36. Douglas, *Purity and Danger*, p. 2.
37. *The Speeches of Charles Dickens*, p. 129.
38. *Nineteenth Century Fiction*, vol. XXV, pp. 199–215.
39. Barnett also draws attention to the ways in which contagion is explicitly used as a metaphor for a contamination of the mind caused by greed.
40. The next chapter explains the specifically Christian dimension of the revelation he offers.
41. His inability to read the city churches places Jo in a different category to characters such as Ralph Nickleby, who can and do read their message – and deliberately reject it. The latter commands church bells to

> ring chimes for the coming in of every year that brings this cursed world nearer to its end. No bell or book for me; throw me on a dunghill, and let me rot there to infect the air!
>
> (*NN* 62 p. 906)

Our Mutual Friend provides the most concrete example of a society that values the dustheaps more highly than the cross.
42. Sicher, *Rereading the City, Rereading Dickens*, p. 340.
43. Welsh, *The City of Dickens*, p. 176.
44. Ibid., p. 143.
45. Walder, *Dickens and Religion*, p. 114.

4 'Angel and devil by turns': The Detective Figure in *Bleak House*

1. *Collected Poems*, 1909–1962, p. 70.
2. *Dickens* (London: Minerva, 1991), p. 55.
3. Outside the British context, a 'detective' who had already achieved international celebrity was the French informer Eugène François Vidocq. Dickens is likely to have shared the widespread public interest in this character prevalent in the early nineteenth century. Edgar Allan Poe's Dupin in the short stories 'The Murders in the Rue Morgue' and 'The Mystery of Marie Rogêt' is another example of interest in the detective predating *Bleak House*.
4. For a fuller discussion see D. G. Browne, *The Rise of Scotland Yard* (London: Harrap, 1956).

5. F. Moylan, *Scotland Yard and the Metropolitan Police* (London and New York: Putnam, 1929), pp. 78–9.
6. *Household Words*, vol. I (1850), pp. 368–72.
7. Ibid., pp. 409–14, 457–60.
8. Ibid., pp. 577–80.
9. Ibid., vol. III (1851), pp. 265–70.
10. 'A "Detective" Police Party' in ibid., vol. II (150–1), p. 409.
11. To Sir Edward Bulwer-Lytton, 9 May 1851, Letters, vol. IV, p. 380.
12. Household Words, vol. III (1851), p. 265.
13. Montclair, N J: Patterson Smith, 1975.
14. Manchester: Manchester University Press, 1976.
15. *Household Words*, vol. III (1851), p. 265.
16. D. Kiberd (ed.), (Harmondsworth: Penguin, 1992), pp. 107–47.
17. See, for example, Mark 4:11.
18. *Household Words*, vol. III (1851), p. 266, as for the three following quotations from the same article.
19. *Charles Dickens: The World of his Novels* (Cambridge, MA: Harvard University Press, 1959), pp. 104 ff.
20. Berkeley and Los Angeles: University of California Press, 1988, p. 75.
21. For the argument summarised here, see *The Novel and the Police* (Berkeley and Los Angeles: University of California Press, 1988), pp. 83 ff.
22. Ibid., p. 89.
23. *Literature and Medicine*, vol. IX (1990), p. 99. The following quotation is taken from Schwarzbach's article in *Literature and Medicine*.
24. See Chapter 3 for the chilling implication that even Woodcourt's efforts here may not have been enough.
25. To W. H.Wills, 18 September 1853, *Letters*, vol. VII, p. 151.
26. Mr Inspector in *Our Mutual Friend*, 'posting up his books in a whitewashed office, as studiously as if he were in a monastery on the top of a mountain' (I 3 p. 33) also represents, at least metaphorically, an order that can provide a peace by its ability to assemble knowledge of London into an organised system of information. That this order is secular, unlike the religious order evoked in the simile, may suggest that the police force has replaced this function in the metropolitan age. On the other hand, he also educates the reader, if not Eugene himself, to trust reliable guides who (as we shall see in Chapter 6) name-check a more traditional religious Providence. Note that Mr Inspector also shares Bucket's love of disguise and secrecy even for its own sake (I 13).

5 'A road of ashes': London's Railway and the Providential Timetable

1. *Interpreting Interpreting* (Baltimore and London: The John Hopkins University Press, 1979), p. 34.
2. This kind of hermeneutic issue is familiar to theologians, who, for example, must decide whether the yeast in the parable of Matthew 13:33 has any connection with 'the leaven ... of the doctrine of the Pharisees and of the Sadducees' of Matthew 16:11. If the same signifier should be read as denoting the same signified concept in both instances, the disciples are being warned that the kingdom of Heaven is vulnerable to the rapid spread of legalistic teaching.

If the same image is being used to illustrate two separate meanings locally within the same text, the context of the parable would probably lead us to read it as denoting the rapid spread of the kingdom throughout the world.

3. Chatto & Windus: London, 1965, pp. 306–11.
4. L. T. C. Rolt, *Red for Danger A History of Railway Accidents and Railway Safety* (Newton Abbot and London: David and Charles, 1976), p. 21.
5. See ibid., pp. 127–30.
6. *Longfellow's Poetical Works* (London: Oxford University Press, 1910), p. 141.
7. *The Imagination of Charles Dickens*, p. 103.
8. See Chapter 1.
9. J. Richards and J. M. Mackenzie, *The Railway Station: A Social History* (Oxford: Oxford University Press, 1988), p. 124.
10. Letter to Thomas Beard of 2 May 1835 narrates a horse-drawn race with a *Times* reporter to bring the text of a speech by Lord John Russell from Exeter to the offices of the *Morning Chronicle* in London. For the first edition of the *Daily News*, on 21 January 1846, by contrast, George Hudson had laid on a special train to report an Anti-Corn Law meeting in Norwich. See letters to Thomas Beard and Joseph Paxton, 16 January 1846.
11. The final chapter of this book deals with the eyes of the crowd penetrating the enclosed milieu of the concealer.
12. See Chapter 4.
13. J. Pendleton, *Our Railways; Their Origin, Development, Incident and Romance*, 2 vols (London: Cassell, 1986), vol. I, p. 118.
14. For the argument summarised here, see D. A. Miller, *The Novel and the Police*, passim.
15. See Chapter 3.
16. *The City of Dickens* (Oxford: Clarendon, 1971), p. 189.
17. Amongst the best-known recent readings of the passage, see Terry Eagleton, 'Ideology and Literary Form: Charles Dickens', in Steven Connor (ed.) *Charles Dickens* (London and New York: Longman, 1996), pp. 155–7; Jeremy Tambling, *Dickens, Violence and the Modern State* (Basingstoke and London: Macmillan, 1995), pp. 58–63; John Sutherland, 'Visualizing Dickens', in John Bowen and Robert L. Patten (eds), *Charles Dickens Studies* (Basingstoke and New York: Palgrave Macmillan, 2006), pp. 114–21. All are useful, but they do not explicitly discuss why Dombey associates the train with Florence's face. David D. Marcus's article, 'Symbolism and Mental process in *Dombey and Son*' reads the connection as demonstrating the arbitrary nature of all symbolism, which tells us more about the interpreter's needs than either signifier or signified. The introduction of Florence's face to Dombey's clearly limited perspective on the railway shows that his pathology seizes on his daughter with equal arbitrariness to represent his own fears to his mind (*Dickens Studies Annual*, vol. VI (1977), pp. 57–71). Nina Auerbach opposes the heroine's characteristics with the train's phallic, emotionless masculinity ('Dickens and Dombey: A Daughter After All', in Alan Shelston (ed.), *Charles Dickens: Dombey and Son and Little Dorrit*, London: Macmillan, 1985, p. 105).
18. See Chapter 1.
19. Welsh, *The City of Dickens*, p. 190. The image of the train striking Carker in the novel's frontispiece demonstrates the railway's role as destroying agent in the mind of Browne, presumably acting in consultation with Dickens.

20. The railways are often credited with establishing punctuality as a British national virtue – and one on which Dickens notoriously insisted. See, for example, M. Baumgarten, 'Railway/Reading/Time: *Dombey and Son* and the Industrial World' in *DSA*, vol. 19 (1990), pp. 67 ff.
21. The necessity of this was demonstrated by a collision on the East Lancashire Railway in 1849 in which a passenger and a goods train were dispatched by different clocks.
22. See Rolt, *Red for Danger*, p. 47.
23. 'Railway/Reading/time', p. 68.
24. *Master Humphrey's Clock and A Child's History of England* (London: Oxford University Press, 1958), pp. 107, 109.
25. The excitement surrounding these buildings can be seen in William Frith's painting, *The Railway Station* (see Colour Plate 2).
26. In actual fact, the omnibus was introduced only in 1814 in Paris and 1829 in London – only seven years before the first London station.
27. Mayhew, *London Labour and the London Poor*, vol. III, p. 337.
28. At the start of the 1830s, there were 1265 in operation in the capital. By 1863, this was increased to 6800 and in 1888, the total is estimated at 11,000 (Richards and Mackenzie, *The Railway Station: A Social History*, p. 311).
29. See Chapter 7.
30. *The Works of Ruskin*, vol. VIII, p. 246.
31. See Damrosch, *God's Plot and Man's Stories*, passim.
32. In 'Dickens's Plots: The Ways of Providence or the Influence of Collins?', *Victorian Newsletter*, vol. XIX (1961), pp. 11 ff.
33. *Darwin and the Novelists* (Chicago and London: Chicago University Press, 1991), p. 139.
34. Ibid., p. 293.
35. For discussion of Dickens's plot structures as reflecting a shifting contemporary attitude towards Providence, see Thomas Vargish, *The Providential Aesthetic in Victorian Fiction* (Charlottesville, VA: University of Virginia Press, 1985) and Elizabeth Deedes Ermarth, *The English Novel in History 1840–1895* (London and New York: Routledge, 1997). For Dickens and Providence, see Chapter 1.
36. G. K. Chesterton, *Tremendous Trifles* (London: Methuen, 1909), p. 219.
37. Quoted in Jean Dethier (ed.), *All Stations, a Journey through 150 Years of Railway History* (London: Thames Hudson, 1981), p. 6.
38. A. W. Ward, *Dickens* (London: Macmillan, 1909), p. 81.
39. *The Works of John Ruskin*, vol. VIII, p. 159.
40. H. J. Dyos, 'Railways and Housing in Victorian London' in *The Journal of Transport History*, vol. II (1955), pp. 12–13.
41. J. Betjamin, *London's Historic Railway Stations* (London: John Murray, 1972), p. 12.
42. J. Richards, 'The role of the Railway', in M. Wheeler (ed.), *Ruskin and Environment – the Storm-cloud of the Nineteenth Century* (Manchester and New York: Manchester University Press, 1995), p. 124.
43. Quoted in S. Marcus, 'Reading the Illegible', in Dyos and Wolff, *The Victorian City*, p. 268.
44. Quoted by H. J. Dyos, 'Railways and Housing in Victorian London', p. 15.
45. In Connor, *Charles Dickens*, p. 155.
46. Indeed, I have attempted to refute Eagleton's backhanded compliment that Dickens had 'no ideological resources by which to secure a reconciliation of

"tradition" and "progress"'. He had several in a state of ongoing debate with one another.
47. See Chapter 2.
48. *Collected Poems, 1909–1962*, pp. 77–8.
49. Perhaps it has an even greater resonance for our generation, hoping for a better world order after the events of September 11, 2001.
50. Van Wyck Brooks's *The Confident Years* quoted in (ed.) Graham Clarke, *T. S. Eliot: Critical Assessments* (London: Christopher Helm, 1990), 4 vols, vol. I, pp. 333–40, presents an account of Eliot's vision in *The Waste Land* that reads it as expressing mid-twentieth century anxieties and hopes as much as those of the inter-war period.
51. See Chapter 1 for discussion of the specifically Christian nature of the transformation undergone internally by Mrs Clennam and then externally by the city.
52. Walder, *Dickens and Religion*, p. 195.
53. There is another such example in *Great Expectations* (III 14 p. 430), which underlines the change that has taken place within Pip as he embraces a less egocentric attitude with a new view of the city of London in its Christian aspect.

6 'The secrets of the river': The Thames within London

1. *The Violent Effigy* (London: Faber & Faber, 1973), p. 105.
2. Ibid., p. 130.
3. See Chapter 5.
4. *Charles Dickens: His Tragedy and Triumph*, 2 vols (London: Hamish Hamilton, 1952), vol. II, pp. 1043–44.
5. *T. S. Eliot: The Waste Land* (London: Edward Arnold, 1973), pp. 40–1.
6. 'Time, Death and the River in Dickens' novels', in *English Studies*, vol. LIII (1972), p. 449.
7. *The Imagination of Charles Dickens*, p. 107.
8. Ephraim Sicher sees the railway as a contrast to the river. The dominance of the former is the triumph of 'the mechanical at the expense of the organic, which serves the mercantile interests of the Dombeys' (Sicher, *Rereading the City, Rereading Dickens*, p. 124), while the tranquil eternity of the river ... reassures us that there is a transcendent power that can resist modernity. ... beyond the fragmenting experience of the city' (p. 141). He even goes as far as to say that 'the lines and branches of the railway are blind to the time of Providence, which watches over Paul' (p. 132). See Chapter 5 for an alternative view – that the gap between the railway timetable and Romantic-era conceptions of Providence as represented by the river is suggested early in the novel, only to be proven illusory.
9. 'Dealings with the Firm of Dombey and Son: Firmness versus Wetness', in J. Gross and G. Pearson (eds), *Dickens and the Twentieth Century* (London: Routledge & Kegan Paul, 1962), pp. 124, 126.
10. *The Violent Effigy*, p. 108.
11. See Chapter 4.
12. *All The Year Round*, vol. III (1860), p. 349.

13. *Household Words*, vol. VI (1853), p. 481, as for following reference to this article.
14. *Household Words*, vol. III, p. 269.
15. London: George Allen & Unwin, 1984, p. 54.
16. London: Penguin, 1997, p. xi.
17. *Violent Effigy*, p. 108. Incidentally, it is by no means clear to me that Dickens handles the theme of self-sacrifice clumsily in *A Tale of Two Cities*.
18. Ephraim Sicher, *Rereading the City, Rereading Dickens*, p. 367.
19. Summarised in J. Forster, *The Life of Charles Dickens* (London: Dent, 1966), vol. I, p. 146.
20. See to Forster, 3 October 1846.
21. *Collected Poems 1909–1962*, p. 72.
22. To W. W. F. de Cerjat, 7 July 1858.
23. 'On Duty With Inspector Field', in *Household Words*, vol. III (1851), p. 269.
24. Sicher, *Rereading the City, Rereading Dickens*, p. 346.
25. Sicher sees this too as a metaphor for the author's task of attempting to restore deadened matter to the potential for representing life, see ibid., p. 346.
26. Ibid., p. 332.
27. J. H. Miller, *The Novel and the Police*, p. 315.
28. For a fuller analysis of these two young women, among many others, as angels and agents of rebirth (although with a slightly different emphasis to my own), see Welsh, *The City of Dickens*, Chapter 12.
29. *Collected Poems 1909–1962*, p. 79.
30. *A Reader's Guide to T. S. Eliot* (London: Thames Hudson, 1955), p. 151.
31. Cockshut, *The Imagination of Charles Dickens*, p. 176.
32. 'Entering the Kingdom: Charles Dickens and the Search for Spiritual Regeneration', Unpublished doctoral thesis (Ann Arbor, MI), 1969, p. 110.

7 'A dream of demon heads and savage eyes': Dickens's Metropolitan Crowd

1. The strict focus of this chapter on the relationship between the crowd and the religious symbolism of the river to which it is so frequently linked has unfortunately precluded discussion of the crowd's richly ambiguous role in embodying the flow of historical time, its questionable justice and its drive towards violence in *A Tale of Two Cities* and of Carlyle's influence on such representation. Nevertheless it is to be hoped that some of these points will still be clear from my discussion of the fiction up to 1848.
2. *Collected Poems 1909–1962*, p. 65.
3. *The Divine Comedy of Dante Alighieri*, J. D. Sinclair (ed. and trans.), (London: Bodley Head, 1958), vol. I, pp. 49–51.
4. See Cleanth Brooks, '*The Waste Land*: Critique of the Myth', in C. B. Cox and Arnold Hinchcliffe (eds), *T. S. Eliot: The Waste Land* (London and Basingstoke: Macmillan, 1968), pp. 128–61.
5. See Chapter 6.
6. R. Williams, *The Country and the City*, p. 146.
7. George Rudé, *The Face of the Crowd* (New York and London: Harvester, 1988), pp. 224–5.

8. J. A. Banks, 'The Contagion of Numbers', in Dyos and Wolff, *The Victorian City*, vol. I, pp. 105–22.
9. London and Toronto: Dent, 1923, Author's note, p. xii
10. See Chapter 4.
11. Most importantly for the government, it allowed Catholics to join the army to fight in America.
12. Gordon Spence has helpfully compiled a comprehensive list of these in Appendix B of the Penguin Classics edition of *Barnaby Rudge* (Harmondsworth, 1973).
13. To John Cay, 21 July 1841.
14. 15 November 1841.
15. Cockshut, *The Imagination of Charles Dickens*, p. 73.
16. 'The Gordon Riots: A Study of the Rioters and their Victims', in *Transactions of the Royal Historical Society*, vol. VI (1955), pp. 105–6.
17. *King Mob* (London: Longmans, Green & Co., 1959), pp. 59–61.
18. Ibid., p. 92.
19. Philip G. Zimbardo defines this phenomenon in his paper, 'The Human Choice: Individuation, Reason, and Order versus Deindividuation, Impulse, and Chaos', *Nebraska Symposium on Motivation*, vol. 17 (1969), pp. 237–307.
20. London: Ernest Benn, 1896, p. 26.
21. Ibid., pp. 36–40.
22. *The Imagination of Charles Dickens*, p. 66.
23. London: Macmillan, 1892–7, vol. III, p. 120.
24. *The Crowd: A study of the Popular Mind* (London: Ernest Benn, 1938), p. 33.
25. Ibid., p. 19.
26. Summer 1851.
27. 3 vols (London: Chapman & Hall, 1896), vol. I, pp. 178–9.
28. Ibid., p. 188.
29. Ibid., p. 194.
30. Michael Goldberg, in *Carlyle and Dickens* (Athens, GA: Georgia University Press, 1972), sees this tension as fundamentally unresolved in *The French Revolution*, saying that Carlyle, 'Certainly … brightened his pages with illuminating references to his characters, but he finally undermined their full humanity by making them appear as powerless creatures of the historical process' (p. 116). Dickens's fictional account in *A Tale of Two Cities*, however, attracts praise for blending a sympathetic understanding of causality with a constantly vivid and vital account of the members of the crowd: 'They are simultaneously the victims of terrible oppression and a mob of howling ruffians' (p. 102).
31. Harold F. Holland usefully lists the comparisons made between the mob and the water in 'The Doer and the Deed: Theme and Pattern in Barnaby Rudge', in *Publications of the Modern Language Association of America*, vol. LXXIV (1959), pp. 406–17.
32. *Hunting Mr Heartbreak* (London: Picador, 1991), pp. 357–8.
33. 20 September 1846.
34. See Cockshut, *The Imagination of Charles Dickens*, p. 79.
35. To John Forster, 18 September 1841.
36. *Dickens and Crime* (London: Macmillan, 1962), p. 45.
37. To John Forster, 30 August 1846.

38. Quoted in Kate Flint, *Dickens* (Brighton: Harvester, 1986), p. 13.
39. This vision resembles the 'Men and bits of paper, whirled by the cold wind' which evoke the deadness and directionless erosion of identity experienced by the metropolitans in T. S. Eliot's 'Burnt Norton', ll. 104–110, *Collected Poems 1909–1962*, p. 193.
40. R. Williams, *The Country and the City*, p. 155.

Conclusion: 'What is the city over the mountains'

1. Welsh, *The City of Dickens*, pp. 141–2.
2. Ephraim Sicher, *Rereading the City, Rereading Dickens*, pp. 364–5.
3. *Dickens and the Sprit of the Age* (Oxford: Clarendon, 1999), p. 121.
4. *Rereading the City, Rereading Dickens*, p. 330.
5. *Dickens and the City*, p. 205.
6. In *Dickens and the Dream of Cinema* (Manchester: Manchester University Press, 2003), Grahame Smith suggests that London's function in Dickens's fiction as a means of externalising the mechanisms of the plot fashioned ways of perceiving and experiencing the city that were taken up with enthusiasm by early cinema at the beginning of the twentieth century. This idea that Dickens both reflected and helped to form nineteenth-century tendencies in looking at the metropolis in ways that were conducive to the particular development taken by an early twentieth-century art form is analogous to my own discussion of Dickens's role in the Modernist poets' vision of the city.
7. *Collected Poems 1909–1962*, p. 65.
8. Ibid., p. 68.
9. Ibid., p. 73.
10. R. Williams, *The Country and the City*, pp. 154–5.
11. Ibid., p. 164.

Bibliography

Primary texts by Dickens

All references to novels by Charles Dickens are to the Clarendon editions (Oxford, 1966–99), except where these are not yet available, in which case Penguin Classics editions (Harmondsworth, 1965–1999) have been used. In addition, please note:

Household Words. London: Bradbury and Evans, 1850–9.

All the Year Round. London: Chapman and Hall, 1860–70.

Master Humphrey's Clock and A Child's History of England (ed. by D. Hudson). London: Oxford University Press, 1958.

The Life of Our Lord. London and Edinburgh: Morrison & Gibb, 1934.

Fielding, K. J. (ed.). *The Speeches of Charles Dickens*. London: Clarendon Press, 1960.

House, M., Storey, G. and Tillotson, K. (eds). *The Letters of Charles Dickens*, 12 vols. Oxford: Clarendon Press, 1965–2002.

Critical works on Dickens

Ackroyd, P. *Dickens*. London: Minerva, 1991.

Barabara Hardy. 'The Change of Heart in Dickens's Novels' in *Victorian Studies*. Vol. V (1961), pp. 49–67.

Barnett, E. B. '*Little Dorrit* and the Disease of Modern Life' in *Nineteenth Century Fiction*. Vol. XXV (1971).

Baumgarten, M. 'Railway/Reading/Time: *Dombey and Son* and the Industrial World' in *Dickens Studies Annual*. Vol. XIX (1990), pp. 65–89.

Berry, L. C. 'In the Bosom of the Family: The Wet-nurse, the Railroad and *Dombey and Son*' in *Dickens Studies Annual*. Vol. XXV (1996), pp. 1–28.

Bloom, H. (ed.). *Modern Critical Views*. New York: Chelsea House, 1987.

Bowen, J. and Patten, R. L. (eds). *Charles Dickens Studies*, Basingstoke and New York: Palgrave Macmillan, 2006.

Brooks, C. *Signs for the Times*. London: George Allen & Unwin, 1984.

Carey, J. *The Violent Effigy*. London: Faber & Faber, 1973.

Cheadle, B. 'Mystification and the Mystery of Origins in Bleak House' in *Dickens Studies Annual*. Vol. XXV (1986), pp. 29–47.

Cockshut, A. O. J. *The Imagination of Charles Dickens*. London: Collins, 1961.

Collins, P. *Dickens and Crime*. London: Macmillan, 1964.

Collins, P. (ed.). *Dickens: Interviews and Recollections*. London and Basingstoke: Macmillan, 1981.

Collins, P. (ed.). *Dickens: The Critical Heritage*. London: Routledge and Kegan Paul, 1971.

Connor, S. (ed.). *Charles Dickens*. London and New York: Longman, 1996.

Flint, K. *Dickens*. Brighton: Harvester, 1986.

Ford, G. H. and Lane, L. (eds). *The Dickens Critics*. New York and Ithaca: Cornell University Press, 1961.

Forster, J. *The Life of Charles Dickens*. 1870. London: Dent, 1966.

Frank, L. 'Through a Glass darkly' in *Dickens Studies Annual*. Vol. IV (1975), pp. 91–112.

Giddings, R. (ed.). *The Changing World of Charles Dickens*. London and Totowa, NJ: Vision, 1983.

Gold, J. *Charles Dickens: Radical Moralist*. Minneapolis: University of Minneapolis Press, 1972.

Goldberg, M. *Carlyle and Dickens*. Athens, GA: University of Georgia Press, 1972.

Gross, J. and Pearson, G. (eds). *Dickens and the Twentieth Century*. London: Routledge and Kegam Paul, 1962.

Grubb, G. G. 'The Personal and Literary Relationships Between Dickens and Poe' in *Nineteenth Century Fiction*. Vol V (1950), pp. 1–22.

Hattaway, K. A. K. 'Entering the Kingdom: Charles Dickens and the Search for Spiritual Regeneration'. Unpublished doctoral thesis: Ann Arbor, MI, 1969.

Hibbert, C. *The Making of Charles Dickens*. London: BCA, 1967.

Hirsch, G. D. 'The Mysteries in *Bleak House*' in *Dickens Studies Annual*. Vol. IV (1975), pp. 132–52.

Holland, H. F. 'The Doer and the Deed: Theme and Pattern in *Barnaby Rudge*' in *Publications of the Modern Language Association of America*. Vol. LXXIV (1959), pp. 406–17.

Hollington, M. 'Dickens the Flâneur' in *Dickensian*. Vol. LXXVII (1981), pp. 71–87.

Horton, S. *Interpreting Interpreting*. London and Baltimore, MD: The John Hopkins University Press, 1979.

House, H. *The Dickens World*. London: Oxford University Press, 1942.

Humphreys, A. 'Dickens and Mayhew on the London Poor' in *Dickens Studies Annual*. Vol. IV (1975), pp. 78–90.

Hutter, A. D. 'Dismemberment and Articulation in *Our Mutual Friend*' in *Dickens Studies Annual*. Vol. IV (1975), pp. 135–75.

Jarrett, D. 'The Fall of the House of Clennam' in *The Dickensian*. Vol. LXXIII (1976–7), pp. 155–61.

Johnson, E. *Charles Dickens: His Tragedy and Triumph*. London: Hamish Hamilton, 1952.

Knight, M. '*Little Dorrit* and Providence' in *Dickens Studies Annual*. Vol. XXXII (2002), pp. 179–90.

Larson. J. L. *Dickens and the Broken Scripture*. Athens, GA: University of Georgia Press, 1985.

Leavis, F. R. and Leavis, Q. D. *Dickens the Novelist*. Harmondsworth: Penguin, 1972.

Mackenzie, N. and Mackenzie, J. *Dickens: A Life*. Oxford: Oxford University Press, 1979.

Malone, C. N. '"Flight" and "Pursuit": Fugitive and Identity in *Bleak House*' in *Dickens Studies Annual*. Vol. XIX (1990), pp. 107–24.

Marcus, D. D. 'Symbolism and Mental Process in *Dombey and Son*' in *Dickens Studies Annual*. Vol. VI (1977), pp. 57–71.

Marcus, S. *Dickens: From Pickwick to Dombey*. London: Chatto & Windus, 1965.

Maxwell, R. 'G. M. Reynolds, Dickens and the Mysteries of London' in *Nineteenth Century Fiction*. Vol. XXXII (1977).

Maxwell, R. *The Mysteries of London and Paris*. London and Charlottesville, VA: University Press of Virginia, 1992.

Miller, J. H. *Charles Dickens: The World of His Novels*. London: Oxford University Press, 1958.

Nelson, H. S. 'Staggs's Gardens: The Railway Through Dickens' World' in *Dickens Studies Annual*. Vol. IV (1974), pp. 41–53.

Nelson, H. S. 'Dickens's Plots: The Ways of Providence or the Influence of Collins?' *Victorian Newsletter*. Vol. XIX (1961), pp. 11 ff.

Palmer, W. J. 'Dickens and Shipwreck' in *Dickens Studies Annual*. Vol. XVIII (1989), pp. 39–52.

Poe, E. A. 'Prospective Notice of *Barnaby Rudge*', reprinted in *The Dickensian*. Vol. IX (1913), pp. 274–8.

Poole, A. 'Introduction' to *Our Mutual Friend*. London: Penguin, 1997.

Quiller-Couch, A. *Charles Dickens and Other Victorians*. Cambridge: Cambridge University Press, 1925.

Robison, R. 'Time, Death and the River in Dickens' Novels' in *English Studies*. Vol. LIII (1972), pp. 436–54.

Sanders, A. *Charles Dickens: Resurrectionist*. London and Basingstoke: Macmillan, 1982.

Sanders, A. *Dickens and the Spirit of the Age*. Oxford: Clarendon Press, 1999.

Schlicke, P. (ed.). *Oxford Reader's Companion to Dickens*. Oxford: Oxford University Press, 1999.

Schwarzbach, F. S. *Dickens and the City*. London: Athlone Press, 1979.

Schwarzbach, F. S. '*Bleak House* – The Social Pathology of Urban Life' in *Literature and Medicine*. Vol. IX (1990), pp. 93–104.

Shelston, A. (ed.). Charles Dickens: Dombey and Son and Little Dorrit. London: Macmillan, 1985.

Sicher, E. *Rereading the City, Rereading Dickens*. New York: AMS Press, 2003.

Slater, M. (ed.). *Dickens 1970*. London: Chapman & Hall, 1970.

Smith, G. *Dickens and the Dream of Cinema*. Manchester and New York: Manchester University Press, 2003.

Smith, K. A. 'Little Dorrit's "Speck" and Florence's "Daily Blight": Urban Contamination and the Dickensian Heroine' in *Dickens Studies Annual*. Vol. XXXIV (2004).

Tambling, J. *Dickens, Violence and the Modern State*. Basingstoke and London: Macmillan, 1995.

Walder, D. *Dickens and Religion*. London: George Allen & Unwin, 1981.

Walton, J. 'Conrad, Dickens and the Detective novel' in *Nineteenth Century Fiction*. Vol. XXIII (1969), pp. 446–52.

Ward, A. W. *Dickens*. London: Macmillan, 1909.

Welsh, A. *The City of Dickens*. Oxford: Oxford University Press, 1971.

Wilson, A. *The World of Charles Dickens*. London: Martin Secker & Warberg, 1970.

Wolfreys, J. *Writing London: The Trace of the Urban Text from Blake to Dickens*. London and Basingstoke: Macmillan, 1998.

Other critical works

Aguirre, M. *The Closed Space*. Manchester and New York: Manchester University Press, 1990.

Beer, G. *Darwin's Plots*. London: Routledge and Kegan Paul, 1983.

Clarke, G. (ed.). *T. S. Eliot: Critical Assessments*. 4 vols. London: Christopher Helm, 1990.

Cox, C. B. and Hinchcliffe, A. (eds). *T. S. Eliot: The Waste Land*. London and Basingstoke: Macmillan, 1968.

Crawford, R. *The Savage and the City in the Work of T. S. Eliot*. Oxford: Clarendon, 1987.

Damrosch, L. *God's Plot and Man's Stories: Studies in the Fictional Imagination from Milton to Fielding*. Chicago and London: University of Chicago Press, 1985.

Ellis, K. F. *The Contested Castle*. Urbana and Chicago: University of Illinois Press, 1989.

Ermarth, E. D. *The English Novel in History 1840–1895*. London and New York: Routledge, 1997.

Gardner, H. *The Art of T. S. Eliot*. London: Cresset, 1949.

Grant, M., T. S. *Eliot: The Critical Heritage*. London: Routledge & Kegan Paul, 1982.

Greenslade, W. *Degeneration, Culture and the Novel*. Cambridge: Cambridge University Press, 1994.

Heyns, Michael. *Expulsion and the Nineteenth-century Novel*. Oxford: Clarendon, 1994.

Hoeltje, H. H. *Inward Sky: The Mind and Heart of Nathaniel Hawthorne*. Durham, NC: Duke University Press, 1962.

Howells, C. A. *Love, Mystery and Misery: Feeling in Gothic Fiction*. 1978. London and Atlantic Highlands, NJ: Athlone Press, 1995.

Hutter, A. D. 'Dreams, Transformations and Literature: The Implications of Detective Fiction' in L. Pykett (ed.). *New Casebooks: Wilkie Collins*. Basingstoke and London: Macmillan, 1998.

Levine, G. *Darwin and the Novelists*. Cambridge, MA. and London: 1988.

Miller, D. A. *The Novel and the Police*. Berkeley and Los Angeles: University of California Press, 1988.

Moody, A. D. *Thomas Stearns Eliot, Poet*. Cambridge: Cambridge University Press, 1979.

Murray, G. *The Classical Tradition in Poetry*. Cambridge, MA: Harvard University Press, 1927.

Punter, D. *The Literature of Terror*. 2 vols. London and New York: Longman, 1996.

Qualls, B. V. *The Secular Pilgrims of Victorian Fiction*. Cambridge: Cambridge University Press, 1982.

Rajan, B. T. S. *Eliot: A Study of His writing in Several Hands*. London: D. Dobson, 1947.

Sage, V. *Horror Fiction and the Protestant Tradition*. Basingstoke and London: Meredith, 1988.

Sedgwick, E. K. *The Coherence of Gothic Conventions*. New York: Arno, 1980.

Sandison, A. *Robert Louis Stevenson and the Appearance of Modernism*. London and Basingstoke: Macmillan, 1996.

Smith, J. H. and Kerrigan W. (eds) *Interpreting Lacan*. New Haven, CN: Yale University Press, 1983.

Traversi, D. *T. S. Eliot: The Longer Poems*. London: The Bodely Head, 1976.

Vargish, T. *The Providential Aesthetic in Victorian Fiction*. Charlottesville, VA: University of Virginia Press, 1985.

Wheeler, M. *Heaven, Hell and the Victorians*. Cambridge: Cambridge University Press, 1994.

Wheeler, M (ed.). *Ruskin and Environment: The Storm-cloud of the Nineteenth Century*. Manchester and New York: Manchester University Press, 1995.

Williams, H. T. S. *Eliot: The Waste Land*. London: Edward Arnold, 1973.

Williams, R. *The Country and the City*. London: Chatto & Windus, 1973.

Williamson, G. *A Reader's Guide to T. S. Eliot*. London: Thames Hudson, 1951.

Works on other subjects

Betjamin, J. *London's Historic Railway Stations*. London: John Murray, 1972.

Browne, D. G. *The Rise of Scotland Yard*. London: Harrop, 1956.

Burke, E. *A Philosophical Enquiry into the Origin of our Ideas of the Sublime and the Beautiful*. Oxford: Oxford University Press, 1990.

Chadwick, E. Report on the Sanitary Condition of the Labouring Population of Great Britain. Edinburgh: Edinburgh University Press, 1965.

Coleman, B. I. (ed.). *The Idea of the City in Nineteenth Century Britain*. London: Routledge and Kegan Paul, 1973.

Dennis, R. *English Industrial Cities of the Nineteenth Century*. Cambridge: Cambridge University Press, 1986.

Dethier, J. (ed.). *All Stations: A Journey through 150 Years of Railway History*. London: Thames Hudson, 1981.

Douglas, M. *Purity and Danger*. 1966. London and New York: Routledge, 1984.

Dyos, H. J. 'Railways and Housing in Victorian London' in *Journal of Transport History*. Leicester: University College of Leicester, 1955.

Dyos, H. J. and Wolf, M. *The Victorian City: Image and Reality*, 2 vols. London and Boston: Routledge and Kegan Paul, 1973.

Handlin, O. and Burchard, J. (eds). *The Historian and the City*. Boston, MA: M. I. T. Press and Harvard University Press, 1963.

Hibbert, C. *King Mob*. London: Longmans Green, 1959.

Hohenberg, P. M. and Lees, L. H. *The Making of Urban Europe*, 1000–1994. Cambridge, MA and London: Harvard University Press, 1994.

Jones, G. S. *Outcast London*. Oxford: Clarendon, 1971.

Moylan, F. *Scotland Yard and the Metropolitan Police*. London and New York: Putnam, 1929.

Mumford, L. *The City in History: Its Origins, Its Transformations, and Its Prospects*. London: Secker & Warberg, 1961.

Pendleton, J. *Our Railways, Their Origin, Development, Incident and Romance*. London: Cassell, 1896.

Protheroe, E. *Railways of the World*. London and New York: Routledge, 1914.

Raban, J. *Soft City*. 1974. London: Harvill, 1988.

Richards, J. and Mackenzie, J. M. *The Railway Station – A Social History*. 1986. Oxford: Oxford University Press, 1988.

Rolt, L. T. C. *Red for Danger A History of Railway Accidents and Railway Safety*. Newton Abbot and London: David and Charles, 1976.

Rudé, G. *The Face of the Crowd: Studies in Revolution, Ideology and Popular Protest – Selected Essays* (ed. by H. Tinge). New York and London: Harvester, 1988.

Rudé, G. 'The Gordon Riots: A Study of the Rioters and their Victims' in *Transactions of the Royal Historical Society*. Vol. VI (1955), pp. 93–114.

Sennett, R. (ed.). *Classic Essays on the Culture of Cities*. New York: Meredith, 1969.

Warner, M. *The Image of London*. London: Trefoil, 1987.

Weber, A. F. *The Growth of Cities in the Nineteenth Century – A Study in Statistics*. 1899. Ithaca, New York: Cornell University Press, 1967.

Wohl, A. S. *Endangered Lives*. London: Dent, 1983.

Young, K. and Garsine, P. C. *Metropolitan London*. London: Edward Arnold, 1982.

Zimbardo, P. G. 'The Human Choice: Individuation, Reason, and Order versus Deindividuation, Impulse and Chaos' in *Nebraska Symposium* on Motivation. Vol. 17 (1969).

Index